Praise for Peter James' Detective Superintendent Roy Grace series

'Peter James has penetrated the inner workings of police procedures, and the inner thoughts and attitudes of real detectives, as no English crime writer before him. His hero, Roy Grace, may not be the most lively cop, nor the most damaged by drink, weight or misery, but he's one of the most believable'
The Times

'Peter James is one of the best crime writers in the business'
Karin Slaughter

'James just gets better and better and deserves the success he has achieved with this first-class series'
Independent on Sunday

'Meticulous research gives his prose great authenticity . . . James manages to add enough surprises and drama that by the end you're rooting for the police and really don't know if they will finally get their men'
Sunday Express

'No one can deny James's success as a crime novelist . . . The Grace stories almost always go to the top of the bestseller lists, not least because they are supremely well-told. James writes meticulously researched police procedurals, so informed that you can smell the canteen coffee . . . enthralling'
Daily Mail

'In my thirty-four years of policing, never have I come across a writer who so accurately depicts "The Job"'

'Full of gripping twists and turns'
Guardian

'Very accomplished . . . I loved it'
Observer

'Another great effort from the accomplished author
with a thrilling climax'
Sun

'An incredibly strong book in a strong series. Peter knows
how to spin a yarn!'
Simon Kernick

'Such a skill to write so gripping a detective story, but also
deal with really serious issues and it not get preachy.
Masterful, Mr James!'
Kate Mosse

'Peter James is on a roll with his Roy Grace novels . . . an
authentic, well-researched and compelling read'
Daily Express

'What sets James apart is his extraordinary attention to detail
and sheer authenticity of his police procedurals'
Daily Mirror

'The latest crime thriller from Peter James is just as gripping
and detailed as ever – you'll be hooked!'
OK!

DEAD MAN'S TIME

Peter James is a UK number one bestselling author, best known for writing crime and thriller novels, and the creator of the much-loved Detective Superintendent Roy Grace. Globally, his books have been translated into thirty-seven languages.

Synonymous with plot-twisting page-turners, Peter has garnered an army of loyal fans throughout his storytelling career – which also included stints writing for TV and producing films. He has won over forty awards for his work, including the WHSmith Best Crime Author of All Time Award, Crime Writers' Association Diamond Dagger and a BAFTA nomination for *The Merchant of Venice* starring Al Pacino and Jeremy Irons for which he was an Executive Producer. Many of Peter's novels have been adapted for film, TV and stage.

Visit his website at www.peterjames.com
Twitter @PeterJamesUK
Facebook.com/peterjames.roygrace
Instagram @PeterJamesUK
Youtube.com/peterjamesPJTV

NOT DEAD YET

Terror on the silver screen;
an obsessive stalker on the loose.

DEAD MAN'S TIME

A priceless watch is stolen and the powerful
Daly family will do *anything* to get it back.

WANT YOU DEAD

Who knew online dating could be so deadly?

YOU ARE DEAD

Brighton falls victim to its first serial killer
in eighty years.

LOVE YOU DEAD

A deadly black widow is on the hunt for
her next husband.

NEED YOU DEAD

Every killer makes a mistake somewhere.
You just have to find it.

DEAD IF YOU DON'T

A kidnapping triggers a parent's worst nightmare and
a race against time for Roy Grace.

DEAD AT FIRST SIGHT

DS Roy Grace exposes the lethal side
of online identity fraud.

Also by Peter James

DEAD LETTER DROP
ATOM BOMB ANGEL
BILLIONAIRE
POSSESSION
DREAMER
SWEET HEART
TWILIGHT
PROPHECY
ALCHEMIST
HOST
THE TRUTH
DENIAL
FAITH
PERFECT PEOPLE
THE HOUSE ON COLD HILL
ABSOLUTE PROOF
THE SECRET OF COLD HILL

Short Story Collection
A TWIST OF THE KNIFE

Children's Novel
GETTING WIRED!

Novella
THE PERFECT MURDER

Non-Fiction
DEATH COMES KNOCKING: POLICING ROY GRACE'S
BRIGHTON (*with Graham Bartlett*)

DEAD MAN'S TIME

PETER JAMES

PAN BOOKS

First published 2013 by Macmillan

This edition published 2019 by Pan Books
an imprint of Pan Macmillan
The Smithson, 6 Briset Street, London EC1M 5NR
EU representative: Macmillan Publishers Ireland Ltd, 1st Floor,
The Liffey Trust Centre, 117–126 Sheriff Street Upper,
Dublin 1, DO1 YC43
Associated companies throughout the world
www.panmacmillan.com

ISBN 978-1-5098-9889-3

3 5 7 9 8 6 4

A CIP catalogue record for this book is available from the British Library.

Printed and bound by CPI Group (UK) Ltd, Croydon, CR0 4YY

Visit **www.panmacmillan.com** to read more about all our books
and to buy them. You will also find features, author interviews and
news of any author events, and you can sign up for e-newsletters
so that you're always first to hear about our new releases.

FOR PAT LANIGAN

This book would never have happened without your generosity in sharing your family history with me.

1

The boy's father kissed him goodnight for the last time – although neither of them knew that.

The boy never went to sleep until he had had that kiss. Every night, late, long after he had gone to bed, he would lie waiting in the darkness, until he heard the door of his room open, and saw the light flood in from the landing. Then the shadowy figure and the sound of his father's heavy footsteps across the bare boards. 'Hey, little guy, you still awake?' he would say in his low, booming voice.

'Yep, big guy, I am! Can I see your watch?'

His father would take out the watch from his pocket, and hold it up by the chain. It was shiny, with a big, round face, and there was a winder on the top with a hoop the chain was attached to. In the top half of the face was a section that showed the phases of the moon. The sky behind the moon was dark blue and the stars were gold. Sometimes the moon was barely visible, just peeping out. Other times it was whole, an ochre disc.

Every night the boy would ask his father to tell him a story about the Man in the Moon. His father always did. Then he would tousle his hair, kiss him on the forehead and ask, 'You said your prayers?'

The boy would nod.

'You go to sleep now.'

Then his father would clump back out of the room and close the door.

That's how it was the very last time.

2

Four men lurched their way up the street towards the house of the man they had come to kill. Three of them were unsteady because they'd drunk too much; the fourth because he had drunk too much and had a wooden leg.

They had been boozing to steady their nerves, to get some Dutch courage, they had reassured each other a while earlier, over clinking glasses and slopping beer and whiskey chasers, in the packed Vinegar Hill bar. The one with a wooden leg wasn't convinced they were doing the right thing, but he went along with his mates, because that's what you did when you were part of a gang. You either went along with them or they killed you too.

It was a few minutes to midnight and the street was dark and deserted, steady rain glossing the cobblestones. Each of them had a handgun, and two of them carried baseball bats as well, concealed inside their coats. It was a cold night. Cold enough for Hell to freeze over. They all wore fingerless mittens.

'This is it,' their leader said, peering at the number on the front door of the row house. Vapour trailed from his mouth and nostrils like smoke.

Number 21, it read.

'Are we sure this is it?'

'This is it.'

'Where's Johnny?'

'He'll be here; he's just up the road now.'

Even in the darkness, the house looked shabby, like all

its neighbours in this Brooklyn waterfront district. There was a curtained window to the right of the door, with no light on behind it. They tugged their balaclavas out of their pockets, and wrestled them down over their damp heads. Their leader raised his baseball bat in his hand, and stepped forward.

3

The boy lay in the darkness, snug in his pyjamas beneath the heavy bedclothes, listening to the ticking of the big, round clock in his room. Listening to the familiar sounds of the night. The drone of a passing ship on the busy, inky water of the East River close by. The clatter of a train, high overhead. The creaking of bed springs through the thin wall to his parents' bedroom; moans from his parents. His mother crying out. His father's loud grunt. The gentle patter of rain on the roof above him. The night had its own sounds. Its own music.

The tinkle of breaking glass was not part of it.

He froze. It sounded like it came from downstairs, right below him. Had the cat knocked over the whiskey bottle and glass his dad left out, empty, every night? Then he heard footsteps coming up the stairs. Not his dad's. His dad was already upstairs, in bed.

Several sets of footsteps.

He lay, motionless, his fear increasing. The door opened. A powerful torch beam struck his face, blinding him, and he shut his eyes. Heard footsteps in his room. He could sense a whole group of people, and was shaking with fear. Could smell tobacco and alcohol and wet clothing and sweat. He felt his throat was closing in, he couldn't breathe, and his heart was going crazy. He opened his eyes and all he could see was dazzling light. He closed his eyes again, shivering, quaking in terror. Heard footsteps approaching the bed.

A hand patted his head, then his right cheek, playfully, the wool itchy against his skin.

Then a voice, coarse but soft, an Irish accent, right above him. Breathing heavily. 'Just checking you out, kid.'

'You – you – you'll wake my ma and pa,' he stammered to the stranger, suddenly finding the strength to speak and then to open his eyes again. But all he could see was the glare of light.

'And where would we be finding them?'

He pointed, squinting. 'Through there.' He put a finger in front of his mouth. 'They're sleeping. Be quiet. You'll wake them, and my sister.' Maybe now he'd told them that they would go away.

The flashlight moved off his face. But still dazzled, all he could see for some moments were pink flashes of light. He heard the sound of footsteps, on tiptoe, moving away. A floorboard creaked. Then his door closed.

Maybe they had gone home. People often came into this house, at all hours of the night. Drinking, smoking, shouting, laughing, arguing. Mostly arguing, and sometimes fighting. When they fought, his dad would throw them out. He was a big man. No one argued with his dad.

He pulled the bedclothes over his head so they would not see him if they came back.

Moments later, he heard his father bellow something. Then a loud thud, followed by another. He heard his mother scream. A terrible, terrible scream. Then she cried out, 'Leave him, leave him, leave him! Please don't! Please don't. Leave him!'

Then he heard one of the strangers say loudly, 'Get dressed!'

Then his mother, her voice quavering, 'Where are you taking him! Please tell me? Where are you taking him?'

A minute went by. The boy lay frozen beneath the bed-clothes, trembling.

Then his mother screamed again. 'No, you can't! You can't take him! I'll not let him go!'

Then five loud bangs, as if a door, close by, was being slammed repeatedly.

'Ma! Pa!' he screamed back, his whole body electric with fear for his parents. And now the footsteps were much louder, clumping down the stairs as if they no longer cared about being silent. He heard the click of the front door opening, then the roar of an engine and a squeal of tyres. And no sound of the door closing.

Just the echo in his mind of the terrible sound of his mother's screams.

Then the silence that followed.

It was the silence that echoed the loudest.

4

He lay, listening, under the bedclothes. All was quiet. Just a pounding roar in his ears and the puffing sound of his own breathing. Maybe it was just a bad dream? He was trembling all over.

After some moments he climbed out of bed in the darkness, in his pyjamas, into the cold, then hurried across the bare floorboards to where the door was, fumbling around until he found the handle, and stumbled out onto the landing. He could feel an icy draught, as if the front door really had been left open. There was a faint smell of exhaust fumes from a motor vehicle.

And there were unfamiliar smells. A reek of oil, and a sweeter, denser smell that he vaguely recognized from fireworks on the Fourth of July. And a coppery, metallic smell.

He felt around until he found the switch for the electric light and snapped it on. And, for an instant, wished he had not. He wished that darkness could have stayed for ever. So that he had never seen it.

The terrible sight of his mother on the floor beside the bed. Blood leaking from her shoulder; the whole front of her nightdress sodden with a spreading, dark-crimson stain. Blood everywhere, spattered across the walls, across the sheets, the pillows, the ceiling. She lay on her back, her black hair matted by blood. Part of her head was missing, exposing something wet, gnarly, a brown and grey colour. She was twitching and shaking.

Then, as if someone had reached over and pressed a switch, she fell silent.

He ran forward, crying out, 'Mama, Mama!'

She did not respond.

'Mama, wake up!' He shook her. 'Mama, where's Pop? Mama!'

She did not move.

He fell to his knees and crawled up to her and kissed her. 'Mama, wake up, Mama!' He hugged her and shook her. 'Wake up, Mama! Where's Pop? Where's Pa?'

Still she did not move.

'Mama!' He began crying, confused. 'Mama! Mama!' His arms and face felt sticky. 'Mama, wake, Mama, wake up . . . !'

'What's happening? Gavin? What's happening?' His sister's voice.

He backed away, took a step forward, then backed away again, uncertainly. Kept backing away through the door. And collided with his sister, Aileen, three years older than him, in her nightdress, chewing a pigtail as she always did when she was afraid.

'What's happening?' she asked. 'I heard noises. What's happening?'

'Where's Pop?' he asked. 'Where's Pop? Pop's gone!' Tears were streaming down his face.

'Isn't he in bed?'

He shook his head. 'He's gone with the bad men.'

'What bad men?'

'Where's Pop? He has to wake up Mama! She won't wake up.'

'What bad men?' she asked again, more urgently.

There was blood on the landing. Drops of blood on the stairs. He ran down them, screaming for his pa, and out through the open front door.

The street was deserted.

He felt the rain on his face, smelled the salty tang of the river. For some moments, the rumble high overhead of another train drowned out his cries.

5

From a distance, the man cut a dash. He looked smarter than the usual Brighton seafront crowds in their gaudy beachwear, sandals, flip-flops and Crocs. A gent, with an aloof air, in a blue blazer with silver buttons, smartly pressed slacks, open-neck shirt and a natty cravat. It was only on closer inspection you could see the shirt collar was frayed, there were moth holes in the blazer, and his slicked-back hair was thinning and a gingery-grey colour from bad dyeing. His face looked frayed, too, with the pallor that comes from prison life and takes a long time to shake off. His expression was mean, and despite his diminutive stature – five foot three in his elevated Cuban-heeled boots – he strutted along with an air of insouciance, as if he owned the promenade.

Behind his sunglasses, Amis Smallbone, on his morning constitutional, looked around with hatred. He hated everything. The pleasant warmth of this late June morning. Cyclists who pinged their bells at him as he strayed onto the cycle lane. Stupid grockles with their fat, raw skin burning in the sun, stuffing their faces with rubbish. Young lovers, hand in hand, with their lives ahead of them.

Unlike him.

He had hated prison. Hated the other inmates even more than the officers. He might have been a player in this

11

city once, but all that had fallen apart when he'd been sent down. He hadn't even been able to get any traction on the lucrative drugs market in the jails he had been held in.

And now he was out, on licence, he was hating his freedom, too.

Once, he'd had it all – the big house, expensive cars, a powerboat, and a villa in Marbella on Spain's Costa del Sol. Now he had fuck all. Just a few thousand pounds, a couple of watches and some stolen antique jewellery in the one safety deposit box the police hadn't managed to find.

And one man to thank for his plight.

Detective Superintendent Roy Grace.

He crossed the busy four lanes of King's Road without waiting for the lights to change. Cars braked all around him, their drivers hooting, swearing and shaking their fists at him, but he didn't give a toss. His family used to be big players in this city's underworld. A couple of decades ago, no one would have dared, ever, hoot at a Smallbone. He ignored them all, contemptuously, now.

A little way along the pavement he entered the news-agent's, and was taken aback to see the bastard cop's rugged, serious face staring out of a copy of the *Argus* at him. Close-cropped fair hair, blue eyes, busted nose, beneath the front-page splash.

TRIAL OF BRIGHTON MONSTER RESUMES

He bought the paper and a packet of cigarettes, as he did every day, and filled out a lottery ticket, without much hope.

*

A short while later, back in his basement flat, Amis Small-bone sat in the ripped leather armchair with its busted spring, a glass of Chivas Regal on the table beside him, a smouldering cigarette in his mouth, reading with interest about the case. Venner was on trial for murder, kidnap and trading in illegal videos. Last year, one of Detective Superintendent Grace's officers had been shot and wounded during the attempt to arrest Venner. Too bad it hadn't been Grace himself. Shot dead.

How nice would that be?

But not as nice as something he had in mind. To have Detective Superintendent Grace dead was too good for him. He wanted the cop to really suffer. To be in pain for the rest of his life. Oh yes. Much better. Pain that would never ever go away!

Smallbone dragged on his cigarette, then crushed it out in the ashtray and drained his glass. He had gone to prison still a relatively young man of fifty. Now he'd come out an old man at sixty-two. Detective Superintendent Grace had taken everything he had. Most of all he had taken those crucial twelve years of his life.

Of course, Grace hadn't been a Detective Superintendent back then; just a jumped-up, newly promoted Inspector who had picked on him, targeted him, fitted him up, twisted the evidence, been oh so clever, so fucking smug. It was Grace's persecution that had condemned him, now, to this cruddy rented flat, with its shoddy furniture, no-smoking signs on the walls in each room, and having to report and bloody kowtow to a Probation Officer regularly.

He put the paper down, stood up a little unsteadily, and carried his glass over to the dank-smelling kitchenette, popping some ice cubes out of the fridge-freezer into his glass. It was just gone midday, and he was thinking hard. Thinking how much pleasure he was going to get from hurting Roy Grace. It was the one thing that sustained him right now. The rest of the nation had Olympic fever – the games were starting in a month's time. But he didn't give a toss about them; getting even with Roy Grace was all he cared about.

All he could really think about.

He was going to make that happen. His lips curled into a smile. He just had to find the right person. There were names he knew from before he'd gone to prison, and a few more contacts he'd made inside. But whoever it was wouldn't come cheap, and that was a big problem right now.

Then his phone rang. The display showed the number was withheld.

'Yes?' he answered, suspiciously.

'Amis Smallbone?' It was not a voice he recognized. A rough, Brighton accent.

'Who are you?' he replied, coldly.

'We met a long time back, but you won't remember me. I need some help. You have connections in the antiques world, right? Overseas? For high-value stuff?'

'What if I do?'

'I'm told you need money.'

'Didn't anyone tell you that you shouldn't be calling me on a fucking mobile phone?'

'Yeah, I know that.'

'Then why the fuck are you calling me on mine?'

'I'm talking a lot of money. Several million quid.'

Suddenly, Amis Smallbone was very interested indeed. 'Tell me more.'

The line went dead.

6

They were right, thought Roy Grace, all those people who had told him that having a baby would totally change his life. He yawned, leadenly tired from endless disturbed nights with Cleo getting up every time Noah had woken needing a feed or his nappy changing. One of his colleagues, Nick Nicholl, a recent first-time father, had told him he'd taken to sleeping in a separate room so he wouldn't be disturbed by the baby. But Roy was determined never to do that. The baby was a joint commitment and he had to play his part. But, shit, he felt tired; and grungy; it was a sticky August day and, although all of the windows were open, the air was listless, warm and humid.

The television was on, playing the recording of the Olympics closing ceremony from less than a couple of weeks ago. He and Cleo had both fallen asleep watching it live on the night. He could not remember ever feeling so tired in his life, and it was affecting his concentration at work. He was definitely suffering from *baby brain*.

Ray Davies, from one of his favourite bands, The Kinks, was singing 'Waterloo Sunset', and he turned up the sound slightly to listen. But Cleo did not look up from her book.

Grace had recently crossed the Rubicon to his fortieth birthday. For the past couple of years he had increasingly been dreading that milestone. But when it had finally arrived, both he and Cleo had been too tired to think about a proper celebration. They'd opened a bottle of champagne and fallen asleep before they'd even drunk half of it.

Now they had another celebration due. After a long time, the formalities for his divorce from his wife, Sandy, on the grounds of her being presumed legally dead, had this week been completed, and he was finally free to marry Cleo.

Sandy had been missing since the day of his thirtieth birthday, ten years ago, and he still had no clue as to what had happened to her, or whether she was alive, as he still liked to believe, or long dead, as his friends and family all told him, which probably was the truth. Either way, for the first time he was feeling a sense of release, of truly being able to move on. And a further big part of that was that finally a buyer had been found for the home he and Sandy had shared.

He stared down lovingly – and hopelessly proudly – at his seven-week-old son. At the tiny, cherubic creature, with rosebud lips and chubby pink arms and fingers like a toyshop doll. Noah Jack Grace, in a sleeveless white romper suit, eyes shut, lay on his lap, cradled in his arms. Thin strands of fair hair lay, brushed forward, with his scalp visible beneath. He could see elements of both Cleo and himself in his face, and there was one slightly bemused frown Noah sometimes gave, which reminded Grace of his late father – a police officer, like himself. He would do anything for Noah. He would die for him, without a shadow of hesitation.

Cleo sat beside him on the sofa, in a sleeveless black top, her blonde hair cut shorter than usual and clipped back, engrossed in *Fifty Shades of Grey*. The house was filled with a milky smell of baby powder and fresh laundry. Several soft toys lay on the play mat on the floor, including a teddy bear and a cuddly Thomas The Tank Engine. Above them dangled a mobile with brightly coloured animals and birds.

Humphrey, their young black Labrador-Border collie cross, gnawed a bone, sulkily, in his basket on the far side of the room. He had taken a couple of disdainful looks at Noah when he had first come home, then wandered off, tail between his legs, as if aware he was no longer number one in his owner's eyes, and his attitude had remained the same ever since.

Roy Grace clicked his fingers, beckoning the dog. 'Hey, Humphrey, get over it! Make friends with Noah!'

Humphrey gave his master the evil eye.

It was midday on Tuesday, and Roy Grace had sneaked home for a few hours, because he had a long meeting ahead of him this evening. It was with the prosecution counsel on the trial, at the Old Bailey, of a particularly repugnant villain, Carl Venner, the mastermind behind a snuff movie ring, whom Grace had arrested last year. The trial had been adjourned recently for several weeks because the defendant had claimed to be suffering chest pains. But doctors had now cleared the man to continue with his trial, which had restarted yesterday.

At this moment Roy Grace honestly believed he had never felt happier in his life. But at the same time he felt an overwhelming sense of responsibility. This tiny, frail creature he and Cleo had brought into this world. What kind of future lay ahead for Noah? What would the world be like in twenty or so years, when he became an adult? What would the world be like during the next twenty years – at the end of which Grace would be sixty years old? What could he do to change it? To make it a safer place for Noah? To protect his child from the evil out there, of which Venner, sadly, was just one of life's sewer rats?

What could he do to help his son cope with all the shit that life, inevitably, threw at you?

God, he loved him so much. He wanted to be the best father in the world, and he knew that meant committing a lot of time. Time he wanted to spend, yet, in his chosen career, he was painfully aware it was time he would not always have.

Since Noah had been born, Grace had spent much less time with his son than he'd hoped, because of the demands of work. If he got lucky, and there were no major crimes committed, he might have this weekend relatively free. He was the duty Senior Investigating Officer and his week was due to end at 6 a.m. on Monday. Normally, all SIOs hoped for a high-quality murder – one which would hit the national press, enabling them to shine, to get on the Chief Constable's radar. But right now, Roy Grace hoped for a silent telephone.

That wasn't going to happen.

7

The old lady heard the knock on the door for the third time. 'I'm coming!' she called out. 'Bejazus, I'm coming!' She lifted the saucepan of boiling water and green beans off the hob, grabbed her wheeled Zimmer frame, and began making her way across the kitchen.

Then the phone started ringing. She hesitated. Her brother rang every day at 7 p.m. on the dot, whether he was in England or France, to check she was okay. It was 7 p.m. She grabbed the phone, with its extra-large numbers for her failing vision, and shouted, over the *Emmerdale* theme tune blaring from the television, 'Hold on a minute, will you!'

But it wasn't her brother's voice. It was a younger man with a silky purr. 'I only need a moment of your time.'

'There's someone at the door!' she shouted back, fumbling with the TV remote to turn the sound down. Then she clamped her arthritic hand over the mouthpiece. Despite her years, she still had a strong voice. About the only thing left of her that was still strong, she rued. 'You'll have to wait. I'm on the phone,' she hollered at the front door. Then she lifted her hand. 'I'm back with you, but you'll have to be quick,' she said with her Irish lilt.

'A good friend of yours told me to call you,' the man said.

'And who would that be?'

'Gerard Scott.'

'Gerard Scott?'

'He said to say hello!'

'I don't know any Gerard Scott, for sure.'

'We're saving him two thousand five hundred pounds a year off his heating bill.'

'And how would you be doing that?' she asked, a tad impatiently as she stared at the door, worrying about her beans staying too long in the hot water.

'We have a representative working in your area next week. Perhaps I could make an appointment at a time convenient for you?'

'A representative for what, exactly?'

'Loft insulation.'

'Loft insulation? Why would I be needing loft insulation?'

'We are England's leading specialists. The insulation we put in is so effective it will have fully paid for itself in just nine years from savings on your fuel bills.'

'Nine years, you say?'

'That's right, madam.'

'Well now, I'm ninety-eight years old. That would be a high-class problem, I'd say, for me to think I'm going to be worrying about my heating bills when I'm a hundred and seven. But thank you kindly.'

She hung up, then carried on towards the front door. 'I'm coming! I'm on my way!'

Her brother had been trying to convince her for a long time to sell the house and move into sheltered accommodation, but why the hell should she? This had been her home for over fifty years. Here she had lived happily with her husband, Gordon, who had passed away fifteen years ago, had raised her four children, who had all predeceased her, and had created the once beautiful garden, which she still continued to work in. All her memories were in this house, as well as all the fine paintings and antiques she and her husband had collected during their lives – guided by her brother's discerning eye. She'd been uprooted once in her life, and it was not going to happen again. She was adamant that when she left this place she loved so much, it would be feet first.

Her only concessions to her brother's concerns were the panic button that hung from a cord around her neck, and the housekeeper who came twice a week.

She peered through the spyhole in the front door. In the light of the summer evening she saw two middle-aged men in brown uniforms, with identity tags hung from chains around their necks.

She removed the safety chain and opened the door.

They smiled politely. 'Sorry to disturb you, madam,' the one on the right said. 'We're from the Water Board.' He held up his identity card for her to read.

She did not have her glasses on, but she liked his Irish accent. The face on the card was a little blurred, but it looked like the face of the shaven-headed man in front of her. *Richard Carroll*, she thought his name read, but she couldn't be sure.

'How can I help you, gentlemen?'

'We're investigating a water leak. Have you noticed a drop in water pressure during the past twenty-four hours?'

'No,' she said. 'No, I can't say that I have.' But, she knew, there was a lot of stuff she did not notice these days. Much though it angered her, she was increasingly becoming dependent on others. Although she still kept a tight grip on everything she could.

'Do you mind if we come in and check your water pressure? We'd hate you to be charged for water you're not using.'

'Well, I wouldn't be wanting that either,' she said with

a twinkle in her eye, in her soft Dublin accent. All these bastard utilities were trying to rob you blind all the time and she wasn't one to be having any of it. She scrutinized the phone bills, the electricity bills, the gas and the water. 'I've been thinking the water charges are high of late.'

'All the more indication of a problem,' Richard Carroll said, apologetically.

'You'd better be coming in.'

Holding the Zimmer with one hand, she stepped aside to let the men enter, then closed the door behind them.

Almost immediately she did not like the way their eyes began roaming. At the fine oil paintings hanging on the walls, and then at the Louis XIV table in the hallway. The Georgian tallboy. The Georgian chest. The two Chippendale chairs. Bargains, once, all of them, pointed out by her brother, who knew a thing or two about antiques of all descriptions.

'Where would you like to start your investigations, gentlemen?'

She saw the blur of the man's fist only a fraction of a second before it struck her stomach, punching all the wind out of her. She doubled up, her frail hand clutching at the panic button.

But it was ripped off her neck long before she could press it.

8

It is a truth universally acknowledged, that a single man in possession of a good fortune must be in want of a wife, PC Susi Holliday thought. A sturdily built woman of twenty-eight, with brown curly hair and a constantly cheerful face. That line had been running through her head repeatedly ever since she had woken up this morning. She'd had a day off yesterday, and much to her husband James's incredulity had spent much of it watching all six episodes of the BBC production of *Pride and Prejudice*, binge-eating junk food, and smoking an entire packet of fags. She was like that. One week all healthy, working out at the gym, not smoking, then the next being a total slob.

Now, irreverently, she decided that another truth universally acknowledged is that no one looks their best sitting on a toilet seat with their trousers round their ankles.

Especially not if they are dead.

Memo to self. Please, please, please don't die on the loo.

The need to go to the lavatory was a frequent precursor to a heart attack. All too many did die that way.

Like the plump old man in front of them, in the dingy, narrow little toilet in the squalid Housing Association flat with its bare pale-blue walls and unwashed underwear, socks and shirts lying all over the floor in every room. It smelled rank: a mixture of a rancid, cheesy reek and, the worst smell in the world, a decaying human. Its tenant was named Ralph Meeks, and this was whom she presumed, with revulsion tinged with sadness, she was now staring at.

Like all G5s who had been dead for more than a couple of days, he looked more like a waxwork than a real human being. She always found the total stillness of a cadaver both eerie and fascinating.

His bulky frame was wedged between the walls. There were liver spots on his hands, the crimson and green blotches of advanced decomposition on his face and visible parts of his body. An insistent swarm of blowflies crawled over his face and neck and hands, and buzzed around him.

Folds of flesh hung from the man's midriff, forming a canopy over his private parts. His dome was bald with little tufts of hair on either side, he had a hearing aid in his right ear, and his mouth was frozen open in an expression of surprise, one that was mirrored in his startled, lifeless eyes. As if dying had not, she thought, irreverently, been on his list of *things to do* that day, and certainly not in this un-dignified way.

A television was on in the sparsely furnished living room, a daytime chat show on which, ironically, there was a discussion about the plight of the elderly.

She glanced around looking for signs of anything per-sonal. But there were no photographs, no pictures on any of the walls. She saw an ashtray full of butts, with a lighter and a packet of cigarettes beside it, and a beer can with a half-empty glass tumbler. A small, untidy stack of old gardening magazines lay on the floor, next to a pile of *Daily Mirror* newspapers.

Ralph Meeks had clearly been dead for a while, in here all alone. It was a sad but common story in cities. They were on the second floor of a low-rise apartment block. But Ralph Meeks had no friends, no neighbours bothering to check he was okay, no one who had thought it odd that the post was getting more and more jammed in the letter box every day. Not until he had started to decompose, and neighbours had begun to notice the smell out in the corridor, had anyone been bothered to check on Meeks.

The stench in the corridor was nothing compared with that inside the flat. It was a hundred times worse in here. The stench and the buzzing of flies. It was making her gag, and her colleague, PC Dave Roberts, was keeping his gloved hand over his nose.

The two immediate tasks were to call in their Sergeant to help them assess whether this was a natural death, or whether there were any suspicious circumstances, in which case they would involve CID and seal the flat as a crime scene. Their second was to call a paramedic to have the man's death confirmed. Fairly unnecessary in this case, but a legal formality. The next duty would be to ask a Coroner's Officer to attend. And finally, if it was decided no forensic examination of the body was required in situ, a call would be made to Brighton and Hove Mortuary to recover the body.

Sudden deaths – or *G5*s, as the form for them was called – were the least favourite shouts for most Response officers. But Susi Holliday actually liked them, and found them interesting. This was the fifteenth she had attended since joining the Response Team three years ago.

Turning to her colleague, eighteen years her senior, she said, 'Anything bothering you about this?'

He shook his head, feeling queasy. 'Nope.' He shrugged. 'Except – just the thought that could be me one day.'

Susi grinned. 'Best thing is to try to avoid growing old. Growing old kills you, eventually.'

'Yep, guess I'd prefer to die young, with my trousers on.'

She gave him a mischievous grin. 'Wouldn't that depend who you were with?'

9

Whenever Roy Grace left his front door he was always on guard. After over twenty years as a cop, looking around for anything unusual or out of place had long become second nature. It used to irritate his former wife, Sandy. One time, during his early days as a Detective Constable, he'd spotted a man slipping a handbag off the back of a chair in a crowded pub, and chased him a mile on foot, through Brighton, before rugby-tackling and arresting him. It had been the end of their evening, as he'd had to spend the next four hours booking the thief into custody and filling out forms.

Often when he and Sandy were out for a meal, she would notice his eyes roving and kick him sharply under the restaurant table, hissing, '*Stoppit, Grace!*'

But he couldn't help it. In any public place, he couldn't relax unless he knew he was somewhere there were no obvious villains, and no immediate signs of anything about to kick off. Sandy used to joke that while other women had to be wary of their men ogling other women, she had to put up with him ogling Brighton's pond life.

But there was one thing he never told her, because he didn't want to worry her: he knew, like all police officers, there was always the danger of retribution by an aggrieved villain. Most *crims* accepted getting arrested – some saw it as part of the game; some shrugged at the inevitability; some just gave up the ghost from the moment the handcuffs were snapped in place. But there were a few who harboured grudges.

Part of the reason judges traditionally wore wigs was to disguise themselves, so they would not be recognized later by those they had sent down. The police had never had such protection. But even if they had, to someone who was determined enough, there were plenty of other ways to track them down.

*

Such a man, right now, was sitting in his car, in front of an antiques shop that specialized in fireplaces, opposite the gates of a smart town-house development in the centre of Brighton.

He had a grudge against one particular Sussex Police officer, Detective Superintendent Roy Grace.

The cop's baby was in there, in the third house on the left. He'd obtained plans of the house from the Planning Office where they were filed in the original building application, fifteen years ago, to turn the old warehouse into a courtyard development of seven town houses.

The baby would sleep in the tiny room opposite, with the window overlooking the courtyard.

But what interested him most of all right now was an estate agent's sign, fixed to the wall to the right of the wrought-iron gates to the courtyard, advertising, TOWN HOUSE TO RENT.

What fun to be Roy Grace's neighbour. And how convenient?

He'd be able to watch every movement. And bide his time.

Happy days again!

10

Two hours after first entering Ralph Meeks' flat, Susi Holliday and Dave Roberts were back out on the streets of Brighton in their patrol car. Susi drove. She loved her job. Hunting was what she liked to call it, all the time they weren't actually on a *shout* – as calls to incidents were known colloquially.

Dave, at forty-six, was one of the oldest PCs on the unit. Response was considered a young person's game, and it could at times be extremely physical – intervening in violent domestic fights, pub brawls and chasing after robbers and burglars. But he'd been on this unit for twenty years and had no interest in promotion and the desk work that would involve, or in any other area of policing.

If anyone were to ask him what he most loved about his job, he would have replied that it was never knowing what was going to happen in five minutes' time. That, and ripping through the city on blues and twos, which almost every police officer with a Pursuit Driving ticket he had ever talked to admitted was one of the greatest kicks of the job.

They were driving up North Street towards the Clock Tower, one of the city's most prominent landmarks. Watching the faces of people meandering along the pavements on both sides of the road, recognizing the occasional villain among the crowds. And all the time monitoring their radios, clipped below their shoulders. Waiting for the next shout from the Control Room.

It was coming up to midday, on a fine late August

Thursday morning. They'd started their shift at 7 a.m. and would be on until 4 p.m. So far they'd attended a call to a potential firearms incident up at Brighton Racecourse, which had turned out to be a man shooting rabbits. That had been followed by a rip across the city to attend a collision between a motor scooter and a bin lorry, which had, fortunately, been less serious than it had sounded. Then another shout to attend a report of a woman screaming for help. Which had turned out to be an infant having a tantrum. Then the Ralph Meeks G5.

For the past thirty minutes all had been quiet. They were thinking about returning to John Street police station to eat their packed lunches, have a comfort break and fill in the paperwork on Meeks.

'What are your plans for the weekend?' Dave Roberts asked Susi. They crewed together regularly and got on well.

'Going to the Albion with James,' she said. 'You?'

'It's Maxim's fifteenth birthday on Saturday,' he replied. 'Marilyn and I are taking him and some of his friends for fish and chips on the pier – to the Palm Court. Best fish and chips in Brighton!'

'Tiffany going, too?'

Tiffany was his teenage daughter.

As he was about to reply, their radios crackled into life.

'Charlie Romeo Zero Three?'

'Yes, yes, Charlie Romeo Zero Three,' Dave answered.

'Charlie Romeo Zero Three, we've a call from a concerned individual. A man who normally speaks to his elderly sister every day. Says he's not been able to reach her for two days. He's out of the country, otherwise he would have gone round to check on her himself. Her name is Aileen McWhirter. The address is 146 Withdean Road, Brighton. Please check this out, Grade Two.'

All Control Room calls were graded One to Four. *Grade One* was immediate response, with a target time of within fifteen minutes. *Grade Two* was prompt response, with a target time of within one hour. *Grade Three* was a planned response, by appointment, which could be made several days later. *Grade Four* was no attendance by police, but dealt with over the phone.

'Charlie Romeo Zero Three, we're on our way.' Then, doing a quick calculation, Dave Roberts said, 'We'll be there in about fifteen minutes.'

Both officers looked at each other. They'd not had a G5 in several weeks, until this morning. One of their colleagues had joked they were like buses. You had none for ages then two came along together.

11

Sarah Courteney lay back nervously on the blue reclining couch in the doctor's clinic. It wasn't the needle or the pain that scared her; it was a whole bunch of other stuff. Some of it was to do with her hitting forty in two weeks' time, and all the unwelcome shit that went with that particular milestone. Such as the wrinkles that were becoming increasingly persistent; the grey hairs that were starting to appear. Her career as a local TV news presenter was constantly under threat from younger, fresher faces.

But what scared her most of all was her husband, Lucas. More and more every day. He was losing the plot and blaming everything on her, from his increasing gambling debts, his bouts of impotence – not entirely unrelated to his heavy drinking – and his rages. One constant target of his rages was her inability, after eight years of constant trying – including four of IVF hell – to go to term with a baby. She had a son by her previous marriage, but his relationship with his stepfather was disastrous – and not much better with her. There was constant friction in the house.

Royce Revson stood in his small, sterile clinic, studying a monitor displaying an array of turquoise symbols, amid a bank of technical apparatus. Nudging fifty-six, he could have passed for someone in his mid-forties. A stocky, energetic man with short, jet-black hair, who exuded charm, he was wearing a purple short-sleeved shirt, collegiate tie, black trousers, blue surgical gloves, and had an infrared goggle headset clipped to his forehead. He turned from the machine and beamed down at his patient, his winning, boyish smile filled with all the genuine enthusiasm and confidence of a man on a mission.

And he was indeed on a mission: to help women – and frequently men, too – ward off the cruelties of ageing with a little help from cosmetic chemicals. Such as the woman who lay back at this moment on his blue reclining couch. A raven-haired beauty, wearing a black tunic dress over black leggings and black suede sandals with large buckles.

Her husband, she had confided in Revson, the way many of his patients did, was a bully who often hit her. One of the city's prominent antiques dealers, he had a constantly roving eye and a vile temper, which had got progressively worse as the antiques trade had diminished – partly due to the financial climate, but more because of the change in fashion. People wanted a modern look in their homes these days.

Why Sarah did not leave the brute was a mystery that, in Royce Revson's long experience, was repeated by women many times over. He hoped to keep her looking young and attractive enough so when the day finally came that her marriage was over, she'd be able to attract someone new and hopefully kinder. Maybe even himself? But he pushed that thought away almost before it had even entered his head. Fancying his patients was not an option. However tempting. And Sarah Courteney was very tempting indeed.

Unlike some of his clientele, which numbered a high percentage of the city's richest, spoilt bitches, Sarah was a genuinely nice and kind person. For the past two years since she'd become a patient, he'd done a good job of keeping her looking youthful, through Botox, collagen and the lasering away of the occasional unwelcome vein that popped on her cheeks.

To inspire client confidence, it helped, of course, that he'd had a fair amount of non-surgical intervention himself. And a bit of actual surgery that he omitted to talk about – reducing the wrinkles on his neck, and raising his drooping eyelids. He loathed what he called 'the tyranny of ageing', and had devoted much of his life to, if not halting or reversing it, at least cheating it of some of its worst ravages.

'You're looking very tanned, Sarah,' he said.

'I've just got back from Dubai.'

'Holiday?'

She nodded.

'With your husband?'

'No, with a girlfriend – we go every year. I love it there. I do my annual clothes shopping there.'

Revson was relieved that she got some time away from the monster. He noticed the shiny Cartier Tank watch on her wrist. 'Is that new?'

She smiled. 'Yes, got that there. I found a little jewellery place a few years ago that makes really good-quality copies – not like most of the rubbish. He's a proper craftsman, can get anything you want copied in just a few days.'

'My wife wants one of those Cartier bracelets,' he said, then frowned. 'A *Tennis* bracelet, is it? They cost a fortune.'

'He'd be able to make one for you – she'd never know the difference.'

'Is it legal?'

She shrugged. 'I can give you his email address. You can send him a photo of what you want and he'll send you a quote.'

'Hmm, thanks, I might well do that.' Pulling his goggles

down over his eyes, he accepted the hypodermic needle from one of his two assistants dressed in identical navy tunics, and stepped forward across the grey and white speckled floor. 'Okay, ready?'

Sarah nodded. It would hurt, she knew. But the pain was a small price to pay for the difference she felt it would make to her lips. 'No gain without pain' was one of her favourite sayings. She said it now.

Royce slid the slender needle through her upper lip.

She winced.

'Okay?' he asked.

She nodded with her eyes. *No gain without pain . . . No gain without pain . . . No gain without pain.* She repeated the mantra continuously, silently.

Steadily, he worked his way along her upper, then lower lips.

'It'll look like an allergic reaction for a couple of days,' he said. 'Before they settle down.'

'I'm not on television again until Tuesday,' she said.

'You'll be fine by then.'

'You think so?'

'Aren't you usually?'

'Yep.'

He smiled. Sure, it was clients like this that had helped make him a wealthy man, but money had never motivated him. Every time a beautiful woman like Sarah Courteney slipped off his couch with a smile on her face, he wanted to punch his fist in the air and give two fingers to whatever sadist that cruel god of ageing was.

12

Withdean Road was one of the city's most exclusive addresses. Secluded houses were set well back behind high walls or screens of trees and shrubbery in a quiet, meandering, tree-lined street. Susi Holliday drove slowly as Dave Roberts called out the numbers. The even ones were on the right-hand side.

'Here!' he said.

She turned in through old wooden gates that looked in bad repair and drove down a steep, winding, potholed tarmac drive. There were rhododendron bushes to the right, and to the left down below them, beyond a rockery and a steep lawn, the pebbledashed façade of a grand Edwardian house, with mock-Tudor features, leaded-light windows and high gables. Fixed high up on the wall was a red LanGuard alarm box.

At the end of the drive, to the rear of the mansion, was a courtyard in front of two dilapidated garages. Susi stopped the car and they climbed out. A fence to their right, with tall trees behind, screening off the neighbouring house, was in a state of neglect, but the terraced lawns had recently been mown and there were sweet scents of cut grass and roses in the air. The property had a fine view across the valley where the London–Brighton railway line ran at the bottom of a steep chalk escarpment, to the houses on the far side of Withdean and Patcham and the playing fields of Varndean School.

Close up, they could see the house was in poor repair,

with the rendering badly in need of a lick of paint and some chunks missing; the paintwork around the window frames was peeling, the condition that often signalled an elderly occupant. A thrush was washing itself in a stone birdbath in a small rectangle of lawn bounded by rose trees.

'Shame not to look after such a beautiful place,' Dave Roberts said.

Susi Holliday nodded, looking around, thinking how much her dog would love it here, and wondering how many millions it would cost to buy, even in its current state.

They took the pathway around to the front, peering through each of the windows they passed for any signs of the occupant. They walked by a rose garden that needed some TLC, then reached a large, tiled porch. Rolled copies of the *Daily Telegraph* and the *Argus* were rammed into the letter box. More newspapers and some mail lay by the foot of the door. Not a good sign.

Susi Holliday knelt and looked at the dates. 'Yesterday – Wednesday – and today,' she announced.

Dave Roberts rang the doorbell. They waited. But there was no answer. Then he knocked on the door. It was a knock he had perfected, and one, he proudly boasted, that would wake the dead.

It was greeted with silence.

He rammed his hand through the letter box, and it plunged into a whole mass of correspondence. He pulled some out. A mixture of letters and advertising pamphlets. Among them a buff envelope with HMRC printed on it, addressed to Mrs Aileen McWhirter, appeared to confirm they were at the right address.

He pressed his nose up against the letter box, and sniffed for that unmistakable leaden, clingy, rancid smell of death. Unlike at Ralph Meeks' home earlier, he did not detect it, but that gave him no assurance that Mrs Mc-Whirter was still alive. Even in these summer months it could take a week, at least, before a body started to smell.

He gave one more knock, then dialled the phone number that the Controller had given them. They could hear it ringing, somewhere inside the house, but there was no answer. After some moments, it went to answerphone.

They made a complete circuit around the exterior, peering intently through each window for signs of life. The television was on in the kitchen. They saw a copy of the magazine *Sussex Life* on the table. Alongside it was a plate, with a knife and fork. A saucepan sat beside the Aga.

'What do you think?' PC Holliday asked.

In reply, her colleague pulled on a pair of protective gloves, took out his weighted baton, and smashed a pane of the leaded-light window beside the front door. Then he pushed his hand through, careful to avoid the jagged glass, found the door latch and opened it.

They walked through into a large, oak-panelled hallway, on which lay several fine, but worn, Persian rugs. Almost instantly they noticed dark rectangles on the bare walls, as if pictures had once hung there. And the entire hallway, for such a grand house, seemed strangely bare.

As did most of the downstairs rooms they searched.

Leaving his colleague to continue downstairs, Dave Roberts walked up the ornate circular staircase. Only a few moments later he shouted, 'Susi, quick! Up here!'

13

Roy Grace was not due in court until sometime next week at the earliest. And it was a bank holiday weekend ahead of him. Hopefully time to spend with Cleo and Noah. He'd taken a bunch of paperwork home so he could relieve Cleo from baby duties for a while. And, so far so good! Although tomorrow, Friday, was normally a jinxed day for him. So often, just as he thought he was getting away with a quiet week as the duty Senior Investigating Officer, whenever he got to Friday, something seemed to happen. He was really hoping that, for once, he'd be left in peace. He had some great plans for this weekend, if he was.

On Saturday afternoon he'd been invited by a colleague who had a pair of tickets to one of the first football games of the season at Brighton's fabulous new Amex Stadium, which he had only been to once. He really hoped he'd be able to make it. Then in the evening he and Cleo planned to go out for a meal for the first time since Noah had been born.

It was mid-afternoon. He'd changed Noah's nappy and Noah was now sleeping in his cot, with a white dummy in his mouth. Cleo was having a snooze in bed. Humphrey lay in his basket, a rubber bone in front of his nose, still sulking away with jealousy about Noah, despite his master having taken him for a five-mile run along Brighton seafront early this morning.

Roy Grace removed a lengthy form from a large envelope. After several months of having his house in Hove on the market, the estate agents had finally found a buyer for it. A woman with a small boy, currently living in Germany. He had not met them, but she seemed serious and a date had been set for the exchange of contracts. The form was a detailed questionnaire about all aspects of the property, from the woman's conveyancing solicitor.

Cleo's house, where he was now living, was also on the market. Their plan was to pool the proceeds of the two houses and buy a property in the country, a short distance from Brighton, where Humphrey could have a decent-size garden, and maybe even a field, to roam in.

The only person not happy about the whole situation was his colleague and closest friend, Glenn Branson, who had been lodging at Roy's house since splitting up with his wife. Poor Glenn would have to find somewhere new to live; but it was time he moved on, got a place of his own and got his life back together.

Just as Roy focused on the first item on the form, the house phone rang.

He snatched the receiver, not wanting the ringing to wake Noah. 'Hello?' he answered quietly, hoping desperately this was not to do with work.

The male voice at the other end spoke with a silky purr, and almost instantly, Grace felt relieved – and irritated.

'Good afternoon. I'm calling because a good friend of yours told me to call you.'

'Oh really, who was that?'

'Gerard Scott.'

'I'm sorry, I don't know anyone of that name.'

'He says to pass on his very best wishes.'

'I think you must have the wrong number.'

'We're saving him two thousand five hundred pounds a year off his heating bill.'

'Really?' Grace disliked the intrusion of telesales people, although he could not help having a tiny amount of sympathy for them, trying to make a living. 'How?'

'We have a representative working in your area next week. Perhaps I could make an appointment at a time convenient for you?'

'A representative for what, exactly?'

'Loft insulation.'

'Loft insulation?'

'We are England's leading specialists. The insulation we put in is so effective it will have fully paid for itself in just nine years from savings on your fuel bills.'

Quite apart from anything else, with their plans to move, Cleo wasn't about to spend any money on this place that wasn't absolutely necessary. Mischievously, he said, 'Are you aware you're calling a crime scene?'

'A crime scene?'

'I need your name, address, date of birth and your connection with the murder victim. Are you willing to come voluntarily to Brighton police station to make a statement?'

There was a sudden silence. It was followed by the click of the line disconnecting.

Yesss! Grace smiled at his small triumph. He looked down at his sleeping son.

Moments later his mobile rang. He answered. It was the new duty Detective Inspector at Brighton's John Street police station, who had replaced the recently promoted Jason Tingley. Any call from him was unlikely to be good news.

'Sorry to bother you, sir. We have a nasty tie-up domestic robbery in Withdean Road. A ninety-eight-year-old lady has been tortured. She's been taken to the ITU at the

Royal Sussex County Hospital. Looks like her home may have been stripped of antiques and paintings.'

Stepping away from Noah, to the far end of the room, he asked, 'Is she going to survive?'

'Well, she's slipping in and out of consciousness, sir.'

'What do you have on it?' he asked.

'Nothing so far. This is a very vicious attack. I've attended myself and my feelings are this is something for Major Crime to handle. All the indications are that this is a high-value robbery, and I don't think the victim will make it.'

Thugs who hurt elderly people were high up on Roy Grace's list of what made him truly angry. 'Okay,' he said, masking his reluctance to be involved. 'Give me the details.'

He scribbled them down on a pad. Then, when he had finished with the DI, he called Detective Sergeant Glenn Branson, whom he had made an acting Detective Inspector on the last case they had been on together, two months back, when a stalker was threatening the life of a popstar-turned-actress who had been making a movie in Brighton.

'Doing anything important right now, Glenn?' he asked.

'Apart from dealing with the divorce papers from my bitch wife?' he replied.

'Good. Meet me at 146 Withdean Road in thirty minutes.'

'Smart address, that street.'

'So be on your best behaviour!'

14

Yet again he sat in the elderly, borrowed, S-Type Jaguar outside the entrance to the gated development where Roy Grace now lived with his beloved Cleo Morey and their two-month-old baby, Noah. Noah Jack Grace.

The windows of the Jaguar were illegally blackened. No one could see him. No one could see the mask of hatred that was his face.

Noah Jack.

He'd got all the details from the Registry Office at Brighton Town Hall.

Noah Jack Grace.

Leave him alone, friends had said. *Move on.*

No way. You could not just forget a man who had totally screwed your life. You had to take things one step at a time. And this was the first step. You had to level the score. Last night he'd watched, through night-vision binoculars, as one of the residents had punched the code into the number panel beside the gates. Later he'd entered himself, checked there was no one watching and no CCTV cameras, and stood in the darkness outside the Grace house, as he liked to call it. He'd watched through the slats in the blinds as Detective Superintendent Grace and his slut, Cleo, lay curled up on the sofa in front of the television, with the baby monitor beside them.

Such a cosy scene.

How sweet would it be for Cleo Morey, Senior Anatomical Pathology Technician at Brighton and Hove Mortuary, to attend the recovery of a baby, suffocated by a plastic bag over its head, from a rubbish dump? And then find it was her own?

How symbolic would that be?

Rubbish father, rubbish baby.

He liked that image so much. But he also liked the image of Grace coming home to find his beautiful slut permanently disfigured. Acid in her face might teach her not to fraternize with cops.

Options. He liked having options. You didn't have much freedom of choice when you were in prison, but free, you had all the options in the world.

Yes.

He crushed out his cigarette in the ashtray.

And now the gates were opening. Someone was walking out. Suited and booted. Detective Superintendent Roy Grace. Looking a bit tired.

He watched him stride, in the afternoon sunshine, up the road towards the black Alfa Romeo Giulietta in the residents' parking bay a short distance away.

He saw the brake lights come on, then the car drive away into the summer afternoon.

He thought about the pleasure he would get from Detective Superintendent Roy Grace's suffering.

Oh yes. The joy of revenge. A dish best eaten cold.

A cold baby.

He liked that idea a lot.

The unit that was for rent was number 4. The Grace House was next door. The adjoining property. Just a few formalities to settle and then, in a week or so's time, he would become their next-door neighbour.

In Roy Grace's face, for a change, instead of the copper being in his.

How sweet was that going to be?

15

An icy breeze blew, and sleet was falling, as the small boy stood, with his sister and his stern aunt, amid the huge crowd of people along the wharf at Pier 54. He was dressed in a long coat, woollen gloves and a tweed cap, and he looked forlorn. The few possessions he owned in the world were crammed into the small leather valise which sat on the ground beside him. He felt dwarfed by the crowd.

He was five years old, feeling lost and bewildered – and angry at his aunt. She was taking him and his sister away from his ma and pa. His ma was in the cemetery and she wasn't coming home, he understood that much; that she had left for ever. She had gone to another place. She was in Heaven.

But his pa might come home at any time. He wanted to wait, but his aunt wouldn't let him. His pa wasn't ever coming back, she told him. His sister believed her, but he refused to. The big guy, with a silver rabbit on a chain around his neck, who hoisted him up on his shoulders, who pitched balls at him, who took him on the rides at Coney Island, and went swimming in the sea, and kissed him with his bristly face, and smelled of beer and tobacco, and told him stories about the Man in the Moon, and sneaked off with him to the zoo when he had promised his mother he was taking him to church – he was coming home.

He *was*. He knew it.

'I don't want to go,' he said petulantly. 'I want to go home and wait for Pa. I hate you!' Then he stamped his foot on the ground.

'You're going to like Ireland,' she said. 'It's a better place. Safer. Less troubles there.'

'Maybe Pa will be there.'

Oonagh Daly said nothing.

'Maybe? Do you think?' he asked hopefully.

She still said nothing.

There was a tang of salt in the air, peppered with an acrid stench of burning coke, sweet snatches of cigarette and pipe smoke. All around was the constant grinding of machinery, men shouting, the cry of gulls. A crate swung on creaking ropes, and pulleys clanked and squeaked high above him. The dark hull of the ship rose even higher, like a mountain. The boy looked around him. His pa worked on the waterfront; maybe he was working here today? He watched every face. Every single face.

It felt wrong to be leaving. He needed to find his pa. But now they were about to sail thousands of miles away. Away from his pa. He did not understand why.

He stared up at tall people. At the cranes and the derricks, and the massive hull of the ship, the *Mauretania*, with its four funnels and gangways. A rope pulled at a capstan near him, and groaned. He caught a glimpse of the dark-green water of the Hudson between the ship and the quay; heard the slop-splash of the water. It was glossy with oil, with bubbles of froth, and litter suspended in it. They would be boarding soon. The ship was going to take them to a place called Dublin, in Ireland. His ma was in Heaven, and his pa had disappeared, taken by the bad men. They'd killed him, too, his aunt said. But he did not believe her.

Now his aunt Oonagh, whom he barely knew and did not like, was taking them to a new life, she said. A place where they would be safer. To a farm in the countryside where there were chickens, cows, pigs and sheep.

He didn't want chickens or cows or pigs or sheep. He wanted his pa.

He didn't want to leave. He was crying. Every few minutes his aunt would dab his eyes with a handkerchief. His sister, who was three years older, clutched her ragged little bear, Mr Stuffykins, under her arm and was silent. The three of them waited, watching an endless procession of people making their ascent up the gangway, some elderly, but most of them young and many with babies and small children. They carried suitcases, packing cases, wooden and cardboard boxes, and sometimes dogs and cats in baskets. Occasionally one of them lugged a piece of furniture. One man he watched was staggering under the weight of a wooden grandfather clock.

None of them noticed the youth, with a cap low over his face, elbowing his way through the crowd behind them. Not until the boy heard his name called out.

He turned. 'Yes?'

The youth thrust a heavy brown-paper bag into the boy's hand. 'I was told to give you this,' he said. 'For you and your sister. And to tell you, '*Watch the numbers!*'

'Excuse me!' his aunt called out.

But he was already moving away, quickly and furtively.

'Excuse me!' she called out louder. 'Young man, who sent you?'

'A friend!' he replied. Then within seconds, like a sinking stone, he was swallowed by the crowd and vanished.

'Aunt Oonagh, who was that boy?' his sister, engulfed

in a duffel coat too big for her and wearing a bobble hat, asked.

'Let me see that,' their aunt said, snatching the bag from the boy's hand, surprised at how heavy it was. She peered inside it, and frowned. It contained a small black revolver, a broken pocket watch and a folded page from a newspaper.

She removed the paper and opened it carefully. It was the front page of an old copy of the *Daily News*. The headline was the murder of Brendan Daly's wife, and the abduction and disappearance of Brendan Daly, chief contender for the role of boss of the White Hand Gang. The children's parents.

There was a photograph of Daly. A big, handsome, angry-looking guy with a shock of shiny black hair, slicked back, wearing a three-piece suit, with a draped pocket watch chain, a rumpled white shirt and a plain tie, beneath a greatcoat.

Scribbled down the margin in blue ink were four names and twelve numbers.

'What does it say?' his sister asked.

His aunt showed it to her, then turned it over. The boy looked too. He couldn't read what the newspaper said, and he struggled with the names, but he could read the twelve numbers.

9 5 3 7 0 4 0 4 2 4 0 4, the boy read out, slowly. 'What do they mean?' he asked.

'You tell me!' his aunt said, handing it to him. 'They were given to you. You tell me.'

It was something important, he knew. It had to be. But he had no idea what.

'Are they the names of the bad men who took Pa?' his sister said.

His aunt said nothing.

The boy folded the piece of paper and tucked it carefully into his inside pocket. Then he looked at the gun that his aunt had lifted from the bag and was holding nervously, as if scared it was about to sting or bite her. 'I should get rid of this,' she said. 'It's a bad thing to have a gun.' She turned, and started weaving through the crowd towards the edge of the quay. But as she was about to throw it into the water, the boy grabbed her arm.

'No!' he said. 'It may be Pa's! He might want it back! He might come for it, he might!' He burst into tears.

She looked down at him and her expression softened. 'All right, we'll keep it for the voyage. Just in case your pa's waiting for us at the other end.'

He nodded eagerly, wiping away his tears with the back of his right hand.

His aunt put the gun into her purse, then removed the watch. It was a man's gold-case pocket watch, on a chain, with a moon-phase on the dial. The crystal was cracked and the crown slightly buckled. The moon hands were stopped at five minutes past four. He snatched it from her hand and stared at it. 'Pa's watch,' he said. 'It's Pa's.'

There was a long, loud, single blast of the ship's horn. That and the five gunshots in the night and the screams of his mother were the sounds by which the boy would, for the rest of his life, remember New York.

Together with the image of the watch.

16

In the hushed warm air of the Intensive Care Unit of the Royal Sussex County Hospital, the old man, tired from his flight back from the South of France, sat beside the unconscious woman, holding her frail, veined and liver-spotted hand. Somewhere near he heard the swish of a curtain being pulled.

'Aileen, I'm here, can you hear me?'

He felt a faint squeeze back. Her silver hair, normally elegantly coiffed, looked ragged and matted. Her face, beneath the bandages, was puffy, bloated, mottled with black and orange bruises, and there were a mass of what he had been told were cigarette burns all around her neck. The patches of her bare flesh that were unmarked were the alabaster colour of a cadaver.

Anger seethed in him. He was thinking about the long journey through life they had both made. To end up like this. He was not a man who often cried, but at this moment, he was crushing tears with his eyelashes.

She had compound and depressed skull fractures, a lesion to the cervical region of her spinal cord, from where someone had stamped on her, which was likely to leave her a paraplegic if she survived, as well as an almost irrelevant – at this stage – fractured right clavicle and fractured pelvis.

Aileen had been in steady decline throughout the day,

and although he was still clinging to a desperate, increasingly irrational hope, he was starting to sense a terrible inevitability.

Every few moments he heard the *beep-beep-bong* of a monitor alarm. He breathed in the smells of sterilizing chemicals, the occasional tang of cologne, and a faint background smell of warm electrical equipment.

She was in the bed, bandaged and wired, endotracheal and nasogastric tubes in her mouth and nostrils. She had a probe in her skull to measure her intracranial pressure, another on one finger, and a forest of IV lines and drains from bags suspended from drip-stands running into her crinkly arms and abdomen. Eyes shut, she lay motionless, surrounded by racks of monitoring and life-support apparatus. Two computer display screens were mounted to her right, and there was a laptop on the trolley at the end of the bed with all her notes and readings on it.

'Aileen, I'm here with you. It's Gavin. I'm here.'

Then he saw her lips moving, although he could not hear her voice. He leaned down, close to her lips, but still could hear no sound. He looked back at her.

'What did they take?' she mouthed.

'I don't know,' he said. 'I don't know what they took yet, but none of that matters. Only you matter.'

Again she mouthed the words. 'Did they take the watch? It was all we had of him. Remember the message that boy gave you. *Watch the numbers?*'

And suddenly he was back ninety years. To the quay on Ellis Island, waiting to board the *Mauretania*. The youth in the cap with the heavy brown-paper bag. And he remembered those words too now.

'What do you think he meant, Aileen?'

But there was no reaction.

17

The elderly blue Mercedes limousine, with its darkened rear windows, wound down the potholed drive. Music was playing loudly. The 'Ode To Joy' chorus from the Philharmonic Orchestra. His boss's choice. The boss liked cultural stuff like this. Choral, ethereal. Music that sounded like the gods were calling you. That kind of shit.

The grand Edwardian house sat below them, fronted by mature shrubbery, a rockery and a steep lawn. The drive went all the way around to the rear. At the bottom, in the wide space between two decrepit garages, was a whole cluster of vehicles. Two marked police cars, and what looked like two unmarked ones, and a white van with the Sussex Police crest and the words SCIENTIFIC SUPPORT UNIT emblazoned along the side. Blue and white crime scene tape sealed off the pathway to the house itself, in front of which stood a uniformed woman police officer with a clipboard.

The driver got out; a week short of his seventieth birthday, he was thin as a rake and stooped, with ragged silver hair poking out beneath his chauffeur's cap that was two sizes too big.

'Sorry about the bumps, boss,' he wheezed as he opened the rear door.

Gavin Daly put down the SuDoku he was working on, stepped out, steadying himself with his black, rubber-tipped cane. Its silver head was a hawk with a piercing gaze. He ignored his minder's proffered helping hand, and pulled himself upright.

Tanned, with immaculate, veneered teeth and a ramrod posture, Daly could have passed for a man two decades younger. He had a hooked, down-turned flat nose that gave him the air, like the head of his stick, of a bird of prey, a shoulder-length mane of white hair, and electric-blue eyes that were normally filled with warmth and charm, but today burned bright with anger behind his horn-rimmed glasses. He was dressed in a beige linen suit, open-neck blue shirt with a paisley cravat, tasselled brown Ferragamo loafers, and held an unlit, half-smoked Cohiba in his hand. Only the liver spots on his face and hands, his wrinkled neck and his slow pace gave any real clue to his age.

Masking his fury as he walked up to the police officer, he spoke calmly but firmly. 'My name is Gavin Daly,' he said. 'This is my sister's house. Detective Superintendent Grace is expecting me.' His voice was rich and polished, carrying just the faintest trace of his Irish antecedents. When he needed it, he had the true gift of the gab. He could sell snow to Eskimos, sand to Bedouins and bathing suits to fish. He had made his first fortune in clocked old cars, and his second, much greater one, in high-end antiques, specializing in watches and clocks.

She looked down at her clipboard, then spoke into her radio.

A few moments later a tall black man in a white protective oversuit and overshoes approached him. 'Mr Daly, I'm Detective Inspector Branson, the Deputy Senior Investigating Officer on this case. Thank you for coming – and I'm sorry about the circumstances.'

'Not as sorry as I am,' Daly said, with a wry smile.

'Of course, sir. I understand.'

'You do? Tell me what you understand? You know what it feels like, do you, to see your ninety-eight-year-old sister in Intensive Care, and to be told of the vile things that have been done to her?'

'We're going to do everything in our power to catch the despicable people who did this, sir.'

Daly stared back at him, but said nothing. He was going to have his son do everything in his power to find them too. And if his violent son got there first, as he intended, the police weren't going to find them. Ever.

A stocky man, fully suited and hooded, appeared holding a protective suit and boots. 'I'm David Green, the Crime Scene Manager, sir. I'd appreciate it if you would put these on.'

Glenn Branson helped the old man struggle into them. As he did so he said, 'I understand you've flown back from France today – and you've been to see your sister?'

'I have.'

'How is she doing?'

'Not good,' Daly replied, curtly. 'What would you expect? That she's standing on her bed performing a jig?'

Branson was grateful that Roy Grace was here at the scene. This man was not going to be easy to deal with – as he had already been forewarned. David Green handed Daly a pair of gloves, then the three walked around to the front of the house. As they entered the porch, and walked onto SOCO metal stepping plates through the doorway into the hall, Daly saw two Scenes of Crime Officers, a male and a female, both in white oversuits, the woman on her knees making tapings, the man taking photographs.

He looked around at the dark rectangles on the walls. He'd last been here a fortnight ago. Then it had been filled with paintings and beautiful objects. Now it looked like removals men had cleared the place.

'Your sister lived here all on her own, Mr Daly?'

'She has a part-time housekeeper – but the woman's away on holiday. And a gardener who comes once a week.'

'Would you consider both of them trustworthy?'

'The housekeeper's about seventy-five – she's been with my sister for over thirty years – and the gardener for at least ten years. No question.'

'We'll need to talk to them, to eliminate them from our enquiries – if you can let me have their contact details, please.'

Daly nodded.

'Something that's very important is if you could indicate as much as you can of what's been taken. I understand you know this house well, sir?' Glenn Branson said.

'I guided my sister on just about everything she bought,' Daly said. 'She and her late husband. I don't see anything important remaining in this hall. Whoever's done this knew what they were doing. I can list everything that was in here. There should be a photograph album somewhere of all the most valuable items.'

'That could be very helpful.'

Daly was silent for some moments. Then he said, 'Helpful to whom?'

'This enquiry, sir.'

Daly looked at him sceptically. 'You really think so?'

'It would help us if you could identify, as much as possible, everything that's been taken.'

'From what I've seen just in this room, it might be easier to identify what's been left behind.'

Branson looked at him uneasily. 'It does seem like the perpetrators are professionals.'

Daly did not reply. He walked through into the drawing room. Above the mantelpiece used to be one of his sister's most valuable pictures, a Landseer landscape, worth a good half a million pounds. He had long tried to convince her to move it to another location for fear of heat damage from the fire. Now, fire damage was the least of her problems, he thought, staring at the dark rectangle. On the wall opposite had hung a gilded, hand-made, eighteen-wheel Whitehurst clock, made in 1791. It had exposed workings, which showed the time anywhere on the globe. Its auction value, today, would be over three hundred thousand pounds.

He looked around at other dark rectangles on the walls. At empty spaces in the display cabinets, and on the walnut bureau. Everything of high value was gone. Almost everything. But there was one thing he was more anxious about than anything else. He went through into his sister's office and stared at the wall. As he suspected, the safe door was open. He peered in, but the door to the second, secret chamber at the back was open, also.

His heart sank, but anger rose inside him.

'Bastards,' he said, quietly. He shook his head, stared again, just to be quite certain. 'Bastards.'

Then he walked back into the hall, followed by the Detective. There was a pile of mail sitting on top of a Victorian table, one he had never particularly cared for. Ignoring Branson's caution not to touch it without his gloves on, he began sifting through it. Halfway through the pile was a single A4 sheet of paper with a form letter.

It was headed: R. C. MOORE.

Below was an address in Brighton's Kemp Town. And beneath that the wording:

Dear Sir or Madam

In the many years that I have been visiting this area, I have never ceased to take satisfaction from the pleasure people gain from realizing money from some unwanted, often forgotten item. Funds that you can put to good use – items that I, in turn, can sell.

I am always interested in buying items such as:

Old leather and crocodile suitcases

Children's books

Old jewellery

Scrap silver and gold

'Looks like a knocker-boy leaflet,' Glenn Branson said, bagging it to get it fingerprinted later.

Brighton's knocker-boys hailed back to the post-war days of the rag and bone men, and they had been a scourge of the elderly and vulnerable for decades, using leaflets like these to get inside houses and then either rip off the owners or pass on tips about valuable items to professional burglars.

Daly nodded. He knew. He'd been one himself, years back. Then suddenly his phone rang. Excusing himself, he stared at the display. There was no name showing.

'Gavin Daly,' he answered.

'It's Nurse Wilson, Mr Daly. Your sister is weakening. I think you should come back quickly.'

18

Roy Grace, in protective clothing like everyone else in Aileen McWhirter's house, stood alone in her ground-floor study, at the rear of the property, on his phone, with a map of the area in front of him. He paused from his task of putting together his enquiry team, and issuing instructions to each person he called, to text Cleo and warn her he would be very late home tonight.

The only information Aileen McWhirter had been able to give was that two of the men who attacked her were in brown uniforms, saying they were from the Water Board. He needed to cocoon an area around the property, and arrange for a house-to-house enquiry team to approach neighbours to see if any of them had had similar visits. But the officers carrying out this task needed to make these into reassurance visits at the same time so they did not frighten people, and to dispense crime-prevention advice. They needed to see if there were any CCTV cameras in the area that might have picked up anything. Unfortunately Withdean Road and its environs were not covered by the city's police CCTV network, although plenty of the homes had their own. He needed to establish whether there had been any similar crimes in the city, or in the county, recently. And he needed to set up an 'anniversary visit' check, placing Sussex Police billboards on the street, either side and to the front of the property, asking if anyone had seen unfamiliar vehicles in the area either on the night of the attack, or the previous Tuesday evening.

When villains cased a property, he knew from experience, they would often carry this out a week before, checking the movement patterns of the occupants for the same day.

Something felt wrong about this devastating attack on the old lady, but he could not put his finger on it. This kind of brutal tie-up robbery had, sadly, a long history. But all his instincts told him there was something more going on here.

The contents of the bookshelves had been the first thing to catch his eye in here. Then a movement outside distracted him. Through the leaded-light window he saw a sparrow washing itself in an ornamental fountain, totally unaware of the horror that had recently taken place here.

Grace had never been particularly interested in poetry, but there was one poem he remembered from his schooldays, because he'd had to learn it by heart and recite it during an English class. It was by W. H. Auden, and the first two lines seemed so apt here, he thought suddenly.

Happy the hare at morning, for she cannot read
The hunter's waking thoughts . . .

He stared beyond the bathing sparrow across the terrace of lawns and over to the far side of the valley, a mile distant. This time of the year much of the view of the eastern side of the city was obscured by greenery, but he could still make out the large rectangle of Varndean School, where he had been a pupil, before becoming a police cadet.

On the victim's walnut bureau was a large leather diary, some framed photos of children and adults, all discoloured with age, an old-fashioned red leather address book, a Parker pen lying on a blotter pad, her blue headed notepaper, and a birthday card with a blank page inside and a blank envelope that she had obviously been planning to send to someone. *The clue might be in the diary,* he thought, flicking backwards and forwards through a few pages with his gloved fingers. But at a cursory glance the pages were blank except for an appointment note, in three days' time, written with a fountain pen in a sloping, spidery hand: *Dr Parish. 11.30.*

Above the bureau, surrounded by a dark rectangle where a painting had probably hung, there was a safe, with a combination lock, and the door to it open. He peered inside but it was empty. At the back was what looked like a panel on its side, and a second door, as if to a secret chamber in the safe, which was also open.

He turned his attention back to the bookshelves, and ran his eyes over some of the titles again. *The First 100 Years of the American Mafia. Young Capone. Early Street Gangs and Gangsters of New York City. Irish Organized Crime. King of the Brooklyn Waterfront.*

There was shelf after shelf of them.

Why?

The collection was like an obsession.

Why had this lady got all these books on the early gang history of New York?

Aileen McWhirter. That was an Irish name. Did Gavin Daly's sister have some historic link with American organized crime? Did they both?

From what little he had gleaned about Aileen Mc-Whirter since being called out here, she had been married to a stockbroker, and widowed for the past fifteen years. Her own children had predeceased her, but there was a granddaughter and her husband, Nicki and Matt Spiers, and their two children, Jamie and Isobel – Aileen McWhirter's great-grandchildren – whom the police were currently trying to contact. She had no record, other than a traffic offence three years ago, when she had collided with a bollard for no apparent reason, which had resulted in her licence being revoked.

Perhaps she had once written a thesis on the subject? A book? Was trying to learn something about her family history?

Suddenly his phone rang. 'Roy Grace.'

It was Glenn Branson, outside. 'Boss, Gavin Daly has just been. I was going to get you to meet him, but he's been called up to the hospital urgently.'

'What's the latest on Mrs McWhirter?'

'We've got an officer there, guarding the ward. He's keeping me in the loop. It's not sounding good.'

'It never was,' Grace replied grimly.

'Something I want to show you in the hall.'

'I'll be right there.'

Branson was standing on a SOCO board on top of a frayed Persian rug by a hall table, tapping an A4 leaflet, in a bag, headed with an ornate typeface that was, no doubt, intended to convey an air of class, but which, in Grace's view, made it look even more like the work of a spiv.

R. C. MOORE

Roy Grace glanced briefly at it.

Dear Sir or Madam

In the many years that I have been visiting this area, I have never ceased to take satisfaction from the pleasure people gain from realizing money from some unwanted, often forgotten item.

Then he looked at his colleague. 'Shit, I thought knocker-boys were a thing of the past. That everyone now sees *Antiques Roadshow* and *Cash in the Attic* and all those other shows and they don't get suckered in any more by these creeps.' He remembered, with anger, his grandmother getting conned out of almost all her few family heirlooms by knocker-boys when he was in his teens.

'Obviously not completely, boss. I guess wherever there's a pond, you'll find something crawling around in the mud at the bottom.'

Grace smiled grimly. 'We'll need to question R. C. Moore asap.' Then he glanced down at the carpet. 'Strange – such a beautiful home, filled with, presumably, lovely things, and yet she had this tatty hall carpet!'

Branson gave him a sad look. 'You're so ignorant!'

'Thanks. But actually I think I know beauty when I see it.'

'Oh yeah? Do you have any idea of the value of this rug?'

'I'd probably give a fiver for it in a car boot sale.'

'You'd be getting a bargain if you did. It looks Persian to me, probably worth several thousand quid. Ari's dad traded in them, taught me all about them. When they make these rugs they put flaws in them, deliberately.'

'Why?'

Glenn Branson smiled. 'Because in the eyes of those carpet makers, only God is perfect.'

Grace smiled. 'I'll remember that.' He pulled his phone from his pocket and took a couple of close-up photographs of the leaflet. As he was checking to make sure they weren't blurred, he heard Glenn Branson answering his own phone. After a brief exchange of words, Branson ended the call

then looked at Grace with his large and, recently, world-
weary eyes.

'That was our officer at the hospital, boss.'

'And?'

'Looks like we are now upgraded to a murder enquiry.'

19

The boy's aunt was urging him to come in out of the cold, but he refused. He clung for dear life to the stern rail of the RMS *Mauretania*, salty wind tearing at his hair, a lump in his throat, tears streaming down his cheeks, oblivious to the numbing cold. His eyes were fixed on the steadily disappearing Statue of Liberty as they passed through the Verrazano Narrows.

It was tiny now, just a distant speck. It was being swallowed by the mist and cloud, which were relentlessly closing in on it in the falling darkness. He kept his eyes on the statue until it was gone completely, and then he felt even sadder. As if the cord between him and his pa had now been severed, totally and finally.

The deck thrummed beneath his feet. There was a strong smell of paint and varnish, mingled every few moments with a snatch of smoke from the funnels. His aunt was saying his name again, and tugging at his coat sleeve. But he ignored her, and stared down at the foaming wake, a hundred feet below. Every second, the distance between the stern of the *Mauretania* and New York increased. Every second, he was further away from finding his father. The mystery of his disappearance swallowed up by clouds much darker than the ones now cloaking the Statue of Liberty.

From inside his pocket, he took out the crumpled piece

of newspaper that he had been given a few hours earlier on the pier. The wind ripped at it, making it crackle, and he held on tightly, terrified of losing it. He looked at the newsprint photograph of his father, then at the clumsily written names and numbers. 9 5 3 7 0 4 0 4 2 4 0 4. Then back into the distance at New York.

His father was there, somewhere. In a place he did not want to be. The place where the bad men had taken him. The numbers were important, he knew that for sure. They *had* to be.

But what did they mean?

As his aunt tugged his arm even more sharply, he tucked the paper carefully back into his inside pocket, and, staring towards the grey horizon, he made a promise.

One day, Pop, I'm going to come back and find you. I'm going to rescue you from wherever you are.

Above him there were three sharp blasts from the ship's horn. As if signalling agreement.

20

2012

Ricky Moore was fifty-three, with a balding dome, and long, lank grey hair that covered his ears and the top of his collar. He was dressed in a shiny open-neck white shirt, with half its buttons undone to show off his gold medallion, a cheap beige jacket, and his fingers were adorned with chunky rings. With his booze-veined face and sallow complexion, he looked more like an ageing, drug-addled rocker than an antiques dealer; but he knew how to charm his way into any old lady's house, no matter how canny she might be.

It hadn't been hard to find him. He drank here three nights a week.

The Cock Inn at Wivelsfield was a proper pub, in Moore's view. It had bar billiards, a dartboard and shove ha'penny, was decorated with beer mats from all over the world, and had a friendly landlord and staff, especially a barmaid whom he lusted after. It didn't have a stupid, manufactured name, or the ghastly muzak or the pinging electronic gaming machines that blighted so many establishments these days. And it served a good pint.

But none of those were the real reasons he drank here. Situated in the countryside, fourteen miles north of Brighton where he lived, it wasn't convenient, particularly with the drink-driving laws these days – every time he came here it was a risk. But that had to be balanced against the benefits, as with any business.

As one of the few remaining antiques knocker-boys, he made a comfortable enough living, ripping off the low-hanging fruit – picking up bargains in gullible people's homes. He had charm and good patter, and despite his rough appearance, people took a liking to him. Especially old ladies, for some reason he didn't understand – and certainly did not question. He'd carved himself a niche market, a nice little earner. Stuff he could con little old ladies out of. But every now and then, when he entered a home, he would hit a treasure trove.

Like the house in Withdean Road a few weeks ago. That little old lady knew fine well what she had and she wasn't parting with any of it, at least not to him. She'd sent him packing with a flea in his ear.

Now, he had read in today's *Argus* that she was dead. Stupid old bat. She should have sold him the items he had wanted. Then he might have left it at that, instead of phoning his contacts.

Although maybe he would have phoned them anyway.

The five grand in folding, his advance on his commission, was burning a hole in his pocket.

Tax free, too.

The first benefit of this pub was that no one from Brighton drank here. He'd made a fair number of enemies over the years, tucking people up, and sooner or later in Brighton pubs, he'd run into someone bigger than him who hadn't forgotten. The second and far more important one was the rich pickings to be had from this place.

It was the way he had operated for years. Find a pub in a nice, wealthy pocket of the countryside. Get known and liked and trusted. Sit up at the bar, buy the occasional round, nip outside now and then for a smoke. Keep your ears open. Sooner or later you'd hear about nice big isolated properties. And sooner or later the locals would invite you to value some of the stuff in their homes, or their mum's homes, or whatever. You'd secretly take photographs, make the calls, email the pictures, then after a few months, move on.

He raised a pint of Harvey's to himself. He was doing all right, yeah. Life was sweet. A bit quiet in here for a Friday night, he thought. The barmaid he fancied was off sick tonight. But everything was all right. Very sweet.

Yeah.

Out of slight boredom he studied a framed photograph on the wall showing the members of a football team. Written at the bottom in large letters was *WIVELSFIELD WANDERERS*.

Suddenly he felt a vibration in his trouser pocket. He pulled out his iPhone and checked the display; it was a withheld number. He brought it to his ear and answered quietly. 'Yeah?'

'Ricky Moore?' asked the caller.

'Yeah.'

The caller hung up.

He frowned, and waited some moments, in case whoever it was called back. But the caller had no intention of calling back. He had all the information he needed to confirm the man's identity. He was standing out in the darkness, outside the pub, watching through the window as Moore pocketed his phone and drained his pint. His identity proven.

Ricky Moore put his glass down on the counter, then looked around for someone to play bar billiards with, but didn't spot any of his regular players. Deciding to head home soon, he ordered another pint – one for the road – and another whisky chaser.

His missus, Kjersti, the beautiful Norwegian woman whom he had finally decided to settle down and spend the rest of his life with – after two acrimonious divorces – hankered after a Rolex watch. Now, thanks to the McWhirter house, he had the dough to buy one – and with any luck he'd buy a stolen one, below retail, from a bent jeweller he knew.

She'd go nuts when she saw it!

He downed his drinks and left the pub with a smile on his face. He'd phone her when he got to the car; tell her to get her kit off and be waiting in bed for him.

*

Had Ricky Moore been sober, he might have been more aware. But four pints, accompanied by whisky chasers, had dulled his wits. As he stepped out into the darkness, pulling his cigarettes out of his pocket, he didn't notice anything out of place. If he had looked around the car park, he might have wondered about the Mercedes limousine with blacked-out rear windows that really did not belong in a rural pub car park. Nor, above the rasp of a passing motorbike, did he hear its engine start.

He was preoccupied with thoughts about what he was going to do in bed with Kjersti tonight. She had a very dirty mind; and right now, loaded with drink, he was feeling increasingly rampant.

As he made his way, unsteadily, towards his elderly BMW estate, he stopped to light a final cigarette for the evening. Kjersti did not let him smoke indoors. A strong wind was blowing and he had to cup his hands over his lighter to prevent the flame being blown out. He heard a car slowing down alongside him, but concentrating on the cigarette, he ignored it. He ignored the sound of the door opening, too, as he clicked the lighter for the third time.

Then he dropped the lighter and the cigarette fell from his mouth as an agonizing vice clamp gripped his arm so hard he cried out in pain.

'Sorry,' said the Apologist, yanking him into the rear of the car, across his knees, and slamming his head into the offside door, dazing him. Then he pulled the door shut. 'I'm very sorry,' he said, as the car shot forward.

The interior of the car smelled of leather and stale cigar smoke.

'What the—?'

'I'm sorry. I truly am. You have to believe me. I don't like hurting people.' Then he gripped the man's left thigh, trapping the nerve. Moore screamed and writhed in so much agony he was unable to speak.

'I'm sorry. Don't know my own strength.'

Moments later, Moore felt his phone being removed from his pocket.

'Hey!'

The Apologist was six foot seven inches tall and weighed three hundred and forty pounds, most of which was muscle, and not much of which was brain. The last time he had been in prison, he'd thrown a full-size fridge up two flights of stairs. Because he was angry. It wasn't good to be around him when he got angry.

Moore was panting and sweating. In the glare of oncoming headlights, he saw the man's face above him. He looked almost Neanderthal, his high forehead capped with a fringe like a monk's tonsure. 'What do you want?' he gasped. All he could see of the driver in front of them was shaggy hair beneath a chauffeur's cap.

'Nothing,' the Apologist replied. 'I'm just doing my job. It's not a nice job. I need the code for your phone.'

Moore screwed his eyes up in agony. The car was turning left. More streetlights flashed past. 'You've made a mistake. I think you want someone else.'

The Apologist squeezed his leg, making Moore scream again. 'Please trust me, I haven't. I haven't made a mistake. You'll have to trust me on that. I need the code.'

Now the car was turning left again. 'Where – where are we going?' Ricky Moore gasped, both in agony and terror.

'I'm sorry,' the Apologist said. 'I can't tell you. You have to believe me. I'm truly sorry.'

He noticed for the first time music playing. A choral sound. 'Ode To Joy', although he didn't know its name, nor did he appreciate the irony. Classical music wasn't his thing. It sounded sinister and creepy. He saw the tail lights of a vehicle ahead, through the windscreen. They seemed to be following it along a dark country lane.

Then he felt the vice-like grip on his left thigh again.

'Stop!' he screamed.

But the grip kept tightening.

'I'm sorry,' the Apologist said, 'but I have to make sure you don't try to run away. I'm sorry if I'm hurting you, I really am. The gentleman who wants to see you won't be nearly as gentle. Trust me. Now the code, please.'

Moore gave him the four digits. He saw his captor tap them in and the display came alive.

The vehicle in front, a Range Rover, halted and the Mercedes stopped behind it. A man walked up to the rear window, and Ricky Moore became increasingly afraid. He heard the window go down, felt the cool breeze on his face, smelled freshly mown grass, heard the rumble of the Range

Rover's engine. He saw his iPhone being passed through the window, then it closed again.

'Hey! I want that back,' he said.

His captor said nothing. Several minutes passed. The Range Rover remained static in front of them. Then, suddenly, it drove off. The Mercedes followed.

'My phone!' Ricky Moore said.

The Apologist squeezed his thigh again, even harder, and he shouted out in pain, anger and fear.

'Sorry.'

21

A half-smoked cigar, with undisturbed ash on the end, lay in the large glass ashtray, beside a crystal tumbler of Midleton whiskey, Gavin Daly's regular tipple, for which he paid £267 a bottle. The thought of what the rare Irish whiskey cost gave him even more pleasure than the taste. It meant there was a little bit less of his fortune for his idiot, debt-ridden son, Lucas, to get his hands on after he was gone, although he had no problem leaving it to his sister's grand-daughter and family. But at this moment, for one of the few times in his adult life, his son was proving useful.

Dressed in his blue smoking jacket, Daly was seated at his wide, leather-topped desk in the study of his magnificent Palladian mansion, ten miles north-east of Brighton, blinking away tears. Trying to occupy his mind by focusing on the rare J. J. Elliott clock he was checking for a client before freighting it later this week to an important auction in New York, while he waited for some of the people he had phoned today to call him back.

There were only a limited number of dealers in the world who handled really high-end vintage clocks and watches. Most of them were straight, but over the years he'd had a good relationship with the straight ones and the crooked ones. He'd put the word out and reckoned there was a strong chance that if any were approached by some-one trying to sell his father's watch, most of them would phone him.

Although he was ninety-five, he had never really retired,

just gradually wound down over the years. Even now he still kept an eye on the shop that bore his name in the Brighton Lanes, despairing because his son was letting the business slide away. Not that he really cared, he had more than enough money to see out his days in the style in which he liked to live. And he still had a few clients whom he advised on timepieces, and for whom he sometimes bought and sold, such as this clock he was selling for a wealthy English collector, which kept him occupied.

His chest pains from angina, becoming increasingly frequent now, were returning. His doctor had told him to stop drinking and smoking, but what the hell did it matter? He popped a nitroglycerin tablet under his tongue, waited until it had dissolved, then relit his cigar. He'd always had an eye for fine craftsmanship, and this clock was a particular beauty. Its square case, with its fine marquetry and gold inlay, was a masterpiece of carving, and its movement, with a single hammer to strike its large brass gong, was exquisite. It would never tell the time as accurately as one of today's quartz watches you could buy for a few quid, but that was not the point.

He made a small adjustment to the length of the pendulum, then put his tools down. He was tired, and his mind was all over the place. He'd barely slept a wink last night; he just felt sick all the time. Sick with grief. And now he felt utterly alone in the world.

He had everything. This beautiful house, a staffed villa on Cap Ferrat on the French Riviera, more money than he could ever spend, and none of it mattered; that was the damned irony. He stared bleakly out through the sash window into the darkness. All around him in the oak-panelled room were reminders of his past. The black-and-white photograph of his stern, deeply religious maiden aunt,

Oonagh, who had raised him and his sister. Next to her was a row of framed photographs of his father, Brendan Daly.

One, a youthful picture, showed the big guy striding towards the camera, wearing a three-piece suit, white shirt, black tie and a boater at a jaunty angle; he was flanked by two of his White Hand Gang cohorts, Mick Pollock – later known as Pegleg Pollock after he lost a leg to gangrene following a shooting incident – and Aiden Boyle. Two of the men whose names were written on the reverse of the front page of the *Daily News* from February 1922, in which the shooting of his mother and the abduction of his father was the headline story. The paper he had been given all those years back by the messenger boy on Pier 54.

Next to that was a photograph of his father in bathing trunks, on Brooklyn's Brighton Beach. He was grinning, his jet-black hair tousled, a chain with a silver rabbit hung around his neck. The chain had belonged to Gavin's grandfather, his aunt had once told him; he had been one of the lieutenants in the New York Irish Mafia's Dead Rabbits Gang in the 1880s. Another photo showed his father, sharply dressed, wearing a Derby.

He heard a knock, then the door behind him opened. It was Betty, his faithful housekeeper, only a few years junior to himself. 'You've not touched your supper, Mr Daly,' she chided.

He raised a hand in acknowledgement, without turning around.

'I'm clearing up,' she said. 'Would you like a hot drink or anything before I go to bed?'

'I'm fine,' he said. 'I'm expecting visitors, but I'll see them in.'

She wished him goodnight and closed the door.

The house felt gloomy and lonely since his second wife,

Ruth, had died. In front of him sat a framed photograph taken way back when she was in her late-thirties and he was in his mid-fifties. The two of them on a terrace in the South of France, with the flat blue Mediterranean Sea behind them. She had been a red-haired beauty then; Irish, like his first wife Sinead; but unlike Sinead she had been faithful, he was certain, for all the time they were together. Sinead, his son's mother, had died of an overdose of barbiturates after years of addiction to booze and affairs. He did not have her photograph anywhere in his home. Lucas, his son, was a bitter enough reminder of her.

Lucas had tried for some time to persuade him to think about moving into sheltered accommodation, but he wouldn't hear of it. He loved this place and remembered thinking, when he had bought it all those decades ago, how proud his dad would have been of him. To be sure, he hadn't made all his money honestly, but then who in the antiques world had? He'd been a player in the Brighton antiques ring, rigging prices at auction, and once – something that still made him smile – at a big country-house auction he had even locked a big London dealer in the lavatory to prevent him from bidding against him.

On another occasion, many years before satellite navigation had come in, he and his ring of Brighton antiques dealers had altered all the road signs the night before one of the largest country-house auctions in the county, so that none of the major London dealers had been able to find the place.

He glanced up, impatiently now, at the CCTV screen showing the front of the house and the driveway, waiting for his son's black Range Rover to appear. Lucas had inherited some of his mother's bad genes. He was a lousy son, a school dropout who had failed to maintain the family business, and who had on several occasions narrowly avoided doing time both for violence and for drug dealing. Gavin felt sorry for his son's wife, who was a decent person and, in his view, deserved someone better.

He drank some more whiskey, then puffed his cigar back to life and stared around the room where he used to bring his most important customers, and where he now spent most of his time these days. It was designed to impress, to give the air of a learned man of culture, an aristocrat who was no more than a curator of all he had inherited from his ancestors and would one day pass on to his heirs.

Except Gavin Daly had inherited nothing. Every item in this room, just as with almost everything in this fine house, he had bought, with great care, with the sole intention of impressing others like him, who were prepared to spend vast sums on antiques to line their grand homes in America, Japan and more recently China, to give the impression they were privileged people of taste.

There were two large, studded red-leather chesterfields. On Doric plinths stood busts of some of his past great fellow countrymen – Oscar Wilde, George Bernard Shaw, William Butler Yeats, J. M. Synge, James Joyce and T. E. Lawrence, whose father had been an Irishman, and whose writings he admired. Wall-to-wall bookcases lined with leather-bound tomes. In daylight, the window looked out on a view, framed by a line of Italian cypresses, of acres of lush gardens, an ornamental lake fringed by statues, and the distant rolling hills of the South Downs.

He removed from his desk drawer a crimson, leather-bound book and opened it. It contained a yellowed, decaying front page of the *New York Daily News* from February 1922, protected in a clear plastic envelope.

There had not been a day in his life when he had not looked at this page of the newspaper, and at the names and numbers on the reverse. Four names that filled him with knuckle-clenching hatred every time he saw them.

Fergal Kilpatrick. Mick Pollock. Aiden Boyle. Cillian Cregan.

The men who, the police had told his aunt, had entered his parents' house, entered his bedroom, shone torches at him. Filled his bedroom with the stench of their booze and sweat.

The men who had shot his mother dead and taken his pa away.

All of them long dead. But that knowledge gave him no comfort, no satisfaction. Just regret. A deep regret that he had never returned to America years ago and gone looking for those who were still alive. And now it was too late.

He had often googled them. All their names were there, lieutenants of 'Wild Bill' Lovett, who had taken control of the White Hand Gang, which controlled the waterfronts of Manhattan and Brooklyn after the murders of the gang's leader, Dinny Meehan, and subsequently his next in line, Brendan Daly.

His father.

He had long studied the photographs of their hateful faces that came up on his computer. Pegleg Pollock had been the first to die, shot dead in a bar in a turf war, his killers never identified.

The other three had vanished, faded into the mists of time. Their surnames popped up, meaninglessly, on his internet searches, along with Daly countless times.

Your old men shall dream dreams; your young men shall see visions.

His aunt, who brought him and his sister back to

Ireland, had a deep faith. She had read them passages from the Bible daily on that voyage from New York, and every night of their childhood outside Dublin.

He'd never had any truck with religion, but the book of Joel had been right in that one passage. He'd had plenty of visions as a young man. And now all he had were his dreams. He looked up at the bust of the handsome, equine face of Lawrence of Arabia. There was a quote from that great man's book, *Seven Pillars of Wisdom*, that had been his mantra throughout life.

> All men dream: but not equally. Those who dream by night in the dusty recesses of their minds wake in the day to find that it was vanity: but the dreamers of the day are dangerous men, for they may act their dream with open eyes, to make it possible.

He had always been a dreamer of the day. But now he realized that maybe he had only been a sleepwalker. He was ninety-five years old and he had failed to keep the biggest, most important promise he had made in his life. A promise he had made standing on the stern of the *Mauretania*, as a small boy, all those decades ago.

One day, Pop, I'm going to come back and find you. I'm going to rescue you from wherever you are.

He looked again, for the millionth time, at the only clue he had ever had. Those twelve scrawled numbers below the names of the four men.

9 5 3 7 0 4 0 4 2 4 0 4

He had tried endlessly. Checking plot numbers at every cemetery in the New York area. Checking prisoner numbers – but the numbers were too long. Checking co-ordinates – but they were too short. Telephone numbers. House numbers. Car indexes. Bank account numbers. Safety deposit box codes. He'd even employed code breakers to see if they represented letters or words of a secret message. But always the same negative result.

Then he was distracted by a steady *beep-beep-beep* sound.

The intruder alert system. It warned of anyone approaching the perimeter of his property. He looked up at the bank of CCTV screens on the wall to the right of his desk. And was pleased at what he saw.

They were here.

About time, too.

22

'*Arrivederci*, sunshine,' the driver said, turning round, showing his face to Ricky Moore for the first time. He looked an old, unkempt git, Moore thought, sullenly.

The Apologist hauled Moore out of the rear of the Mercedes as easily as if he were a cardboard cut-out. Then he held him upright in the ankle-deep gravel, in the glare of the floodlighting and the silence of the night, outside the grand entrance porch of the white mansion.

They were half a mile down a tree-lined private driveway and three miles from the nearest dwelling. From his knowledge of Sussex Ricky Moore had a vague idea where they were, but he wasn't familiar with all the back lanes beyond Lewes. He heard an owl hoot somewhere close. In front of him a burly middle-aged man, with short, gelled hair and a sharp business suit, climbed down from the driver's side of the black Range Rover. Something was bulking out the front of the man's jacket.

A cooling engine ticked steadily, like a clock. The man in the business suit strode up to the porch. In the darkness and the silence and the total absence of any neighbours, Ricky Moore was becoming increasingly frightened with every passing second. He had to escape, but how? His brain was all over the place, almost paralyzed with fear. Then he cried out in pain as one of the nerves in his right arm was agonizingly crushed.

'I'm sorry,' the Apologist said to Moore, escorting him forward, maintaining the excruciating pressure. 'Really, I am. Believe me. You may find it hard to believe, but I am sorry, truly.' He smiled. Most of his teeth needed work. 'I'm just doing my job.'

'Look,' Moore said, urgently. 'I'll pay you good money to take me back to the pub. A lot of money. I mean it, a lot.'

The Apologist was a loyal man. He'd been given his nickname in prison for constantly apologizing to everyone, about everything, and he'd liked the name. He hardly ever used his real name, Augustine Krasniki. Apologizing was his nature; he couldn't help it. As a small boy, in his native Albania, his mother had blamed him for his father leaving her. She'd blamed him for everything, and the only way to calm her was to apologize, constantly, day and night. It was even his fault when it rained, so he learned to apologize for that also. Eventually she had put him into care, for reasons he never understood, but he assumed it must have been his fault. From there he had been moved from foster home to foster home. People felt scared by him, intimidated by the way he looked – and by his physical strength. It had taken him a while to understand and control his own strength. Once he killed a child's pet gerbil by stroking it too hard; another time he crushed a budgerigar to death by accident. Often people screamed in pain when he shook their hand. He tried to remember to be gentle, but his brain did not always work that well.

When boys had picked on him at school for being so ugly, he had tried – but failed – to control his strength. With one punch he would smash their ribs, or knock all their front teeth out, every single one of them, like a ten-pin strike! He couldn't help his temper when other kids taunted him, calling him Boris Karloff, telling him he looked like Frankenstein's monster, so he just got used to hitting them and then apologizing after.

Only one person had ever been kind to him in his life. His boss, Lucas Daly. He gave him money, let him have the flat above the shop in the Lanes, which he guarded fiercely, and had him sit in on all his drug deals. No one ever messed with Lucas Daly, not after they had taken one look at the Apologist. He was unswervingly loyal to his boss.

'I'm sorry,' the Apologist said to Ricky Moore. 'I'd like to say yes, really I would. I'd like to say yes and take your money. But I can't. You'll have to trust me on that one.'

The man in the business suit opened the front door with his key and Ricky Moore, propelled by the grip of the Apologist, stumbled in. The door closed behind him. They were in a huge hallway, with a black and white chequered floor. Two suits of armour, each with a lance in their steel right hands, stood either side of a grand stairway. Fine, classical oil paintings hung from the walls, the kind of paintings that would normally have piqued Ricky Moore's interest. But tonight he barely noticed them through his tears of pain.

There was a strong smell of cigar smoke. Moore was craving a cigarette. An elderly man with flowing white hair, wearing a smoking jacket and monogrammed black velvet slippers, walked towards them, with the aid of a silver-headed cane. He held a large cigar in his free hand, and fury blazed in his cornflower-blue eyes.

'Ricky Moore?'

He nodded sullenly.

'I'm Gavin Daly. I appreciate your dropping by.'

'Very funny,' Moore said defiantly.

Daly grinned back. There was a flash of warmth that was gone in an instant, like a fleeting glimpse of the sun behind a storm cloud. 'Funny? You like jokes, do you? Think it's funny to con vulnerable old ladies out of their possessions?'

'I dunno what you're talking about.'

'Get nice kickbacks, do you, for your information? Send your leaflet out in advance, then go into houses and take photographs of anything of value?'

'Nah, not me. I honestly dunno what you're talking about.' He gasped in pain as the Apologist crushed the nerve in his arm again, as if to remind him not to bother thinking about trying to get away. 'It's not me.'

'A house in Withdean Road.'

'Never been there.'

'There's a lady in a house there who has one of your leaflets on her hall table.'

'Not that I recall.'

'Let me jog your memory,' said the man in the business suit in a snide, assured voice. Then he sniffed. He looked taller than when Moore had seen him outside, and more immaculate, with black hair gelled back. He reminded Moore of photographs he had seen of those gangsters, the Kray twins.

Moore glanced around, wondering if he could make a break for it the moment the gorilla let go of his arm.

'This your iPhone?' the Kray lookalike asked, holding it up in front of him.

Moore nodded, and gasped in pain as the gorilla squeezed his arm even harder.

'Sorry!' the Apologist said.

'I'm Lucas Daly, by the way,' the Kray lookalike said. 'It was my auntie who got robbed and murdered, thanks to you. My dad's sister. Neither of us are very happy about it.'

'I didn't have nothing to do with it!' Ricky Moore said.

Lucas Daly frowned, looking down at the phone. He tapped it several times, then held the phone up in front of Moore's eyes.

'Recognize that, do you?'

Ricky Moore stared, reluctantly, at the close-up photograph of the gilded case of the Whitehurst clock that had been hanging in the drawing room of Aileen McWhirter's house. 'No,' he said. 'No, I don't.'

'You must have a fucking short memory.' He sniffed again.

Moore said nothing, his brain racing, trying desperately to come up with something convincing – and failing.

'What about this?'

Moore stared at another photograph. This time of a swan-necked Georgian tallboy. Again he shook his head.

The man tapped the iPhone again. 'This?'

Moore stared at a Chippendale gateleg table.

'Never seen it before, honest! Not my photos. I didn't take them. I didn't!'

Then the man dug his hand inside his jacket, and pulled out the implement that had been bulking it out. It was a pair of electric curling tongs, with a flex trailing. 'How about these, Mr Moore?'

'I've never seen them before, honestly!'

'These are like the ones used on my auntie,' Lucas Daly said. 'They were used to make her give up her safe code and her bank pin codes. Do you think they might make you talk, too? We'd like some names from you. Starting with the men who did Auntie Aileen's house in Withdean Road.'

'Lucas!' the old man cautioned. 'No violence. That's not what I want. We've had enough of that. I don't operate that way.'

'I don't know no names, honestly, sir,' Ricky Moore addressed the old man, sensing hope.

'Go to bed, Dad, it's late,' Lucas Daly said.

'I don't want violence, you understand?' Gavin Daly said to his son.

'Go to bed, Dad. Let me deal with this.'

'I just want the names of the people who did this to my sister, Mr Moore,' the old man said. Then he turned and walked away down the hall.

Moore stood, staring at Lucas Daly, then up at the large, blank face of the Apologist.

'My dad's a gentle person, Mr Moore. So we're going to take you away from here; he wouldn't like to see what we're going to do to you – to help jog your memory, you see?'

Ricky Moore gurgled with terror as he felt himself being propelled towards the front door. Moments later he felt a damp patch down the front of his trousers.

He had pissed himself.

23

Once, way back when she had a life, Sarah Courteney used to love Friday nights. The start of the weekend, a time to kick back, watch rubbish TV, *Big Brother* or whatever, followed by an even trashier, smutty 10 p.m. show on Channel Four. But not any more. Friday nights now meant her husband, Lucas, arriving home even drunker than all the other nights of the week. If he arrived home at all.

She woke up with a start. The television was on, muted, an old film playing. Peter Sellers, as Inspector Clouseau, standing in Herbert Lom's office. It was 2.30 a.m. Upstairs she could hear awful heavy metal pounding from her bolshie teenage son's room. And the sound of bed springs creaking. Accompanied by the faint smell of marijuana. That was all Damian seemed to do these days. Listen to God-awful music, get stoned, and wank.

Ever the dutiful wife, she had cooked Lucas a meal, made it ready for eight o'clock, when he'd said he would be home, and kept it in the warming oven ever since. She heard the sound of the front door opening, then banging back against the wall – the stop had long ago been ripped out of the floor and never replaced – then her husband's clumsy footsteps.

They stopped as he entered the large, open-plan living area of their house on Hove's smart Shirley Drive. A house they were only still living in because of her earnings paying the mortgage.

'What the fuck have you done to your face?' he slurred, then sniffed.

'We talked about it last night. Your dinner's in the bottom oven,' she replied.

'I said, *What the fuck have you done to your face?*'

'Are you deaf? I said we talked about it last night. You wanted dinner at 8 p.m.'

'Stop ignoring me, bitch. I've had business to deal with. Yeah? My auntie who got murdered, yeah? Where's your sympathy?' He tapped his chest. 'You have any idea how I feel? Had to deal with the bastard that done it. Wasn't nice. Had to have a couple of beers to get over it. Know what I'm saying?'

He staggered over and stood above her. *I loved you once*, she thought. *God almighty, I really, really loved you. You pathetic beer-sodden wreck. I loved the way you used to make me feel, the way you used to look at me. I loved your knowledge of antiques. I loved the way you could walk into a room and tell me everything about every piece of furniture in it.*

'You've had that Botox again, haven't you? Lovely Dr Revson. Paying him money we don't have. Are you fucking him or something?'

She held her composure. 'More losses at the casino today?'

'I've had a shit day.'

'Just for a change? I've had my face done,' she said calmly, 'to try to preserve my career. So I can afford to put food on our table – and beer in your fat, stupid belly. I had it done so you don't have to go running to your dad for more money every few months—'

She never got the rest of her words out. His right fist smashed into her chest, knocking her to the floor. The bastard was clever. He always hit her where it wouldn't show.

Tomorrow, she vowed, she would leave him. And yet she knew tomorrow he would weep, and apologize, and tell her how much he loved her and that he could not live without her. Tomorrow he would promise, as he always did, that they would make a fresh start.

24

Peregrine Stuart-Simmonds was a tall, cheery man in his mid-sixties, with a portly figure elegantly parcelled inside a double-breasted chalk-striped suit. He sported a full head of wavy silver hair, and his narrow, horn-rimmed spectacles, worn right on the end of his nose, gave him a rather distinguished, academic air.

He sat at the round meeting table in Roy Grace's small office, exuding the smell of a masculine soap, and stifling a yawn. 'Apologies!' he said, cheerily, in a booming, salesroom voice. 'Been up most of the night working on the inventory for you.'

It was 7.20 on Saturday morning, another weekend shot to hell. Grace yawned, too. He'd also been up most of the night. He'd stayed at work with several members of his team until after midnight, then Noah had barely let him or Cleo sleep a wink. 'Can I get you some coffee?' he offered.

'With a hypodermic syringe, I'll take it intravenously! Black, no sugar, and as strong as you can make it, please.'

Grace stepped out, and returned a few minutes later holding two steaming mugs. 'I really appreciate your moving so fast, Mr Stuart-Simmonds,' he said.

'Have to, Detective Superintendent, if we're to have any chance of playing catch-up. You can be damned sure this has been carefully planned, and most of the items, if not all, are already overseas. What time does your briefing start?'

'Eight thirty. I'd like to use this hour to learn as much

89

from you as I can. If we could run through the highest-value items that have been taken from Mrs McWhirter's home, what their identifying features are, and how rare they are. Also, in your experience, how they might have been transported, where they are likely to have been shipped to – and which agencies overseas are most likely to be able to help us locate them. Then you could help me set some parameters for my team, as well as giving us a crash course in how the global antiques world works.'

An ASDA lorry rumbled up the hill outside. The expert blew on his coffee, then sipped. 'More to the point, how the global antiques *black market* operates – I think you'll find that more helpful.'

'I'll be guided by you.'

'What you have to understand is that small stuff such as low-value porcelain, jewellery, pictures, silverware – items worth only a few hundred quid – can be fenced easily in a city like Brighton, with all its antiques stalls and little shops. But these days important pieces are recorded on an international register, along with photographs and their details, which every reputable international dealer sub-scribes to. None of them would touch a stolen item on it with a bargepole.'

'So that works in our favour?' Grace said.

'Yes and no. What happens in reality is the stolen items go underground, which is the bugger. Most, if not all, are likely to have been stolen to order or presold to private buyers. In twenty, thirty or fifty years' time, if those buyers want to sell, the items will have long since dropped off the register.'

'Where do we begin looking?'

'I understand Mrs McWhirter's brother is Gavin Daly?'

'Yes.'

The antiques expert nodded. 'He has a tremendous reputation. At one time he was one of the most important dealers in this country – and very respected.' He smiled. 'That's not to say possibly a bit of a rogue.'

'Oh?' That piqued Grace's interest.

'Most of the old dealers in Brighton were. They operated an illegal cartel called the *Ring*, where they'd band together to rig prices at auction, for instance. But that's not to deny Gavin Daly's expertise. It's clear from looking through the list of items taken from Mrs McWhirter that she had some jolly fine stuff. Clearly someone was advising her when she bought them – I would imagine her brother. But, like everyone, she'd have had some less good stuff as well.' He raised a finger. 'I think one of the first areas you should be looking at is the low-hanging fruit.'

'Low-hanging fruit?' Grace frowned and took a tentative sip of his scalding coffee. Light rain was falling outside and it felt chilly in the room. Almost autumnal. Outside, in the large open-plan detectives' area, a phone warbled, unanswered. He felt desperately tired, and it was going to be a struggle to make it through the very long day ahead, although he had no option but to get on with it. And more importantly, he wanted to get on with it. He wanted the bastards who did this. Very badly.

'Well, from the amount taken, and the size of some of the pieces, we can assume there were at least two men, probably three, if not even a fourth. In my experience, when hired hands are sent to steal to order, they almost always help themselves to some extra items not on the list, and pass them on to fences for a bit of extra cash.' He blew on his coffee again. 'Almost certainly Mrs McWhirter would have photos, taken for insurance purposes, of the contents in each room. If you can get hold of them, then you can check what has been taken and what is still there, beyond the high-value items her brother has already identified. If there are other items missing, then I'd put some officers out, with their photographs, around all the antiques shops, street stalls and car boot sales in the area, as well as getting them to carefully trawl through eBay.'

Grace made some notes. 'When you say *steal to order*, that implies insider knowledge.'

The antiques expert nodded. 'You said you found a knocker-boy leaflet in the house?'

'Yes. Someone called R. C. Moore.'

'This has all the classic hallmarks,' Stuart-Simmonds said. 'The knocker-boy charms his way into the house, and sees a treasure trove of beautiful things. He makes a note, and often takes surreptitious photographs. Then he sells on the address and a contents summary. Some of the big players have connections to the insurance companies – an employee they bribe within them – and they get the full inventory that way.'

'Interesting,' Grace said. 'The one item that wasn't insured was the pocket watch.'

'Why on earth not?'

'For the very reason you've just told me. Gavin Daly reckoned if it was registered with an insurance company, it would be a target. No one knew it was there, in her safe. Also, it was an extremely well-concealed safe. He designed it himself as a double safe.'

'Double?'

'Yes, very ingenious. If you opened it, you would think that was it. But the wall at the back of it is false; you insert an Allen key, twist and it opens, and there is a second combination lock behind. Ordinarily that false wall would fool any burglar.'

The expert chewed the inside of his mouth for some moments. 'If they didn't know about the watch, then it won't have been presold. Whether they handed it to whoever hired them or try to sell it themselves, a Patek Philippe from 1910 is a damned rare thing. I'd say finding possible buyers for that should be a major line of enquiry for you, Detective Superintendent. That watch will lead you to the perpetrators, for sure.'

'If it surfaces,' Grace said.

'It will, I guarantee. It may be the biggest value item they've taken, but it's also the most dangerous for them.'

25

You don't have to be crazy to work here. But it helps!

Some offices had that sign up as a joke, but there was no sign here. You had to be crazy to do this job. Really, you did. Being crazy was probably the best qualification, Gareth Dupont thought. And he was crazy all right, he knew that. He'd done drugs, done time for GBH – the jerk he'd beaten up had deserved it for goosing his girl in a pub, but maybe it hadn't been worth the two years he'd served in prison and the criminal record, he reflected. And more recently, he'd done serious time for burglary.

Gareth Dupont was thirty-three. He had handsome, olive-skinned looks and shiny dark hair from his mother's Hispanic genes, along with a toned body from obsessive weight training in gyms and his passion for Salsa dancing. He'd made a shedload of money in a Spanish-based tele-sales stock market scam – most of which had gone up his nose – sold loft insulation until Friday, and now, at the start of this new week after the Bank Holiday, was selling advertising space in sports club magazines for the Brighton-based company Mountainpeak Publishing. In addition he had his sideline, which could, on occasion, become a nice little earner. Also, he talked to God a lot. Occasionally God talked back, but not as often as he would have liked. Recently, he reckoned, God was pretty displeased with him. Quite rightly. But hey, you couldn't always be perfect. God had to understand that.

After school, he'd toyed with becoming a monk. Except,

he realized at the last moment that he liked women too much. And booze. And coke. And the money to buy them. But the pull was always there. Something about a monk's cell. A sanctuary. One day, but not right now. Right now, telesales gave him good money, which he needed because he was always skint by the end of every weekend, and all the more so after a long weekend. Skint and usually hungover. And today he was very skint and badly hungover.

And in love.

Hey, that's what weekends were for, weren't they? Partying and getting trashed – oh, and going to church, but the less said about that the better. Not really his thing, church, he was starting to think. He wasn't much enjoying spending time either with old ladies with hatpins and elderly rectors with clattering teeth, or the happy clappy alternatives. You could do God without doing church, right? God was inside you: in your heart, in your head, in your eyes.

God was in the vision of Suki Yang. She was Chinese-American, over here working for an IT media company; he'd met her late on Friday night in Brighton's hip Bohemia bar. They'd slept together in the small hours of Saturday morning, and spent most of the rest of the weekend heavy-duty shagging, fuelled by all kinds of stuff they'd swallowed and snorted.

The slight problem was the few lies he had told her. Like he hadn't mentioned the other lady he was seeing, he didn't actually own the flat, as he had claimed, but only rented it, and he didn't at the moment have enough dough for the next quarter's payment – due in seven weeks' time. And he'd lied about the great job he had in media. Well, Mountainpeak was a media company. Sort of.

There were six teams of five telesales people and a manager – all men – in this second-floor office on the industrial estate just outside the port of Newhaven, ten miles east of Brighton. Each of them in shirtsleeves, some with ties at half-mast, some open-necked, seated at bland modern desks. No one in here, apart from the pleasant boss, Alan Prior, seated over the other side, was older than thirty-five. Each of them had a flat screen in front of him, a keyboard, a phone, coffees and bottles of water. It was 9.30 and Gareth had only been at his desk for thirty minutes, but the morning was already feeling several hours old. Nine calls so far and no sales. Maybe now he'd get lucky.

Gareth sucked on a small scab on his right knuckle, then dialled the number in front of him, abdicating responsibility to God for the call when it was answered. Hey, despite everything, God owed him a whole bunch of credits. *This one's down to you, God*, he mouthed silently, his eyes momentarily closed.

A female voice, sharp, brittle. You could tell from the way they answered if it was going to be a tough or an easy sell. This already felt tough. He looked down at the script in front of him and read from it, sounding all bright and breezy.

'Hi there, it's Gareth Dupont here. I'm calling on behalf of the North Brighton Golf Club. May I speak to the business owner or whoever's in charge of your marketing and advertising, please?'

Silence at the other end. He wondered if the cow had already hung up. Then she said, 'What is this about, exactly?'

He skipped down the script to the paragraph that dealt with this kind of a response, then read aloud, still sounding breezy and chatty. 'The reason I'm calling is that we're producing the official annual corporate brochure for the North Brighton Golf Club in a couple of months' time, and we're going to be distributing extensively across the area. Thousands of homes and most businesses in the area will be covered, not to mention the club itself.'

'We don't have any connection with golf in our business,' she replied icily.

'Well, you might not think that. But I've been asked to source well-established businesses and offer them an opportunity to get involved. With your particular category, we see it as an ideal match. We're targeting a demographic of wealthy and affluent people who have the money to pay for your services, and I've been asked to make sure that only reliable and professional companies go in. What I'm doing is making it so there's only one of each profession or trade available within the entire publication. It literally locks out all of your competitors and means you're the only company available to turn to.'

'We are funeral directors,' she replied. 'Why would we want to advertise in a golf club brochure?'

'The club is bound to have many elderly members. Sooner or later they're going to die. I'll give you the broad strokes, briefly—'

There was a click.

The bitch had hung up.

Thanks a bunch, pal, Gareth Dupont mouthed to God. He moved on to the next name on his list, took a swig of his water, and punched in the number.

*

By five o'clock, when the office was winding down for the day, Gareth had sold one half-page, to a flooring company in Portslade called D. Reeves. Not a great start to his new job, he knew. But hey, maybe tomorrow would be better. It needed to be.

He left the office, pulled on his Ray-Bans against the bright, afternoon sun, climbed into his leased black Porsche cabriolet, started the engine and lowered the roof. He sat for a moment, pensively. He was thinking about the apartment rental, and the next lease payment due on the Porsche. Maybe a bit of prayer was needed, which he hadn't done in a while, not in any serious way. Although he was always wary of praying too soon after he had pissed off God. Better to leave some distance.

He drove off, heading down into Newhaven. Then, as he threaded through the town, heading for the coast road that would take him home to the Marina Village, the *Argus* newspaper banner hoarding outside a newsagent's proclaimed, in large black letters:

McWHIRTER MURDER £100,000 REWARD

Ignoring the car behind him, Gareth Dupont slammed on the brakes and pulled over onto the kerb. He ran into the shop, bought a copy of the paper, then stood in the entrance reading the front-page splash, ignoring the traffic jam along the narrow street his car was causing.

> Gavin Daly, brother of Aileen McWhirter, who was murdered in her Withdean Road mansion last week, has announced a reward of £100,000 for information leading to the arrest and conviction of his sister's brutal killers.

He read on. There was a phone number to the CID Incident Room, and also the one for anonymous calls to Crimestoppers.

He grinned. Sometimes in life you got lucky! He mouthed, silently, *Thank you, God. All's forgiven!*

26

The Scenes of Crime Officers had finished at his sister's house, and the rota of scene guards had been stood down. Now, at six o'clock in the evening, beneath a clear sky, Gavin Daly sat in the back of his Mercedes at the top of the driveway down to the house.

Yellow police signs had been placed a short distance apart, either side of the driveway, each with the same wording on them:

WERE YOU HERE BETWEEN
6 P.M. AND 10.30 P.M. LAST TUESDAY, 21 AUGUST?
DID YOU SEE A VAN HERE?
IF SO, PLEASE CONTACT THE POLICE AND ASK FOR
THE INCIDENT ROOM FOR OPERATION FLOUNDER.
01273 470101
OR PHONE CRIMESTOPPERS ANONYMOUSLY ON:
0800 555 111

He instructed his driver to take him down to the house. Then he climbed out, told the driver to leave, that he would call him when he needed him back, walked around to the front of the silent house, and entered the porch.

His hand was shaking as he put the key in the lock of the front door, and he had a lump in his throat.

Then he hesitated, unsure if he actually wanted to go in. Except that he had work to do.

It was a warm evening, the garden was alive with birdsong, wasps, butterflies, and he could hear, a short distance away, the swish . . . swish . . . swish of a secluded neighbour's lawn sprinkler. Summer was officially coming to an end in a few days. How many more summers would he see? he wondered.

How many more did he want to see?

Any?

Everyone he had ever loved was now dead. His mother in a hail of bullets in her bedroom. His father dragged away into the night. He had buried two wives and his brother-in-law. Now, when the Coroner released her body, he would be burying his sister.

He did not know how many years he had left before his son would be burying him. He was still mobile, and, despite the walking stick, he remained fairly agile. Thanks to the skills of a local plastic surgeon, his face still looked two decades or so younger than his years. He'd beaten off heart trouble with a triple bypass, although he had angina now. He'd had his prostate removed. He'd reached what everyone called a ripe old age. But he did not feel ripe. He felt rotten.

And unfulfilled.

He twisted the key and pushed the door open, then stepped inside, carefully using his walking stick to steady himself on the floor plates the SOCOs had laid down, the smells of the place instantly saddening him further. Old age. Furniture polish. Decaying fabrics. And the new smells of the Crime Scene chemicals. He looked at the empty space, a darker colour than the rest of the floor, where a particularly fine hall table had stood for decades. At the rectangles on the walls where his sister's stunning art collection had once hung. The silence was so leaden he felt it on him like a heavy coat.

His aunt used to take him and Aileen to church every Sunday. But he'd not had any time for religion as a child. And even less so now. Sure, there had been a time when he was happy – or at least content. He'd been one of the biggest players in antiques in the country. He'd enjoyed the entertaining, the celebrity that went with it, the customers he befriended. But all the time it had been clouded by his sadness that he and Ruth could not have children. The Daly name would live on with his one idiot son from his first marriage, to Sinead.

Now, as he looked around the emptiness in here, it seemed to him that life was little more than a bad joke. An endurance test. Every person a Job if you were into that Old Testament stuff.

Well, one thing he was determined to do, was to get an item back, even if it killed him. And he had a name to begin the search with. The name of a very nasty little shit.

He walked through into the drawing room, with its faded green flock walls, green sofas and armchairs. More shadows on the walls. The marble mantelpiece, on which had once sat a stunning Giacometti sculpture, was bare, apart from one framed photograph of happier times.

Aileen, a beautiful, raven-haired twenty-eight-year-old, with the love of her life, Bradley Walker, a USAF pilot and Cary Grant lookalike. He'd flown as a B24 bomber pilot on Operation Tidal Wave, a huge and unsuccessful mission to bomb the oil refineries around Ploiesti, in Romania, in August 1943. His was one of fifty-four Liberator aircraft that never returned, and he was one of hundreds of airmen reported missing, presumed killed.

For years she had harboured a hope that somehow, miraculously, he had survived. She'd kept up her spirits, somehow. She'd kept them up better than he ever had. That was women for you, he rued. Many seemed to have inner resources that were denied to males.

He climbed the stairs to the landing, past the radiator that Aileen had been left chained to for two days, and went into her bedroom, which was directly opposite. After her husband had died she'd had their marital double bed replaced with a single. It looked strange to see it in this large room that still smelled very faintly of her scent. Propped up against the pillows was Mr Stuffykins, the ragged little one-eyed, one-eared bear she'd brought from New York. He made a mental note to ensure he put it in the coffin with her. He removed a pair of her long black Cornelia James gloves, from her dressing table, to put those in the coffin with her as well. Aileen would like that, he thought; she always believed a woman was not properly dressed unless she was wearing gloves. He took a brief walk through into her bathroom, then went downstairs and into her book-lined study.

First he peered inside the opened wall-safe again, just to double-check nothing had been overlooked. But it was bare. And that dark void pained him, and angered him in so many ways. It had contained their father's pocket watch. The only truly personal thing belonging to him that either of them had.

He sat down at Aileen's walnut bureau. A black Parker pen, in a holder embossed with gold letters reading *HSBC* – probably a Christmas gift years ago from the bank, he thought, sat on the curling leather surface of the writing area. Tiny oval-framed photographs of her husband, her children and himself were arranged on the top of it. The drawers were stuffed with correspondence, bills, stamps. There was a fresh sheet of blue headed writing paper, with an envelope beside it, and an unwritten birthday card. A letter she had been going to write to someone, which now would never be written, and a card that would never be sent. Her diary was gone, he noticed, and assumed the police had taken it.

He pulled open one of the deep side drawers and immediately, along with a faint woody smell, caught a whiff of her scent again. After a few moments of rummaging through papers, he pulled out a leather photograph album containing pictures that had been taken of the highest-value items in the house, mostly for insurance purposes. His sister had a fine collection of oil paintings, clocks and furniture, all of which he had advised her on, and some of which he had bought for her, at knock-down prices, at rigged auctions.

He laid it in front of him and opened it up. The first photograph should have been the uninsured gold Patek Philippe pocket watch, still with a slim gold chain attached, that their father had always worn in his waistcoat. The glass had splinter cracks, and the crown was bent at an angle, the winding arbor frozen, with the pinion inside disconnected from the centre wheel so that the hands would not move when the crown was rotated. He hadn't seen the watch for a long time, since he'd moved it to Aileen's safe. But he could still picture every detail, vividly. The last time he had looked at it was to check the serial number, after he had become an expert in watches and realized it possibly had a high value. He had been right.

The watch was extremely rare and even in its busted form had a value of at least two million pounds today. Not that he or Aileen needed the money or would ever have sold it. They had both wanted to keep it as it was, the day he had been given it. Often he had thought of having it repaired and using it, wearing it with pride, but he could never bring himself to do it. With this busted watch he felt a connection with his father and he was scared to lose that.

He had never questioned in his mind how his father, a humble stevedore, had come by something so valuable. He'd stolen it from somewhere, almost certainly.

As executor of his sister's will, Gavin knew she'd left everything to her granddaughter, with the exception of some bequests to her staff and to charity. As he stared at it, tears welling in his eyes, a voice from the past came back to him, like a ghost. It was long, long, ago.

On the Manhattan wharf in 1922. As he stood there, a small boy, with his sister and his aunt, the youth with a cap, pushing through the crowd, thrusting a heavy brown-paper bag into his hand, containing a gun, the watch and the newspaper front page.

Watch the numbers.

He had been trying to puzzle out what the boy had meant for ninety years. He was scared he would go to his grave never knowing.

Tears rolled down his cheeks. He felt an unbearable emptiness.

He thought of the watch. *I'm going to get you back*, he promised silently. *I don't care what it costs, I'm getting you back.*

27

Gareth Dupont liked modern churches. In particular he liked the Church of the Good Shepherd in Portslade. The district to the west of Brighton, inland from Shoreham Harbour, was where he had lived as a child, and he had always been drawn to the sharp, angular brick building. *Surely God didn't just do old stuff?* he always thought. He always felt more in tune communing with God in here than in some dusty old place.

He entered beneath a sign which proclaimed: THERE ARE NO STRANGERS IN THIS CHURCH, ONLY FRIENDS YOU HAVEN'T MET. He breathed in the smell of dry wood, polish and candle wax, and walked a short distance along the aisle and sat down, placing his copy of the *Argus* next to him. Then he knelt, closed his eyes and pressed his hands together, the way his mother had taught him, the way you were supposed to pray. He was *supposed* to be in a Catholic church, but he preferred Anglican, and he figured that would be okay with God. Particularly as the Anglican church was okay with divorce, thanks to Henry VIII, and, by inference, infidelity. And he was currently mixing it with two ladies: one single and one very married. Playing with fire. He liked fire.

When he left it was 7.15 p.m. He needed to hurry home to shower and change; he was picking up Suki Yang at 8 p.m. and taking her for a meal at Spoons. A couple of hours ago he'd been worrying about taking her to such an expensive place and wondering whether to go for something cheaper. But now he felt much better about it.

He climbed into the Porsche, but kept the roof shut, and keyed in a number on his phone.

A crisp, hostile voice he recognized answered.

'It's Gareth Dupont,' he said.

'I don't like being called on my mobile – what do you want?'

'I just saw the *Argus*.'

'What about it?'

'It's pretty tempting.'

'Are you insane?'

'Not at all. I'd like to talk business. Like – renegotiate terms?'

'I'm not talking any more on this phone. I'll meet you at the Albion pub, Church Road, Hove at 8 p.m.'

Dupont was thinking about his date with Suki Yang. 'Eight's difficult.'

'Not for me it isn't.'

28

Trudie's was one of the few perks of Sussex House, Roy Grace thought. The former CID HQ – now renamed, in the ever changing police world, as the Force Crime and Justice Department – was situated on a dull industrial estate. But this mobile cafe, a short walk away, produced the best bacon butties to be had in the county, along with the cheeriest staff behind the counter. Despite Cleo's best efforts at persuading him to eat a healthy diet, Roy Grace had picked up a fried egg and bacon sarnie from them on his way in at 7 a.m.

Then he had become so absorbed in checking through the overnight logs of serious crimes in Sussex, responding to a ton of emails, and answering some more questions from the Prosecuting Counsel on the Venner court case, he had forgotten to eat it.

He munched it now, not caring that it had gone cold, washing it down with mouthfuls of coffee as he sat, suited and booted, in Major Incident Room One going through his briefing notes for Operation Flounder as he waited for his team to assemble, and listened to the pelting rain outside. The names of operations were thrown up at random by the Sussex Police computer. At the moment it was working its way through fish. *Flounder* was particularly appropriate, Grace thought, because at this moment, exhausted after yet another sleepless night thanks to Noah, he truly felt that he was floundering on this case.

It was a week since Aileen McWhirter had died. The time of the robbery was estimated sometime between 6 and 9 p.m. on the night of Tuesday, 21 August. If there had been three perpetrators, it was estimated it would have taken them a good couple of hours to have physically removed the items they took and wrapped and stowed them in a vehicle. The perps had vanished into thin air with ten million pounds' worth of antiques and fine art. And in ninety minutes' time he was going to have to give his mercurial boss, ACC Rigg, an update on progress.

Great.

Running murder enquiries was the job Roy Grace loved, and it was what he wanted to do for the rest of his career. He had been fascinated by homicides ever since the first one he had attended, many years back as a young DC. Normally at the start of each new day of an enquiry he would feel energized, however late he might have gone to bed. But this morning, thanks to a case of *baby brain*, he was struggling.

He stared up at the large colour photograph of the old lady's wrinkled, but still handsome, face, which was stuck to a whiteboard. Next to it, on another whiteboard, were SOCO photographs of three different shoeprints, and catalogue illustrations of the trainers they had come from, and two other whiteboards were almost covered with photographs of antique furniture, pictures and jewellery that had been stolen from the house in Withdean Road.

Aileen McWhirter's white hair, elegantly coiffed, was held in place by a ruby-studded barrette. Her blue eyes, pin-sharp but twinkling with warmth, peered out through the lenses of her tortoiseshell glasses. She was wearing a white blouse with an embroidered collar and pearl earrings. An antique pearl pendant hung around her crinkly neck. She looked serene and wise and elegant.

She must have been very beautiful when she was

younger, he thought. Anyone would have been proud to have her as their grandmother. Throughout his career he had carried a particular hatred for the creeps who breached the sanctuary of people's homes, and even more so for those who harmed vulnerable, elderly people.

He thought about the small, ring-bound crime scene photograph album in his desk drawer, locked to prevent any snooping cleaning staff from coming across it. Despite being hardened to most sights, he found some of the pictures, taken by a Crime Scene Officer, James Gartrell, in the mortuary, almost too distressing to look at. Thinking now about those images of some of the terrible injuries inflicted on her, he squirmed with anger and revulsion.

Eighteen months short of her one hundredth birthday – and the traditional missive from the Queen that would have come with it – Aileen McWhirter had been the victim of brutality on a level that had profoundly upset even the most hardened members of the investigating team. The post-mortem revealed she had burns to her body that were consistent with a pair of heated curling tongs found on her bedroom floor.

But the post-mortem had revealed few clues about who had attacked her. There was no flesh under her fingernails, which meant she probably had not succeeded in scratching any of them. Shame, Grace thought. It would have been nice to think she had managed to gouge at least one of their eyes out.

The only clues found in the house were three sets of shoeprints that did not match up with any of her regular visitors – her part-time housekeeper who normally came twice a week, her gardener, her nephew Lucas's wife, Sarah, and her brother. Copies had been sent to forensic podiatrist Haydn Kelly, who had previously produced some outstanding gait identification results for Roy Grace using the latest technology, and a match had been found to the trainers they believed the perpetrators had worn.

It was strange, he thought, how in these past two months since Noah's birth, violence was affecting him in ways it never had previously. One of the many books he had read on parenting had predicted that would happen.

Above the photograph in front of him on the whiteboard was handwritten, in clear but untidy capitals, in black marker pen:

OPERATION FLOUNDER

DECEASED. AILEEN McWHIRTER. D.O.B. 24 APRIL 1914.
RELEVANT PERIOD (ESTIMATED)
SUNDAY, 19 AUGUST – WEDNESDAY, 22 AUGUST.

Below was an inventory, provided by the dead woman's brother, Gavin Daly, of the items he was certain had been stolen from her home.

But what absorbed Roy Grace at this moment were two sheets of computer printout showing standard family-tree icons and graphs.

He followed the horizontal then the vertical lines. There was a horizontal black one, with an arrow to *Gordon Thomas McWhirter. Deceased. DOB 26.03.1912.* Her husband, he presumed.

Then a vertically descending red arrow to the deceased children, and a further arrow to the grandchild. Then to their left, another vertical red arrow pointed to Brendan Daly and Sheenagh Daly. Beneath Sheenagh Daly was written, *DOB 19.09.1897. Deceased. 18.02.1922.* Beneath Brendan was written, *DOB 07.08.1891. Missing, presumed dead.*

He frowned, thinking back to the books in the dead woman's library on the early history of New York.

'Ever see that movie, *Gangs of New York*?' Glenn Branson said, suddenly, standing over his shoulder.

Grace turned. 'A while ago, but I fell asleep during it.'

Branson grinned. 'Yep, well, that's what happens at your age!'

'Sod off!'

Branson patted him on the shoulder. 'Don't take it personally; it's a fact.'

Grace levelled him with his eyes.

'All that stuff predates Aileen McWhirter. But it gives interesting background during the time the lady was a kid,' Glenn Branson said, serious now. 'Back in the 1800s there were gang wars between the native Americans and the Irish immigrants. We're picking up decades later, when the White Hand Gang was the principal mob of the Irish Mafia. They controlled the Manhattan and Brooklyn waterfronts – all the wharfs and piers. Their boss was a character called Dinny Meehan – he was the guy who kicked Frankie Yale and Johnny Torrio, who headed the Black Hand Gang, out of New York, along with Al Capone, which was why Capone ended up in Chicago. Capone came back to New York with a vengeance in the late-twenties, wiped out the Irish Mafia and took control. Dinny Meehan was murdered in 1920. Brendan Daly was one of his lieutenants, who was missing, presumed murdered, in a power struggle for control of the White Hand Gang.'

'Thanks for the history lesson!'

Branson looked at him then shook his head. 'Didn't they teach you anything at school?'

Grace gave him a wry smile. 'Obviously nothing that mattered!'

Branson tapped his own chest. 'Yeah, well, we descendants of slaves need to know about history.'

'You're not descended from a slave,' Grace said with a grin. 'Your dad was a bus driver in London.'

Ordinarily, his mate would have come back at him with some riposte or a movie quote – he was a total movie buff. But this morning he gave him a strangely sad smile. Grace could read defeat in his eyes, and that upset him.

Glenn Branson's marital life was a train wreck. Grace had helped him out for most of this past year by letting him lodge in his empty house, and the Detective Sergeant managed to keep that looking, most of the time, like a train wreck too. Feeding Grace's goldfish, Marlon, seemed to be the limit of Glenn Branson's housekeeping skills.

Behind him was a familiar rustling sound. He turned to see that Detective Sergeant Bella Moy was now seated at her workstation, red Maltesers box in front of her. She seemed to live on the chocolates. Yet she never appeared to put on weight. And recently, he'd noticed, she seemed to have blossomed.

In her mid-thirties, living with and looking after her sick, elderly mother, Bella used to wear drab clothes, had dull hair and seemed permanently melancholic. But lately she looked a lot more glamorous.

He watched her pop a Malteser in her mouth. Heard the crunch. And suddenly he found himself rather fancying one himself. As if clocking this, she held the box out towards him. He took one, and instantly regretted it, because the moment he had eaten it, he immediately wanted another.

There was one absentee from the team of twelve people: DS Norman Potting. Grace looked at his watch. It was 8.35 a.m. Five minutes late in starting already. He was due to meet with his Assistant Chief Constable Peter Rigg at 10 a.m., and Rigg was a stickler for punctuality.

Suddenly he was distracted by his thoughts. He'd long

had a near-photographic memory, and as he looked up again at Aileen McWhirter's serene face, he could picture those books packing the shelves on her study walls so clearly. Title after title, including *The Gangs of New York. American Gangsters Then And Now. The First 100 Years of the American Mafia. Young Capone. Early Street Gangs and Gangsters of New York City. Irish Organized Crime. King of the Brooklyn Waterfront.*

There were fifty titles, probably more. She hadn't been an academic or a writer, and this number of books amounted to more than just a passing interest in a subject – this was bordering on an obsession. They might of course have been her husband's books. Both Daly, which was her maiden name, and McWhirter were Irish names.

He decided, later, to run the names Daly and McWhirter through some Internet searches. Then he turned to his notes, and began the meeting.

29

Ten minutes after the start, Norman Potting shuffled into the briefing looking very gloomy. The Detective Sergeant, who was in his mid-fifties, had joined the police force relatively late in life and was not popular, being regarded as a politically incorrect dinosaur by many, but Roy Grace tolerated him, because he was one of the most reliable and doggedly persistent detectives he had ever worked with.

'Sorry I'm late, chief,' he said in his gruff voice. 'Had to see the quack.' Then, lowering his voice, he whispered to Grace, 'Not very good news.'

'I'm sorry, Norman. Do you want to tell me about it later?' Grace quizzed, genuinely worried for the man.

Potting shrugged, then gave a defeatist grimace and sat down. Roy Grace frowned as he noticed the exchange of glances between Potting and Bella Moy. He had wondered for a couple of months now if something was going on between them. They seemed too different, and Norman, with his bad comb-over and constant reek of pipe tobacco, never struck him as an appealing man. Yet he'd had four wives, and Grace had long ago learned that life never ceased to surprise you.

Other assembled members of his team included recently married – and now pregnant – DC Emma-Jane Boutwood, Crime Scene Manager David Green, DS Guy Batchelor, Ray Packham from the High Tech Crime Unit, two indexers, a HOLMES (Home Office Large Major Enquiry System) analyst, a crime analyst, the manager for the analysts and indexers, an Intelligence Officer, several Detectives and Press Officer Sue Fleet, a striking redhead. The Chief Constable placed particular importance on keeping the public – or *the customers we serve*, as the public were now called in the latest police newspeak – properly informed.

Roy Grace had never been able to get his head around that word *customers*. The police force, in his experience, had always kept a distance between themselves and the general public. But he had no option but to go along with changes, however absurd he felt some of the government's diktats to be. He looked around fondly at his team, here to serve their *customers*.

The one regular who was missing was DC Nick Nicholl, who had recently been transferred to the Serious and Organized Crime Branch. He was sorry to lose him, but since becoming a father, Nick had definitely become a less effective detective – in part from lack of sleep. Grace made a mental note not to go the same way. Somehow.

Then he said, 'Okay, this is the tenth briefing of Operation Flounder.' He looked at Bella. 'Can you update us on the actions from the Outside Enquiry Team?'

'We're continuing with house-to-house enquiries, sir,' the DS replied. 'One problem, as we know, is that Withdean Road is not exactly a closely knit neighbourhood. They're all large houses in their own grounds; only a few of the people we've talked to have ever met their neighbours. We believe the perpetrators must have used at least one substantial van, if not two, for all the items they took, but no one in the area noticed anything – and there is no CCTV on that road or any intersecting roads. There is just one thing of possible interest.'

'Yes?'

'It's a call we had in response to our boards out on the

street. What makes this particularly interesting is it was possibly an *anniversary visit*. The Tuesday night, exactly a week before the robbery.'

Bella had everyone's attention now.

'A neighbour in the street, a few houses along, phoned in to say he remembered seeing a black Porsche parked on the kerb outside the victim's house as he drove home, about 7 p.m. A man was sitting in the car. He said he didn't think anything of it at the time; he assumed the driver had stopped to make a phone call or something.'

'Did he get a description of the driver or the car's registration?'

'No, sir.'

'Black Porsches are not uncommon in Brighton,' Grace said. 'But there can't be that many. Get a list of all the ones with Sussex registrations and see if that throws up any names.'

'Yes, sir. Oh, and there's one other thing that may be significant, although I don't think so. There was a G5 in Brighton last week, a man called Ralph Meeks, found dead in his house. He used to work as a gardener for Mrs McWhirter – I understand he was sacked by her about fourteen years ago. Possibly he had a grudge – although his estimated time of death was some days before the robbery.'

'All right, see if you can find out any more.'

'Yes, I have someone on it, sir.'

Grace thanked her. Then, looking around the team, said, 'Okay, how's the checking of van rental companies going?'

'I'm working through them, sir,' said a young DC, Jack Alexander, who Grace had brought in to replace Nick Nicholl. 'There's a huge number – quite apart from the national rental companies, there are hundreds of small van hire firms.'

Grace thanked him and turned back to Bella. She glanced down at her notes. 'We've covered eBay and all the antiques dealers in the Brighton and Hove area for the minor stolen items. We've circulated all the photographs of the high-value items that we know to be missing to all of Sussex's principal dealers, and I'm working through a list of all other UK dealers who might handle these valuable items, as well as compiling a list of international ones – and we are liaising with the insurance company's loss adjusters. It's very possible they're being shipped abroad – and might already have been. We're keeping an eye on Shoreham and Newhaven harbours and have officers searching all containers being exported. One area we are also looking at is any upcoming specialist auctions. The highest-value item taken was the 1910 Patek Philippe pocket watch, which is uninsured and worth over two million pounds.'

'Sir Hugo Drax wore a Patek Philippe in the novel of *Moonraker*!' Glenn Branson announced. 'But it was changed to a Swatch in the film!'

'Very helpful, Glenn,' Grace said tartly. Then he turned to Bella. 'Good thinking,' Grace said, making a note. 'Don't restrict your auction search just to the UK. A watch would be easily portable to anywhere in the world.'

'Two million for a watch? Strewth!' Potting said.

Bella nodded, then glanced at her Swatch. 'Obviously a bit posher than mine!'

There was a ripple of laughter. Grace noticed Norman Potting laughing the loudest, and the old sweat making eye contact with Bella, and he thought, just possibly, that she blushed.

'Actually it's a bit ironic about the watch. It belonged to both her and her brother, Gavin Daly. He's always had a high profile in the antiques world and lives in an isolated country house where in the past he's had two burglaries. So it's been at his sister's house for safekeeping for a few decades.'

'Chief,' DC Exton said, 'Surely a watch of that sort of value is going to be very identifiable – presumably unique in some way. So how would it be sold?'

Grace nodded. 'Yes, I've been thinking the same thing. As you've raised the question, I'll give you the task of obtaining all the information about it – what records of it might the manufacturers still have? How many of its kind are there in existence? What identification is on it – presumably a production serial number? Was it monogrammed with any initials? And what kind of world market exists for watches of this value? Who are the likely buyers? Are there any big collectors? Where do watches of this kind of value change hands – is it through dealers or auctions? Are there specialist watch or watch and clock auctions?'

'Car boot sales?' said Potting, facetiously.

'I don't think so, Norman,' Grace said. Then he turned to DS Annalise Vineer, the manager for the analysts, indexers and typists on the enquiry. 'Do you have anything to report?'

'We've run a nationwide check for home-invasion robberies with a similar MO, chief. So far all but one of the matches show the perpetrators of those to be in prison.'

'And that one is?' Grace asked.

'Amis Smallbone.'

The room went quiet for a moment. Then Glenn Branson's mobile phone rang. With an apologetic glance at Roy Grace, he answered it.

'Oh, no!' he said. 'Oh, shit. I'll be right there.'

He stood up, looking ashen. 'I'm sorry, I have to go to the hospital. It's Ari.'

Ari was Glenn Branson's wife. Grace followed him outside. 'Tell me, mate, what is it?'

'I dunno exactly. They said she's broken some bones. Knocked off her bike by a pedestrian on the seafront cycle lane.'

'Call me.'

Branson nodded and hurried off.

30

It was meant to be summer, but the relentless late-August rain rattled against his basement window, with its dismal view of a row of dustbins and stained walls. The meagre light leaking into this crummy bedsit made it feel, at 4 p.m., that summer really was at an end. His first summer as a free man for twelve years.

But Amis Smallbone, in his busted armchair, cigarette smouldering in the ashtray beside the half-drained bottle of Chivas Regal, was feeling in a particularly upbeat mood. A lot of money was about to come his way. A shedload!

Just one wrinkle. A very greedy wrinkle. Gareth Dupont. He knew the man was a bit flaky by reputation, but after twelve years inside, a lot of his best contacts had gone away, or died, which was why he'd gone to him in the first place. Now he regretted that. And he cursed the reward money on offer. He was damned if he was going to be blackmailed by that little shit. Dupont was a problem and had to be dealt with. He would figure something out.

At least, on the brighter side, in a few days he was out of here. Into much nicer accommodation, provided his Probation Officer approved, and he had no reason not to. It was a rented town house in a gated development in the centre of Brighton's North Laine district. His mate Henry Tilney, who, unlike himself, had managed to avoid any residency at Her Majesty's Pleasure, had stood referee and guarantor for him on the tenancy agreement. And very soon he would be able to repay Tilney the five-grand deposit he'd put down on his behalf.

And equally soon he would be able to repay Detective Superintendent Roy Grace for depriving him of twelve years of his life, which he had spent in some of England's biggest shithole prisons.

The floor plans of his soon-to-be neighbours' house lay unfolded on the crappy coffee table in front of him. Cleo Morey's house. There was what looked like an easy route across the rooftop fire escape to her house. In his original thinking, he was going to hire someone to do the deed. But why should he pay good money for an act that would give him so much pleasure to commit himself? Whatever that act was. Maiming Cleo, perhaps. Or killing the baby.

There were endless possibilities. He could visualize lifting the baby from its cot. The stupid, dumb little infant, Noah, and hurling it through the air onto the cobblestones below.

Thud.

He liked that sound.

Thud.

Oh yes.

But far more he looked forward to seeing Detective Superintendent Grace's pain. His grief.

Then he heard a thud. Followed by another. On his door.

He glanced down at his gold Rolex, which had been stored these past twelve years in a safety deposit box that the police had not managed to find. 4.20 p.m. He wasn't expecting any visitors. But he *was* expecting his pay-off anytime now. A cut of the ten million pound haul from the Withdean Road heist. He stood up, swaying from the alcohol inside him, and made his way towards the door.

The cheapskate landlord of this dump hadn't put in either a spyhole or a safety chain, so he had no way of finding out who his visitor was other than shouting through the door. 'Who is it?'

'Father Christmas!'

The voice was dimly familiar. If they were coming to pay him off, he did not want to turn them away. But he did not feel entirely comfortable. He unlocked the door, and the two safety bolts, top and bottom. Then he opened it a fraction. An instant later, it smashed him in the face, sending him hurtling backwards on his unsteady legs, before falling flat on his back.

A big brute in a dark suit picked him up off the floor by his shirt collar, half-throttling him.

'You fucking moron!' his assailant said, his face tight with fury. 'You enjoy killing frail old ladies, do you?' The other man stared down at him, silently.

When the pressure was released from his throat he replied, apologetically and shit scared, 'I said that she was a vulnerable old lady. Hurting her was never the plan.'

'Said? Said to *who*?'

He was shaken so hard he felt his teeth move. 'Why should I be a grass?' he gasped.

'Because you're the biggest fucking dickhead on the planet.'

'Takes one to know one,' Amis Smallbone retorted, defiantly.

Then he instantly regretted his drunken bravado, as a fist slammed into his mouth, destroying thousands of pounds worth of expensive reconstructive dentistry he'd had after the last fight he'd been in. Then another fist slammed into his rib cage.

'You're not in a good place to get smart on me right

now. I want names. I want the bastards who did this, and I want to know where all the stuff's gone – my dad and I want it back. All of it.'

Smallbone stared back at him sullenly, winded, blood pouring down his face. 'I'm not getting killed for being a grass.'

Then he screamed in agony as a hand, hard as a mechanical pincer, grabbed his groin and began to crush his testicles. Then let go.

Smallbone fell to the floor, gasping in agony.

'Want to tell me the names? He won't be so gentle next time. Next time he'll rip them off.'

With tears streaming from his eyes, Amis Smallbone looked at the giant of a man standing beside him, and believed him. 'If I tell you, they'll kill me,' he gasped.

'If you don't, I'll kill you, except I'll have to get rid of your body – and that's a hassle. Just make it easy for me. Names, Smallbone. Okay?'

Then his balls were crushed again, even harder than before.

Through his agony, he screamed out names. But he held back Gareth Dupont's; even through his excruciating pain, he was able to think clearly enough to realize if Dupont was beaten up, he'd reckon he was behind it. And with that £100k reward out there, that could be a dangerous thing.

They left him vomiting on the skanky carpet. As the tall man closed the front door behind them, he turned and said, 'Sorry.'

31

Roy Grace was still smarting from the grilling he'd had from ACC Rigg this morning. On his list of crimes that affected the quality of life of the Sussex community, housebreaking was at the top of the ACC's priorities.

Just three years ago, Graham Barrington, the Divisional Commander of Brighton and Hove, had reported proudly at the daily meeting for all senior police officers, known affectionately as *morning prayers*, that for the first time since records had begun there had been no overnight domestic burglaries in the city of Brighton and Hove. It had seemed then that one aspect of crime in the community was firmly under control.

But since then, with the deepening recession, that had begun to change. Even so there had not been an incident as nasty as Aileen McWhirter's savage attack for some time. The ACC had rigorously questioned Grace about the progress of the investigation.

To be fair to his boss, Roy Grace knew the man was under pressure from a number of different directions. The nationwide publicity from this case was doing a lot to foster Brighton's long-held, and not strictly fair, reputation as a haven for criminals.

He needed to produce suspects, and fast. Amis Smallbone was the only name he had so far that he could give to the Assistant Chief Constable. But would Smallbone, out on licence for only a couple of months, having served twelve years of a life sentence, be so stupid to risk his freedom?

The answer, he knew from long experience dealing with criminals, was that yes, he could be that stupid, or desperate. And it certainly had the scumbag's hallmark.

Aileen McWhirter's brother, Gavin Daly, had contacted him, saying he wanted to offer a one million pound reward for information leading to the arrest and conviction of the perpetrators. Grace had convinced him this was far too much and would result in the incident room being swamped with unhelpful calls. They had settled on one hundred thousand pounds, and informed the *Argus* as well as passing this on to the charity Crimestoppers to put on their website and posters for anonymous informants, and to Sue Fleet in the press office.

He was worrying about Glenn Branson. Twice when he had called, Glenn had told him he couldn't speak at the moment and would bell him back.

As Grace looked down at his notes, preparing to start the 6.30 p.m. briefing, David Green said, 'Chief, I thought that little turd Smallbone was inside.'

'He's out on licence,' DS Guy Batchelor replied. 'This has his handwriting all over it. High-value house with the victim tortured. Never him personally, of course. He gets scrotes to do his dirty work, gives them a cut. He's his father's son – except not as smart.'

'I'd dearly love to go and have a chat with him myself, but I don't think that would be too productive,' Grace said, bearing in mind their past animosity. He turned to a new addition to his enquiry team, DC Sam Tovey, a slim, quiet-natured woman with short, dark hair and a pleasant, if slightly brisk, no-nonsense air about her. Smallbone was a bully, but like all male bullies he'd find it less easy to bully strong women, and Grace remembered him being intimidated by smart women officers in the past. As he looked around the team he thought hard about the best people to send, and decided Bella Moy should be one of them. At thirty-five, she was mature enough to stand up to Amis, who was sixty-two. 'Sam and Bella, I'd like you to go and have a chat with Smallbone. Ask for an alibi for the night of Tuesday, August the 21st. I have an address for him on file, but he may have moved. The Probation Service will have it. Best not send him my regards!'

There was a titter of laughter. Several members of the team knew Roy Grace's past history with Amis Smallbone, one of the Brighton underworld's nastier specimens. Almost thirteen years ago, Grace, then a young Detective Inspector, had been his arresting officer, and almost single-handedly responsible for putting Smallbone away for life. Just over two months ago, Smallbone had been released from jail on licence.

Smallbone's late father, Morris, the brains behind what was, at one time, a widespread crime empire, had slipped through police hands countless times. Other people did time inside for him, but never Morris – he was too smart. Less so his son, whose sadistic streak had been his undoing.

Amis Smallbone had gone down on a charge of murdering a rival drug dealer in the city, by dropping an electric heater into his bathtub. At the time of his arrest, the villain had threatened retribution against Roy Grace personally, and against his wife, Sandy. Three weeks later, with Smallbone in prison, someone had sprayed every plant in the garden of Grace's home with weedkiller.

In the centre of the lawn had been burned the words:

UR DEAD

Smallbone had been on Roy Grace's radar right from his very earliest days as a detective, after he had been the prime suspect in a number of scams involving tricking elderly, vulnerable people out of their cash and valuable possessions, using threats and actual violence whenever necessary. There wasn't an area of the Brighton and Hove crime scene, including burglary, drugs, protection racketeering, prostitution, fake designer goods, vehicle theft and car clocking, that Smallbone's family didn't have a finger in. But what interested Roy Grace now was that Smallbone's credentials included fencing high-end antiques – most of which were shipped overseas, predominantly to Spain, within hours of being stolen.

If an offender was freed on licence, as Smallbone had been, then if that person committed just one offence, of any nature, they would be straight back inside for many years. 'Is there anything to connect Smallbone with this?' he asked.

'Surely he wouldn't be that stupid so soon after coming out, would he?' Emma-Jane Boutwood said.

'If it's in the blood, it's in the blood,' Norman Potting said. Grace noticed he was perspiring heavily. 'Smallbone was used to living high on the hog,' Potting continued. 'From memory, we pretty much cleaned him out after his conviction. He'll be needing to earn again.'

Grace nodded, then addressed Sam Tovey and Bella Moy. 'Smallbone will have an alibi for last Tuesday evening, I'll guarantee. He'll have spent the evening in a pub where he's known, and there'll be a dozen people there who can vouch for him. But just rattle his cage, let him know we think he may be involved. It'll make him nervous – and the more nervous he is, the more likely he'll make a mistake.'

'Could we get surveillance on him, chief?' Guy Batchelor said. 'Or a phone tap?'

'We don't have hard enough evidence to justify the cost

of surveillance,' Grace said. 'And I'm afraid a phone tap is a non-starter at this stage.' Surveillance was extremely costly in terms of specialist manpower and Grace could not see the ACC sanctioning it. The criterion for obtaining a phone tap order was evidence that a human life was in immediate danger. It had to be signed by an ACPO and the Home Secretary or a Secretary of State. He turned to DS Potting, who had been given the action at a previous briefing of seeing if any activity had taken place on the dead woman's credit cards or bank account.

'Norman, do you have anything on her credit cards?'

Again, Grace noticed a quick, almost imperceptible, glance between the old detective and Bella Moy.

For some moments, Potting's gloom lifted, as he looked distinctly pleased with himself. 'I do, chief. During the twenty-four hours between the night of August the 21st and 22nd, two hundred pounds was withdrawn from Aileen McWhirter's bank account with her debit card. During this same period, three hundred pounds was withdrawn on her Amex card, three hundred pounds on her MasterCard and two hundred and fifty on her Visa. All CCTV footage from the cashpoints has been checked. In each case the money was withdrawn by someone with their face hooded.'

Grace frowned, then said, 'The estimated value of the articles stolen from the victim's house is in the region of ten million pounds. It seems odd that anyone would bother with such relatively small amounts of cash in addition, with the risks involved.'

'Well, chief,' said Potting, 'to me that would indicate hired thugs. They're either on a flat rate or a small percentage of what they nicked. So they helped themselves to a bit more, perhaps?'

'Quite possible,' Grace agreed. 'Her brother, Gavin

Daly, is a major player – or was – in the antiques world. And his son, Lucas, has the business now. Any thoughts on whether either or both of them might have had a hand in this?'

'I've interviewed the old man and the son, boss,' DS Guy Batchelor said. 'Gavin Daly's grief seems pretty real. The son seems pretty upset too. He doesn't have a record but Operation Reduction have had an eye on him for some time.' Operation Reduction was the long-term operation of the Brighton Drugs Squad.

'Can you tell us more on that?' Roy Grace asked.

'They're building a file on him. He's running his father's shop in the Lanes and he's married to the television news presenter Sarah Courteney.'

'She's a bit of all right, she is!' Norman Potting said. 'Phwoar!' Then Grace noticed Bella glare at the detective and he fell silent, blushing slightly.

'But no history of involvement with robbery?' Grace asked Batchelor.

'No, but I did find one thing, running a search on him through the serials. Two years ago a crew were called to his home – his wife had phoned for help saying he was attacking her. He was arrested, but subsequently released, because she refused to press charges.'

Roy Grace nodded. 'Useful to know. Thanks, Guy.' On the long list of members of the human species that the Detective Superintendent despised were men who hit women.

'The only other person with regular access to Mrs McWhirter's property,' Guy Batchelor continued, 'is the housekeeper who comes twice a week. She's seventy-five, bless her, and has worked for Daly and his family for thirty years. Other visitors to the property include the gardener, who's almost equally ancient, the milkman, the newspaper boy, a plumber called Michael Maguire, who did some work on a toilet about four months ago, and a builder, Bryan Barker, who did some roof-tiling work in April. We're checking them all out.'

'Good. Thanks, Guy.' Grace turned to the Press Officer. 'What's the situation on press and media interest, Sue?'

'I'm getting a lot of calls and emails asking whether we've established a motive, other than burglary, and if we have any suspects.'

'At this moment I'm regarding Amis Smallbone as a Person of Interest, but no more than that,' he replied. 'I don't want that announced. Is there any urgency on holding another press conference?'

'Not at the moment, sir, but we'll need to by the end of the week,' she said.

'Okay. Friday afternoon.' He turned to David Green, the Crime Scene Manager. 'Anything to report?'

'Not until we get the detailed footprint analysis back from the forensic podiatrist, Haydn Kelly, chief. We haven't found anything else in Aileen McWhirter's house yet.'

Normally, Grace kept his cool, but his tiredness and the grilling from the ACC were getting to him. 'Bloody hell!' he exploded. 'The woman's been tortured, and her house has virtually been stripped bare. No one could have done that without leaving a damned trace! There has to be more than three sets of shoeprints!'

'If there is, we'll find it, boss!' Green said.

He turned to Ray Packham, from the High Tech Crime Unit, a man in his mid-forties who could easily have been mistaken for a provincial bank manager. 'Anything for us from the victim's phone, Ray?'

'Very little traffic, chief. I don't know if it is in any way significant, but she received a call only moments before she was attacked.' Packham checked his notes for a moment. 'We traced it to a mobile phone belonging to an employee of a telesales company selling loft insulation. The man who made the call, Gareth Dupont, left their employment at the end of last week and started with a new company called Mountainpeak this Tuesday. I would not consider this significant, ordinarily, except for one thing.' Ray Packham gave Grace a smile, then said nothing further, as if enjoying his moment in the sun.

'Which is?' Roy Grace asked.

'Gareth Dupont has form. Four previous convictions. Possession of cannabis. That was minor. More significant is one for GBH, one previous conviction for handling stolen goods – and even more significant is he's out on licence for aggravated burglary.'

'Good work, Ray,' Grace said. 'I've had one of those calls about loft insulation as well – but I got rid of him smartly. Do you have any details on his aggravated burglary conviction?'

Packham nodded. 'Yes, chief. Five years ago he was arrested following a burglary at a country house near Lewes. The owners were an elderly couple who were tied up and tortured with a very similar MO to Aileen McWhirter. They were burned with cigarettes by perps wanting their credit-card pin codes. Dupont claimed only to be the driver and got a reduced sentence for giving evidence against the other two perpetrators. I think he's a fairly nasty piece of work. He also has links to an organized crime ring in Spain – Russian Mafia – specializing in fencing valuable paintings.'

DS Batchelor raised his hand. 'Boss, there could be something significant here.'

'Tell us,' Grace said.

'I was on a case of country-house burglars some years ago. They used a trick similar to this: phoning the occupant under the pretext of selling something, while knocking on the front door at the same time. It creates confusion, puts people off their guard – especially elderly people.'

Roy Grace made a note on his pad. 'Good thinking, Guy. Do a full background on him, and what he's up to now. Who he associates with, and any intelligence we have on him. Then I'd like you to go and have a chat with him.'

'Do we have a residential address for him?'

'His Probation Officer will know it. Otherwise you can go to Mountainpeak tomorrow where he's working. Let me know; I'd like to come with you – I'm interested in this person.'

'Yes, chief.'

Grace turned to DS Moy. 'Bella, the knocker-boy who left the leaflet in Aileen McWhirter's house – R. C. Moore. I had a phone call earlier this morning from Andy Kille, the Ops One Inspector. A senior nurse from the Royal Sussex County Hospital contacted Sussex Police at 5 a.m. today. She'd read in the *Argus* about Aileen McWhirter being tortured with burns, and reported that a man giving his name as Ricky Moore had been admitted early last Saturday morning, after stumbling into A&E with burns across his body – as well as internally. Without going into graphic detail, I understand it will be several weeks before he's going to be able to sit down – or have a crap in comfort.'

'You mean he's a fudge-packer, chief?' Norman Potting said.

'Not a willing one, Norman, no,' Grace said, irritated at his language. 'I've never heard of anyone getting pleasure out of heated curling tongs up their rectum.'

'Ouch,' Potting said.

'Could not have put it better myself,' he replied tartly. 'I'd like you to go and have a chat with him, Bella.'

'Yes, chief.'

As Roy Grace ended the meeting, Norman Potting came up to him and said, 'Do you think I could have that word with you, chief? Need a bit of advice.'

Roy Grace glanced at his watch, mindful of his promise to Cleo to be home early. 'In my office – give me five minutes. It'll have to be quick.'

32

To Roy Grace's irritation, Norman Potting followed him straight out of the briefing, along the corridor, towards the open-plan office area of the Major Crime Suite. He had hoped for a bit of breathing space after the briefing to call Cleo and tell her he would be home soon.

He checked his emails on his BlackBerry as he strode along the zig-zagging corridors, annoyed to hear Potting's footsteps almost on his heels.

As he opened the door to his office and went in, peeling off his jacket and hooking it on the back of the door, Norman Potting followed. Grace squeezed into the space behind his small desk, and the DS sat down heavily on the chair opposite. Grace could smell the reek of pipe tobacco smoke on his clothes, but he didn't mind it. An occasional smoker himself, he loathed the draconian anti-smoking laws the nanny state in the UK had come up with. In truth, he envied Potting's total insouciance in ignoring them at every possible opportunity.

'So, Norman?' he said, glancing at his BlackBerry, flashing red again, then his watch. 'Tell me?'

Potting was looking uncharacteristically nervous. 'Well, chief, the thing is, umm, you see . . .' he said in his rural burr. The old detective blushed, then touched his eyebrows with the fingers of both hands. 'I – ah – went to see the quack last week – and I had to go back to him this morning for the results; that's why I was late for the briefing. The thing is, he sent me to have some tests – I'd been having a bit of irregularity with the old waterworks. Peeing a lot during the night, that kind of thing.' He looked at Roy Grace quizzically.

The Detective Superintendent smiled back, patiently waiting for him to get to the point. 'Sorry to hear that, Norman.'

'Yes, well, you see – ' He looked around, conspiratorially, then lowered his voice, despite them being alone in the office. 'Turns out I have a bit of a problem in the old prostate department.'

'What kind of problem?'

'A touch of the *old favourite.*'

Grace had heard that expression before. It was mostly used by old rogues, rather than saying the C word. 'God, I'm sorry, Norman.' Grace genuinely was.

'The doc says I have choices. One option is surgery – have the whole thing cut out, but that could result in a total loss of – you know – *winky action,* if you get my drift?' He curled his index finger to illustrate the problem. 'A one in five chance of that happening.'

Roy Grace nodded. Although he felt sorry for the man, Norman Potting talking about sex did not float his boat. 'It wouldn't come back afterwards?'

Potting shook his head glumly. 'Not in the majority of cases, apparently. The other option is to have radiotherapy. From what I understand that way the old winky action would continue – but they might not get rid of it. Meaning, I suppose – you know – a few years, then curtains. I need to talk it through with someone, but I don't really have any close male friends these days. You've got a wise head on you, chief. I need a bit of guidance.'

Grace thought that Norman Potting, suddenly, for the first time in all the years he had known him, looked lost.

Like a small kid seeking teacher's approval of a piece of work. Despite his frequent irritation at the man, he felt intensely sorry for his dilemma.

'I don't know what to say, Norman. I'm just not qualified to give this kind of advice. What's your doctor's view?'

'That I have to make the decision. I did talk to the Nurse Specialist after – she was a bit of all right, phwoar! But you're the only person whose judgement I trust – you know – to be impartial.'

Grace took a deep breath. 'I just don't know enough about the subject to give you an informed decision. You're obviously very upset at the moment. I think you need to get all the facts clear in your mind before you make any decision.'

'I don't know if I would want to take the risk of not being able to shag. A difficult choice, know what I mean?'

Grace did and shuddered. He'd read stuff in the press about this disease over the years. But at forty he'd never been troubled enough to think about it. Now he was being asked to help someone make a possible life or death decision. 'Get all the facts, Norman, okay? If you can get all the facts, then I'll talk through them with you.'

'Imagine it's you, not me. What would you do?'

Grace shrugged. 'I don't know, really I don't. I guess my immediate reaction would be there's a lot more to life than sex. But I'll tell you one thing. From all I've seen of it, old age has some good points, but a lot of bad ones. I believe in quality of life rather than the length of it. If you feel that sex is an important part of your life, then you have to weigh up whether you are willing to sacrifice that in order to gain a couple more years playing tiddlywinks and pissing into a nappy in an old folks' home.'

Potting grinned. 'You're a diamond geezer!'

Grace shook his head. 'I'm not. Maybe one day I'll understand what life is all about. Then I could give you proper advice – you see—'

Grace was interrupted by his mobile phone ringing. Glancing at the display, he saw it was Glenn Branson's personal number. Apologizing to Potting, he answered it, and instantly heard his mate in tears.

'Shit, Roy,' he said. 'Oh shit. Ari's just died.'

33

The fat man, in his white yachting cap, sat behind the wheel of his white convertible Rolls-Royce Phantom, looking, for all the world, like Mr Toad. He was driving at walking pace, steering, with just one pudgy finger, through the midday hordes shuffling leisurely along the quay of Puerto Banus.

Cars were parked in white-painted bays, elegantly chained off. Beyond them were the fuck-off yachts, mostly painted brilliant white and sporting all kinds of flags of convenience. *ACE. FAR TOO. TIO CARLOS. SHAF.* Some of them came and went; others, like his, were berthed here all year round. His was one of the biggest, and he liked knowing that.

He liked this place. The bling, the bright colours, the designer sunglasses; there was a smell of opulence in the air. And he was part of it – and few things, including his three ex-wives and the twenty-four-year-old pole dancer he was currently shagging, ever let him forget that. One day he would die here, a contented man!

The car purred past smart bars and restaurants, the Bulgari shop, Jack's Bar, then Chloé, American Brasserie and Dolce & Gabbana. Yachts were berthed stern-in, Mediterranean style, along the pontoons of the marina to his right, and white Moorish villas with red pantiled roofs rose up the hillside ahead of him. Even the brilliant sun, beating down its dry, dazzling heat, felt as reassuringly expensive as everything else here.

Wearing a baggy white shirt, Bermuda shorts and Gucci

sandals, and breathing in the smell of the car's fine leather interior, he drove on slowly, at the crowd's strolling pace. He was in no hurry; he had plenty of time for lunch and a round of golf before he needed to think about catching his plane, and he was enjoying himself. He was in a very contented mood indeed – an even more contented one than usual. He was enjoying the admiring glances his Roller got, nodding his head to the tune that was blasting from its sound system: 'The Millionaire' by Dr Hook. He liked to play that song over and over, because that was him, little Eamonn Pollock, from the wrong side of the tracks, now a millionaire over and over again.

'*I've got more money than a horse has hair!*' he sang out loud, to Dr Hook's words, then beamed as a pretty woman grinned at him and he grinned back, waving his fleshy little pinky finger at her, then braking to a halt as a couple in front of him wheeling a pushchair stopped to retrieve a stuffed toy the baby had thrown from it. As he did so, his phone rang. Number withheld.

He pulled the handset to his ear, because you never knew who in the crowd might be listening. 'Eamonn Pollock here,' he said cheerily.

'It's me. How are you?'

'How am I? I am a very contented man, thank you! The sun is shining, and I am very contented indeed. What's not to be contented about, eh?'

'We have a problem. Someone's not a very happy man.'

'So how do we spread a little sunshine for him?'

'You could start by bringing his dead sister back to life.'

The sun felt as if, momentarily, it had slipped behind a cloud. But the sky was an unbroken deep blue. 'She died?'

'Your goons killed her.'

He turned the music right down. 'Well, that was not my instruction to them.'

'What are you going to do about it?'

'I'll tell you what I'm going to do about it. I'm going to have a very nice lunch, then I'm going to play a round of golf at my favourite golf course, and then I have a plane to catch. What about you?'

'When do I get my share?' the caller said sullenly.

'Good boy, now we're talking the same language! In time, you will get it, after I've concluded all the sales.'

'You said you'd pay me based on your valuation.'

'Did I really?'

'Yes.'

'That's not my style at all. I'm afraid you'll just have to be patient, dear boy.'

'You bastard, that's not our deal!'

A youth in bright red trousers was taking a photograph of the car. Eamonn Pollock beamed obligingly. 'So nice to hear from you!' he said, and ended the call. He selected the Dr Hook track again. He was looking forward to his lunch. A grilled lobster today and a glass – or two – of Chablis. Nothing like a good meal before a nice round of golf.

Life was so good!

He checked the time on his gold Vacheron Constantin Patrimony watch, which really did cost more pound notes than a horse had hairs – or would have done had he acquired it honestly and paid the market price of two hundred thousand pounds.

But *honest* was not a word in his vocabulary, any more than *conscience* was. He patted his large pot belly. Yes, he was definitely in a lobster mood today.

And very contented. And about to be very much richer than just a week ago.

DEAD MAN'S TIME

He turned the volume of the song up again, and sang happily along to the words, beaming at the world around him. *'Please don't misunderstand me! I've got all this money, and I'm a pretty ugly guy!'*

34

In the sparsely furnished basement consulting room in Schwabing, close to Munich's Isar river, the woman, with her brown hair cropped short with a boyish fringe, lay prostrate on the psychiatrist's couch. She was in her thirties, with a slender figure, dressed appropriately for the sweltering Munich summer day in cut-off jeans, a white tank-top and Havaiana flip-flops.

'So?' Dr Eberstark said, at the end of one of Sandy's habitual lengthy silences. 'Is there anything you would like to say?'

Sandy shrugged.

'More non-verbal communications with me? Maybe you would find talking easier?'

'I don't understand it,' she said.

'You don't understand what, exactly?'

'Why I hate him so much.'

'You left him, yes?' It was old ground, but the psychiatrist repeated it, as he did periodically.

'Yes.'

'When you were pregnant with his child?'

She said nothing.

'And you never told him you were pregnant?'

'We'd been trying for a child for several years.'

'So why did you not tell him?'

'Because . . .' She drifted into a long silence, and then she said, 'Because if I had . . .' then she lapsed back into silence.

'Because if you had?' he prompted, sensing they were getting somewhere.

'I would have had to stay.'

'Would that have been so bad?'

She nodded.

'Why?'

'You should marry a cop, then you'd understand.'

'What is so bad about marrying a cop?'

She was silent for some moments, then she said, 'I always came second. Job first, me second – when he had time.'

'Don't you think having a child might have changed that?'

'Actually, no I don't.' Then she hesitated. 'There's another thing about the baby.' She fell silent and her face reddened.

The psychiatrist looked at his watch. 'Okay, we'll have to leave it there. I'll see you again on Monday? You can tell me that *other thing* then. Okay?'

'Montag,' she said.

35

A nurse led the way along the maze of corridors at the Royal Sussex County Hospital, which smelled strongly of floor polish, to the High Dependency Unit where Ricky Moore was being treated. Instantly the air was fresher and smelled better. She led Bella Moy through the ward towards the bed at the far end. Its occupant was awake, staring blankly ahead, dressed in pale-blue hospital pyjamas, with a sheet partially covering him. An old-fashioned television on a swing arm was switched on but silent. A solitary greetings card lay on a table in front of the pale-looking man, who rested on a bed of pillows, next to a glass of water, some tablets in a small container and an unopened copy of the *Argus* newspaper. There was a chair beside the bed.

With the assistance of another nurse, the curtains were drawn around the bed to give them privacy. Then Bella Moy sat down. 'Ricky Moore?' she asked, to confirm.

He gave her a suspicious frown, but said nothing.

Her first impression of the man was that he was the very double of the television actor Dennis Waterman, for-mer co-star of *Minder* and now of *New Tricks*.

She held up her warrant card. 'Detective Sergeant Moy of Sussex CID – are you up to answering a few questions?'

He winced, painfully forcing one word out at a time. 'If – you – want – the – capital – of – Peru – it's – Lima.'

She smiled. 'Very witty.'

He winced again.

'I understand you were assaulted last Friday night, Ricky? Okay if I call you that?'

He stared at her for some moments. Then he nodded.

'Do you know the people who did it?'

He shook his head.

'Are you sure about that?'

He fell silent.

'So, Ricky, you're in the antiques business, right?'

'Yes.'

'You look in pain – does it hurt you to speak?'

He nodded.

'I'll be brief. Someone hurt you quite badly – is that right?'

He stared into space.

'How badly, Ricky?'

He continued staring into space.

'I don't get it, Ricky,' she said. 'So why did they hurt you?'

Nothing.

'The doctors say you've suffered very serious internal damage. You have a perforated bowel, and permanently damaged nerves. How do you feel about that?'

Again he was silent.

'I'd be pretty upset if that had happened to me. Are you upset?'

Again he said nothing.

She looked at the greetings card. 'That from your wife?'

'Girlfriend.'

'Does it worry you that you might not be able to make love to her again? And that you might be incontinent for the rest of your life?'

He gave her a sullen glare.

'You've been the victim of a very brutal attack. I understand you have severe rectal burns. Is that right?'

'I never – touched – the – old – lady,' he said. His voice was low and pained.

'Is that why this happened to you?'

He did not reply.

'Would you like to tell me who hurt the old lady? And who hurt you?'

'No one hurt me.'

'I'm told something very hot was pushed up your anus. With your perforated bowel you're lucky not to be dead from septicaemia. Was someone torturing you?'

He shook his head. 'Nah, I was doing some electrical repairs. I just sat down on my soldering iron. Dunno how I did it.'

'You were doing electrical repairs in the nude, were you?'

He closed his eyes.

'Is there anything you would like to tell me?'

He remained silent.

After ten minutes a doctor and a nurse opened the curtain and told Bella that Moore needed to sleep now.

As she walked out of the hospital, Bella dialled Roy Grace's number.

36

'You know the worst thing?' Glenn Branson said through his tears, cradling his second pint in the booth at the rear of the pub a short distance down the road from the Royal Sussex County Hospital.

'Tell me,' Roy Grace said, one arm around his mate's shoulder, his glass of a single Glenfiddich on the rocks on the table in front of them. He should not be drinking on duty, he knew, and he still had work to do tonight. But for the moment he was making an exception. He was deeply shaken by Glenn's news.

'It's knowing Ari'll be having a post-mortem in the morning.' He stared, heavy-lidded at Roy Grace. 'We both know what that means.'

All Grace could do was nod.

'They're going to cut her open. They're going to saw off her skull cap, and lift out her brains. Then they're going to slice open her chest and then . . .'

He broke down, sobbing uncontrollably.

'Don't go there, mate,' Grace said.

'But they will, won't they?' Branson said, helplessly. 'We're talking about the woman I loved. The mother of my kids. I can't bear that, Roy.'

'They have to know what happened,' Grace said, and immediately regretted it.

'I know what happened. She was cycling along the cycle lane on the seafront. Someone, not looking where they were going, stepped out in front of her. She came off the bike, broke her arm in three places and dislocated her shoulder.'

Grace frowned. 'Was she wearing a helmet?'

'Always wore one. Made the kids, too.'

'But she must have had a head injury, surely, to have died?'

'No. They took her to the hospital, where she had to have corrective surgery on her arm – it needed metal pins putting in – and they had to reset her shoulder. They put her under anaesthetic and she had an allergic reaction to it – called something like *malignant hyperthermia*. Apparently it happens; one in a hundred thousand or a million or some statistic.'

Grace was silent for a moment. Then he touched his friend's arm, and squeezed gently. 'I've heard of things like that happening – allergic reactions to anaesthetics – but I never – you know. God, poor you, poor kids.'

'How am I going to explain to them that their mummy's never coming home again?'

'Maybe you need some advice from a child counsellor. Take a few days off – compassionate leave.'

He shrugged. 'Thanks, but I'll see.'

'You'll have a lot of stuff to sort out.'

'Yeah,' he said, pensively.

He looked so helpless, Grace thought. Even when Ari had kicked him out, Glenn had coped, but he was all at sea now, overwhelmed.

'It really is unbelievable,' Grace said. 'Talk about *shit happens*. She comes off her bike, the kind of accident every cyclist has, then dies in hospital from the anaesthetic. I – I know you weren't together, but I'm sorry.'

Branson shrugged. 'Yeah. I wish – you know – me and

her – I wish we could at least have stopped disliking each other – that we could have been – at least – ' he choked. 'Friends, yeah?'

Grace had no answer.

'Stupid woman who walked onto the lane in front of her probably won't even get a fine. And I get to bury my wife, and the mother of my kids.'

'You need to be strong for your kids,' Grace said, trying to find a positive for his friend out of the tragedy. Glenn's relationship with his tricky, demanding wife had hit the rocks nearly a year ago. Privately, Grace had never liked her. The DS had moved out and had been lodging at his house ever since. Meantime, to Glenn Branson's chagrin, Ari's new man had moved into their marital home.

Branson gulped down some of his pint and nodded bleakly.

'What's happening with the children?'

'Ari's sister's staying over.'

'What about the boyfriend?'

'He's packed up and gone. Out of there. Shows his moral fibre, right?'

'Already?'

'Speedy Gonzales.'

Grace shook his head. 'They're going to need their father. Have you seen them yet?'

'No.'

'I think you should go round there right now. It's your house, your home. You need to take charge, mate.'

'She's poisoned them against me.'

Grace shook his head. He was out of his depth in a situation like this, he knew. But all his instincts told him that Glenn had to take charge. 'I'll drive you there.'

'My car's in the hospital car park.'

'You're not driving anywhere in your state. I'm going to take you.'

Branson smiled bleakly at him. 'What am I going to do, Roy?'

'I'll tell you exactly what you are going to do. Do you remember, a few years back, telling me why you had become a copper?'

'What did I say?'

'You told me that you were a night club bouncer. When your son Sammy was born, you looked down at him and realized that one day someone at school would ask him what his dad did for a living. You didn't want him having to say his dad was a bouncer. You wanted him to be proud of you. That's why you joined up. Doesn't matter how much Ari poisoned them against you. I'm going to drive you home in a few minutes, and you are going to walk in through the front door and hug them. And one day, very soon, they're going to forget all the shit they've been told and they will be very proud of you indeed. Because you're a very special guy, and they are damned lucky to have you as a dad.'

Branson gave him a bleak smile. 'You know, after my second, Remi, was born I looked down at both of them one day – and I had this weird thought. I thought, one day you are going to think I'm a better person than I really am. So I'd better try to improve myself, in order to cushion their eventual disappointment!'

Roy Grace raised his glass and clinked it against Glenn's. 'You're going to be okay. Know that? I love you, mate. I really love you.'

Branson squeezed his friend's arm and blinked away tears. Then he took a deep breath. 'Let me tell you something. It's a warning, okay?'

Grace frowned. 'A warning?'

'I don't want the same thing to happen to you that happened to me. You've been through enough shit in your life. You've got to realize that ever since Noah was born, your relationship with Cleo has changed for ever. You are no longer the most important thing in her life, and you never will be again. You'll always take second place to your son, and to any other kids you might have. I'm just telling you that because I know you're a decent, caring man, but you're overloaded with work and it might take time to sink in – it did for me. Our kids didn't bring Ari and me together, and I blame myself.'

Roy Grace shook his head. 'You don't have anything to blame yourself for. You're a good man, mate.' At that moment his phone rang. He answered, then looked at his watch. It was a quarter past eight. He had planned to take his work home and help Cleo, who was sounding stressed, by looking after Noah. But this was too important.

Reluctantly, he said to the caller, 'Okay, I'll meet you there at nine. Forty-five minutes.'

He ended the call and turned back to Glenn. 'Drink up, you're going home. *Home.* To your house and your kids!'

'What – what do I say to them when I get there?'

Grace balled his fist and touched his friend's cheek lightly with his knuckles. 'You just say, "I'm your dad, and I'm home."'

37

'In your dreams,' Amis Smallbone said, through his missing teeth. Seated in a booth in the busy pub, opposite a glass tropical fish tank that acted as a dividing wall, he cradled a whisky, feeling particularly ratty as he hadn't had a smoke for over half an hour because it was pissing down with rain outside, waiting for this fuckwit who was late, and hurting all over from his beating. He was dressed in his regular summer rig of blue blazer, open-neck shirt with a paisley cravat, chinos and Cuban-heeled boots.

'I don't think so,' said Gareth Dupont, with a pint of Diet Coke in front of him and a packet of cheese and onion crisps. He was feeling equally ratty because he was running very late for his date with Suki Yang. He sat there in a thin leather bomber jacket over a white T-shirt, jeans and flashy loafers. 'And what the fuck happened to you?'

'I walked into a door.'

Dupont nodded, not expressing any interest in the details.

'We made a deal,' Smallbone said. 'You don't renege on a deal. And you don't grass up people in this city.'

'I don't need to grass up anyone,' Dupont said. 'You weren't straight with me. You didn't tell me how much value was involved here – and you didn't tell me I was going to be at the wrong end of a murder enquiry. I'm out on licence like you. You asked me to find a home for some paintings. You never told me I was going to be the driver for some psychos and ten million quid's worth of gear.'

'And you really think you can grass us all up and collect the reward? You're fucking dreaming.'

Dupont shook his head. 'You've been inside a long time, Amis. But don't tell me you've been out of touch.' He dug his hand into the crisp packet. 'You must know about Crimestoppers?'

'What about them?'

'They're a charity. Any member of the public can call them with guaranteed anonymity. They will never, ever reveal the caller's identity to the police or to anyone else. But if that anonymous call results in arrest and conviction, the caller will get the reward. Are we on the same song sheet now?'

'You're forgetting that I know everyone, Gareth,' Smallbone said. He spoke kindly, like an uncle to an errant nephew.

'You're forgetting you've been inside for over twelve years, Amis. Most of your contacts are inside or have gone away. That's why you contacted me.'

'So what do you want?'

'You offered me ten grand for this deal, right?'

'That's what you accepted, and very gladly,' Smallbone replied.

'Yep, well, now I want one hundred grand. Or you're going back inside.'

'In your dreams.'

38

Grace sat outside Glenn Branson's house in Saltdean, in his new – new to him at any rate – black Alfa Romeo Giulietta, which he had bought from the second-hand lot of Frost's at a bargain price. Hard summer rain drummed on the roof. Cleo had sounded exhausted on the phone, and he wanted to get back to her, and to see Noah.

'I have to meet this guy, darling, it's really important.'

'I thought you were going to be home early today,' Cleo said.

'I had to see Glenn. His wife died – I told you, right? Dead from an allergic reaction. It's unbelievable.'

'You did tell me, and I can't imagine how he is feeling. Poor, poor guy. Aileen McWhirter died and that's terrible, too. You have to find her killers, and you have to find them quickly, and you will, darling, because you're the best. But a few hours aren't going to change anything, Roy.'

Sandy had never understood – or at least, accepted – how the work hours of a homicide detective could be so totally unpredictable. But Cleo was different. Until only a short time before she had given birth, she ran the Brighton and Hove City Mortuary, and had equally unpredictable hours, recovering bodies from wherever they had died. People were rarely courteous enough to drop dead or get murdered within office hours. But all the same, he really wanted to be at home with her, wanted to spend every precious minute with Noah that he could.

'I'm doing all I can to keep the weekend clear, darling,' he said.

'So you can go to the footy?' There was humour in her voice.

'If I go, it's for work. How is Noah?'

'He's cried, pooed and vomited for five hours, non-stop.'

'I'll be on Noah watch all night, after I get home, I promise.'

'That's sweet of you to say, darling, but you won't. You'll fall asleep and I won't wake you, because I know you have to be at work at 6 a.m. And besides, you don't have breasts.'

'Couldn't I bottle-feed him to give you some sleep?'

'I'm so tired,' she said, 'I can barely think straight.'

'I'll be home as soon as I can.'

He hung up with a heavy heart. How the hell was he going to be a good father and a good detective at the same time? The task in front of him seemed daunting. Was it possible?

Others had done it, it had to be. But at this moment he wasn't sure how.

39

Hector Webb was a tall man with a ramrod-straight back and a military bearing. He had close-cropped fair hair and a rugged, pockmarked face. He was seated at the bar, with a half-drunk pint of Guinness in front of him, as Roy Grace entered the Royal Pavilion Tavern on Brighton's Castle Square.

Before crossing the threshold, out of habit Grace clocked all the faces in the room. But none of them rang any bells. Webb, twenty years ago, had been the Detective Inspector in charge of Brighton and Hove's Antiques Squad – a unit that had been disbanded, for economic reasons, shortly after his retirement. Since then he had written a series of non-fiction books about his big passion, Second World War aviation.

'What can I get you?' Roy Grace asked.

'My shout,' Webb insisted.

After his conversation with Cleo, he felt badly in need of a drink, but he was still working and he should not even have had the one with Glenn. 'A Diet Coke on the rocks, thanks.'

Webb ordered, and when the drink was poured, they retreated to a quiet table.

'So?' Webb asked.

As a young Detective Constable, Grace had served for a short time under Webb, who had then been a DS at Brighton's John Street, and had liked the man a lot.

Grace brought him up to speed on the Aileen Mc-

Whirter case, then said, 'What I need help with, Hector, is where to look for all the stuff that's been stolen. I don't know the world of antiques, although I'm having a crash course in it right now and some very good help from Peregrine Stuart-Simmonds. Do you know him?'

'Yes.'

'Do you still keep in contact with any of the old dealers?'

Webb drank a large draught of his pint. 'It's a changed world from my time, Roy. But I still keep up with a few of my old contacts and they tell me most dealers have had a rough time, particularly since 9/11 when the Americans stopped coming over here. They also tell me fashions have changed a lot in the Western world. People have modern furniture in their homes these days.'

Grace nodded.

'Cost's a big factor,' Webb said, draining his pint.

Grace fetched him another, then queried, 'Cost?'

'People used to furnish their homes largely with antiques because they were cheaper than buying new furniture. Ikea has a lot to answer for in hurting the antiques trade. My youngest daughter recently got married. They bought lovely dining chairs from Ikea at thirty quid a pop.' He helped himself to a handful of nuts. Chewing them, he said, 'One thing's for sure, a raid of this magnitude was pre-planned – and I wouldn't be at all surprised if a lot of the items weren't already pre-sold. It would have been out of this country pretty damned quick. I wouldn't rule out the Russian Mafia being involved, Roy. More likely they'd have their tentacles wrapped around this crime and those expensive items than anyone in Spain. But Marbella is a good starting point for the Russians – and the Irish, of course.'

'Irish?'

Webb nodded. 'People forget them, but the Irish Mafia were around long before the Italians. The White Hand Gang? Al Capone may have kicked them out of New York in the late 1920s, but they've never gone away. Drill down through the IRA and you'll find Irish Mafia at their heart.'

Grace gave him a wry smile. 'Interesting.'

'In New York in the twenties they slugged it out with the Italians,' Webb continued. 'Now in Marbella, Spain, ninety years later, they're slugging it out with the Russians – and the Albanians. That Patek Philippe watch, in particular. There are plenty of rich Russians who would desire a rare, vintage Patek Philippe, and pay big money for one. When I was on the squad, we knew that two of our Brighton knockers had travelled to Moscow to buy stolen Russian icons which were then later traded in Finland – and I would imagine by now that even better links have been made.'

Grace sipped his Coke. 'What routes abroad should we be watching – assuming the stuff is even still here in this country?'

'Which is unlikely,' Webb said. 'The watch could have been taken over the Channel to France within hours of the crime by a trusted "donkey" travelling with it in his pocket on a day trip on the Newhaven ferry – where virtually no checks are made – and a meeting made at an autoroute cafe for the exchange. The paintings could have been cut out of their frames, and laid at the bottom of a suitcase for a similar exchange. Furniture would be harder.' He drank some beer, then wiped his mouth with the back of his hand. 'Furniture is a bit more difficult and would probably need a container – out of Shoreham or Newhaven ports. Expensive pieces placed among ordinary furniture with a cover story for HM Customs that it's to be used in decorating a home in France. The ordinary Customs Officer has no idea about antiques.'

'Great,' Grace said gloomily. 'So if it's already overseas, where do I start looking?'

'I'd start here at Shoreham and Newhaven. Have all the bills of lading checked on every shipment out of both ports that took place within hours of the robbery, and check everything waiting to leave. I'd take a particular look at anything being shipped to Russia or Spain. Second-hand cars – stuff can be hidden inside them; container ships with timber cargoes on board – and cargoes of steel, where a container full of antiques could be smuggled aboard. I'd look beyond the local ports, too. At Dover, Portsmouth, Southampton, Harwich, for starters.'

Grace drank some more of his Coke. 'You're talking about a massive operation, Hector.'

'I am, yes.' He shrugged. 'You're dealing with an horrific murder and a huge-value crime. I don't envy you this one.'

'Any chance of luring you out of retirement to come and help me on this?'

Webb shook his head and smiled. 'And get involved in all the politics again? No, thank you. I'm happy doing my gardening, tinkering with my sailing boat and spoiling my four grandchildren. I just got my Yacht Master's Certificate in July, which I'm pretty pleased about. Know what I learned in my thirty years with the Force?'

'Tell me.'

'Fighting crime is like lying down in front of a glacier and trying to stop it. If I could have my life over again, and had an ambition to be rich – which I never did – I'll tell you which businesses I'd go into: security, food or armaments.

People are always going to steal, they're always going to have to eat, and they're always going to kill each other.'

'You're a pessimist!'

'No, I'm a realist, Roy.'

*

It was dark outside as Roy Grace left the Royal Pavilion Tavern. His watch said a quarter to ten by the time he walked down the concrete steps of the Bartholomews car park, wrinkling his nose at the stench of urine.

He needed to go home, and stopped to text Cleo that he was on his way. But the moment he had done so, he regretted it. Something had been preying on his mind for many hours, and now he realized what it was, and what he needed to do.

40

Cleo's house was less than half a mile north from the car park. But instead of heading home after exiting, Roy Grace made a U-turn, then drove the Alfa west along the seafront. Cleo was not going to be pleased, and he was not happy about that. But he could not help it. Whoever had tortured Aileen McWhirter was out there, and might well be planning their next attack on a helpless, elderly victim. Cleo was wrong to say that a few hours weren't going to change anything. In the early stages of a murder enquiry, every minute of every hour mattered. It was quite possible that the people behind this robbery had already selected their next target.

All kinds of emotions tugged at him, and for a moment he found himself envying Hector Webb, who appeared to have little to worry about beyond his garden and maintaining his boat and how to spoil his grandchildren. He thought for a moment about Glenn Branson's warning about what having children did to a relationship. Reflecting on Sandy, and her tantrums whenever his work wrecked their plans, he wondered if it was not only children, but the nature of a homicide detective's work. Like it or not, trying to solve the crime took priority over everything else in his life. It always had done, and for as long as he remained in this job, he knew it always would. His first responsibility was justice for the victim and closure for the victim's family. That was the reality.

He kept thinking about Glenn Branson.

He selected a Marla Glen track, 'The Cost of Freedom', on his iPod, plugged into the car's sound system. Her deep, rich, soulful voice often helped him think clearly. It filled the car now, as he headed along by the winged figure of the Peace Statue, one of his favourite monuments, which sat exactly on the border between Brighton and Hove, then along past the Hove Lawns, street lights flashing by overhead. He turned right at the Queen Victoria monument and up Grand Avenue, a wide, handsome boulevard. This section, close to the sea, was lined with high-rise blocks, many of them populated by wealthy retired people. He crossed the lights at Church Road, and continued; on this section, The Drive, most of the original, imposing terraced Victorian town houses remained – many now housing law firms and medical practices, or converted into flats.

Half a mile on, he waited at the lights at the junction with the Old Shoreham Road, and then drove up Shirley Drive, the start of the area that Glenn Branson always jokingly referred to as *Nob Hill*. It was an appropriate sobriquet, Grace reflected. Few of the smart, detached houses in the area adjacent to the park were within the price range of police officers. Many of the great and the good of this city lived here, along with a fair smattering of its successful villains.

He turned right up Woodruff Avenue and reached Dyke Road Avenue, which ran along the spine of the city, where the houses became even larger. He turned left, then moments later he made a right, then a left into Withdean Road, one of the city's most exclusive addresses of all. It was a winding, tree-lined road, with a semi-rural feel, the imposing houses set back behind high fences, walls or hedges.

Something was bothering him about this case. Something that did not feel right. Something they were missing. He needed space, quiet time; to be alone at the crime scene without being distracted by anyone and try to think through the sequence of events, and walk through them.

A few hundred yards further on, the road curved left, and he turned right and coasted down Aileen McWhirter's steep, winding drive, the headlights making shadows jump from the fir trees and rhododendrons. He could see the grand, secluded house down to his left, dark and forlorn, and in truth a little creepy. At the bottom, he turned the car around, and held the beam of the headlights on the rear of the house, staring at the windows, the rear door, the walls, the roof.

He switched the engine off, but kept the lights on full beam. The rain had stopped and the blue and white crime scene tape fluttered in the light breeze. He was thinking through all that he knew about the robbery. There had been no sign of forced entry, and it sounded like those responsible had posed as Water Board officials to gain entry. The loft insulation salesman, Gareth Dupont, had made a call to Aileen McWhirter around the time they estimated the attack to have taken place. It was quite possible Dupont had nothing to do with it, but in Grace's view, the man's previous record for aggravated burglary and handling stolen goods could well place him at the crime scene. There was something too coincidental about the timing of that call. He would be interested in the man's alibi.

It was also a strange coincidence, he thought, that he'd had a cold call himself about loft insulation two days after Aileen McWhirter was attacked. But could there possibly be any connection? He dismissed it, climbed out of his car and removed his powerful torch from his go-bag. He snapped on a pair of protective gloves, then walked around to the front of the dark, silent mansion. The red eyes of a rodent suddenly lit up, then vanished. He reached the porch and took the duplicate key he'd borrowed from the Crime Scene Manager out of his pocket, opened the front door and, once inside, noticed the alarm was not pinging. Had someone forgotten to set it?

With the aid of the beam he found a row of old-fashioned wall switches, and pulled one down. Several sconces, with pink, tasselled lampshades, lit up dimly. He made his way past the dark shadows along the nearly bare hall and through to the kitchen, where an open saucepan, with mouldy-looking green haricot beans at the bottom, lay beside the gas hob, and a wooden spoon lay next to it, beside an elderly Aga, which was stone cold. A range of pans was stacked on a rack to the right of it. Near it sat a modern, push-button phone with extremely large numbers for people with poor eyesight. Had she lifted the saucepan off the hob to answer the front door, he wondered.

The front door had a safety chain and a spyhole. So either she knew her assailants, or she had been tricked into feeling comfortable enough with them to open the door. Who among the people she knew might have done this? In his mind he went through the people who had access to this property: not her elderly housekeeper, or her almost equally elderly gardener. Her brother? But he did not need the money. Her nephew? A slim possibility. The knocker-boy, Ricky Moore, was high on his list.

The way the insurance company kept their records of high-value items, and who might have access to them, was currently being investigated. So was the window cleaner, the plumber she used, Michael Maguire, the painters and decorators. The building firm, Bryan Barker, and the washing-machine man. Most household burglaries were opportunistic, but this robbery was in a different league. The city of Brighton and Hove had many rich, elderly, vulnerable people like Aileen McWhirter. If the perps thought they could get away with this, for sure they would strike again. He had to stop that, and there was only one way to do that – lock up the perps. But first he had to find them.

Ten million pounds was, as Webb had said, an enormous sum. During the past few days he had spoken to several local antiques dealers, including a Chinese and Japanese porcelain expert called Chris Tapsell, a jewellery expert, Derek le-Warde, and Simon Schneider, who appeared regularly on one of Cleo's favourite TV programmes, *Secret Dealers*. All of them had told him that it was likely to have been a planned burglary, using insider information, and that there would have been customers lined up for many of the stolen items. The Oriental porcelain would have Chinese buyers. Much of the furniture was likely to be destined for, or already have been shipped to, Russia. The paintings would likely be bought by US, German, Dutch or Russian clients.

Insider knowledge about the contents of the house could have come from someone bent at the company which insured Aileen McWhirter's contents. But far more likely, all his contacts told him, was that the knocker-boy, Ricky Moore, had sold information about the contents to someone. That was a regular business for knocker-boys who had managed to gain entry to houses rich in old treasures.

Moore had subsequently been tortured, Bella Moy had informed him over the phone a couple of hours ago. For what reason? And by whom?

His phone vibrated, then pinged with an incoming text. He looked at the display. It was from Cleo.

Roy, darling, you OK?

He tapped out a quick reply.

Another 30 mins. Sorry. XXXXX

Then he went back into the hall and stared up the staircase at the dark landing. He looked around but could not see a light switch. So he climbed up the stairs, then turned on the torch, again looking for a switch, and still could not find one.

He flashed the beam up and down, still without seeing any switch. Then he pushed open the door into Aileen McWhirter's bedroom and, as he pointed the beam into the darkness and stepped forward, something hard struck his shins with such force he shouted out in pain, lost his balance and fell to the carpeted floor, the torch rolling away from him.

41

All his life, Roy Grace had been able to think clearly under pressure. At this moment, in the pitch darkness, as his torch stopped several feet away, he knew his assailant would be expecting him to lurch forward to grab it. So instead, he rolled sharply away from it, connecting with something hard but yielding right behind him.

'Ouch! Shit. Owwww.'

Someone cursing dropped something which thudded onto the floor. A torch? A gun? Then he heard the heavier thud of someone falling over. He twisted around in the darkness, balling his right fist, ready to punch out, rolled fast, grabbed his torch and shone it in the direction of the sounds.

And saw Gavin Daly, in a green suit, flat on his back, tie askew, eyes shut. For a moment, he thought he had killed the old man. He knelt and shone the beam directly on his face; after a few moments, Daly blinked.

'You okay?' Grace asked.

The old man blinked again, worriedly. Grace shone the beam on his own face for a few seconds, so Daly could see who it was. 'Jesus!'

'Are you okay?' he repeated.

'I'm okay,' Daly gasped.

'You scared the shit out of me.'

'Next time come in a bloody marked police car,' Daly gasped again. 'And what the hell are you doing here anyway?'

He struggled with his arms, pushing himself upright, then exhaled.

'Perhaps you can tell me what you're doing here, sir,' Grace said. He stood up and switched on the bedroom light, then helped the old man to his feet. Then he saw his silver-headed cane on the floor – and realized that was what he had been hit with. He handed it back to Daly.

'I've just lost my sister, the only person I had left in the world who I loved.' He shrugged. 'I just wanted to be here – to feel her presence. Okay? And one of your officers told me I should keep an eye on this house. He said the bastards might return and take more stuff, or tell others about the things they didn't take. I've had the most valuable items they left moved into storage. But someone has been here and taken something.'

'What was it?' Grace knelt, and examined the painful weals above his ankles.

'Sorry if I hurt you.'

'You're bloody strong – especially for a man your age,' Grace said, unable to conceal the admiration in his voice.

'Apologies, but I didn't know who the hell you were. I thought you might be the bastard who took the photograph of the Patek Philippe watch from Aileen's album, coming back for something else.'

'Aileen's album?'

'It was here, in her bureau, on that Thursday evening when I came here, minus the photograph of the watch.'

'It wasn't removed by one of my team?'

Daly shook his head. 'No, I asked your Detective Branson colleague. It was the album with the pictures of all the high-value contents. It must have been one of the burglars who came back and took that one photograph to make it harder for you lot to identify the watch, do you think? My guess is they took that photo, as the watch is not insured, so the insurance company would have no record of it.'

Grace frowned. If that was the case, it meant the robbery team was even bigger than they had suspected. 'It's a possibility, sir, but that must have happened in the past forty-eight hours – no one would have had access while the house was sealed as a crime scene.'

'Well, I decided to lie in wait for them if they did come back,' Daly replied. 'I barely sleep these days, anyway. But I thought you were meant to have a round-the-clock guard on this house?'

He was right, Grace knew. But he couldn't tell him that budget cuts meant that wasn't possible. 'It's being patrolled hourly, sir.'

'It is? Well, I've been here since six o'-bloody-clock and I haven't seen a police car all evening.'

'How old are you, Mr Daly?'

'Ninety-five.' He exhaled sharply again.

'You're damned fit. You're damned fit for a man twenty years younger! What's your secret?'

Daly's eyes twinkled for a moment. 'Whiskey, cigars and the occasional wild, wild woman, Superintendent.'

Grace grinned. Then he returned to serious mode. 'I know you've been asked this before, but how long did your sister live here?'

Daly thought for some moments. 'It would have been since 1962.'

Grace thanked him.

'Is that useful information, Detective?'

'It might be. Tell me, sir, you know the antiques world better than anyone in this area – do you have any thoughts on who might have been behind this? Anyone local who has the ability to handle something of this size?'

'Someone knew about the contents all right,' Gavin Daly said. Grace stared at the single bed, which looked far too small for this huge bedroom.

'The watch,' Daly said. 'You know, ultimately, that's all I care about. Whatever else the bastards took, they can keep.' He sat down on the bed, looking defeated.

'Presumably the insurance will cover much, if not all, that was taken, sir?'

'To hell with the insurance. I don't need the money. I hope they don't pay out. My asshole son will only put it up his nose after I'm gone, anyway.'

'Lucas?'

'Yes.' He sat in silence for some moments, then looked sheepishly up at Grace. 'You probably think I'm a hard old bastard, and you'd be right.'

Grace shook his head. 'No, I don't.'

'Do you have children, Detective – Detective Chief – Chief whatever? Do you?'

'I have a young son.'

Daly nodded, then dug his hand into his inside pocket and pulled out a leather cigar holder. He removed the cover then held it out to Grace. There were three cigars in it.

Grace shook his head. 'Thank you. I'd love one sometime, but not at this moment.'

Daly replaced the top, with a wistful smile. 'That black detective feller I spoke to, your colleague?'

'Detective Inspector Branson?'

He nodded. 'Quite a comedian, isn't he? Bit of a film buff.'

'He's a walking encyclopaedia of movies,' Grace acknowledged.

Daly pursed his lips. 'I told him something he didn't know.'

'Oh, really?' Grace prepared to commit this nugget to memory, to rib Glenn with it.

'That miserable old bastard, W. C. Fields. Know what he said when he was asked how he liked children?'

He shook his head.

'Fried.'

Grace grinned.

'Children, Detective Grace. I'll tell you something. They're almost always going to disappoint you. But that's enough about me and my problems. What do you think? You seem to be a smart guy. Everyone tells me I'm lucky to have you on this case.'

'I don't have enough information at this stage to give you an informed opinion, sir. But I will tell you what my gut's telling me. Someone with inside information did this.'

Gavin Daly nodded. 'That knocker-boy. That's where you need to start looking.'

'We're looking at him,' Grace replied. 'But someone's already been looking at him even harder.' He gave Daly a questioning stare. 'Any idea who that might be?'

The old man's eyes darted to the right for an instant; then he returned his stare, silently and resolutely for some moments, before shaking his head. Then he said, 'You said you like cigars.'

'I do.'

'Come out into the garden. Let's smoke a cigar together. I want to tell you my life story, about my sister and me. Maybe it will help you to understand.'

42

To reassure Gavin Daly about security, Grace requested a patrol car to sit at the top of the drive of his sister's house, while Daly called his chauffeur to come and collect him. Grace then stayed on in the house for a while, on his own, thinking about his conversation with the old man.

Thinking about why the old man had lied to him. He could tell from the direction the old man's eyes had moved that there was a high probability he had lied. When he had asked Daly his age a short while ago he'd had no reason to lie; as he thought about the answer his eyes had moved to the left, to the *memory* side of his brain. Similarly his eyes had moved to the left when he had asked him the secret of his fitness, and how long his sister had lived in the house; but they had not moved left when he'd asked him who might have tortured Ricky Moore, they'd moved right, to the *construct* side of his brain. Where lies came from.

Was he taking the law into his own hands?

All his checking out on Gavin Daly so far had revealed him to be a man with a great deal of charm, but an utterly ruthless business streak. He was a rogue, or certainly had been once, like so many of the Brighton antiques fraternity. But he had no criminal record. His son appeared to be in the same mould, but without the charm. He needed to get Ricky Moore to talk, but apart from the man being in hospital, in great pain, Bella had reported he was clearly far too scared to give any names. Maybe putting pressure on Moore when he was feeling better might be a route to follow. Threatening to arrest him on a murder charge might persuade him to talk. Suspects on murder charges did not get bail. It could be a year to eighteen months for Moore to sweat before the trial came up. Faced with that time in jail, or naming names, Moore might well squeal.

One thing he felt certain about was that the knocker-boy was involved – whether in the planning and execution of the burglary, or simply selling on the information. The fact that Moore was tortured with a similar – but uncommon – torture implement to that used on Aileen McWhirter was evidence enough. If Moore was innocent, he would have made a complaint to the police, so he was clearly hiding something, scared of someone. But why had he been tortured? And by whom? Old man Daly knew about it, and might have ordered it. For what reason? Most likely, Grace thought, it was to get the names of the perpetrators, and go after them. And if the old man was involved, it was likely his son was too. People taking the law into their own hands, assuming they could do better than the police, always worried him, because they invariably made a mess of everything. And he still felt that the reward Daly had put up was bigger than he would have liked.

He needed to have Lucas Daly interviewed as soon as possible. And to find out his whereabouts late last Friday night around the time of Moore's torture. A richly funded vigilante campaign was something Roy Grace seriously did not need.

It was just after 11.30 p.m. when he set the alarm and drove away from the house. He turned onto the forecourt of the Esso garage at Dyke Road Park, went into the Tesco Express and looked at the depleted selection of flowers. Most of them looked as tired as he felt. The best of the bunch was a small bouquet of crimson roses. He bought them for Cleo, then walked back out to his car and drove down to his own house, just off Hove seafront.

The sale board outside had an UNDER OFFER sticker on it. *Please God, whoever you are, buy the damned place*, he thought, as he unlocked the front door. It would be one headache less. He switched on some lights, then hurried through into the kitchen, and went over to the goldfish bowl.

The fish, which he had won at a fairground well over a decade ago, was swimming around and around, as if on a quest, as he always did. And, as Grace had suspected, his food hopper was empty.

Grace filled it, and for good measure sprinkled several pinches of food onto the surface of the water. Marlon rose and began gulping it down.

'How are you doing, old chap?'

Marlon continued eating.

He was a surly creature, who had never been much of a conversationalist. But he was the last living link Roy Grace had with Sandy, who had been with him when he had won him, shooting an airgun at targets at a funfair in Hove Park. They'd bought a companion for Marlon on a couple of occasions. Each time, a couple of days later, they'd come down in the morning to find just one fish in the tank – Marlon, looking a tad fatter and smugger.

If Glenn was really going to move back home, and stay there, he would need to transport the fish to Cleo's house at some point. But, at Marlon's age, he was worried about him surviving the journey and the transition. It was pathetic, he knew, to have this little fish, with its fading gold colour, being the only link to his former life. But he couldn't help it.

He thumbed through the stack of post on the table that

Glenn had forgotten to bring over to his office. Mostly it was junk, but almost at the bottom was a letter from the estate agent's, Mishon Mackay. He ripped open the envelope.

Inside was a letter from Darran Willmore, the negotiator at the agency who was handling his property. It contained the good news that the offer, at the full asking price, had now been confirmed by the solicitors for the purchaser. *Our client, currently resident overseas, has assured us that she is in funds, and has lodged the deposit with her solicitors here in Brighton, subject to contract.*

Grace felt a quiet thrill of excitement. Finally, finally, he could truly move on.

*

Twenty minutes later as he drove slowly past the wrought-iron gates, which were the entrance to Cleo's town house, he noticed the TO LET sign on the outside wall had been removed. It was for the adjoining house in the old factory that had been converted into seven urban dwellings. The house had been empty for some months – Cleo's neighbours were overseas, working on a long-term contract in Dubai.

He found a parking space a short distance away, then sat in the car for some minutes, debating whether to call Glenn and see how he was. It was bad to think ill of the dead, he knew, but he was finding it hard to be sad about Ari's death. She had been a total and utter bitch, treating Glenn, who was one of the loveliest guys on the planet, like complete dirt for this past year. It was terrible for their two lovely kids to have lost their mother so suddenly. But now they had their father back, who was, frankly, an infinitely better person.

Holding the flowers, he walked back, let himself in through the gates, and then into Cleo's house. Humphrey came bounding over to greet him, stamping his paw expectantly, demanding a walk.

Roy Grace bent down and stroked him. 'I'll take you out in a minute, okay?'

Then he listened for any sound of a greeting from Cleo. But there was none. Hopefully she was asleep.

Starving hungry, he tiptoed through into the kitchen area. On the worktop was Humphrey's red bowl, filled with dog food. It was covered with cellophane and had a handwritten note taped to the top.

Please feed Humphrey.
He is starving.

Grace frowned. *Great*, he thought. *Thank you so much, darling.*

Humphrey looked up at him expectantly.

'That's all I am, isn't it, boy? Your servant, and Marlon's servant. Right?'

Humphrey barked. Instantly he hushed the dog, not wanting to wake Noah. He removed the cellophane and lifted the bowl. Beneath it was another note.

Yours is in the fridge.
You don't deserve it.
But I love you.
XXXXX

43

This region of the southern Spanish coast, officially named in all the sunny tourist brochures as the *Costa del Sol*, had long been known to the British police by the less welcoming sobriquet the *Costa del Crime*. In the immediate aftermath of the Second World War, its main town, Marbella, was rumoured to have offered open house to fleeing wealthy Nazis. And until 2001 it had no properly enforceable extradition treaty with England. For decades it was a safe haven for British crooks on the run, who could live the good life with impunity.

If corruption were an Olympic sport, two of its recent mayors, both jailed, would have had gold medals in their trophy cabinets, and ninety-four dignitaries, also jailed, would have slugged it out for silver and bronze. Today the area played host to brutally active Russian, Albanian and Irish Mafia clans, along with a thriving community of British gangsters. Yet despite the occasional shooting, the crime rate was relatively low, and with its year-round benign climate, it was a long-established playground for expats and tourists.

Several miles west of Malaga airport, Lucas Daly drove the rented Jeep fast up a twisting highway cut through the mountains, keeping an eye on the arrow on the satnav. He used to know the area well, having owned an apartment in Marbella's bling suburb of Puerto Banus for some while, until he had been forced to sell it to pay gambling debts four years ago. He had not been back here since.

It was 11.30 a.m. local time. Down below them to their left was a town of white houses, and the cobalt-blue Mediterranean beyond. Although the air-conditioning was whirring away on maximum power, Daly kept his window wound down, savouring the blast of 34-degree heat on his face after the crap English summer he'd endured. 'Shit, it's hot,' he said, shaking a Marlboro Light out of the pack.

'I'm sorry,' the Apologist said.

'You don't always have to apologize for everything.'

The Apologist said nothing for some moments. Then he said, 'Okay, I'm sorry.'

Lucas Daly grinned then patted his henchman on the shoulder. 'You know why I like you, Augustine?'

'No.'

'Coz you're a moron! You're always fucking apologizing!'

'I'm sorry.'

Daly lit the cigarette, then answered a phone call from his bookmaker in Brighton. Immediately his mood soured. He'd placed a bet on a horse race, and paid on his Amex, but it had not gone through. It was a long-odds hot tip, a dead cert, from a bent trainer he knew who had a horse running at Brighton. He'd bet far bigger than usual. If the horse, Fast Fella, won, it would give him some welcome respite from his immediate problems.

He pulled into a layby, and hastily gave his bookie the details of another card, which he kept for emergencies and which was not yet maxed out. Then they drove on in silence, which was usual. The Apologist didn't have a lot of conversation, unless the subject was football, about which he could talk for hours. He knew everything there was to know about every football team in the whole of Britain, their strip, their key players' names, their goal count for the season.

Lucas avoided talking football with him; it was like pressing the switch on a machine that had no *off* button.

And besides, he had other stuff on his mind. A lot of stuff. Bad stuff.

Total shit.

One particular loan shark, who had recently bailed him out of his latest problem, was turning nasty. He'd been stiffed on a major deal. And his cantankerous father was refusing to help him. His best hope was for the old bastard to die soon. Alternatively a change in his run of bad luck with the horses and at the gaming tables. Hopefully this bet would be the start of it.

Driving past Marbella and Puerto Banus and on for a few more miles, they headed along the main drag into the neighbouring town of Estepona. To their left was the pyramid shape of the Crown Plaza. To their right, a large Lexus dealership and a closed-down car wash. The arrow on the satnav was pointing right, but Lucas Daly knew where he was.

They drove up past a short promenade of shops and bars into a residential area of small, white houses and apartment blocks. Ahead on their left was a row of shops, at the end of which was a bar with an outside terrace and the name LARRY'S LOUNGE printed in red capital letters on a scalloped awning. Two shady-looking men in their thirties, in dark glasses, accompanied by a bored, tarty-looking younger woman, were seated at an outside table. One man was smoking a huge cigar.

Daly pulled into a parking space a short distance past the bar. They climbed out into the searing heat, and headed towards the bar. Daly, a lightweight bomber jacket slung over his shoulder, was dressed in white T-shirt, jeans and brown suede Gucci loafers, and walking with his customary swagger; the Apologist, a foot taller than him, wore a T-shirt, tracksuit bottoms and trainers.

Inside the bar was a cool blast of air. Half a dozen men lounged in front of a TV screen, mounted high on the wall, showing a replay of some football game. Three of them, heavily tattooed, wore singlets and cut-off jeans, like a uniform. All of them were holding beer cans, and shouting at the screen. A few years ago, Lucas would have known the faces in here, but these were strangers to him.

The Apologist stopped and stared at the screen for some moments. 'Manchester United and Sunderland. Not a good game.'

Two of the men glared up at them suspiciously. They walked on.

The interior was a cross between an ersatz English pub and a bodega, with an L-shaped oak bar, wooden stools, beer pumps, oak barrels on the wall lined with bottles, and shelves stacked with spirit bottles. Tiffany lamps hung from chains all the way around, and British football club pennants decked the walls, along with framed signed photographs of past Manchester United, Newcastle, Arsenal and Chelsea teams.

Behind the counter stood a tall, wiry man, with short thinning hair, dressed in a grey button-down shirt, opened to the navel. A tall glass of lager stood in front of him. He looked at Lucas Daly. 'Seen you before, haven't I?'

'Yeah, you might have done. Used to own a place in Banus. Drank here a few times – until that fellow got shot.'

'You and half of the Costa del Sol. Screwed my business totally,' he said, in an East London accent. 'That was five years ago, but people got long memories. No one comes here no more – apart from a few regulars.' He pointed at the slobs watching the footy. 'I have to work as a window cleaner some days, to make ends meet. Thing is, you see—'

Lucas Daly interrupted him. 'I'm looking for Lawrence Powell.'

'Yeah? You've found him.' He gave him a stony stare.

'I'm a mate of Amis Smallbone. He told me to tell you that you're a tosser.'

Lawrence Powell grinned. Then, looking uneasily, first at the Apologist then back at Daly, he said, 'Thought he was still inside.'

'He's out.'

'He's a fucking idiot, that one.' He shook his head, then tapped the side of it. 'Nutter. So what can I get you, gentlemen?'

'A San Miguel and a Diet Coke.' Daly glanced at the Apologist for approval, and got it. The man never drank alcohol. 'Do you have any food?'

'Crisps.'

'That all?'

'Plain or cheese and onion?'

'One of each.'

The drinks arrived, with the crisps. Daly dug into them hungrily, while the Apologist drained his Coke. The barman stood, silently and patiently, behind the bar. 'So, Amis is all right?' he asked.

'He was needing a good dentist, last time we saw him.' Daly smirked at the Apologist, who nodded pensively, but distractedly, as if his mind was on some forgotten sadness.

'I'm looking for some people living out here,' Daly said. 'I'm told you know them. Eamonn Pollock, Tony Macario and Ken Barnes?'

'You've got nice friends,' Powell replied.

'I only do quality.' Lucas Daly glanced at a barstool, two away from where he was sitting. He could see the bullet hole in the top of the seat, where a previous occupant had been shot through the groin in an argument over a woman. He'd been in here when it had happened, and still winced, five years on, at the screams of pain from the .38's recipient.

'They shouldn't be hard to find,' Larry Powell said. 'Eamonn Pollock's halfway up his own asshole. You just need a powerful torch. Tony Macario and Ken Barnes are all the way up it. They're so far up it they could clean his teeth through his throat. They're easyJet gangsters, them two.'

'Meaning?' Daly asked.

Powell shot a glance at the group in front of the television, to make sure none of them was listening, then leaned forward conspiratorially. 'They do jobs for Pollock. He keeps his nose clean and his belly filled with the proceeds of their labour. Nice work. He fixes jobs for them in England, pops them on an easyJet flight. Twenty-four hours they're back here. He makes sure never to use anyone with a British criminal record. No dabs, no DNA.' He shrugged, and sipped his lager.

'And if someone I knew wanted any of them whacked?' Daly asked.

Lawrence Powell shrugged again. 'Not a problem. Give a Moroccan a Bin Laden.'

Daly swigged down some of his beer, straight from the bottle, frowning.

'What? Did you say, *Give a Moroccan a Bin Laden*?'

'Yes.'

'Can you talk in English?'

Lawrence Powell led them outside onto the terrace, and pointed out across the Mediterranean, at two hazy shapes on the horizon. 'That lump of rock is Gibraltar. The other's North Africa. Morocco,' he said. 'Their police have a useless fingerprint database and an even more useless national DNA database. A Moroccan can come over here, do a hit and be back in his own country before the police have even reached the crime scene. He'll be harder to find than a specific grain of sand in the desert.'

'And a *Bin Laden*?' Lucas Daly asked.

'A five-hundred-Euro note. They say they're as elusive as Bin Laden was.' Powell grinned. 'Morocco's a short ferry ride away from Ceuta.' He jerked a finger to his left, west. 'A Moroccan can live a couple of years on that kind of dough. Life's cheap there.'

'And you have access to these Moroccans?' Daly asked.

'I have access to everything.' Lawrence Powell rubbed his index finger and thumb together.

Behind them, in the bar, there was a loud cheer as someone scored.

Back inside, Daly put a hundred Euro note on the counter, followed by four more.

Powell slipped them behind the bar. 'So what's in it for me?' He looked at them expectantly.

'How long does it take you to deliver?'

'Same day service. Just bell me.' He pushed a business card across the counter.

Daly slipped it in his wallet, then pulled another hundred Euro note out and placed it on the counter. Powell looked at it like it was a dog turd. Daly added a second. 'Pollock, Macario and Barnes. Where do I find them?'

Powell raised three fingers, indicating he wanted another banknote.

Lucas Daly nodded at the Apologist. The Albanian grabbed him by the throat and lifted him in the air. Powell, choking, shook his head vigorously, making yammering sounds. No one behind them looked round; they were engrossed in the football.

The Apologist let Powell's feet touch the floor, but kept hold of his throat. 'My boss is not a hole-in-the-wall cash dispenser. He asked you a question. He'd like an answer. Sorry to hurt you.'

'*Contented*,' Lawrence Powell croaked. 'At Puerto Banus.'

'It's okay, let him go,' Lucas Daly said. '*Contented* at Puerto Banus?' he said to Lawrence Powell. 'That the name of a house or apartment block?'

Powell, rubbing his throat, and gulping down air, croaked, 'It's a boat. A sodding great yacht, okay?'

'You'd better be right,' Lucas Daly said. 'I'd hate to have to come back and disturb you again.' He turned to the Apologist. 'We don't like disturbing people, do we?'

'I'm sorry,' the Apologist said to Lawrence Powell. 'For the inconvenience.'

44

Mountainpeak Publishing, where Gareth Dupont worked, was on the third floor of a shiny modern building, on an industrial estate close to Newhaven Port, the commercial harbour a few miles to the east of Brighton. Its affable proprietor, Alan Prior, had made Roy Grace and Guy Batchelor comfortable in a conference room, organized tea, coffee and biscuits, and then left to fetch Gareth Dupont.

Earlier, Grace had spoken to Glenn, telling him to take whatever time off he needed; he had to deal with the Coroner's office in order to get Ari's body released, and register her death, then start making the funeral arrangements. Glenn had sounded very down, unsurprisingly, and Guy Batchelor was in a subdued mood, as everyone on the team had been at this morning's briefing.

There was a chill from the air-conditioning and a strong new-office smell in the room, from the carpet, paint and furniture, which was overpowered, the moment Gareth Dupont entered, by the cloyingly aromatic cologne he was wearing. He greeted the two detectives cheerily, oozing self-confidence, his demeanour more than a tad cocky, Grace thought. He looked flash, every inch a salesman: white shirt rolled up at the sleeves, neatly creased black trousers, shiny black shoes, and sporting two vulgar rings and a showy watch.

Grace carefully studied the man seated opposite them throughout the interview. Dupont was in his early thirties, with Hispanic good looks, short gelled black hair, tattooed arms, with the muscular physique of someone who worked out regularly. There was a scab on the knuckle of his right pinky finger. Grace did a quick mental calculation. The robbery was ten days ago; about the right length of time for a scab to still be present after a nasty gash.

Dupont poured some coffee, helped himself to a biscuit, then dunked it carefully in his coffee. Grace wondered if he'd been dunked in cologne. Then he waited until the man had eaten it, so he had his full concentration.

'We appreciate time is important to you, so we won't detain you longer than necessary, Mr Dupont,' Grace said. 'Can you tell me your date of birth?' He watched Dupont's eyes closely.

'Twenty-fifth of July, 1979.'

'So you're thirty-three?'

'Yeah. Not good, eh? Fast turning into an old git.'

'I think you have a way to go before that,' Guy Batchelor said.

'What is your home address?' Grace asked, watching him carefully all the time.

Dupont gave him the address of an apartment block in Brighton Marina.

Grace wrote it down. Then he stared at the man's wrist. 'Nice watch.'

'Thank you!' He held it up for them to see. 'Vintage Bulgari. My ex gave it to me a couple of years ago.'

'Really?' Grace said. 'Bit of a coincidence, but it looks just like one that was stolen from a home in Withdean Road, in Brighton, last week.'

He felt Batchelor shooting him a glance. For an instant, it felt to Roy Grace that the temperature in the room had dropped even further.

'Is that so?' Gareth Dupont said dismissively. 'Tell me, gentlemen, how can I help you?' He glanced down at his watch anxiously. 'We're on targets here, you see.'

'Don't worry, Mr Prior kindly said we could take as long as we need,' the Detective Sergeant said.

Dupont glanced at his watch again, looking increasingly uncomfortable. 'Well, he would, you see, because he doesn't pay us any wages. We're all on commission only, so time is a bit important, like.'

'We'll be quick,' Grace said. 'I'd like you to cast your mind back to the afternoon and evening of ten days ago, Tuesday, August the 21st. Could you talk us through that?'

Despite the low temperature in the room, both detectives noticed the tiny beads of perspiration popping on the salesman's brow. He touched his nose.

'Umm, let me think. Umm.' He pulled out his phone. 'Just check the diary. Ah – yeah – well, I was working. Yeah.'

'Where were you working?' Grace asked him.

'At my last company. Ransom Richman.'

'In the office?'

Both detectives noticed the brief hesitation. 'No, I was at home. Do a lot of my work from home. Early evening's a good time to catch the householder in – and before they've settled down for the evening.'

'At 7 p.m. you made a phone call from your mobile to this number,' Batchelor said, and handed him a slip of paper.

Dupont looked at it. 'A Brighton number, yeah, could have – well, that code covers a big area I'd been working.'

'Would you remember anything about this particular number?' Roy Grace asked.

The salesman shot a glance at both of them, hesitating,

before shaking his head. 'No, sorry, I make dozens and dozens of cold calls every day and night. I remember the names, of course, of anyone who becomes a prospect.'

'Might you remember the name Aileen McWhirter?' he asked, watching the man's face intently again.

'Aileen McWhirter?'

'Yes.'

He shook his head a little too quickly, Grace thought. Then he raised a finger in the air. 'Wait a sec – she's been in the news, right? A nasty robbery at her home?'

'Very nasty,' Grace said. 'She died.'

'Yeah, I read that, that's why I recognize the name.'

Grace pointed down at the piece of paper bearing the phone number, lying on the table. 'You ought to recognize that number. You phoned her the evening she was attacked.'

'I did?'

'She was in pretty poor shape,' Grace said, 'but she told officers it was about 7 p.m., Tuesday, August the 21st. The records show you phoned her at that time. Quite coincidental, wouldn't you say?'

'I – I dunno what to say.'

'You claim you were at home, Mr Dupont?' Guy Batchelor cut in. 'Why didn't you phone on a landline?'

'Coz it's cheaper on my mobile. I got one of those deals with O2, one thousand free minutes per month. In the office I use a landline; at home it's cheaper on my mobile.'

'Can anyone vouch for where you were at 7 on the evening of Tuesday, August the 21st?' Grace asked.

'I was home alone. I guess God could.'

'God?' Grace smiled at him.

Dupont shrugged.

'You could get an affidavit from Him, could you?'

Dupont looked down at his watch. 'I've told you all I can – I really need to get back to work.'

'Of course. We're sorry to have bothered you.' Grace smiled again. 'It's just that on a murder enquiry we have to check out everything, so we can eliminate people. I hope you understand that?'

'I do – perfectly. I hope you catch the bastards who did it.'

'Oh, we will, Mr Dupont. You needn't worry about that. We will.' He gave him a confident smile. 'By the way, what car do you drive?'

He hesitated for a moment, then replied, 'A Golf GTI.'

'Nice car,' Grace said. 'I don't suppose you remember the registration?'

'Just one moment.' Dupont left the room, then returned a minute later holding a set of keys, with the registration tag attached. He handed them to Grace.

'Almost brand new,' Grace said.

'Much less grief, having a car under warranty,' Dupont said.

'And who wants grief, eh?' Grace said, handing him the keys back.

As the two detectives left, Gareth Dupont sauntered back into the open-plan office, looking more carefree than he felt, and handed the keys back to a colleague whose car it was. 'Thanks mate,' he said. 'I owe you one.'

45

The two detectives said nothing until they had left the building and climbed back into Roy Grace's work car, the standard silver Ford Focus estate issued to all superintendents. As they buckled up, Grace turned to his colleague and said, 'So, what do you think?'

'The little shit was squirming.'

'He lied about working at home. He lied about not recognizing the number. He lied about not recognizing her name – then quickly covered his tracks.'

'I don't remember seeing a Bulgari watch on the inventory of stuff that was taken, Roy?'

'There wasn't one.' He started the engine. 'I just wanted to rattle his cage a little – and then watch his eye movements on something he didn't need to lie about.'

'Don't you think we've enough to arrest him?'

'We need something to place him at the crime scene,' Grace said, driving off. He headed out of the industrial estate, and down towards the coast road back to Brighton. 'Dupont's involved, for sure. You saw that scab on his knuckle?'

'Yes.'

'Maybe he left some blood at the scene. If SOCO find it, and we get a match, then we'll have him banged to rights. And I've a feeling he could lead us to the other perps. He looks a slimeball who'd sell anything, especially his colleagues, for a reduced sentence. If he's left just one drop of blood there, however tiny, those two SOCOs will find it.'

'Dunno if I'm putting two and two together and getting five, Roy, but—'

'That would be a lot more than we have on anything at the moment, Guy,' Grace said with a grin.

Batchelor grinned back. 'I'm thinking about Bella's report of her interview with Smallbone.'

'I've been thinking about it, too.'

'He had a black eye, and was missing some of his front teeth. Bella said it seemed to be hurting him to walk. He claimed he'd walked into his fridge door after a glass or two too many.'

'Oh yes? What was the fridge's name?'

'Exactly.'

'The day after Aileen McWhirter is found, Ricky Moore is beaten up – tortured. A few days later, Amis Smallbone is beaten up. Maybe tortured too.'

'Moore is linked to Aileen McWhirter's house, and Smallbone has previous for this kind of crime,' Grace said. 'As does our slimy friend Gareth Dupont.'

'What's your hypothesis at this point, guv?'

'Historic knocker-boy modus operandi is for them to case a place and if it's got value higher than they can handle, they sell it on to someone for a cut. I'd say at this stage it's possible Ricky Moore passed the information to either Smallbone or Dupont. Old man Daly, Aileen's brother, saw that leaflet. He might have taken the law into his own hands, had Moore tortured for names – and was given Smallbone. So he had him tortured for names next.'

The Detective Sergeant nodded. 'I think we're both on the same page, guv.'

*

Many things about policing these days really irked Roy Grace. High among them was parking. It used to be that on a major enquiry, you could park anywhere in the city. Not any more. You had to park, like anyone else, legally. Which meant driving around until you found a car park with vacancies, and paying an exorbitant amount to leave the car there. What the cost was to the taxpayer, in terms of parking fees, and police time, he had, in despair, long given up thinking about.

He emerged with DS Batchelor from the Bartholomews seafront car park, and headed into the Lanes. They zigzagged through the narrow alleyways, passing one landmark, the jewellery store of Derek le-Warde. Then they reached the large shop, filled with a wide range of antiques including a stuffed ostrich, a George III writing desk, a gilded chandelier, and a display of Chinese vases, the gilded sign above the door proclaiming: GAVIN DALY AND SON.

They entered. Seated behind a glass display shelf in the centre of the room containing a range of tiny ornaments was a man in a wheelchair, with a short ponytail, tiny oval glasses, his head tilted back, which gave him a hint of arrogance. He was dressed in a baggy Hawaiian shirt, with even baggier cavalry twill trousers.

'Hello, gentlemen. Can I help you?' His accent was Southern Irish.

Grace showed him his warrant card. 'Detective Superintendent Grace and Detective Sergeant Batchelor. We'd like to have a word with your proprietor, please. Mr Lucas Daly.'

'Ah, I'm afraid he's away right now – he'll be back in on Monday.'

'Do you know where he's gone?'

'Yes, he's in Spain having himself a golfing weekend. Can I give him a message?'

'Where in Spain has he gone?'

'The south. Marbella.'

Grace gave him his card. 'Thank you – please ask him to call me on this number as soon as he gets back.'

'Anything I can help you gentlemen with in the meantime?'

'How much is the ostrich?' Guy Batchelor asked.

'Four thousand pounds.'

'Yeah, right, thanks. I'll think about it,' the DS said.

'They are very hard to come by,' the man said.

'A bit like your boss, you mean?'

He didn't get it.

As they stepped out of the shop, into the late-morning sunshine, Roy Grace dialled Gavin Daly's number. The old man answered almost immediately.

'It's your sparring partner from last night, Mr Daly. Detective Superintendent Grace. I should have you for assault.'

'I'll tell you something, if I'd been twenty years younger, you would not have got up!' Grace detected humour in his voice.

'I don't doubt it.'

'So, what news? You've got some good news for me?'

'Your son Lucas is a keen golfer, is he?'

Instantly he sensed the cagey tone of Gavin Daly's voice. 'Why do you ask?'

'What club is he a member of?'

'I actually don't know, Detective Grace.'

'But he's a good golfer, is he?'

'My son and I are not that close. I'm not able to tell you how he spends his leisure time.'

'*Not that close?* Would you like to elaborate, Mr Daly?'

'No, I would not. We have our issues, but I can tell you that following the death of my sister we are united.'

'Because you don't trust us to find the perpetrators?'

'Not at all.'

'Even though you put up the reward of one hundred thousand pounds?'

'Is your father alive, Detective Grace?'

'No. He died some years ago.'

'Do you have anything belonging to him that you hold dear?'

'A few things, yes.'

'My sister and I only had one thing. His pocket watch. As you probably know, it's worth about two million pounds. But that's of no consequence. She and I were lucky in life, we both made a lot of money. We never ever put that watch on the market; it was the only thing of our father's – in fact of our parents' – that we had. Those bastards took it. I don't care about the rest of the stuff that was taken, but I care about that watch. I want it back. Just so you understand.'

'I understand, loud and clear,' Roy Grace said. 'I just want you to understand one thing, too, sir, equally loud and clear. We are doing everything we can to find out who carried out this crime, and to recover the stolen property. But we have to do it within the law.'

Gavin Daly said nothing.

46

Lucas Daly removed his Ray-Ban sunglasses as he drove the Jeep down the entrance ramp into the large, communal underground car park of Puerto Banus. All the time he was looking warily around for CCTV cameras. He did not want anyone to be able, later, to plot their movements. To his annoyance he saw several, and drove back up the ramp again. He was feeling edgy as hell.

The Apologist gave him a strange look. 'Plenty of spaces there, boss.'

'I didn't like the shape of them.'

'I'm sorry.'

Daly put his glasses back on as they emerged into the dazzling early afternoon sunlight. He looked at the car clock, then, as if he did not trust it, he checked his wristwatch: 2.26 p.m. They were an hour ahead of the UK here, which meant that in a little under an hour, the first race of today's meeting at Brighton races, the 2.15 p.m. Reeves Flooring Cup, would be under way. With Fast Fella running at 33/1.

He'd bet the ranch on the horse, which was part of the reason he felt so nervous. But only part. He knew why he was here, and what he had to do, but carrying it out was going to be another matter. As yet he hadn't fully worked out a plan, and he wanted to have all his ducks in a row.

But they had time; too much of the damned stuff; they had to wait for the cover of darkness, and with the clear sky at this time of year it wouldn't start to be fully dark until around 9.30 p.m. Still, he remembered all the scantily dressed young women who swarmed around the port, seriously attractive totty, so passing a few hours over some cold beers in a quayside bar would not be too much of a hardship, even if he did have to endure the Apologist's company – or rather, lack of it.

He drove around for a while, happy to be killing time, until he found a parking space in a narrow shady street that did not appear to have any surveillance. They left the car, walked down to the port, then ambled along, seemingly casually, just a couple of guys amid the early afternoon throng of holidaymakers admiring the swanky boats berthed along the quay. He clocked their names on their gleaming sterns. *TIO CARLOS*. *SHAF*. *FAR TOO*. *FREDERICA*. *CONTENTED*. Their flags hung listlessly in the still heat.

The bar owner, Lawrence Powell, had been right when he'd said *Contented* was a sodding great yacht. It was considerably longer, taller, fatter and even more gleaming than its neighbours. Two men in white uniforms were working on the rear deck, one cleaning with a mop and pail, the other polishing the chrome rails. The one with the mop had a shaven head and a tattooed neck; the other had short dark hair and worked with a cigarette in his mouth.

Surreptitiously, as they strolled past, Lucas Daly snapped both men with his phone camera, then stopped a short distance on, pulled the card Lawrence Powell had given him from his wallet, entered his mobile-phone number and texted him the photographs.

They seated themselves at an outdoor table that gave them a perfect view of the *Contented*. The Apologist studied the plastic menu, while Daly checked his watch. Fifteen minutes to the race now. The Apologist ordered a Coke and a lasagne with chips. Daly ordered a large beer. He was too knotted up to eat anything, and he shouldn't be drinking, he knew; he needed to keep his wits clear for this evening. But that was still a long time away.

As their drinks arrived, his phone vibrated. He looked down. It was a reply from Lawrence Powell.

Dark-haired one on left Macario. Shaven head on rt Barnes.

'We're on,' he said to the Apologist. He stepped outside the bar to make a phone call.

Five minutes later he returned, drained his beer in three gulps and ordered another. He looked down at his horse-racing app, and tapped on it for the tenth time, trying to log into the Brighton race meeting, but the connection was too slow and nothing happened. Twenty anxious minutes and a third beer later, whilst the Apologist was shovelling his food into his face, he lit a cigarette and phoned his bookmaker.

'It's Lucas Daly. Have you got the result of the 2.15 at Brighton?'

'One moment. Yeah. First number seven, Connemara, second number four, Kentish Boy, third number ten, Voyeur.'

Daly felt a cold sensation in the pit of his stomach. 'Are you sure that's the 2.15 at Brighton?'

'Yeah. The Reeves Flooring Cup.'

He dragged on his cigarette, his hands shaking. 'What about Fast Fella?'

'Fast Fella? Hang on, I'll check.'

As he waited, Daly dragged deeply on the cigarette again. 'Shit,' he said. 'Fuck.'

'Something not good, boss?' the Apologist said.

Moments later Daly heard the male voice of the bookie. 'It was left at the post.'

'What do you mean, it was *left at the post*?'

'Fast Fella planted its feet. Refused to come out of the starting gate.'

'So it was withdrawn from the race? It didn't run. Do I get my bet returned?'

'Afraid not; it was under starter's order. All bets on that horse are lost.'

'Shit, shit, shit,' Daly said, ending the call.

The Apologist looked at him. 'Bad?'

Daly nodded and shook another cigarette out of the pack. 'Bad.'

'Sorry.'

47

Shortly after 2.30 p.m. Roy Grace pulled up outside his favourite bookshop, City Books, an independent store on Western Road. He loved the way it truly smelled of books, and despite the small exterior, it opened up inside to a maze of crammed shelves. Whenever he had time, which was not often these days, he loved to go in and just get lost among its shelves.

'Do you have anything on the early gang history of New York?' he asked a young, brown-haired woman behind the counter, who had a studious air. Behind her stood a serious-looking man, with short grey hair, pecking at a computer keyboard. He looked up in recognition and smiled broadly.

'Detective Superintendent Grace, nice to see you! Early gang history? How far back do you want to go? The start was really the Irish Dead Rabbits Gang in the 1850s, or their later White Hand Gang, or Al Capone's Italian Black Hand Gang.'

'I need to cover everything,' he replied.

Ten minutes later, with five books lying in the shop's carrier bag on the rear seat, Roy Grace drove slowly up Shirley Drive, passing Hove Recreation Ground on their left, while beside him Guy Batchelor looked at the numbers on the detached houses on the north side.

A quarter of a mile on he said, 'Here, boss!'

They pulled up outside a smart detached house. A silver Mercedes SLK sports car occupied one of the two spaces on the driveway, in front of the integral garage; the other one was empty. They climbed out and walked to the front door, entering the porch, and Grace rang the bell.

They could hear an aggressive beat of music coming from somewhere inside the house.

'*The Number of the Beast*,' Guy Batchelor said.

'Iron Maiden?' Grace asked.

He nodded.

'Didn't know you were into music, Guy?'

'Yeah, well, when you have a teenage daughter . . .'

Grace grinned, and at that moment the heavy oak front door was opened by a barefoot woman in a cream silk dressing gown. She looked smaller in real life, and without make-up her face looked a little bleached out; her long, dark hair was pushed up inside a towel, wrapped around like a turban. For a moment he hesitated in recognizing her as the strikingly attractive local TV news anchor he had so often seen. She also looked a little nervy, a little frightened. Not at all the confident, assured woman on his television screen.

'Hello?' she said suspiciously. 'Who are you?'

'Sarah Courteney?'

'Yes.'

Grace held up his warrant card, and Batchelor did likewise. 'I'm Detective Superintendent Grace and this is Detective Sergeant Batchelor of Sussex and Surrey CID, Major Crime Branch,' he said. 'Would it be possible to have a quick word?'

She glanced down at her watch. 'This is to do with my husband's aunt, presumably?'

'Yes,' Grace replied.

'So dreadful. I still can't quite believe it. Okay, come in. I can only give you a few minutes – the car's on its way to take me to the studio. But I'd rather you came in than stood out here – I've been besieged by the press over this.'

'Of course. I'm a big fan of yours by the way!' Grace said, then blushed, aware just how cheesy that had sounded.

She gave him a genuinely warm smile. 'Thank you so much!'

They entered a hallway which smelled of fragrant potpourri. It was decorated with an exquisite antique table, two high-back chairs and a long-case clock. Photographs of the newscaster lined the walls. One was of her with Fatboy Slim, another, together with the man Grace presumed to be her husband, with sports commentator Des Lynam. Another was her with Dame Vera Lynn, and another with David Cameron. The music, coming from upstairs, was much louder in here. 'Apologies for the din,' she said with a grin. 'My son, home from uni for the summer. That's all he does all day long.' She led them through into the drawing room. 'Can I offer you something to drink?'

'No, we're fine, thank you. We'll be very quick.' Grace's eyes roamed the large, elegant but comfortable room; it was furnished almost entirely in antiques, with a view out onto a well-kept lawn and a swimming pool. Two large, brown leather chesterfields faced each other in front of a marble fireplace, separated by an ornate wooden chest which served as a coffee table. A huge television screen peeped out of what looked like an adapted mahogany tallboy. A trophy cabinet sat in one corner, and the mantel above the fireplace was stacked with invitations. The room had a masculine feel, with just a few feminine touches. *The sign of a dominant husband*, Grace thought. Her dressing gown gaped open momentarily, before she clamped it shut defensively, and in that moment he noticed some bruises high up on her chest. Had her husband done that? A man who might brutally torture someone, who also beat his wife?

'Have you had any luck on the case?' she asked.

'We're making progress,' Grace replied. 'But no arrests yet.'

'These people are monsters – I hope you get them.'

'We're very hopeful,' he said.

'I can't believe what they did to her.'

'Were you and your husband close to Mrs McWhirter?' Batchelor asked.

She was quiet for a moment then she said, 'I'm afraid no, not really. She and I always got on really well – we actually became quite close – but she had issues with Lucas.'

'What kind of issues?'

'Well, the thing is that Lucas and his father don't get along.'

'So I've gathered,' Grace said. 'What is the problem there?'

'His father's a tough act to follow – a highly successful self-made man. I think he put a lot of pressure on Lucas, and my husband's a strong man – it's like fire against fire.'

'I think there's often a problem when a relative works in a family business.'

She shrugged. 'I suppose the truth is my husband doesn't have his father's business acumen. He's lost a lot of his father's money over the years in trying to diversify the business – you probably know the antiques trade isn't what it used to be. Lucas set up a large bar and restaurant in Brighton which failed. He's sunk big sums of money into other businesses and for one reason or another they didn't work out. When he came into the business, Gavin Daly

Antiques was one of the biggest dealers in the UK – they had six stores in Brighton and two in London. Now they have just the one.'

Grace nodded. 'What about the relationship between your husband and Aileen?'

'I'm afraid the old man rather poisoned his sister against Lucas. He convinced her to cut him out of her will.'

'Why did he do that?'

She hesitated. 'I rather feel I'm talking out of turn.'

'You don't have to tell us if you don't want to.'

'I think he felt Lucas needed a reality check. That if he inherited a large amount from her, he'd just blow it. Squander it.'

'Families and money,' Grace said with a wry smile.

'Maybe this terrible thing will bring Lucas and his father closer together.'

'But you and Aileen got on well?'

'Yes, Aileen and I got on very well. I used to pop in and see her every now and then – and she'd pour me a massive sherry! She was fiercely independent, still going really strong at ninety-eight. Her brother's amazing for ninety-five – they have some good genes in that family, for sure. And they've been through a lot in their lives.'

'Oh? Such as?'

'They were born in New York. Their father was, I guess, what you'd call a gangster. He was high up in the White Hand Gang. One night their mother was shot dead by a bunch of men who entered the house – they actually went into Gavin's bedroom first, then they shot the mother dead and took the father away. Gavin and Aileen never saw him again. A few months later an aunt took them to Ireland, thinking they'd be safer there than in New York. Then in their teens – I suppose that must have been in the early thirties – their aunt met and married a man from Brighton and they moved over here.'

Grace listened intently, the books he had seen in Aileen McWhirter's study starting to make sense now, together with the conversation he had had with Gavin in the garden. Then he walked over to the cabinet, and peered in at the trophies. 'Are these yours or your husband's, Mrs Courteney?'

She blushed slightly. 'All of them are mine – mostly broadcasting, and a couple of tennis trophies and one for Salsa dancing. I go to classes – a good way of keeping fit. Actually I'm Mrs *Daly*, but Courteney is my professional name.' She gestured for them to take a seat, then sat on the sofa opposite them, crossing her bare feet, and looked at them expectantly.

'We need to have a word with your husband, Lucas,' Grace said. 'I understand he's away at the moment.'

'For the weekend.'

'Where's he gone?' DS Batchelor asked.

'Marbella. A boys' golfing trip.'

'He's a regular golfer, is he?' Grace asked.

She hesitated. 'He's a social golfer.'

'What club is he a member of locally?'

Suddenly, she looked very uncomfortable. 'Umm, well, you know, he only plays occasionally. Societies, mostly. I'm not actually sure what club he's a member of here – I don't know for sure if he is actually a member of any of them.' She hesitated. 'I mean – he plays at different ones.'

'Very expensive game,' Guy Batchelor said. 'I nearly gave up membership to my club because I don't play enough. It would be cheaper just to pay green fees.'

'Does your husband play regularly in Spain?' Grace asked.

'No – not at all.' She shrugged, looking increasingly

uneasy. 'He – we – used to have a place in Puerto Banus and we still have friends there.'

She showed none of the confidence she exuded on air as a newscaster, as she nervously twisted her wedding band. Grace was almost certain she was lying. Covering up for her husband. Covering what up?

'So he doesn't often make you a golf widow?' Grace said with a smile.

'No.' She smiled, then shot a pointed glance at her watch.

'We'll be gone in just a second. When will your husband be back?'

She hesitated. 'Sunday. Late Sunday.'

Guy Batchelor handed her his card. 'I wonder if you could ask him to call me when he returns – as soon as convenient.'

'Of course.' She laid the card on the coffee table.

'If you don't mind me saying, you're a very good newsreader,' Grace said.

'Thank you so much!'

'Are Fridays one of your regular nights?' he asked.

'Well, they rotate, but this past month I've been doing the Friday evening regional news, after the 6 p.m. and 10 p.m. national news.'

Sounding as nonchalant as he could, Grace continued, 'I suppose with these long summer evenings, your husband plays golf while you're working?'

She blushed, looking very uncomfortable now. 'Well – not that often.'

'Out of interest, can you recall if he played last Friday evening?'

She looked at her watch again. 'Last Friday. No, he went over to see his father – Gavin's very upset about

Aileen. I think he had dinner with his father while I was at work.'

'Have you had to read out any of the coverage on this story yourself, on air?' Guy Batchelor asked.

'No,' she said. 'And I'd rather not. Not sure I could cope with that emotionally.'

The two detectives stood up. 'Thank you for your time, and we'll have a chat with Mr Daly when he's back.'

'I'll make sure he gets your card.'

*

Back in the car, Grace said, 'I didn't see a single golfing trophy in there.'

'So maybe he's a crap golfer. Where are we going with this, boss? Sorry if I'm being dumb.'

'I don't think he plays golf at all. Golfers always have trophies, even if just a wooden spoon.'

Batchelor pulled over, got out of the car, shook a Silk Cut cigarette out of a pack, and offered the pack to Grace. 'Want one?'

'No, not right now, but go ahead.'

'Have you given up?'

'I gave up a long time ago, but I still have the occasional one with a drink in the evening.' He shrugged. 'I enjoy them, so sod it!'

'Why's Daly's shop manager and his wife saying he's on a golfing holiday, Roy?'

Grace was silent as the DS leaned against the outside of the car, lit his cigarette, and blew a perfect smoke ring.

'I've always wondered how to do those,' he said.

The DS grinned and blew two more in rapid succession. For an instant, as they closed together, they looked like handcuffs.

'I'm impressed!' Grace said.

'My party trick.'

'Then you wave a magic wand and turn them into steel?'

'Depends whose party I'm at.' He grinned back. 'So we're safe to assume that whatever Lucas Daly's doing in Marbella, golf isn't a feature?'

'Once again we're on the same page. Or maybe I should say the same *fairway*.'

'Or *bunker*?'

48

At 7 p.m. Lucas Daly and the Apologist watched Tony Macario and Ken Barnes lock the gate at the top of the *Contented*'s gangway, and strut ashore.

They were rough-looking men; neither of them was tall, but they both had a wiry meanness about them. Macario, with short dark hair, sported several days' growth of stubble, and even from this distance Daly could see a long scar beneath his right eye. Both men wore jeans, and white T-shirts with the yacht's name stencilled across the front. They headed off along the quay, Macario in flip-flops, and shaven-headed, tattooed Barnes in trainers.

'They coming back or should we follow?' the Apologist asked.

'They'd sodding well better come back. Wait here.' Daly got up and sauntered after them.

The two crewmen did not walk far. After a couple of hundred yards they made a left into an alley lined with buzzing bars and restaurants, then a right, and entered O'Grady's Irish Pub. The word GUINNESS and its harp logo were etched onto the windows and the glass panes of the open doors. Daly waited, watching them make their way slowly through the crowd towards the bar. Then as he saw their drinks being served, he returned to fetch the Apologist.

Ten minutes later the two of them were positioned with their drinks in the pub, a safe distance from Macario and Barnes, watching them attempting to chat up a small group of uninterested teenage girls. Daly hoped to hell they wouldn't pull, as that would complicate his newly formed plans.

An hour and a half later, to his relief, the girls left, despite the entreaties of the two men, who were clearly a little sloshed, to stay. Just after 11 p.m., Macario and Barnes staggered out of the bar and up the alley. Daly and the Apologist followed them, and saw them stop at a takeaway pizza joint.

Then, carrying their large polystyrene boxes, they headed unsteadily back to the *Contented* and boarded the yacht, disappearing through the saloon doors.

It was approaching 11.30 p.m. The evening was warm, and the streets seemed to be getting even more crowded. Daly and his colleague entered a bar opposite. He ordered a Metaxa brandy, to steady his nerves, and another Coke for the Apologist. Ten minutes later he said, 'Okay, time to rock and roll.'

'Sorry, I don't dance very well,' the Apologist said.

Daly grinned and slapped him on the back. 'I'm talking about rocking the boat.'

'Rocking the boat?'

'It's a joke.'

'I don't get it.'

Daly pointed at the *Contented*.

The Apologist grinned. 'Ah. Sorry.'

49

The quay was almost deserted, apart from one young couple eating each other's faces, who weren't going to be noticing anything else happening around them. Lucas Daly, needing a cigarette to steady his nerves, put one in his mouth, then clicked his lighter to no avail; it was out of gas.

'Shit.'

He walked over to the couple and, ignoring the fact they were snogging, said loudly, 'Either of you speak English?'

They both turned. 'We are English,' the male said. 'What do you want?'

'Don't suppose you've got a light?'

'Bloody hell!' He dug in his pocket, clicked a lighter and held the flame up to Daly's cigarette.

'Thanks, mate,' he said, grabbing the lighter and walking away with it, drawing on the cigarette.

'Don't sodding mention it.'

When he had finished the cigarette the couple had disappeared. He handed the Apologist a pair of surgical gloves, and snapped on a pair himself. Then the Apologist followed him up the gangway of *Contented*, through the gate, which the two henchmen had left unlocked, and onto the wide deck of the yacht. It felt plush and smelled of teak, polish, varnish and leather. They could feel the faint floating motion of the vessel.

Daly opened the patio doors and entered the huge rear saloon. All around the sides were white leather banquettes, and in the centre was a curved bar, with stools also covered in white leather. On the wall behind were shelves stacked with an array of spirits. There was a distinct smell of pizza in here.

Behind the bar were shiny wooden steps, with a roped handrail. They could hear the sounds of a football commentary coming from a television somewhere down below them. Raising a hand to keep the Apologist a distance behind him, Lucas Daly walked slowly down. In front of him, at the bottom, he saw a large dining room. Its centrepiece was a twelve-seater table, with white leather-covered chairs arranged around it, and a huge television screen, showing a football match, at the far end of the room. Macario and Barnes, facing away from them, were eating their pizzas out of the opened cartons, and swigging from cans of lager.

He beckoned the Apologist down, pointed at his own chest, then at Macario, then pointed at the Apologist and indicated Barnes.

The Apologist nodded.

Both men hurried forward, as silently as they could. Just as Macario was putting a slice of pizza in his mouth, Daly felled him with a single karate chop to the back of his neck. He fell sideways off the chair, and onto the floor, where he lay still. The Apologist hauled Barnes up, out of his chair, onto his feet.

'What the—?' Barnes said, before the Apologist tightened his grip on his throat, turning the rest of his words into an incomprehensible gurgle. Then the Apologist stamped really hard on his foot.

The shaven-headed man cried out in pain.

'Sorry,' the Apologist said.

'Who the hell are you?' Barnes croaked, his quavering voice betraying his fear.

'I'm *Mr Pissed Off,*' Lucas Daly said. 'And this is my friend, *Mr Even More Pissed Off*. And you are Ken Barnes?'

He said nothing.

'Cat got your tongue?'

Again he said nothing.

'Tell you what. My friend here has some tongs. Curling tongs. He could plug them in, heat them up, then pull your tongue right out of your mouth. Would you like that? Then you'd have an excuse for not speaking, wouldn't you?'

Barnes's eyes filled with terror.

'Hurt him a little again, Augustine. He's not being very talkative.'

The Apologist stamped on the man's foot again, this time even harder.

Barnes screamed in pain, tears shedding from his eyes.

'So you're able to scream. If you can scream, you can talk, yeah? So what's your name?'

'Ken Barnes.' He could hardly speak for the pain.

'I need some information from you. Like, did you have a nice time in Withdean Road, Brighton, last week? Was it fun torturing that old lady with the curling tongs?'

'It wasn't me,' he yammered.

'No?'

'No. Wasn't me. I was – I was . . .' He fell silent.

Daly nodded at the Apologist. He stamped even harder, and this time Daly heard the crunch of breaking bones, accompanied by a howl of agony from Barnes.

'Barcelona just scored,' the Apologist said, nodding at the television screen.

'He did that. It was him, the stupid bastard,' Barnes gasped.

'Your friend, Mr Macario?' Daly asked.

'Yes.'

Daly nodded, then looked down at the slumped, unconscious figure of Tony Macario. 'The strong, silent type, is he?'

'I was just hired to do the job. They needed someone to help hump the furniture, that's all I was doing there.'

'Hired by who? Your boss, Eamonn Pollock?'

Barnes said nothing.

Daly turned to the Apologist. 'You'd better stamp on his foot again.'

'Noooooo! Please! I'll tell you what you want.'

'That's better,' Daly said. 'Because you're going to tell us anyway, so the less pain for you, the less aggro for us. Now, I've a list of things I really want to know. First, where is the Patek Philippe watch you stole from that house? Second, where is the rest of the stuff? Third, where is the safe on this boat, and how do we open it? And fourth, where is your boss, Eamonn Pollock?'

'I don't know about any watch, that's the truth. I don't remember a watch.'

'Remember getting the safe code from that old lady?'

He shook his head.

'You know something, I don't believe you,' Daly said. 'Why is that, do you think? Because you're a crap liar?'

'The gorilla's broken my fucking foot.'

'He'll break the other one in a minute. That old lady was my auntie. That watch belonged to my grandfather. I can't get my auntie back because she's dead. But I'm sure as hell going to get that watch back. And you know where it is.'

Barnes shook his head.

Daly cupped the man's chin in his hand, forcing him to

look straight at him. 'Listen to me, Ken. If you don't tell me where that watch is, my friend's going to kill you. Simple as that. I'll give you ten seconds to think it over.'

Daly stood staring at his own watch for the ten seconds. Then he looked at the Apologist and rotated his wrist. Moments later, Barnes was hanging upside down, suspended by his right ankle.

'That helping to clear your mind?' Daly asked.

'I've drunk too much,' he slurred for the first time. 'Please put me down. I – I—'

'Maybe you need another drink, to help the old brain cells?' Daly asked.

He shook his head. His eyes were like two frightened little birds.

'Be back in a tick,' Daly said, and climbed up the stairs.

'Sorry to keep you hanging about,' the Apologist said.

Moments later Lucas Daly reappeared with a bottle of Macallan Scotch in one hand, and a small plastic funnel in the other. 'Put him on the deck,' he instructed the Apologist. 'Then open his gob.'

The henchman obliged. Barnes tried to wriggle free, but the Apologist knelt on his chest, pinioning him to the floor, and held his head with his hands, as firmly as a vice. Daly knelt, unscrewed the cap of the bottle, pushed the funnel into his mouth, then began pouring in the whisky.

The man spluttered and choked.

'Am I pouring too fast?'

Barnes tried to shake his head, but it was held in the Apologist's iron grip. In less than five minutes, the bottle was empty.

Their captive's eyes were rolling. Daly shot a glance at Macario, who was slowly starting to stir, then returned his attention to Barnes. 'Where's the watch? The Patek

Philippe? Where's the safe? And where's your boss, Eamonn Pollock?'

'Safe's in the master bedroom.' Barnes's eyes rolled again. Then, moments before he passed out, he murmured something barely decipherable.

*

Fifteen minutes later, as Tony Macario opened his eyes, fully conscious again now, the first thing he saw was his colleague, Ken Barnes, suspended upside down by his ankles, unconscious, being swung, head first and extremely hard, into a stanchion studded with rivets.

Then he realized, through a haze of alcohol and blinding headache, that he was bound hand and foot and could not move.

Barnes was dumped, unceremoniously, on the floor. Blood leaked from a gash in his head.

'Your mate's not very chatty,' Daly said. 'Maybe you can help us? We've had a look at the safe but it's empty.' He was silent for a moment, sniffing. 'What's that pong? I've got a very strong sense of smell. Have you shat yourself?'

Macario shook his head.

'That's all right, then. You will in a minute.' He pulled out his cigarette lighter and flicked it on and off. 'Like hot things, do you?'

'Hot things?'

'Yeah. Burning people.'

'I never burnt no one.'

Daly eyeballed the man. 'Want to tell us about Withdean Road, Brighton? A little old lady you burned? Who put you up to it? Eamonn Pollock, right?'

Macario stared back impassively for some moments. Then he said, 'Withdean Road? I never heard of that street.'

'That's not what your mate said. He said it was your idea to torture the old lady for her safe code and the pin codes for her credit cards. Was he lying? Fitting you up to save his skin?'

'He what? That fucking shitbag . . .'

'Now, that's much more like it!'

'My idea? I had to fucking pull him off her.'

'Tell us more.' He nodded at the Apologist. 'My friend hates to hurt people, really he does. He much prefers not to. My dad and I don't care a toss about all the antiques and paintings. But we want that watch back. It's sentimental, right? Know the meaning of that word?'

Macario nodded.

'Your friend says he doesn't know where Mr Pollock is. How about you?'

'He doesn't tell us anything. I don't know. Really, I don't know.'

'Is that right? What do you think this boat's worth? Ten million quid? Twenty? Fifty? One hundred? You two jokers are guarding it while he's away, and you don't have an address for him? A contact number?' He tapped his chest. 'Do I look stupid or something? Do I look like I just rode into town in the back of a truck?'

'No.'

Leaving the Apologist with him, Lucas Daly went back up to the bar and returned with a litre bottle of Grey Goose vodka, and proceeded, with the funnel, to pour half of it down Macario's throat.

A couple of minutes later, under Daly's coaxing, Macario slurred out that he might have gone to New York, but he didn't know where, he swore.

'Now tell me what you did with all the rest of the stuff?' Daly said. 'What happened to all of my auntie's precious antiques and paintings? Eight million quid's worth. What did you do – vanish it into thin air?' He flicked the lighter and brought the flame close up to Macario's eyes. 'Don't think I won't,' he said. 'I'll burn your face off with pleasure.'

'Delivered to warehouse . . . barn . . . sort of place.' His voice was slurring.

'What warehouse? Down at the docks? Shoreham or Newhaven Harbour?'

He shook his head. 'Industrial estate. Lewes. Back of Lewes. By the tunnel.'

'Where was it going after the warehouse?'

'Overseas.'

Then he passed out.

Daly untied his bindings. Then with the help of the Apologist, he untied Barnes. They left both men unconscious on the saloon floor, climbed back up the stairs and went out, through the patio doors onto the stern deck. Then they walked ashore across the gangway, and strode a short distance along the quay towards the shadowy, dark-skinned figure who was waiting for them, smoking a cigarette.

'Mr bin Laden?' Daly asked.

The Moroccan grinned.

50

Humphrey was snoring. The dog was lying on its back on the sofa beside Roy Grace, paws sticking up in the air like a mutant dead ant. Grace patted its belly. 'Hey, fellow, quiet! Can't hear the television!'

Humphrey ignored him.

Daniel Day-Lewis was looking murderous on the screen in the video of the *Gangs of New York* that Glenn Branson had lent him. Piled up on the coffee table were four of the volumes on the early gang history of New York he'd bought from City Books. The fifth, *Young Capone*, lay open on his lap. The baby monitor was turned up loud enough for him to hear the sound of Noah's breathing. His son had been sleeping soundly since his last feed at 9 p.m.

Grace patted Humphrey's belly harder. 'Shh, boy! I can't turn the TV up, don't want to wake your mistress, or Noah. Okay?'

Humphrey farted silently. Moments later the horrific stink reached Grace's nostrils. 'Hey! That's not playing fair!' He gave Humphrey a playful slap, which the dog ignored. He held his nose until the stink passed. He gave him another tap. 'No farting, okay? Two can play at that game!'

A hand suddenly squeezed his shoulder. He looked up and saw Cleo, her hair up, in a pale-blue nightdress. 'What are you watching?'

'It's for work. You okay? Do you want anything?'

'Yes, I do. I want to lose my bloody baby fat and my varicose veins. I want to stop feeling so damned tired all the time and bad-tempered from loss of sleep,' she moaned. 'I'm sorry, but they don't tell you how rubbish you are going to feel in any of the books – at least not the ones I read.' She kissed his forehead.

He took her hands and squeezed them tenderly. 'If I had a magic wand, I'd wave the damned thing!'

'Shit, Roy, why didn't anyone tell me what having a baby's really like?'

'Maybe because no one would have one if they really knew.'

She nodded. 'Yes, that's true!' Then, changing the subject, she said, 'Where do you keep your handcuffs?'

'Handcuffs?'

'Uh huh.'

'I have some in my go-bag – but I don't really have any reason to use them in what I do.'

She gave him a strange smile that he could not read. 'So you do have some?'

'Yes.'

'I thought maybe – you know – perhaps I could try them out on you – sometime when I'm feeling less sore.'

He grinned. 'That book you're reading?'

'I'm into the second one,' she said. She grinned again.

'Not sure about my handcuffs,' he said. 'They've been on some pretty scuzzy people. Maybe we could try silk ties?'

'I think we should try a few things. But I'd hate to distract you from your work. Lock up all the bad guys first. Then you can start on me.' She kissed him on his forehead again. 'Not tonight, though. I'm still really sore, and I'm too tired.'

He watched as she headed back up the stairs. 'Love you,' he said.

'Even fat like this?'

'More to love.'

'You're a good bullshitter.' She pointed across the room. 'See, your goldfish agrees!'

High up on one of the fitted black bookshelves on the far side of the room, Marlon had his nose pressed up against the side of his bowl, endlessly opening and shutting his mouth. Grace was relieved he had survived the transition to his new home. He'd developed a strong affection for the fish over the years following Sandy's disappearance. He would be sad, he knew, the day Marlon died.

He'd brought the fish here as Glenn was now moving back to his home to take care of his children. And with the exchange of contracts on his own house sale imminent, he'd needed to start clearing everything out, putting it into storage until Cleo and he decided what they would need once they had found a new house.

He focused on the film, shocked by the brutality of the Dead Rabbits Gang. If this movie was even remotely accurate, life in several boroughs of New York from the 1850s up until the time of the Depression was hellish. *Hell's Kitchen* was an apt name.

Gavin Daly was a tough old bird, for sure. He wondered if he could be that energetic and sharp at ninety-five – if he ever made it that far, which was unlikely. Historically, life expectancy for retired police officers was among the lowest of any profession. His father had been a textbook example. Dead within three years of retiring.

He looked at the baby monitor. Listened to the sound of Noah's breathing. And wondered if he would live long enough to be a grandfather.

Daly was going strong at ninety-five. From all accounts Aileen McWhirter had been on course to live well past a hundred, until she had been savagely cut down. That made him feel very sad. Civilization, he knew, was a fragile veneer. You only had to read or watch or listen to the news every morning to witness the hell in which so many people on this planet existed. He never forgot how lucky he was to have been born in England, and to have grown up in a country which was relatively peaceful. But there were threats here all the time. Terrorist threats from within the UK and outside. And threats from villains.

He was in a rare position, he knew, to be able to do something for the citizens of Brighton and Hove, and of Sussex, which he loved so much. Aileen McWhirter should have died peacefully in her sleep, from old age, a few years from now. After all she and her brother had endured in their early childhood, as he had learned from him over a cigar in her garden, she deserved at least that. Instead she had died from terrible injuries in hospital.

He had never felt more determined in his life to find the perpetrators of a crime and lock them up. Hopefully for ever. If he got lucky and didn't end up with a woolly-minded liberal of a judge.

He looked back across at Marlon. And momentarily was distracted by the thought of packing up the house, and all those past years of his life. Then he focused back on the film and what he could learn from it that might, in any way, help him with this case.

51

Someone else was packing up his life too, and it was hurting. It wasn't the memories that were painful – Amis Smallbone didn't have any memories he wanted to pack into a suitcase, other than a photograph of his father and his mother that had been the only decoration in his cell. He no longer had photographs of his ex-wives, or his two long-estranged children, whom his wife had taken to Australia twenty years ago.

The packing, little though it was, hurt him physically. Every moment. His whole body was in pain from the beating he'd had. But what upset him most of all was the damage to his mouth. Not long before his arrest, thirteen years ago, he'd paid a fortune for work on his teeth. Now, five of his front teeth were missing, and his jaw was broken, and hurting like hell. His dentist told him he needed surgery on it. He didn't have time for surgery, so he dulled the pain as best he could with Nurofen and whisky. He'd get it fixed when he got paid on this deal; until then, in public, he'd have to keep his mouth shut.

It was just past midnight, but he was wide awake, with a cigarette clamped between his lips, as he double-checked the cupboards in his basement flat. The last night in this shithole, he thought with some relief. He was spending the weekend with his mate Benny Julius in his Dyke Road Avenue mansion, just a few doors away from the huge house he used to live in himself, with his Ferrari parked outside. He'd had his villa in Marbella, and a boat in Puerto Banus, too.

All he had here now was one large, cheap suitcase, only half full. How great was that? He was sixty-two years old and his worldly possessions – his clothes and washing kit – did not even fill half a suitcase.

He laid his parents' photograph down carefully on top of a folded shirt. Morris Smallbone had been a tall man, with big shoulders and a lean, handsome face, his hair, dyed dark brown to the end of his life, brushed straight back. His mother had been tall and elegant, too. So why the hell was he only five foot one inch? Why had life dealt him such a shitty hand?

Why had Roy Grace picked on him all those years back? Everything he used to have was gone, thanks to Roy Grace's determination to destroy him. Grace assured him at the time it wasn't personal, but it was. Amis Smallbone knew that. And Grace was not going to get away with it.

His friends told him to forget it, that Grace had merely been a copper doing his job, but Smallbone didn't see it that way. He found out from an old lag in prison that Grace's father, also a detective, had spent much of his career pursuing his father, and that one of his big regrets was never potting him.

So it was personal for Grace. The detective had been in his face for years. Even after he had done his time, Grace had continued to go after him. Accusing him of etching a message on his girlfriend's car, kidnapping him after a funeral and dumping him on top of the Devil's Dyke, leaving him to walk five miles home in the pissing rain.

Thanks to this one man, not only did he have nothing in his life, but most of his old acquaintances didn't want to know him any more, as if he was some kind of pariah, a has-been. His father had been the big guy of the Brighton crime scene. Everyone feared and respected him. No one dared touch Morris Smallbone, not even the police, most of whom he'd had in his pay back in his heyday.

What the fuck had gone wrong?

Detective Superintendent Roy Grace would go to his grave regretting what he had done. You didn't take away twelve years of someone's life; and all the other shit that went with it. The prison doctor had warned him about not getting angry, because of his high blood pressure. But fuck that. He stubbed the butt out and lit another cigarette. Then spotted something he had missed. Another framed photograph of his father outside Lewes Crown Court. His father was beaming, arms wide out like he owned the world – and actually he had owned a handsome slice of it. In this photograph, taken minutes after being acquitted by a coerced and frightened jury, his father was walking free from a whole bunch of charges.

Amis Smallbone had not been so lucky, following in his dad's footsteps.

Thanks to Detective *Inspector* Roy Grace, as he had been back then.

Promoted now. Huh.

A father now.

On Monday he would become Detective *Superintendent* Grace's neighbour. Renting the three-storey house next door to where he was living with his blonde slapper, Cleo Morey. His Probation Officer, who had to approve any change of address, had queried how he would pay the rent in his new abode. Smallbone had explained that his mate Henry Tilney, who owed him a favour, would be paying it for him, until a new business they were setting up, dealing in second-hand cars, was up and running. The Probation Officers had swallowed it.

Roy Grace thought his slapper and baby would be safe inside that little gated residence, did he?

Smallbone smiled. As the saying went, *if you can't beat them, join them.*

Roll on Monday!

52

Roy Grace had to hold the Saturday morning briefing in the Conference Room of the Major Incident Suite in order to accommodate his growing team. He had a full turnout, including, he was pleased to see, Glenn Branson, who told him his sister-in-law had taken the kids swimming and was looking after them for the day.

Bella Moy was the first to speak. 'Working on the information from your contact Hector Webb, who felt it likely the major portion of the items stolen would have been shipped out of the UK in a container, I've been focusing on ships capable of carrying containers out of our local harbours.'

Grace noticed that she shot two glances at Norman Potting while she was speaking. He was becoming increasingly curious about whether there was something going on between the two of them.

'I talked to the Harbour Master at Shoreham Port yesterday afternoon, sir, in his office,' she said. 'I went through with him the list of all cargo ships that sailed after 8 p.m. Tuesday the 21st – the earliest time that the items stolen from Aileen McWhirter's house could have arrived there. Cargo ships can only enter and leave four hours either side of high tide. The next relevant high water was at 02.38 Wednesday the 22nd and then at 15.03.'

She shot Potting another glance and this time Grace caught the old sweat's wink back to her. Surely not? Bella with an old lech like Potting? But few things truly surprised him.

Bella held up several sheets of paper clipped together. 'All ships over 500 gross tons weight have to have CERS transponders switched on. It stands for Central European Reporting System – it's a progression from the Royal Navy's wartime IFF system, *Identification Friend Or Foe*. Basically it works exactly the same way as the system for identification of planes for air traffic control. All cargo ships around the world are plotted constantly at sea – this was something brought in after 9/11.'

'What happens if they switch them off?' Dave Green, the Crime Scene Manager, asked.

'They need to have a valid reason,' she responded. 'For instance, if they're in waters known to be at danger from Somali pirates, they're permitted to turn them off, but only in situations like that.' She pointed to her sheets of paper. 'This is a list of all ships that have sailed since 8 p.m. August the 21st, together with their bills of lading. The *Torrent*, carrying scrap metal. The *Anke Angela*, carrying oats. The *Walter Hamman*, carrying fertilizer—'

'Do we have their intended destinations, Bella?' Glenn Branson asked, interrupting her.

'Yes.'

'Good work, Bella,' Grace said. 'First thing is we need to see if any of these ships divert from their stated destinations. Second we need the co-operation of Interpol to check everything they offload against those bills of lading. I need you to circulate the inventory of everything stolen from Aileen McWhirter to Interpol.'

'Yes, sir.'

'What about trucks on the roll-on/roll-off ferries, Bella?' DC Alec Davies asked.

'I'm getting a log of all of them within one hundred miles of Brighton,' the DS answered. 'It's a mammoth task.'

She glanced down at her notebook. 'Just one thing more, sir,' she said to Roy Grace. 'We're still working on black Porsches with Sussex registrations, but so far none of the owners is on our radar. I'd like to widen the parameters.'

'Yes, do a nationwide search. It could easily be a second-hand car bought elsewhere.'

DC Jon Exton raised his hand. He had a stack of magazines in front of him. 'Sir, I've got copies of the *Antiques Trade Gazette*, which I think might be helpful for everyone on the team to read. There's a Turkish crime family in London who have a very good distribution system to the London antiques markets. This lists all the fairs and markets, as well as the auction calendar both here and overseas. It might be worth the team looking at to learn a bit more about the antiques trade – and just how many outlets there are.'

'Thanks, Jon,' Grace said. 'Please circulate them.'

Exton handed a copy to DS Potting. 'Sorry, Norman,' he said, 'there's no Page Three girl. Not really your kind of reading.'

There was a titter of laughter. Even Roy Grace grinned.

Potting pursed his lips. 'Actually, Jon, did you hear the one about the lady married to the archaeologist?'

Again Grace noticed the exchange of glances between Potting and Bella Moy.

'No,' Exton said.

'She said, "The good thing in this relationship is that the older I get, the more interesting he will find me."'

Everyone, except for Glenn Branson, laughed and Grace was happy to see his team smiling. In his experience, it was teams that had some kind of camaraderie that produced the best results. But he was concerned about his mate, and wanted to ensure he was kept involved.

'Glenn, I'm giving you an action. I want you to liaise with Interpol in Spain. I want to know if there were any suspicious deaths reported in the Marbella area this weekend, or anyone attacked or beaten up, okay?'

'Want me to go and check it out, boss? Could do with a weekend in the sun.'

Grace smiled. 'Not at this stage.' Then he turned to the analyst Annalise Vineer. 'Have you found any similar MOs anywhere else?'

'There's one in Newcastle, sir, and one in Glasgow. I'm looking into them.'

Grace looked around at his team hopefully. 'Anything else, anyone?'

There wasn't.

'I'm making this evening's briefing at 5 p.m. If there's nothing significant then, I'm giving you all the evening off, so you're fresh in the morning. Okay?'

No one objected.

53

His day began at 5 a.m. It was nice, if a tad ironic, Gavin Daly thought, that the older he became, the less sleep he needed. There'd be plenty of sleep soon enough, he thought. Oh yes. The great bard understood.

> To sleep: perchance to dream . . .
> For in that sleep of death what dreams may come
> When we have shuffled off this mortal coil,
> Must give us pause.

He had pause, all right. Three nights a week for the past ninety years he had dreamed of that night his mother was shot dead and his dad was taken. In that dream, the same dream every time, he saw the blood pulsing from her; then the Statue of Liberty fading into the mist beyond the Verrazano Narrows. And then his promise.

One day, Pop, I'm going to come back and find you. I'm going to rescue you from wherever you are.

The words of Hamlet returned.

> The undiscovered country,
> From whose bourne no traveller returns.

He could not die without having found his father. It was still not too late. So long as he was alive, it was never going to be too late.

54

'Still feeling in the mood for fish?' Roy Grace asked.

'Very definitely!' Cleo said. 'And I have a craving for oysters. Followed by a great big Dover sole!'

'I thought you were only meant to have cravings when you were pregnant?' Roy Grace looked apologetically at Marlon, swimming around his bowl. 'Don't take it personally, old chap,' he said.

'Unfortunately I'm not meant to eat shellfish while I'm breastfeeding. So you'll have to eat some and I'll just stare at them and enjoy them vicariously!' She grinned wickedly. 'Apparently they make men horny as hell.'

'I don't need oysters,' he said. 'Just being with you makes me horny as hell, all the time!'

'Cravings aren't restricted to pregnancy. I've got new cravings now.'

'Oh?'

'Some rather interesting stuff I didn't know about that I've just learned.'

'From that book you've been reading?'

'I'm on the third one now. I went shopping this afternoon and bought a few things we could try out when I'm up to it again.' She gave him a sideways look.

'You took Noah into a sex shop?'

'He loved it! He looked around quite excitedly – I think he liked the red and pink colours in Ann Summers.'

'He's two months old and you're getting him into bad ways!' Grace grinned.

She said nothing for a moment, then she frowned. 'You do still fancy me, don't you? Even though I'm fat and I've got varicose veins? I read that some men get put off sex after their wives have given birth.'

He took her in his arms and kissed her. 'You look stunning.' She did look really stunning, he thought. She was wearing a loose cream linen summer dress, suede ankle boots with killer heels, her hair, the colour of winter wheat, shining and smelling freshly washed. 'I fancy you like crazy. I fancy you more than ever.' He kissed her again.

The doorbell rang.

Cleo took a reluctant step back. 'That'll be the Aged Ps!'

Grace glanced at his watch. It was 6.45 p.m. Cleo's parents, who he really liked, always arrived at least fifteen minutes early for anything. They were babysitting their grandson tonight, giving Roy and Cleo their first evening out since Noah's birth.

*

Although many people considered summer officially over at the end of August, in Roy Grace's experience September was often the most glorious month of all. Normally he did not like to take any time out during a murder enquiry, and he had felt torn between spending the night working on the Aileen McWhirter case and taking Cleo out.

It was Cleo starting to sound a little tetchy last night that had been a reality check for him. It reminded him so much of Sandy. Sandy had never accepted how dead people could be more important than she was. How his work took priority over their life together. He had tried to explain, back then, the words instilled in him when he had been at the police training college, learning to be a detective. An instructor had read out the FBI moral code on murder investigation, written by its first director, J. Edgar Hoover: *No greater honour will ever be bestowed on an officer, nor a more profound duty imposed on him, than when he or she is entrusted with the investigation of the death of a human being.*

He would never stop fighting his corner for his murder victims. He would work night and day to catch and lock up the perpetrators. And mostly, so far in his career, he had succeeded.

But he was a father now, too. And soon to be a husband again. And that gnawed at him; the realization that there was someone in this world now who needed him even more than a murder victim. His son. And his wife-to-be.

He was glad he had made that decision as he walked hand in hand along Gardner Street with this beautiful woman he was so proud of. They passed Luigi's clothes shop, where some months ago Glenn Branson, as his self-appointed style guru, had coerced him into spending over two thousand pounds to transform his wardrobe. He was wearing some of the gear now: a lightweight bomber jacket over a white T-shirt buttoned at the front, tapered blue chinos and brown suede loafers. Men turned and looked at Cleo as they passed. Roy Grace liked that, and wondered, with a private smile, if they would still ogle her if they knew what she did for a living, and might one day, if they were unlucky enough, be preparing them for a post-mortem.

They walked the narrow Lanes he loved so much, passing packed restaurants and bars, and came into the square, Brighton Place, dominated by the flint façade of one of Brighton's landmarks, the Sussex pub. English's restaurant was directly across, with a long row of outside tables roped off, Mediterranean style.

'Inside or outside?' the restaurant manager asked.

'I booked outside,' Cleo said decisively, and glanced at Roy Grace for approval. He nodded enthusiastically.

They were led down the line to the one table that was free. From long experience, Cleo indicated for Roy to take the chair with its back to the wall. 'You take the *policeman's chair*, darling.'

He squeezed her hand. After a few years in the force, most police officers only felt comfortable in restaurants and bars if they had their backs to the wall and a clear view of the room and the entry points. It had become second nature to him.

They took their seats. Behind Cleo, an endless stream of people walked along the alley from Brighton's trendy East Street into the Lanes. He picked up the leather-bound wine list and opened it. Just as he began casting his eye up and down, looking for the dry white wines he knew Cleo liked, and which he liked best, too, he suddenly saw two people he recognized.

'Bloody hell!' He pulled the wine list up, covering his face, wanting to spare them the embarrassment of being spotted. Although the Machiavellian streak in him almost wanted them to see him.

'What is it?' Cleo asked.

He waited some moments, then lowered the list, and pointed at a couple, arm in arm, strolling away from them. 'I thought they were coming in here!'

She stared at the couple. The man had a large bald patch, and was wearing a brown jacket and grey trousers.

The woman had brown hair cut in a chic style, and wore a pretty pink dress. 'Who are they?'

'You've met them both, individually, at the mortuary over the years. DS Norman Potting and DS Bella Moy!'

'They look rather a mismatched couple, from here anyway.'

'They're even more mismatched close up, believe me!'

'She's the one on your team who doesn't have a life, right? She cares for her elderly mother?'

He nodded.

'And he's been married – what – four times?'

'Yup.'

Their waiter appeared. Grace ordered two glasses of champagne and some olives.

'That's terrible.'

'He is pretty terrible. But hey, good on Norman pulling Bella!'

'*Good on Norman pulling Bella?*' she quizzed. 'What is it with you men? Why do men treat pulling women like a sport? What about, *Poor Bella, lumbering herself, in desperation, with a serially unfaithful old lech?*'

He laughed. 'You're right.'

'So why do they, Roy?'

'Because, I suppose, for most people, life's a compromise. That writer – philosopher – you like, whose work you introduced me to a few months ago. What was his great line? Something about so many people *living lives of quiet desperation?*'

'Yes. Don't let us ever get like that, Roy.'

He stared back into her clear, green eyes. 'We never will,' he said.

'Is that a promise?'

'It's a promise.'

Their champagne arrived. He raised his glass and clinked it against hers. 'No desperation,' he said. 'Ever.'

'None!'

A short while later he ordered six oysters. Then, when he saw the mischievous look in Cleo's eyes, he upped it to a dozen.

55

At 11 a.m. on Monday, Gavin Daly sat at his desk, thumbing through his ancient Rolodex looking for a name from the past, ignoring the grinding blatter of the old ride-on mower as his gardener went up and down the lawn, cutting immaculate stripes.

He had heard the news, an hour earlier, that the Coroner had released his sister's body, and her funeral could go ahead tomorrow, as he had planned.

His thoughts were interrupted by a perfunctory knock, followed by the sound of his door opening, and he turned to see his housekeeper, Betty, enter with a tray containing a wine glass, an opened bottle of Corton-Charlemagne white Burgundy, a Robaina cigar, perfectly cut, and a dish of green olives.

The first of his two glasses of white wine a day, which would be followed by his evening two fingers of whisky. Everything in moderation was his recipe. All the people he knew of or had read about who'd made it to his kind of old age had their own particular secret. For some, it had been total abstinence from alcohol. For others, it had been a life of celibacy. Poor, miserable sods – they might have lived a long time, but strewth, it must have seemed so much longer! What they all ignored was England's oldest ever man, Henry Allingham, who had died only a few years ago at 113, and had attributed his longevity, in a radio interview he'd heard on the great man's 112th birthday, to 'Cigarettes, whisky and wild, wild women.'

Every morning, as Betty filled that first glass for him, he raised it in a silent toast to Henry Allingham, before lighting his cigar.

In front of him lay the front page of the *Daily News* from February 1922, in its protective plastic. He thanked Betty, drank some wine, and waited until he heard the door shut behind him. Then he continued his search through the ancient, battered Rolodex index cards, until he found the name and telephone number he was looking for. A genealogist called Martin Diplock, whose service, years back, he had used regularly to check the background history of high-end antiques.

He dialled it, and as he half-expected, heard a *number discontinued* tone. But just in case the man was still alive, he googled his name. To his surprise he found a simple website giving an email address and what looked like an overseas phone number. He dialled and it rang. Three times. Four. Five.

Then he heard a click, followed by Diplock's very distinguished, cultured voice.

'You're still alive?' Daly said.

There was a moment's pause. 'Who's that?'

'Gavin Daly!'

'Well, well, well! It sounds like you're still alive too!'

'Just.'

'It must be twenty years.'

'All of that.'

'So, to what do I owe this pleasure?'

'I need some family history checked out. Are you still working?'

'I live in Tenerife – retired here over fifteen years ago. But I keep my hand in – thanks to the Internet, it's easy to keep up with old acquaintances and developments. Why?'

'This is probably a long shot, I don't know. I guess I'm long enough in the tooth to have learned not to dismiss coincidence.'

'You know what Einstein said about coincidence?'

'Something about *God's calling cards*?'

'Kind of. He said it was *God's way of remaining anonymous*.'

Daly smiled and drank some more wine. 'It's good to speak to you, Martin. How's Jane?'

'She's well. She's in rude health. Sunshine is good for people.'

'It's bad for antiques.'

'So, what information do you have for me?'

'There's a man named Eamonn Pollock,' Daly said. 'His current main residence is on a yacht based in Marbella called *Contented*. As I said, it's a long shot. But I'm happy to pay whatever you charge these days to find out if he is related, in any way, to a man in New York back in the 1920s called Mick Pollock. I think he would have been Irish, and a member of the White Hand Gang.'

'Do you have any more details than that, Gavin?'

'Back then, Mick had only one leg – I gather he got gangrene in it after being shot in a gang fight. He had the nickname of *Pegleg*.'

'*Pegleg Pollock*. Anything else?'

'No, I'm afraid not. Could you try to prepare as detailed a family tree as you can?'

'I'll see what I can do, but I can't promise anything.'

'Give me an address to wire some money to.'

'There's no charge. Tell you the truth, I'm bored. Be good to have a challenge. Is there any urgency?'

'Everything's urgent at our age, Martin.'

56

Like most police officers he knew, Roy Grace always felt uncomfortable entering a prison. In part it was the knowledge that prisoners had a pathological hatred of the police, and in part it was the loss of control. As a police officer you were normally in control of any environment you found yourself in. But from the moment the first of the prison's doors was locked behind you, you were in the hands of the Prison Governor and his or her officers.

Convicted policemen, given custodial sentences, were treated by other prisoners on a par with paedophiles.

Sussex had two prisons: Ford, an open, Category D prison, filled mostly with relatively minor and low-risk offenders, as well as some lifers approaching the end of their custodial terms, gradually getting accustomed to the world they were soon to re-enter. The other, Lewes, a Category B, was a grim, forbidding place. Roy Grace had passed it many times, as a child with his parents, and back then it had always both fascinated and scared him.

Built like a fortress, it had high, flint walls and tiny barred windows. When as a small boy his dad once told him that the *bad people* were locked up in there, Roy Grace used to imagine *bad people* as monsters who would rip people's heads off, if given the chance. Now, with his years of experience in the force behind him, he knew a little different. But he was only too aware that if anything were to kick off when a police officer was inside a prison, for any reason, he – or she – would be damned lucky to get out unharmed.

Which was why, to Roy Grace's relief, having checked in at the registration office where he had to leave his private and police phones in a locker, he was greeted by Alan Setterington, the duty Governor, who told him he had an interview room reserved for him in the main office section.

Setterington, a lean, fit-looking man with a fine physique from being a weekend racing cyclist, was dressed in a smart suit and a bright tie with his white Prison Service shirt. As with every prison Grace had ever been inside, all the doors were unlocked then locked again behind them as they made their way further through into the gloomy, windowless interior with its cold stone floors, drab walls decorated with the occasional Health and Safety poster, fire buckets and large, strong doors.

Alan Setterington made him a coffee, then went off to fetch the informant who was prepared to talk to Grace. For favours, of course.

Donny Loncrane came into the room in his green prison work tunic. Aged fifty-five, he looked as most long-term prisoners did: a decade older than his years, from the lifestyle and badly cut drugs. Roy Grace was shocked at his appearance. Last time he had encountered the serial car thief – and police informant – had been a good ten years ago. Setterington tactfully left them to it, closing the door behind him.

Loncrane, tall, with bad posture, his short, grey hair brushed forward over his forehead, gave him a sheepish grin, shook Grace's hand with his own damp one, as if he had just washed it in deference, and sat down opposite him. 'Hello, sir,' he said. He exuded a sharp, earthy smell of clothes that were in need of a wash.

Grace shook his head. 'What are you doing still inside? You told me you were going straight last time I saw you.'

Loncrane shrugged. 'Yeah, well, I was. Problem is, you see, I love motors.'

'You always did.'

'The thing is, they're harder to nick these days. The high-end jobs, right? The Audis, Beemers, Mercs, Ferraris, Bentleys? I used to be able to hotwire one in thirty seconds. You know how long it takes now?'

'How long?'

'Well, with all their security systems it takes about four hours. So the only way is either to get one on the road, taser the driver, pull him or her out – or else break into the owner's house and nick the keys.'

'Last time we talked you told me you were doing a degree in fitness and nutrition. That you had plans to start a gym when you came out, Donny.'

Loncrane shrugged again. 'Yeah, that was the plan.'

'So what went wrong?'

'It's not so easy out there. Not so many people want to help an old con like me. You need references, bank loans, stuff like that. I don't exactly have the world's best CV.' He grinned wistfully.

Grace smiled back. Donny Loncrane wasn't a fool. But he'd never had a chance in life. His father had been busted for drugs when his mother was pregnant with him – her fourth child. She'd been on drugs too. He'd always been obsessed with fast cars and had his first conviction, for joyriding, at fourteen. At seventeen he was making good money, and having fun, stealing exotic cars to order for an organized crime gang in London. 'You know, it's never too late, Donny.'

The old lag nodded. 'Yeah. I have my dreams, sir,' he said with a sad expression.

'What are they?'

'I'd like to be married again. Live in a nice house. Have kids. Have a nice car. But it ain't going to happen.'

'Why not? You're only fifty-five. I'm sure you could start over.'

He shrugged yet again, a forlorn look on his face. 'I'm fifty-five, with one hundred and seventy previous. No one wants to know me outside of here, except other crims. And you know what, sir? I don't mind it inside. I've got me telly; the electricity's paid for; the grub's all right; I've got me mates here.'

'Can't I help you?' Grace asked.

'Yeah, you could give me the keys to a Ferrari 458. Not driven one of them yet.' He grinned. 'So what do you want from me?'

'You're not doing this stretch just for nicking cars – it's for nicking antiques also, right?'

Loncrane nodded. 'Yeah, well, the thing is, like I said, the easiest way to nick a fancy motor these days is to break into the house where it's parked. And if you're inside, you might as well take some stuff while you're there.'

'Of course.' Grace couldn't help grinning at the man's warped logic.

Loncrane looked at him hard for some moments. 'If you don't mind me saying so, if you hadn't chosen to be a copper, I think you'd have made a good burglar, sir.'

'I'm flattered.'

'No, I'm serious. You're a good detail man. Burglary's all about planning and detail. Anyhow, you ain't come here for career counselling. How can I help you?'

'There was a nasty tie-up robbery, just under a fortnight ago, in Withdean Road, Brighton. Ten million quid's worth of antiques taken and the house owner, an old lady called Aileen McWhirter, was tortured and died subsequently. Ten million is a lot of stuff by anyone's reckoning. I was curious if you'd heard any word in here?'

Loncrane was silent for some moments. 'And if I had?'

'Two hundred quid, Donny – and the possibility of a good word to your governor.'

'I thought the going rate was ten per cent of value?'

Grace smiled. 'That was in the days before our budget was slashed to ribbons.'

There was a time when informants could receive as much as a tenth of the value of the stolen goods they helped recover; the payment was good because being an informant was a highly risky business, particularly in a prison. Loncrane would have had to have given a very plausible reason to his fellow prisoners why he was going through to the Governor's office area – and would undoubtedly be getting a lot of suspicious questions about it afterwards from his fellow inmates.

The prisoner shot him a wary glance. 'Know what happens to grasses in here?'

'I've a fair idea.'

'Boiling water thrown in your face. Razor blades in your food. It's not clever.'

Loncrane fell silent, and for a moment Roy Grace worried that he was going to clam up on him. But then the prisoner held up his hand, showing three fingers.

'Okay, three hundred, we have a deal. Who do you want the money paid to, Donny?'

'I'll give you the number of my Swiss bank account,' he said with such a deadpan look that Grace believed he really might have one.

'Dicky bird tells me that if I were you, Detective Superintendent, sir, I'd be looking hard at an expat called Eamonn Pollock who might be behind this.'

Roy Grace stared back at him; in the overall scheme of things, three hundred pounds was neither here nor there, but he would still have to justify the expenditure to his seniors. He hoped it was money well spent. 'Pollock rings a faint bell,' he said, frowning in thought.

'Used to be involved with Amis Smallbone going back some years.'

'Amis Smallbone?' Grace said.

'Yeah. They were pretty thick at one time.'

'Tell me more about Pollock.'

'A fat bastard who stitches up everyone he deals with. Lives abroad, Marbella. Used to live in Brighton. He's flash, likes expensive watches. High-end fence; wouldn't touch anything below ten grand value. Also got a loan-sharking business with extortionate interest rates. Always kept under the police radar, somehow, but made a lot of enemies. I'm told he lives on a boat in Marbella, surrounded by henchmen. Only people who are desperate do business with him.'

'Sounds a nice man.'

'He's a regular sweetheart.'

Grace's first action, after recovering his mobile phone, and walking out through the prison gates, was to phone Emma-Jane Boutwood at the Incident Room, and instruct her to drop everything and start working on an Association Chart for Eamonn Pollock.

Then he turned right and walked down the slope towards the visitors' car park, thinking hard. Pollock. The name was very definitely ringing a bell, but he could not immediately place it.

57

PC Susi Holliday took the call on her radio as they were driving west along Portland Road in Hove, approaching the spot where they had attended a fatal accident earlier this year, where a cyclist had gone under a lorry. Her colleague Dave Roberts, who was driving the response car this morning, could hear the conversation on his, too. 'Old Rectory, Ovingdean. Know that?' she asked.

He frowned. 'No.'

'Sounds like another potential G5.' She punched the address into the satnav. 'Spin her round.'

'Thought we'd had our quota for this year,' Roberts replied.

'Dead people can't count,' she retorted, cynically.

As he indicated left, then turned down towards the seafront, her radio crackled again with the voice of the Controller. She inclined her head, listening, then said to Roberts, 'Been called in by a lady called Carol Morgan. She has a tenant in a cottage and is worried about him.'

Ovingdean, a village to the east of Brighton's Kemp Town, just a mile north of the sea, behind Roedean Girls' School, surrounded by stunning rolling farmland, was a place that Dave Roberts had often thought he would like to retire to, if he could afford it. 'Do we have his name?'

'Lester Stork.' She grinned. 'Funny name.'

'Lester Stork? He's a shitbag.'

'Oh?'

'Small-time fence. He was one of the first people I ever

nicked when I first started on the force. Must be as old as God, I'm surprised he's still alive.'

'Sounds like he might not be.'

They turned left on the seafront and headed east, passing the marina, Roedean, and made another left just before St Dunstan's, the famous home for blind ex-servicemen, and threaded round uphill, into the village. A short distance on, the satnav told them they had arrived.

Almost immediately on their left was an imposing Sussex flint farmhouse, with a large paddock behind it. 'This is it!' Susi said, reading the name, THE OLD RECTORY, smartly sign-written.

He turned the car into the circular drive and pulled up in front of the porch. As they got out, into a strong wind, an extremely attractive woman in her mid-forties, with long, wavy blonde hair, dressed in jodhpurs, riding boots and a sleeveless puffa, appeared from around the side of the house, leading a horse, which was pulling reluctantly against its reins.

'Henry!' she remonstrated, in one of those naturally posh voices that Susi secretly envied. Then she saw the police car and the two uniformed officers climbing out of it, pulling on their hats, raised a hand, turned to the horse again, spoke sternly to it, then waited for the officers. 'It's all right,' she said. 'He's in a bit of a strop this morning, that's all.'

'Mrs Carol Morgan?' Susi Holliday asked.

'Yes, that's me. Thank you for coming. Gosh, you're jolly prompt. I had visions of you taking a couple of days!'

'We'd hope not,' Dave Roberts said. 'We had a report that you are concerned about a tenant.'

'Yes, that's right.' She pointed at the side of the house. 'We have a little cottage at the rear that we've rented out for the past five years. He's a strange character, very pleasant, nothing bad to say about him, sort of keeps himself to himself.' She frowned. 'But last night I heard his van – it has rather a distinctive sound; my husband, John, thinks it needs a new exhaust – coming home just before midnight. Then this morning, when I woke up, I could hear the engine running. I went out to feed Henry at 7 a.m. The front door of the house was shut. I rang the bell, but there was no answer. I gave it a few hours, then tried again at midday. That's when I decided to phone you. I really hope I'm not wasting your time . . .'

'Not at all,' Susi Holliday said. 'You did exactly the right thing.'

'I was worried, you see. I read an article in the *Argus* a couple of weeks ago about the number of false emergency calls made.'

'My colleague's right, Mrs Morgan,' PC Roberts said. 'Your tenant's name is Lester Stork?'

The horse pulled, as if impatient, and she gave a sharp tug on the reins. 'Henry!' Then she turned to the police officers. 'That's right. Lester Stork.'

'Could you show us where the cottage is, please?' Susi Holliday asked.

'Yes, of course. Let me just tie Henry up, then follow me.'

She tethered the horse to a wooden rail, then they walked around the side of the house, up a short, steep farm track. It led to a small red-brick cottage, more recently built than the main house, with a decrepit garage annexed to it. A rusty white Renault van was parked outside, and they could clearly hear the engine idling as they neared it.

Dave Roberts, holding on to his hat to stop it blowing off in the wind, peered into the driver's window of the van, then opened the door, which was unlocked, and peered inside. The cab was empty and apart from a petrol can, a wheelbrace and an old newspaper, the rear was empty, too. As a precaution, in case fingerprints became important, he took out his handkerchief, gloved his hand inside it, and turned off the ignition.

Then he entered the porch, rang the doorbell, and moments later, rapped hard on the cheap front door with his knuckles. When there was no response, he knelt, pushed open the letter box and sniffed. He couldn't smell anything untoward. To the left of the door there was a window onto a small sitting room, with an elderly television, which was off.

'Midnight, yesterday, he came back, Mrs Morgan?'

'Yes, a bit before.'

'Do you have his phone number?'

She gave it to him. Susi Holliday dialled and all three of them heard it ringing, until it fell silent and the answerphone kicked in, with a chirpy voice. 'You've reached Lester Stork. I might be busy, I might be dead. Take a chance, leave me a message!'

The three of them walked around the house, peering in the rest of the downstairs windows. They saw a small, empty kitchen, and tried the side door, but it was locked. At the rear of the house the curtains were drawn. On the far side, where the garage was, there were no windows. Back around the front they stopped outside the porch. Roberts studied the locks on the front door. 'Do you have a spare key, Mrs Morgan?'

'I do, but I'm not sure where it is.'

'Would you mind if we broke in?' he asked.

She shook her head. 'Go ahead.'

He braced himself, then kicked the front door hard. It

did not move. He tried again, even harder. Still it did not move. He frowned at his colleague. 'Feels like it's reinforced.' He went over to the window, pulled on a pair of gloves, then pulled out his baton and hit the glass hard. It shattered, a chunk of it falling into the sitting room. Then he put his hand through, feeling for the latch. But could not move it. 'Bugger!' he said, then turned apologetically and said, 'Forgive my language.'

Carol Morgan grinned.

'Window lock,' he said. 'Not making it easy for intruders.'

'He must have fitted them himself,' she said.

He smashed out the rest of the glass with his baton, then climbed into the little room, which smelled like a million cigarettes had been smoked in it without a window ever being opened. A couple of dull, framed horsey prints were on the otherwise bare walls. The furniture, on a threadbare carpet, was meagre and tired. He called out, 'Mr Stork! This is the police! Mr Stork?' He waited some moments then walked through into the hallway. And stopped.

It had been many years since Dave Roberts had last seen the old crook, but he had no difficulty recognizing him. Lester Stork, a wizened shrimp of a man, who might have been a jockey in a better life, was dressed in a shabby herringbone jacket, crumpled cream shirt, grey trousers and cheap black shoes. He looked like he had been heading upstairs, but never made it. He lay sprawled across the bottom steps, eyes wide open and sightless, dark-brown wig askew.

The PC knelt, peeled off one glove and touched his face. It was stone cold. He felt for a pulse, even though it was obvious the man had clearly been dead for some hours. He checked his face carefully and his position, looking for any signs that he might have died violently, but could see none. But the immediate thoughts going through his experienced mind were why had he shut the front door behind him, leaving his van engine running?

'Maybe the wind shut the door? But why would anyone arrive home close to midnight and go into his house leaving his van's engine running?' Dave asked.

'You'd only do that, surely, if you were planning to go out again,' PC Susi Holliday said, staring at the body.

'So where is a seventy-five-year-old man going at midnight on a Sunday, in an old van?' he queried.

'Not clubbing, that's for sure.'

'Probably not to church either,' Dave Roberts said. He radioed for their Sergeant to attend, then requested a Coroner's Officer.

While he was making his calls, Susi walked through into the room at the rear, little bigger than a box room, and switched on the light, and immediately realized why the curtains were drawn.

There was a stash of antique items on the floor. She saw bronze statuettes; Chinese vases; a silver tea set; an ornate clock; several oil paintings; a gold plate. Immediately, well aware of the major domestic burglary that had taken place in the city less than a fortnight ago, she pulled out her phone, selected the camera icon, and took a rapid series of photographs. Then she contacted the Incident Room for an email address, and sent them with a brief note:

Found this stash at a G5 of an old fence. In case any of it might have come from your Withdean Road robbery.

58

'I do horrible things sometimes,' she said.

'Go on.'

There was a long silence. After several minutes the Munich psychiatrist, Dr Eberstark, asked, 'What kind of horrible things, Sandy?'

She lay on the couch, facing away from him so they had no eye contact. 'I put an advertisement in their local paper's Deaths column that their baby had died.'

'Roy Grace's baby?'

'His and his bitch girlfriend.'

'But you're not with him any more. It was your choice to leave him, wasn't it?'

'I didn't think he'd replace me with some bloody bitch.'

Dr Eberstark sat impassively, his face revealing nothing. After several minutes he asked, 'What did you expect after nine years? For him to be celibate for the rest of his life?'

It was Sandy's turn to be silent for some minutes. Then she said, 'I did something else horrible too.'

'What did you do?'

'I vandalized the bitch's car. What's her name? Cleo? I carved on the bonnet, with a chisel. *COPPER'S TART. UR BABY IS NEXT.*'

'Nine years after you'd left him?'

'Almost ten years, actually.'

'What did you think you would achieve by doing that?'

'Sometimes I feel I'm like the scorpion in that fable.'

'Which fable?'

'The one where the scorpion asks the turtle to give him a ride across a river to the other side. The turtle replies, "I can't do that. You might sting me to death."

'The scorpion says, "Look, I'm not dumb. If you carry me across the river and I sting you, we will both die – you from my sting, and I will drown."

'So the turtle says, "Okay, that makes sense!"

'They get halfway across the river and the scorpion stings the turtle. The turtle, in agony and starting to sink, turns and looks at the scorpion and says, "Why did you do that? Now we're both going to die."

'The scorpion replies, "I know. I'm sorry, I couldn't help it. It's in my nature."'

'So you're the scorpion, you think?'

She said nothing.

'Is that what you like to think, to justify your anger?'

'It's not rational, I know. I should be happy that he has moved on, but I'm not.'

'Do you want him back? Does he represent the past, something you want but can't have back? None of us can.'

'Maybe I'm a psycho and should be locked away,' she said.

'The fact that you recognize that tells me you are not. You have all this anger inside you, and it has to go somewhere, so you vent it on him, and on the woman you think is stopping him coming back to you.'

She sat, thinking, in silence.

After some moments, changing the subject, he said, 'In our last session you were going to tell me something about the baby. Do you want to tell me now?'

She shrugged. Then she said, 'The thing is, I'm not sure it was Roy's.'

'Oh?'

'I was having an affair. With one of his colleagues.'

59

'Eamonn Pollock's not been flavour of the month for a long time,' Glenn Branson said. 'Not among the Brighton antiques fraternity. Your mate Donny Loncrane was right.'

Grace turned the car in through the entrance to the Downs Crematorium. Of Brighton's two multi-denomination crematoriums, Roy Grace much preferred the municipal one, Woodvale, with its air of a village parish church, and its woodland setting. But the private one, the Downs, was the one chosen by most of the city's wealthier people.

He had always considered it a courtesy to attend the funeral of murder victims whose cases he was working on, but he always had another, ulterior motive, which was to scrutinize all those attending, and any lurkers in the background who might be watching. Sometimes, sick killers turned up to observe. And the perps who had killed Aileen Mcwhirter were, unquestionably, very sick indeed.

He reversed the unmarked Ford into a space, giving himself and Glenn Branson beside him a clear view of the arriving cortege.

It wasn't a long procession. Out of the first limousine following the hearse emerged Gavin Daly, his son Lucas and his wife Sarah. From the next a couple emerged, along with two young children. Aileen McWhirter's granddaughter and her husband, Nicki and Matt Spiers, Grace presumed, and her great-grandchildren, Jamie and Isobel. From the one behind that emerged a number of elderly people, one of whom Grace recognized as Gavin Daly's housekeeper; he wondered if two of the others were Aileen's housekeeper and her gardener.

They were followed inside by a woman he knew and liked a lot, Carolyn Randall, the hardworking Area Manager of Sussex Crimestoppers, presumably one of the charities the dead woman had supported. Next he recognized the Head of Fundraising for Brighton's hospice, the Martlets.

Glenn Branson unclipped his seat belt, slipped his hand inside his suit jacket and took out an envelope, which he handed to Grace. 'His mugshot. Eamonn Pollock.'

Grace shook it out of the envelope and stared at it. A morbidly obese man in his mid-sixties, with a generous thatch of short, wavy grey hair, and an unbearably self-satisfied grin, stared back at him. He was wearing a white tuxedo and holding up a glass of champagne in a mock toast to the photographer. 'What intelligence do we have on him?'

'He's on a few historic Association Charts, but only one previous: for handling stolen watches and clocks – that was back in 1980. He got two years' suspended.'

Grace's interest was instantly piqued. 'Watches and clocks?'

Branson nodded.

'I think someone had better go and have a chat with him.'

'Yeah, I wouldn't mind a trip to Marbella – in normal circumstances.' He shrugged and suddenly looked deeply forlorn.

Grace put his hand out and squeezed Glenn Branson's. 'You okay, matey?'

Branson nodded. Grace could see the tears suddenly welling in his eyes.

'Did Ari ever say what she wanted?'

'She didn't want to be burned.' Glenn Branson sniffed. 'So I guess I have to respect that. I've told the funeral directors I want a plot for her at Woodingdean Cemetery. Will you come with me to the funeral?'

'Of course. Do you have a date yet?'

The DS shook his head. 'I'm waiting for the Coroner to release her body.'

A young couple climbed out of a small Audi, then lifted a baby out of the rear seat. Looking at his watch, Grace saw it was five minutes to go. 'Rock'n'roll?'

'Yep.'

As they opened their doors and climbed out into the warm sunshine, the Detective Superintendent's phone rang.

'Roy Grace,' he answered.

It was the Crime Scene Manager, Dave Green, sounding excited. 'Roy, thought you'd like to know we've found a tiny blood spot, down the inside of a double radiator we removed from the house.'

'The one that Aileen McWhirter was chained to?'

'Yes, it's microscopic, but it looks in good enough condition to give us DNA.'

Grace thought immediately of the scab on the knuckle of the arrogant telesales man, Gareth Dupont, and what Donny Loncrane had said to him in Lewes Prison yesterday. 'Can you get it fast-tracked?'

'It's en route to the lab now.'

Only a couple of years ago, DNA results took several weeks. Now, less than twenty-four hours was sometimes possible. 'Brilliant work, Dave!' he said.

'Thanks, boss, but let's see.'

'Of course.'

He ended the call, and was about to tell Glenn Branson the news as they approached the chapel door when Branson's phone rang.

They stopped and stood still. 'Yeah, you're speaking to him,' Glenn Branson said. 'Sorry, not a good line – can you say that again?' He was silent for a moment; then, his face lighting up with excitement, he said, 'Shit! Really? You've confirmed the IDs?'

Grace watched his friend looking more animated than he had seen him in a long while. After a couple of minutes, the DS terminated the call and turned to Roy Grace. 'I think you're going to like this!'

60

Returning home from the funeral at 4 p.m., the large house felt emptier than ever and unusually gloomy. Gavin Daly, drained, sat in his study, drinking a larger than usual glass of wine and smoking a cigar. He had gulped the first glass straight down. He stared out through the window.

Aileen's family had invited him to a restaurant for a meal after the funeral, but he wanted to be alone with his thoughts. At 6 p.m. he walked along to the dining room and sat down, with the local Brighton paper the *Argus* in front of him, a little smashed and in need of an early supper.

And if you couldn't drown your sorrows in one of the world's finest wines at the age of ninety-five, then when the hell could you? he liked to tell people, particularly Betty, his housekeeper, who sometimes chided him for his drinking. But he knew she always kept a bottle of Bristol Cream sherry concealed in a kitchen cupboard – and it got replaced at very regular intervals.

Betty had prepared him his favourite supper, one he ate at least twice a week: smoked salmon from the local Sussex smokery, Springs, with a large wedge of lemon and scrambled eggs on the side. Oily fish. Something else to which he attributed his fitness in old age. Not that he cared if he keeled over right now, in his current mood.

But this evening he finished his meal more quickly than usual, anxious to return to his study.

Back at his desk, with his study lights on, he removed the brown envelope, containing a photograph of the broken

Patek Philippe watch, from a drawer. But to his surprise, the envelope was empty. He frowned, wondering where he had put it. He could visualize it so clearly; the bent crown. The hands, frozen permanently since 1922. The Man in the Moon forever invisible, behind the quarter yellow disc against the blue background and gold night stars.

Then he fretted again over the numbers that had been handwritten, in now fading ink, on the reverse of that page from New York's *Daily News*.

9 5 3 7 0 4 0 4 2 4 0 4

Watch the numbers, the messenger who had given him the gun, the watch, and the page of the newspaper had said.

He drank some more wine, then clipped the end of his next cigar. Something was staring him in the face. Something blindingly obvious. So damned obvious it had taken him nearly ninety years, and countless experts, to still not see it.

It was there. He knew that. It was there as loudly and clearly as if his father was whispering into his ear, from the grave.

Hey, little guy, you still awake?

Yep, big guy, I am! Can I see your watch?

Time was running out on him.

People said that life was a gift. Maybe. Or perhaps a curse. In his view, life was a journey. A kind of circular journey. He was back in New York, in 1922, as a child. Remembering that night his mother was killed and his father abducted. Remembering his promise, on the stern of the *Mauretania*.

One day, Pop, I'm going to come back and find you. I'm going to rescue you from wherever you are.

There was a Hemingway quote he repeated often to

himself. He did not fully understand it, but he knew it applied to him.

There are some things which cannot be learned quickly, and time, which is all we have, must be paid heavily for their acquiring. They are the very simplest things, and because it takes a man's life to know them the little new that each man gets from life is very costly and the only heritage he has to leave.

What, Gavin Daly asked himself often, had he got from life?

Vast riches. No one to share them with, and just Aileen's granddaughter and family to leave it to. Just a small bequest to his son, on legal advice, to make it hard for Lucas to challenge the will. What the hell had been the point of it all?

Sure, at times he had enjoyed the ride. For several decades he'd been the undisputed King of the Brighton antiques scene. And now?

And now?

Ever since Black Monday, and then 9/11, when Americans had stopped coming here, the antiques trade, particularly in *brown furniture*, had died a rapid and brutal death.

That was all history now. None of it mattered. Within the next few years he'd be out of here. And a few decades after that, his name would be completely forgotten, as if he had never even been born. How many people, he often wondered, could remember their great-grandparents? Could anyone? Certainly not many. That was how it was.

Then his phone rang. 'Gavin?'

It was the treacly-rich New York accent of a very charming Manhattan rogue, Julius Rosenblaum, who had carved a good living from handling valuable timepieces of dubious provenance. He had contacted Rosenblaum because one of his specialities was rare nautical watches and clocks. But all kinds of precious watches and clocks, whether illegally looted from sunken ships or stolen in robberies and burglaries, had passed through his hands with few questions asked. 'Gavin, thought this might be something in relation to our conversation earlier. I got a call a short while ago from a guy with an English accent saying he has a Patek Philippe pocket watch circa 1910, asking would I be interested in taking a look at it. Says he's looking for the best offer over three million dollars.'

'Oh?'

'Well, there's a few things that didn't feel right. He was pretty evasive on the timepiece's history; his terminology when I asked him about the watch's *complications* was real layman stuff – you'd expect a guy who has a timepiece that rare to have a little knowledge, right?'

'Ordinarily, yes,' Gavin said. 'Did you get a phone number or anything?'

'No, but he's going to bring it in – he said he'd call me in the morning – he was tied up the rest of the day.'

'Could you take some photos when he brings it in – fax or email them to me?'

'Of course.'

'While you're at it, get a photograph of him, too.'

'No problem, I have CCTV here.'

'Did he give you his name?'

'Robert Kenton.'

'Robert Kenton?'

'Do you know him?'

'No, I've never heard of him.'

'No guarantee that's his real name.'

'Indeed.' Gavin thanked him and hung up. He debated

for some moments whether to phone Detective Superintendent Grace, then decided against it.

Instead, he poured himself another drink, relit his cigar and thought hard.

61

'Team, we have a result,' Glenn Branson announced, rejoining the evening briefing after having stepped out to take a phone call. 'Boss, that call I had this afternoon at the funeral, right? The two bodies found in the harbour at Puerto Banus close to the yacht, *Contented*? Its upturned dinghy near them. The boat owned by the man your informant in Lewes Prison told you about, yeah?'

Grace looked up at the large rectangle of paper that had been slightly crookedly Blu-Tacked to a whiteboard. On it was written, OPERATION FLOUNDER – ASSOCIATION CHART. EAMONN POLLOCK. Computer-generated, it looked like a family tree from school history books, but with modern heads and shoulders, the men in blue, the women red.

'The one who has previous for fencing, you were told,' Branson continued.

'Yes, that's right – with another old friend of ours.' Grace pointed at a line running to a small box to the right on the Association Chart. 'Look what we have here, our very own Six Degrees of Separation. Except there's no separation. On the fencing job Pollock was done for – a haul of watches – Amis Smallbone was known to be involved. I had a look at the file; Smallbone was charged but released for lack of evidence.' He turned to the indexer, Annalise Vineer. 'Nice work, Annalise,' he said, then turned back to Branson.

'I think you got your money's worth from your informant, chief.'

'Tell me more.'

Glenn Branson had everyone in the Conference Room's attention. Roy Grace shot a glance at Bella Moy then at Norman Potting. Although they were both on his team, they both deserved some happiness. So as far as he was concerned, good luck to them.

'That was my Spanish Interpol contact calling me. They've got positive IDs on both of the bodies. One's called Anthony Joseph Macario and the other Kenneth Oliver Barnes. Both – despite Macario's name – Irish citizens.' He looked at the indexer. 'Can you do a nationwide check on those names as quickly as possible and see if that throws up anything?'

'Yes, sir.'

'Good work, Glenn,' Grace said. 'So, we have the knocker-boy, Ricky Moore, who we think may have been the originator of this burglary, apparently tortured within twenty-four hours of Aileen McWhirter being found. Then Gavin Daly's son goes to Marbella on a "golfing" holiday, despite there being no evidence he's ever picked up a golf club in his life. Eamonn Pollock becomes a possible Person of Interest. And now two bodies are found in the vicinity of his boat. If we could connect Macario or Barnes to the house in Withdean Road or to Pollock, we might be getting somewhere.'

Grace looked at DC Alec Davies, one of the younger members of his team. 'Alec, I'm tasking you with finding out if Lucas Daly flew to Spain alone or was accompanied. Start with the airlines, like easyJet; they should be able to tell you if he was on his own or not.'

'Yes, sir.'

He looked at Potting. 'Norman, I'd like you to fly out to Marbella and see what you can find.'

'Yes, chief.' Potting's eyes darted momentarily towards Bella, then back to Grace. 'Should I take someone with me?'

'Not with our current budget, I'm afraid.'

'Don't forget your bucket and spade, Norman,' Guy Batchelor said. 'Nice beaches there, I'm told.'

'I got the shits last time I was in Spain,' Potting replied. 'From a dodgy paella.'

Grace's phone, on silent, vibrated with an incoming call. He was about to kill the call, then thought better of it, and took it. 'Roy Grace,' he said quietly.

Two minutes later he ended the call, feeling a real buzz for the first time on this case. He looked at Potting. 'Got your Holy Bible with you, Norman?'

A titter of laugher rippled through the assembled company of thirty-five police officers and civilian support staff.

'Think I must have left it on my regular pew, chief,' Potting replied with a grin.

Bibles were needed when a police officer requested a search warrant from a magistrate.

'Lucky I keep one in my office, then,' Grace said. 'I think we'd better get a search warrant in case our friend isn't in when we turn up to spin his drum.'

'Whose drum is it, boss?' Guy Batchelor asked.

Roy Grace smiled. 'I'll tell you whose it isn't. It's not Ringo Starr's. So don't bother bringing your autograph album. That was the Fingerprint Department calling me. A bronze statuette that was found in Lester Stork's house, among his hoard of nicked goods, was identified by Gavin Daly as belonging to his sister.'

'We've got a result?'

Grace grinned.

62

It was 10.35 p.m. by the time Roy Grace had all his ducks in a row. Norman Potting had sworn a search warrant in front of a magistrate called Juliet Smith, and had the document signed. Roy Grace, who wanted to be there himself, had assembled a group of police officers from the Local Support Team. One carried the 'big yellow key', as the battering ram was known, and another held the hydraulic ram for pushing out doorframes. Alongside them was a POLSA – a Police Search Advisor – Lorna Dennison-Wilkins, with her team of specialist search officers.

They climbed out of their vehicles in the Brighton Marina yacht basin, in front of the steep escarpment of the white chalk cliff. A strong breeze was blowing in off the English Channel. Rigging clacked and pinged, and there was a steady creak of mooring ropes and squeak of hulls against fenders from the dark, empty yachts moored a short distance away. In front of them was a modern, low-rise apartment building.

'Flat 324, guv?' said the Sergeant in charge of the LST.

'Yep,' Grace said, then looked at DS Potting for confirmation.

Potting checked his notepad and confirmed, 'Three-two-four.'

There was a row of parking bays in front of the building. In number 324, Grace clocked a black Porsche cabriolet. He memorized the registration.

Their first task when raiding a flat in a block was to get

into the building without being seen. With advanced planning, they could usually get a key or entry code from the caretaker, but tonight they'd not had sufficient time. Grace despatched three of his team to cover the fire-escape exits from the building, and the rear entrance to the block.

Norman Potting pressed a couple of buttons on the entry phone and waited. After some moments, he tried another two flats.

A young, cheery female voice responded to one of them. 'Hello?'

'FedEx delivery,' Potting said.

'FedEx?'

'Flat 221?'

'Yes, that's me!'

'I've a FedEx delivery.'

'Ah – you from Amazon?'

'Yes,' Potting said.

There was a loud click. He pushed the door and they were in.

'Is there a name on the package?' the woman's voice said. But she was history now.

The rest of the team of officers walked quickly along the corridor, ignoring the lift, and took the stairs. They assembled outside the front door on the third floor. There was a faint whiff of curry. All eyes turned to Roy Grace.

Grace was aware that he and Potting were the only officers not wearing body armour, or even a stab vest. So he kept Potting back with a restraining hand. 'Go!' he said.

One officer rang the doorbell, then waited. After thirty seconds, he rang again.

They waited for some moments, then, in unison, they shouted, 'POLICE! THIS IS THE POLICE.' They stepped aside as an officer put the door in with the bosher. Then, all of them, in a standard shock-and-awe tactic, shouting 'POLICE' at the tops of their voices, crashed into the apartment. Grace and Potting brought up the rear. It was a smart, minimally furnished modern flat, with a huge picture window looking onto a row of berthed yachts, barely illuminated in the darkness.

Moments later there was a shout from one of the LST. 'Guv, in here!'

Grace ran in the direction of the voice, followed by Norman Potting, through an open-plan living and dining area and into a bedroom. Then stopped in his tracks.

A king-sized four-poster bed almost filled the softly lit room. Occupying the centre of the bed was the telesales man, Gareth Dupont. He was lying on his back, his hands and feet secured with silk ties to the bedposts. And he had an erection that, by any standards, Grace considered impressive. A gravelly, sultry female voice was singing in Italian on the sound system.

Standing beside Dupont, and holding a stick on the end of which was attached a bright red feather, was a woman wearing a sinister, black Venetian mask, naked except for a pair of shiny, wet-look thigh boots. She had an attractive body, Grace thought, but not in the first bloom of youth. In particular he noticed the bruises below her right collar bone.

A female member of the team handed her a dressing gown.

'Tickling your fancy, is she?' Norman Potting asked Gareth Dupont.

'That's not even funny,' Gareth Dupont said. 'She's got nothing to do with this.'

Grace stared in growing disbelief at the bruises. He knew them, and he wished to hell he did not. Then, with difficulty, he focused his attention on the suspect.

'Gareth Ricardo Dupont,' Roy Grace said, 'evidence has come to light, as a result of which I'm arresting you on suspicion of robbery and the murder of Mrs Aileen Mc-Whirter. You do not have to say anything. But it may harm your defence if you do not mention when questioned something which you later rely on in court. Anything you do say may be given in evidence. Is that clear?'

'You sure know how to pick your moment.'

'It's known as getting your comeuppance!' Norman Potting said to Dupont. Then, unable to resist, staring pointedly down at the man's rapidly shrinking member, he added, 'Or in your case, more of a *comedownance*.'

Grace stared at the woman in the mask. He hoped she would keep it on, to preserve her anonymity and her dignity for just a little while longer. This was not about her.

But Sarah Courteney went ahead and removed it.

63

From an upstairs window of his new home, where he had set up an observation post and where he sat in darkness, Amis Smallbone waited for Roy Grace to arrive home. It was half past midnight.

Smallbone had rented the place fully furnished. It was modern stuff, really not to his taste, but it was a lot better than the shithole he had just vacated.

Tomorrow, he was expecting delivery of two pieces of electronic kit. One was an up-to-date, encrypted police radio from a bent technician who had worked in the Police Communications Department. The other was a scanning device, which he had bought through a contact of Henry Tilney, that could pick up any phone call, whether a landline or mobile, within a two-hundred-metre radius, and read any email or text.

He looked forward to becoming fully acquainted with his new neighbours' movements. But what he was looking forward to most of all was Detective Superintendent Roy Grace discovering who his new neighbour was. After years of the detective being in his face, the thought that he was now going to be in Grace's face was very sweet indeed.

But not as sweet as all the different possibilities for destroying his life that were going through his mind. As if picking up his thoughts through the wall, he heard a baby crying. The Grace baby.

He poured himself another large whisky, and lit another cigarette. Then stiffened.

Someone was walking through the entrance gate: a man in a suit and tie, holding a bulging briefcase.

Hey, Noah! Smallbone mouthed silently. *Daddy's home!*

64

Gavin Daly poured himself another large Midleton whiskey and relit his cigar. It was just gone half past midnight and he was wide awake, fuming. The news, earlier, from the New York nautical timepiece dealer Julius Rosenblaum, had lit the fire inside him. He was a man on a mission. A man on fire.

Laid out on his desk in front of him was a three-foot-tall Ingraham chiming mantel clock. Beside it lay his specialist timepiece tool kit spread out, each item in its velvet sleeve. Also on the table lay the Colt .32 revolver, with six live rounds in the chambers, that he had been handed all those years back on Pier 54. It was heavy and cold and smelled of the gun-oil with which he lovingly cleaned it every year, on the anniversary of his father's disappearance.

Inside the clock's fine inlaid mahogany case was a round brass gong. It was hollow, and comprised two brass discs screwed together. It was a slow and intricate job but finally he carefully removed the gong, laid it down, then began undoing each of the screws. None of them had been touched in over the one hundred and fifty years since the clock had been made, and it took him time to free each one in turn. He was perspiring by the time he had finished. He laid the discs down and then picked up the revolver, and laid it in one. It fitted snugly.

He went through to the kitchen, glad that Betty was up in her room, probably asleep, and helped himself to a couple of J-cloths. Then he returned to his study.

He wrapped the revolver in the cloths, binding them with Scotch tape, then placed the package inside one disc of the gong. He placed the other disc over it, then held the gong up and shook it. To his immense satisfaction, there was no sound at all.

Then, with painstaking care, he began to replace the gong in the clock, and reassemble the chiming mechanism. It was important, if anyone were to take a close look, that it was in perfect working order.

He finished shortly before 3 a.m. But still he wasn't tired.

Still he burned.

A fire that had been lit on a February night in 1922 burned even more intensely now, early on this September morning nine decades later.

He crushed the tiny remaining stub of his cigar out in the ashtray, then looked down once more at the page of the *Daily News*. At the four names written in the margin.

At one in particular.

Pollock.

Mick Pollock.

Pegleg Pollock.

Then at the list of names, scribbled in his shaky handwriting, on the notepad on his desk. The ones given to him by the genealogist Martin Diplock.

Coincidence? God's calling cards?

Or a dead man whose time had come?

65

At 4 a.m. Noah began crying, wanting another feed. Feeling totally exhausted, Grace climbed out of bed and followed Cleo through into his room as she switched on the light.

'Go back to bed, darling,' she said, lifting Noah out of his cot.

'I'll sit up with you.' In truth, he felt wide awake. He was still finding it hard to believe that the lovely Sarah Courteney was having an affair with that little shit, Gareth Dupont. And he sincerely hoped for her sake that her thug of a husband, Lucas, never found out.

Cleo carried Noah back into the bedroom, then sat on the edge of the bed and lowered her nightdress over her right breast. Roy Grace watched, mesmerized. This tiny creature was their son. His son. One day he would play football with him. Cricket. Go swimming. Maybe cycling. This frail human, sucking away on Cleo's breast. They had made this little person. Brought him into the world. They would be responsible for him for ever.

Cleo had a small rash above her breast. Her hair tumbled around her face as she looked down at Noah, with such deep love in her eyes that Grace felt his own eyes filling. Noah's thin, straggling hair was matted forward across his forehead in a way that reminded him of the character of Bill Cutting that Daniel Day-Lewis played in *Gangs of New York*.

Throughout his career, he had confronted a few monsters. But you couldn't pigeon-hole murderers into any one category. Some were tragic people who killed in the heat of the moment out of jealousy, and spent the rest of their lives regretting those few minutes of madness. Some were greedy villains with no conscience, who would kill for a bag of beans. And then there were the predators who slaked a lust by killing.

There was one common denominator among most of the people he had ever locked up. They came from broken homes.

He hoped that Noah would never find himself in a broken home. Cleo had been upset with him a few days ago, for working so late. Looking at the woman he loved and the child he loved, he knew, as much as he loved his job, that if he had to make a choice right now between his career and being a good father to his son, he would quit the police tomorrow.

Then, in his mind, he saw the photograph of Aileen McWhirter's face – like a ghost.

It was followed by the image of Lucas Daly's wife, the broadcaster Sarah Courteney, with her incredibly sexy body, taking off her mask in Gareth Dupont's bedroom. She was shagging him? Shagging a man who had robbed and murdered her husband's aunt?

Just what the hell was all that about?

Different scenarios played in his mind. Had Gareth Dupont targeted her as an unwitting stooge? Perhaps to get information about the old woman's movements? He was casting his mind back to the visit he had paid her at her Shirley Drive home, with DS Batchelor. She had told him then she was close to Aileen McWhirter. She had also seemed genuinely upset over her death. Crocodile tears?

He didn't think so. She had a bullying husband, which made her vulnerable; had Gareth Dupont preyed on that?

That was the most likely scenario, he decided. He'd called her, to try to make an appointment to go and talk to her again – without her husband present – but she told him she was out of town for two days, working on a pilot for a new daytime television show.

'I think we've got new neighbours,' Cleo said.

'Oh?'

'The house next door that was up for rent.'

'The owners are in Dubai, right?'

'Yes, I think on a two-year contract. The TO LET sign's been taken down and I saw lights on in there this evening.'

'You haven't met them?'

'No – and so far they've been very quiet.'

'Do you think we should invite them over for a drink sometime?'

She shrugged. 'I suppose that would be a nice gesture. Sometime when you are actually *here*,' she added pointedly.

He nodded.

'Go to bed, darling,' she said. 'You look exhausted.'

'I was thinking,' he said, and smiled.

'Thinking what?'

'How lucky Noah is to have such an amazing mother.'

'His dad's not bad, either!'

'Sometimes.'

'Yeah.' She wrinkled her nose in agreement, and grinned. 'Sometimes.'

Noah burped.

Grace went back to bed, but sat up, picked up the book he had been reading, and found his place. It was one from the pile of books on the early gang history of New York that he had bought from City Books.

Halfway through the first page of the chapter he saw a name, and froze.

66

Gavin Daly was feeling his age this morning. He'd stayed up until 5 a.m. phoning his old contacts in America, first in New York, then, as it became late, he switched to a contact in Denver, Colorado, followed by one in Los Angeles. He was feeling ready for his eleven o'clock glass of wine and his first cigar of the day. Then he heard the front doorbell ring.

A few minutes later his housekeeper knocked on his study door and entered. 'There's a police officer asking if he could have a word with you, Mr Daly.'

He nodded, his eyes feeling raw. 'Show him in – I'll see him here.'

Moments later, Roy Grace entered. Daly stood up and mustered a cheery smile. 'Detective Superintendent, what a pleasant surprise. Do you have some news for me?'

'I'd like to have a chat with you, Mr Daly.'

He ushered Grace to one of the studded red chesterfields. 'I was about to have a drink. Do you like white Burgundy?'

'I do, but I'm on duty, sir. Some coffee would be very welcome.'

The detective looked and sounded as tired as he himself felt. Daly instructed Betty to bring coffee and his wine, then sat back in his chair and swivelled round to face Grace. 'Do you have some news for me?'

'We made an arrest last night, sir, of a male suspect involved in your sister's robbery.'

'That's extremely welcome news. May I know his name?'

'Do you have any views on possible suspects yourself, sir?'

'I don't, no.'

'Other than the knocker-boy, Ricky Moore?' Grace watched his eyes carefully.

'Other than Moore, no.'

'I'd appreciate your keeping this confidential, for the moment.'

'Of course.'

'The man we arrested is called Gareth Dupont. Does that name mean anything to you?'

Daly shook his head. Then echoed the name. 'Gareth Dupont?'

Grace continued studying his face. 'I can't say too much at the moment, but we have evidence linking him to the scene. You've never heard your sister mention his name?'

'Never.'

'I'm trying to find out if he would ever have had a legitimate reason for being in the house.'

'Not so far as I know.'

'I wonder if you could tell me in a little more detail about the watch that was taken from your sister's safe? To help us try to identify it. It's extremely difficult without a photograph, as I'm sure you can appreciate. We know the make and we have a description, but there are quite a number that may fit that description.'

Daly shook his head. 'No, this was unique. Well, let me qualify that, almost unique. I don't know how much you know about watches, Detective Superintendent?'

Grace glanced down at the sturdy but heavily scratched Swiss Army watch Sandy had given him for his thirtieth birthday, the day she disappeared; its leather strap was almost worn out. 'Very little, I'm afraid.'

'Well, it's pretty fair to say that Patek Philippe & Cie., founded in 1851, is the inventor of the pocket watch, which evolved into the wristwatch familiar to us all today. The firm invented automatic winding, the perpetual calendar, the split-seconds hand, the chronograph, the minute repeater – as a result, vintage Patek Philippes tend to have an exceptionally high value. The world record price ever paid for a watch was $11.3 million, at auction some years ago, and that was for a unique Patek Philippe – it was known as the Patek Philippe Henry Graves Super-complication.'

'So, the one that was stolen from your sister's safe – would there be many identical ones?'

'To be honest with you, it was always a mystery how my father obtained the watch in the first place. He was a humble dockworker – all right, he was in a gang, but the gang basically existed to protect the rights of Irish people on the Manhattan and Brooklyn waterfronts. Even back then the watch would have had a very high value. But you have to remember parts of New York were pretty lawless in those days. I like to think he might have won it in a poker game, or been given it in lieu of a debt, but I know from the history he was a hard man – you had to be to survive then. It's possible he got it some other way.'

The two men smiled at each other, the innuendo hanging, unresolved, in the air.

'Now, as to your question about other identical ones. Some years back when I realized the watch was so valuable, I tried to find its provenance. I contacted Patek Philippe in Geneva and gave them the serial number, but they said that it did not tally with their records; the number was wrong.'

Grace frowned. 'Is that implying the watch is a fake?'

'That's what I thought at first. But then I found out something that was common practice back in those days. You see, at that time, all their watches were bespoke, commissioned by buyers. Many months of work would go into a single pocket watch. Well, apparently, top apprentices would make themselves a duplicate at the same time, secretly of course. I suspect that's what my father's watch is. I believe in the rag-trade, where workers make themselves duplicate garments from left-over cloth, it is called *cabbage*.'

'Some cabbage!' Grace said, and smiled. 'And it doesn't detract from its value?'

'Far from it,' Gavin Daly said. 'It's an important piece. Part of watchmaking history.'

'You never took photographs?'

'Oh, I did, I have them somewhere. But maybe they got misfiled or thrown out. I've searched high and low and so far nothing. And, of course, the photo Aileen had has gone.'

Changing the subject abruptly, Grace asked, 'So how did your son get on with his golfing weekend in Marbella?'

'To be honest, I wouldn't know. Lucas and I are not that close.'

He nodded, then sat in silence for some moments. 'Do you know an Anthony Macario or a Kenneth Barnes?'

'No, I don't.' He answered too quickly, as if he had expected to be asked. And that, together with his eye movements, gave Grace a strong indication he was lying. Daly compounded this by scratching his nose, a further tell-tale sign.

'They were found floating in the water at Puerto Banus yesterday morning, with a capsized dinghy near them. It normally takes two to three days for a body to rise to the surface after being put into the sea in warm water. Your son went to Marbella on Friday. I always like to look at coincidences.'

Grace paused as the housekeeper came in with a tray on which was an opened bottle of wine, a single glass, a china cup and saucer, a small coffee pot and a milk jug. While she was setting down their drinks, he took the opportunity to look around the room, seeing what he could learn about the old man from his lair.

He looked at the crammed bookcases, the busts, some on shelves, some on plinths, and at the beautiful gardens beyond the window. Then at the fine inlaid mahogany clock with a Roman numeral dial on the old man's desk.

The housekeeper departed, and Grace took a grateful sip of his coffee.

Daly was glaring at him, his mood perceptibly different now, bordering on openly hostile. 'Just what are you insinuating, Detective Superintendent?'

'Nice coffee, thank you.' He set the fine bone china cup down in its saucer. Then he pointed at the clock. 'That's very beautiful.'

Daly looked at it, then looked at Grace, with a strange expression. He looked decidedly uncomfortable suddenly, Roy Grace thought.

'It's an Ingraham. Handmade in 1856. A very fine example. I'm shipping it to a client in New York.'

'So you still keep your hand in?'

'Oh, indeed. Keeping active, that's my secret. Keep doing what you love. You're a young man, but you'll understand me, one day.' Gavin Daly caressed the clock, becoming animated. 'This was made by a true craftsman. There's nobody today could make something like this.' Then his mood reverted to anger once more. 'So, would you mind telling me exactly what you are insinuating?'

'Well, let's take Ricky Moore. Your sister was tortured, hideously, with cigarettes and heated curling tongs. The night after she died, Moore was kidnapped and tortured with a hot instrument.' Grace raised his arms and smiled disarmingly. 'Bit of a coincidence, but perhaps no more than that. Then your son went to Marbella the following Friday and just days later, two bodies were found. Their time of death is estimated by our Spanish police colleagues at between Friday night and sometime on Saturday.' Grace picked up his cup, blew on the coffee, and drank some more.

'And just what the hell does that have to do with Lucas?'

'I was hoping you might be able to tell me, sir.'

'I told you, we rarely speak.'

Grace put his cup down, then pointed at the bust of T. E. Lawrence. He recognized him because Cleo had been studying Lawrence for her Open University degree in philosophy, and had encouraged him to read some of his writings. 'You have him there for a reason, I presume?'

'I have all of them for one reason. They were great Irishmen whose works I admire.'

'Then you'll remember something Lawrence once said: "To have news value is to have a tin can tied to one's tail."'

Daly frowned. 'Actually, I don't remember that. What in hell does that mean?'

'It means I can hear the sound of your son clanking every time you move, Mr Daly.'

Daly stood up, his face flushed with rage. He pointed at the door. 'Out, Mr Grace – Detective Superintendent or whatever your damned rank. Out! If you want to speak to me or my son again, I'll give you the number of my solicitor.'

'Mind if I finish my coffee first?'

'Yes, actually I do. Just get the hell out of my house, and don't bother to come back without a warrant.'

The housekeeper let Roy Grace out through the front door. He thanked her for the coffee, and walked across the gravel towards his car with a smile on his face. He was leaving with a lot more than he had dared to hope for.

67

'They're nineteenth century,' Lucas Daly said to the two quiet, polite Chinese dealers in business suits, to whom he had sold items previously, pointing at the pair of baluster-shaped Chinese vases. The Chinese and Japanese were among the few people who still spent good money on antiques these days.

'Cantonese.' He pointed at the panels of Oriental figures. 'Quite exquisite! We acquired them from the home of the Duke of Sussex – he was forced recently to sell off some heirlooms to pay for maintenance of his stately home. We understand from him that these were bought in Canton by his great-great-grandfather, who helped John Nash with many of his acquisitions for the Royal Pavilion. They're really exceptional pieces, I think you'll agree.'

There was no Duke of Sussex. He'd bought them from a local fence, Lester Stork, no questions asked, for one hundred pounds.

'How much?' asked one of them.

'Two thousand five hundred for them both. Very rare to find a pair in such good condition, you see—'

'Lucas?' His assistant, Dennis Cooper, who had on an even more hideous Hawaiian shirt than normal, interrupted him.

'I'm busy.'

'It's your father. Says it's urgent!'

'Tell him I'm with important customers.'

When he turned back, the two Chinamen were walking towards the door.

'Hey!' he said. 'Hey! Make me an offer!'

'Don't like your face,' the one he had been talking to said.

'Fuck you!' he shouted back, as the door closed behind them.

Dennis Cooper wheeled his chair over and held the phone out to him. He snatched it, angrily, from his hand. 'I'm busy, Dad.'

'You twat!' Gavin Daly said. 'You absolute bloody idiot. You were meant to get information from them, not kill them.'

Lowering his voice and moving further away from his assistant, Lucas Daly replied, 'What do you mean?'

'I told you to go to Marbella to find out where the watch is. I didn't tell you to kill anybody. What the hell did you think you were doing? Why did you kill them? I want my watch back. I don't want blood on my hands.'

'I didn't kill anyone.'

'No? So how come the bodies of Tony Macario and Ken Barnes were found floating in Puerto Banus Harbour?'

'I've no idea.'

'No idea? Really? You and your Albanian thug, Boris Karloff, went to see them, right?'

Lucas Daly tried to think fast, on his feet. Not one of his natural talents. 'Yeah – like – we had a chat with them. They were a bit pissed – been out clubbing. They were fine when we left them. Like I told you, they said Eamonn Pollock had gone to New York. We searched the boat and found the safe, which had nothing in it. Then we left.'

'I've just had a visit from the Senior Investigating Officer on the case, Lucas. He made it pretty damned clear he thinks I'm involved in their deaths.'

'They were drunk when we left them, Dad. Maybe they fell overboard.'

'Did you look up at the night sky?'

'Up at the night sky? What do you mean?'

'Did you look up at the bloody night sky when you were there? After you and Boris left them?'

'His name's not Boris; it's Augustine Krasniki.'

'So what did you see when you looked up at the night sky?'

'I don't think I looked up at the night sky at all, Dad.'

'Shame. You know what you'd have seen?'

'No, what?'

'Pigs flying.'

'Yeah, well, it was cloudy that night.'

'Very funny. Listen. I may need to fly to New York at short notice.'

'New York? Why?'

'Because I think the watch might be there and, if it is, I know who has it.'

68

Roy Grace's love of Brighton ran deep in his veins. At his wedding, his best man, Dick Pope, had joked with his typical black humour that if Roy was ever unfortunate enough to be the subject of a post-mortem, the pathologist would find the word *Brighton* repeated right through every bone in his body, like in sticks of Brighton rock.

For over a decade the city's football team, the Albion, known by locals as the Seagulls, had been without a proper home, and forced to use an athletics stadium. But during the past year, thanks to the generosity of an individual benefactor, Tony Bloom, and American Express, they now had the Amex Stadium, a building that by general consensus was one of the finest football stadiums in Europe.

Wednesdays were not usual nights for a game, but this was an important Championship game. As Roy Grace sat in the traffic jam on the A27, staring at the stunning sweep of the building over to the right, he felt a great twinge of pride. The building was not only great for the city, it had rekindled his interest in the game, as it had for thousands of other residents of Brighton and Hove.

Ten minutes later, parked on the kerb between two marked police cars, he was escorted by Darren Balkham, the Police Football Liaison Officer, wearing a high-viz jacket and uniform cap, to the Police Observation Room in the North Stand.

In an elevated position, directly behind the goal posts, the room had a commanding view of the brightly lit pitch and the terraces. The game was in progress and a quick look at the scoreboard told Grace the score, at the moment, was nil-nil.

Over twenty thousand of the twenty-seven thousand fans here today were season-ticket holders and there had been a lot of careful strategizing to minimize trouble when the seating areas had been allocated. One whole section of the East Stand was for families. Next to them were the fans known to be milder mannered. The rowdiest had been placed at the North Stand, close to the observation room. Visiting fans were grouped in an area on the South Stand.

The CCTV controllers behind a bank of monitors in this room could zoom any of the stium's eighty-seven cameras in on a troublemaker so tightly they could read the time on his or her watch.

Balkham introduced Roy Grace to Chris Baker, the Safety Officer, smartly dressed in a grey suit. 'You're looking for someone in the crowd – Lucas Daly?'

'That's right,' Grace said.

'I've already checked out our list of season-ticket holders and he's not one of them. You don't know who he might have come with?'

'No. I tried to get hold of him earlier and his wife said he was coming here.'

Baker led him over to the bank of monitors and sat Grace down next to an operator.

Although monitoring potential hooliganism was the primary object of the cameras, they had a secondary function for the CID, which was to observe Persons of Interest to the police. In particular, to watch where local villains were seated, and who they were with. It was a valuable source of intelligence.

With the assistance of the operator, steadily scanning

the 27,000-strong crowd, it took Grace just under fifteen minutes to spot Lucas Daly, on the twelfth row of the West Stand. He was wearing a leather aviator's jacket with a fleece collar, a roll-neck sweater and jeans, and a blue and white Seagulls scarf draped around his shoulders. Grace recognized him from the photographs in the living room of his home when he had gone to talk to his wife, Sarah Courteney. He also recognized the men seated either side of him. One, Ricky Chateham, was a local wheeler-dealer, in the vending-machine trade as a day job, but a known handler of high-end stolen goods, whom the police had been watching for some time; he was also suspected of being behind the supply of drugs into several clubs around Sussex and its neighbouring counties, but so far there had never been enough evidence to nail him. The Albion records showed he was the season-ticket holder for the three seats they occupied. The other man was a criminal solicitor favoured by many of the city's villains called Leighton Lloyd. Handy, Grace thought, cynically. Daly might well be needing him sometime soon.

It was a lacklustre game, enlivened by a couple of early yellow cards, and then some minutes later by a tantrum thrown by the team manager, Gus Poyet, after a player was sent off in a highly disputed decision by the referee.

The crowd roared and broke into their regular angry chant against the ref. *The referee's a wanker!*

But Roy Grace wasn't following the game. He was glued to Lucas Daly's every movement. Daly wasn't following the game, either. He was engaged in what looked like very intense discussions with the two men. Grace dearly wished he had a lip-reader with him at this moment.

Ten minutes before the final whistle he left the observation room and made his way along past the exits to the

West Stand, then waited. All the supporters would have to pass him, whether heading towards the car parks, the buses or the train station.

As they poured out, his target, flanked by Chateham and the solicitor, stopped less than ten yards from him to light a cigarette. Grace stepped forward, holding up his warrant card. 'Lucas Daly? Detective Superintendent Grace. I'm the Senior Investigating Officers on your aunt's murder. Wonder if I could have a quick word?'

Ricky Chateham gave Grace an uneasy glance of recognition and strode on. The solicitor stood his ground, giving Daly an inquisitive glance.

'See you in the car park, Leighton,' Daly said, dismissing him. Then he looked levelly at Grace, showing no surprise or any other emotion. 'Yes?'

Grace put Lucas Daly's age at around late-forties. He studied his face for any signs of his father in it, but saw none. Unlike his father, whose aged face was etched with character, Lucas Daly had blandly thuggish good looks, with an unreadable expression, and exuded all the personality of an unplugged fridge.

'How was your golf this weekend?'

Daly frowned, then took a moment to reply. 'It was all right.'

'Nice golf courses around Marbella?'

'Does my golf have something to do with my aunt, Detective – er – sorry – didn't get your name?'

'Grace.' Then in answer to the question he said, 'Yes, perhaps it does.' He noticed the man's discomfort, and his eyes all over the place. 'You were in Marbella this past weekend?'

'What of it?'

'On a golfing holiday?'

'Yes.'

'Who did you go with?'

'On my own – went to meet up with some friends who live out there.'

'Expats?'

'What of it?'

'You didn't actually go alone, did you?'

Daly stared at him, looking uneasy, his eyes all over the place. 'What are you saying?'

'You travelled with a gentleman called Augustine Krasniki – you bought return tickets for both of you on easyJet.'

'Oh yeah, right – him.' His eyes continued moving around wildly. 'He's my assistant, you know.'

'Caddies for you, does he?'

'Yeah, exactly.'

'Good golfer, are you?'

'Average.'

'What's your handicap?'

As Daly dragged on his cigarette, Grace watched the man's eyes.

'Twelve.'

Roy Grace had had a go at taking up golf some years back, but had given up after a few months of Sandy complaining about him being away so much during his precious hours of free time. He knew that a twelve handicap was impressive; you didn't get that unless you played regularly. And if you played regularly, every now and then you would win a trophy. Which you would put on display. 'Where do you play locally?'

'Haywards Heath, mostly. I'm sorry, what does this have to do with my aunt – my late aunt?'

'Do the names Anthony Macario and Kenneth Barnes mean anything to you, Mr Daly?'

Daly squinted at him, as if a stream of smoke had gone into his eyes. 'No, never heard of them.'

Grace nodded. 'So it wasn't you or your father who had anything to do with them ending up in the harbour at Puerto Banus, then?'

For a moment Grace really thought, from Daly's ferocious expression, that he was going to be punched in the face; he braced himself to duck. But the punch never came. Instead, Lucas Daly pointed an arm in the direction that the crowd was taking. 'Never heard of them. Okay if I go now? I want to beat this mob out of the car park.'

'You can go, but I want you to know something. No one's above the law, Mr Daly. Okay? I'm very sorry about your aunt. What happened to her should not happen to any human being, ever. But you need to know I don't allow vigilantes.'

Daly dragged on his cigarette again. 'What exactly are you insinuating, Detective Grates?'

'*Grace,*' he corrected. 'I'm insinuating nothing. But I'm not convinced you went to Marbella to play golf and I don't allow people to take the law into their own hands.'

'My father and I are law-abiding people,' he said.

'Good.'

'So can I ask, how are you doing in finding out who killed my aunt, and getting her property back? In particular the watch – it means a great deal to my dad.'

'We're working on it,' Roy Grace said.

'Yeah, well, my dad and I are working on it too. Just in case you don't deliver – nothing personal. We'll see who gets the watch back first, Detective Grace. The longer it's gone, the less chance any of us have of getting it back. True?'

'No one's going to find it easy to sell a rare watch of that high value, regardless of its provenance,' Grace replied.

'That's what worries me, Detective,' he said. 'Maybe some scumbag who knows nothing about watches took it and flogged it to a fence for a few quid.'

'Which is why you went to Marbella, right? To stop the watch from being taken any further distance overseas? Anthony Macario and Kenneth Barnes got in your way, so you had them drowned. Am I warm?'

'Warm? You're the advance guard of the fucking Ice Age. I suggest you stop wasting public money having freebies at football matches, and get back to catching villains.'

69

It was 10.15 p.m. by the time Roy Grace drove out through the congested exit of the Amex stadium car park. There was an accident ahead on the A27, which partially blocked the road, and it took him another forty minutes to finally arrive back at Cleo's house.

He punched in the entry code to the gate and entered the cobbled courtyard, looking at the house next door, which was in darkness, curious about the new neighbours. Seemed like they went to bed early, which was good news. In a small, gated community like this, the biggest nightmare would be someone who stayed up late playing loud music.

He let himself in, happily unaware of the figure behind net curtains in a dark, upstairs room next door, cigarette burning in the ashtray beside his tumbler of whisky, who was watching him with hate burning in his eyes.

All was quiet in Cleo's house, with a few dimmed lights on downstairs. Humphrey bounded over and he patted and hushed the dog. Then he removed his shoes, tiptoed across the lounge to say hi to Marlon, and went into the kitchen. Cleo had left him a plate of cod, mash and beans wrapped in clingfilm and handwritten instructions on how long to microwave it, followed by a row of kisses.

He followed the instructions, gave Humphrey a biscuit, poured himself a glass of rosé wine from a bottle in the fridge, gave Humphrey a second biscuit, then carried his meal on a tray back into the living room, and sat on the sofa, which the dog insisted on sharing with him. He promised Humphrey he'd take him out for a walk later, switched on the television, the sound low, to see if there was anything he wanted to watch. Then he noticed the handcuffs.

They lay on the far right-hand side of the low coffee table, pinning down a handwritten note, which said:

For sometime soon . . . XXXXXXXXXXX

He grinned, then channel-surfed through to Sky News, and watched the banner headlines. When he had finished eating he picked up another of the books on the history of the White Hand Gang and turned to the index, looking for one name in particular. There were six different page references against it. He began to read through them; the further he read, the more he became convinced.

Then he was distracted by Humphrey suddenly sitting up and giving a single bark.

He turned to see Cleo standing at the bottom of the stairs, holding several silk ties in her hand and wearing nothing but a very horny smile.

70

'What you smiling about, old timer?' Glenn Branson asked.

It was 8.25 a.m. Grace looked up from his desk, holding a half-eaten Trudie's bacon sarnie in his hand. 'The report from yesterday's progress at the trial. It's looking good for us.'

Branson swivelled around the chair in front of his desk, and sat astride it, placing his hands on the back. He looked like he had just bitten into a lemon. During the arrest of Carl Venner, Branson had been shot, the bullet, fortunately, missing all of his internal organs. 'Glad to hear it. Would hate to think it went any other way.'

'How's you?'

'Full on damage limitation. Ari did a great job of poisoning my kids against me. I've got an unexpected ally in her sister, who turns out to be a great Ari fan – not.'

'What about the boyfriend?'

'He had the nerve to come round for some of his possessions – and to give me verbal for changing the locks! Told him if he wanted his stuff, he'd better start looking in the local skips. Can you believe it, the kids wanted to see him?'

'I can believe it, matey. Of course they're missing him. Remember, their lives have been turned totally upside down. For the past year or so he's been their father figure. You're going to have to take it one step at a time. One day your kids will realize what a decent guy you are.'

'You think so?'

'Sure. Give 'em thirty years or so to adjust – you know – to the fact you left their CDs all over the floor and regularly forgot to feed their goldfish.'

'I don't know why I like you,' Branson said. 'You know, sometimes you remind me of that bastard Popeye Doyle in *The French Connection*.'

'Didn't he handcuff his girlfriend to his bed?'

'In the opening scene. Or maybe she handcuffed him.' Grace smiled.

'That's a very dirty grin.'

Grace nodded, memories of last night still vivid in his mind. 'Yeah. Very!'

'Cleo's a bit kinky, is she?'

Grace gave him a shrug. 'You're a movie buff. You like Woody Allen, don't you?'

'Not everything, but some, yeah.'

'So don't you remember, in *Everything You Always Wanted to Know About Sex*?'

Branson frowned. Then he nodded. 'Yeah! Someone asked him if sex was dirty. And he replied, "Only if it's done right!"'

Grace smiled, then tried to prise a bit of bacon free from between two of his teeth.

Branson lowered his chin onto his folded arms. 'Ari and me, we used to do it right, once. It goes; that's the bummer. You have kids, and it goes.' He raised a warning finger. 'Don't let it go – despite your age!'

'Thanks for the advice!' Grace looked at his watch. 'Okay, two minutes,' he said.

71

Grace began the 8.30 a.m. briefing by launching straight into the hypothesis that had been churning in his mind all night. 'Okay, team, Gavin Daly's son Lucas went to Marbella and, according to the airline's passenger list, he was accompanied by a character named Augustine Krasniki. Our Interpol sources tell us Krasniki has a string of convictions for assault back in his native Albania. In one of them, he gouged both eyeballs out of a male victim who had defaulted on a debt, leaving him permanently blind. But thanks to our bleeding heart liberal European laws, we have to let this monster in and give him money and free health treatment. Our same Interpol sources tell us that two people were found dead on Sunday morning – Anthony Macario and Kenneth Barnes.' He looked at Annalise Vineer. 'You have some information about them, I believe?'

The indexer looked down at her notes. 'Yes, sir. Both of them were employed as yacht crew by Eamonn Pollock, on his boat *Contented*, which is permanently berthed in Puerto Banus. We know that Pollock has a record for handling stolen watches and clocks. Macario has a string of previous convictions for aggravated burglary, as well as one, seventeen years ago in Manchester, for Class A drug dealing. Ken Barnes is two years free of his licence for ten years for armed robbery on a building society branch in Worthing. He took a hostage – a twenty-year-old woman – who he threatened to kill. I don't think you could find a nicer couple of guys, sir.'

There was a titter of laughter.

'So no great loss then,' Norman Potting said.

Ignoring the DS, Grace thanked Vineer, then looked down at the notes that his assistant had prepared for this meeting. 'I think Lucas Daly went to Marbella to attempt to recover his father's highly valuable Patek Philippe watch. The time of death of these two people found in Puerto Banus harbour coincides with his visit.'

Norman Potting raised his hand. 'Chief, if they'd gone to try to recover the watch, and anything else, what would be the gain in killing those two?'

'My thoughts precisely, Norman,' Grace said. 'The chance to check the boat out, perhaps? Hopefully you'll find out more than Interpol have given us so far when you get out there.'

'Why didn't they just tie the two of them up, in that case?' Guy Batchelor said.

'Because Krasniki's a psycho?' Potting said. 'We've just heard about his past form.'

Grace was thinking about the bruises he had seen on Sarah Courteney's chest, when her dressing gown had slipped open, and then again in Dupont's bedroom. 'We know that Daly was arrested two years ago for assaulting his wife, Sarah Courteney, and then released when she wouldn't press charges. He's a thug. Could be that he and Krasniki went too far.' He held up a sheaf of printed papers. 'I have the post-mortem report on the two men from the Marbella Coroner. It makes interesting reading.'

He paused, the bit of bacon stuck in his teeth nagging him, but he couldn't be seen picking his teeth in front of his team, so did his best to ignore it. 'Summarizing the report,' he said, 'Macario had two broken bones in his foot, and bruising right across it, consistent with it being crushed. He also had severe bruising across the back of his neck, and

Barnes had severe bruising around the front of his. Not injuries I would consider consistent with capsizing a small rubber dinghy.'

'So if Daly and Krasniki killed these two, chief,' Guy Batchelor said, 'was it because they had got the information they wanted, or because they hadn't?'

'This kind of killing tends to be done to silence people,' Grace said.

'Silence them from what, in this instance?' Batchelor asked.

It was a good question. The bacon in his teeth was really distracting him now, and Grace desperately wanted a toothpick. He tried to dislodge it with his tongue, for the twentieth time, without success. 'Possibly to stop them from telling their paymaster who was on his trail. Possibly because, as Norman so succinctly put it, they're both a couple of psychos and Daly lost his temper with them over his aunt's death.'

'Should we bring old man Daly in for questioning?' Glenn Branson asked.

Grace shook his head. 'I think Daly could be ahead of us. We should put surveillance on his son. I've a feeling he'll lead us to the watch. If we find the watch, I suspect we'll find who's really behind this.'

'Eamonn Pollock?' Branson quizzed.

'I'd put him as our prime suspect,' Roy Grace replied. 'We have Gareth Dupont in custody and we'll have to try to make him talk. In his early interviews he gave his first account, and we developed a strategy for the interviews this morning. His detention has been extended. It's a shame we're not allowed to offer murder suspects a deal on sentence. But I think our interview strategy might be to offer him another kind of deal.'

'What do you have in mind?' Potting said.

'Let's recap on what we know about Lucas Daly. This is just my hypothesis – nothing proven yet. The knocker-boy, Ricky Moore, who Lucas Daly considers responsible for his aunt's robbery and murder, ends up in Intensive Care with severe burns. Lucas Daly goes to Marbella, and lo and behold, Macario and Barnes end up as floaters.' He gave Norman Potting a quizzical stare.

'I'm on your bus, chief.'

'Now, with Lucas Daly's record for vengeance, if I was shagging his wife, I think I'd want to keep it quiet. In particular, I wouldn't like hubby to find out. Would you?'

'No.'

'Murder suspects don't get bail. If we can bang Dupont up in the remand wing, and let him know we're going to tell Lucas Daly about him and his wife, I think he'd talk. You don't have many places to hide in prison. But we have one problem to overcome. We haven't got enough to charge Dupont yet; we need something that puts him at the house. He lied to us when we went to see him at his office, and we asked him what car he drove. He told us he owned a Golf GTI. There was a black Porsche parked outside his block of flats. The registration plate gave the owner as a leasing company in London.' He turned to Bella Moy. 'Which is why your search did not reveal anything. I've been in touch with the company, and they tell me it's leased to one Gareth Dupont. At his address. But that still doesn't put Dupont in Aileen McWhirter's house.' He looked around at his team.

'We have his dab on a bronze statuette and the call made from his mobile phone, and now we know he drives a black Porsche, similar to one spotted at the scene exactly a week before the attack,' Guy Batchelor said. 'Isn't that enough?'

Grace shook his head. 'The triangulation report on his mobile phone isn't helpful enough. He could have been anywhere within a quarter-of-a-mile radius of the house at the time of his call. It's too circumstantial. On the fingerprint, his brief would argue that he might have handled the statuette at Lester Stork's house. It's not going to fly – we need something more.'

'Sir,' asked researcher Jacqueline Twamley, 'do we know any more about Lester Stork's death?'

'Yes, I've heard from one of the Coroner's Officers, Philip Keay, that it was natural causes – a heart attack.'

'Probably the excitement of handling all that stolen loot!' Norman Potting said.

'Isn't it a bit too cosy that Dupont was shagging Lucas Daly's wife, chief?' Potting said. 'Doesn't that smack of collusion?'

'I can't rule out that she's involved and we need to talk to her. I'm pretty sure Daly beats her, so she'd have a motive. But when Guy and I talked to her, I got the feeling she was genuinely fond of the old woman.' He looked at the DS.

Batchelor nodded. 'I agree, chief. I'd say it's more likely she was unwittingly targeted by Dupont.' He shrugged. 'Unhappy marriage. Dupont's a fit guy, a charmer. More likely they met somewhere and he pulled. I'm going to talk to her and see what she says.'

The youngest and newest member of his team, DC Jack Alexander, raised his hand. 'I've found out something regarding that Porsche, sir.'

'What's that, Jack?'

The young DC told him. When he had finished, the whole atmosphere in the room had changed.

'That, young man,' Roy Grace said, 'is pure bloody genius!'

72

Like most interview rooms used by Sussex Police, the one at the Custody Suite immediately behind Sussex House had a fitted CCTV camera, perched high up on a wall. By watching and filming arrested suspects, police officers were able to study their body language and generally assess their credibility.

It was a square, featureless room containing a fixed metal table and hard chairs; its internal window overlooked the central area, dominated by a futuristic-looking circular pod made of a dark-green marble-like material that always made Roy Grace think must have been designed by a *Star Trek* fan.

The suspect, unshaven, his shirt crumpled, was seated on one side of the table next to his solicitor, Leighton Lloyd, even more sharply dressed than when he was at the football. A wiry man with close-cropped hair, he had a formidable track record at getting Brighton's villains off the hook.

Grace had chosen his team carefully. Bella Moy and Guy Batchelor were both trained cognitive suspect interviewers. Batchelor, he hoped, would put Gareth Dupont on edge, from having previously visited him at his office. Bella would seem softer, perhaps Dupont's friend, and he clearly had an eye for the ladies.

A narrow, windowless viewing room, where Grace sat in front of a monitor, adjoined the interview room. It comprised two mismatched chairs, which were pulled up against a work surface, and on which sat the squat metal housing of the video recording machinery and the colour monitor in front of him, giving a dreary colour picture of the proceedings.

Grace wrinkled his nose. It permanently smelled in here as if someone with rancid feet had been eating a kebab. He checked the bin beneath the work surface, but it was empty. The interview started. Guy Batchelor asked Gareth Dupont to recount his movements on the night of Tuesday, 21 August.

'Yeah, right, I was at home, working.'

'Working?'

'Doing my telesales.'

'You do that over the phone or in person?'

'By phone.'

'But you drove to Withdean Road, to speak to Mrs Aileen McWhirter, right?'

Dupont shook his head. 'Nah, I was at home in the Marina.'

'Have you heard of mobile phone triangulation, Mr Dupont?'

Leighton Lloyd raised a hand. 'Excuse me, what does this have to do with my client?'

'Give me a moment and you'll understand, sir,' Batchelor said. Then he addressed Dupont. 'Does it mean anything?'

Dupont shook his head.

'I'll explain. All mobile phones, whether switched on or on standby, communicate with base stations. These are sited on masts all over the country. They're programmed to check in every fifteen minutes. You know, a bit like E.T. phoning home. From the base station receiving the signal, we can tell which are the two other nearest, and triangulate from there. You are on the O2 network, right?'

Dupont nodded reluctantly.

'There are two O2 base stations along Dyke Road Avenue, a short distance from Withdean Road,' the DS continued. 'There is a third close to the A23, a quarter of a mile to the north of Withdean Road. The report from O2 shows that you were in the vicinity of Withdean Road around 7 to 7.30 p.m. on the night of Tuesday, August the 21st. So you weren't at home. Would you like to explain that?'

Dupont thought for a moment, then nodded. 'Ah, yeah, I'd gone round to see a lady friend. Quite close to Withdean Road.'

'So she could vouch for you?'

He looked awkward suddenly, and Grace realized why. He was referring to Sarah Courteney. He made a note to check later whether she had been on air that evening.

The solicitor was busy looking at a map on his phone. 'I have the area in front of me,' he said. 'It doesn't cover only Withdean Road – it's a dense residential area, a whole network of streets.'

'Gareth,' Bella Moy said, with a pleasant smile. 'One thing that we don't quite understand is how your finger-print came to be on a bronze statuette owned by Mrs McWhirter?'

Dupont reddened. 'I dabble a bit in antiques,' he said. 'One of my sidelines. It's hard to make a living out of telesales, these days.' His body language, thought Grace, looked increasingly flustered. Then he frowned. 'Like – where was the – the bronze?'

'You tell us,' Guy Batchelor said.

Leighton Lloyd placed a hand on his client's arm. 'No comment,' he instructed him.

'Yeah, no comment,' Dupont said. Then he turned and

whispered something to his solicitor that none of them could hear. Leighton Lloyd shook his head firmly.

'Mr Dupont,' Batchelor said. 'There's something that is puzzling me. When I came with my colleague, Detective Superintendent Grace, to talk to you at your office last Friday, we asked you what car you drove. You told us it was a Volkswagen Golf GTI. But subsequently I've learned you in fact drive a Porsche cabriolet. Is there any particular reason why you lied to us?'

Dupont looked even more of a confused mess, Grace thought.

'Yeah, well, the thing is me and my mate Andre Severs swap cars sometimes. Like, he wants to impress a bird, so he borrows the Porsche. Know what I mean?'

'No,' Guy Batchelor said. 'I've no idea what you mean. I want to know why you lied to two police officers.'

'I guess I didn't want to look too flash.'

Batchelor exchanged a look with Bella Moy, then turned back to Dupont. 'All right, tell me something, how well do you know Withdean Road in Brighton?'

Dupont shook his head. 'Don't know it at all. Never been there.'

'Are you sure?' Batchelor pressed.

He nodded. 'Well, yeah – hang on, wasn't the football there at the Withdean Stadium until last year?'

'Correct.'

'Yeah, well, I'm a Seagulls fan, right. But that's not in Withdean Road exactly.'

'So you definitely were not in Withdean Road on the night of Tuesday, August the 21st?'

'Absolutely not.'

The two Detective Sergeants exchanged a glance. An imperceptible nod passed between them.

'Let's go back to your Porsche for a moment,' Bella Moy said. 'It's a nice car – very expensive, I would imagine, and nearly new, judging from the number plate.'

Dupont shrugged.

'The insurance must be high, I would think?' she continued.

'High enough, yeah.'

'These days, on expensive cars, the insurance companies make all kinds of demands, I'm told. Such as you'd need to have a tracker fitted. Do you have a tracker on your Porsche?'

Dupont suddenly looked deeply uneasy. He shot a glance at his solicitor. 'I do, yes.'

'Smart devices, trackers,' Guy Batchelor said. 'They track your car, every few yards of every journey you ever make. And they keep a log. You're with a company called NavTrak, right?'

Dupont hesitated, not liking where this was going. 'Yes.'

'They've obligingly given us the log of your Porsche's movements for the past four weeks. Every journey you've made, every stop, and the length of time. On Tuesday, August the 14th, you were outside Aileen McWhirter's house in Withdean Road, Brighton, from 6.43 p.m. to 7.21 p.m. Presumably, as you claim not to know it, you were lost?'

'Very witty,' Dupont said.

'You were outside the house again, for a shorter time, on the nights of Wednesday August the 15th, Thursday August the 16th, Friday August the 17th, Saturday August the 18th, and Monday August the 20th, the night before the attack,' Guy Batchelor said. 'Can you explain your reasons?'

Dupont gave Leighton Lloyd a look of desperation. Then turned back to Batchelor. 'Could I have a private word with my solicitor?'

Batchelor and Moy switched off the recording equipment, including the CCTV feed, left them alone in the room, and went outside to have a quick playback of the interview with Roy Grace. After ten minutes the solicitor asked them back in.

'My client is willing to make a statement,' he said, as they recommenced. 'He accepts what your information from the tracker shows, but that doesn't put him inside the house. That's a very important point he wants you to understand.'

The two detectives nodded. Batchelor signalled to Dupont to begin.

Dupont rested his hands on the table, looking confident. 'The thing is, yeah, I was contacted by someone I know, who said I could get good money doing a driving job. A couple of overseas blokes were coming over to do a posh house; they needed a driver who knew the area. So I had to organize a van, meet them at the airport. I admit I drove the van, but I never went in the house.'

Neither detective spoke for some moments. Then Batchelor said, 'Not even to give them a hand with the furniture? There were some big pieces.'

'Well, yeah, I helped them load, outside.'

'You are absolutely certain you never went inside the house?' Bella Moy asked.

'Certain. I'm certain.'

Batchelor frowned. 'You're going to have to help us out here, Mr Dupont. You see, there was a spot of blood found on a radiator on Mrs McWhirter's landing – the one she was chained to. The report from the lab, which we only got in a short while ago, shows it contains your DNA.' Batchelor's eyes fell on Dupont's knuckle; the scab had gone, leaving a small red mark.

Dupont looked stricken. He curled his thumb around the mark, twisting it as if he could make it disappear.

Leighton Lloyd raised a cautioning hand. 'My client has no further comment.'

73

Lucas Daly was having a shit day, and he didn't know yet, but it was about to get a whole lot worse.

He stood outside his shop, in light drizzle, smoking a cigarette, then went back inside, repeatedly dialling a number that went to voicemail. Up until a few days ago he'd been able to leave messages, but now when it answered, it no longer gave him that option. He rang again.

'*Mailbox full; please try again later.*'

'Bastard,' he said. 'You bastard.'

There had been no customers all day, no phone enquiries, not even anyone trying to sell *them* something. 3.30 p.m. His lunchtime beers had worn off and it was too soon to start drinking again. He was feeling in a murderous mood.

Call me. Call me, call me, call me, you bastard. If I have to come and find you, I'll wring your fucking neck.

He went out again, got a couple of coffees for himself and his assistant from a cafe a short distance away, then returned to the shop. He sat at his desk, his email inbox full of spam and online statements, bills he could not afford to pay. He watched the endless stream of people, mostly tourists, wandering along the Brighton Lanes through the window. *Come in and buy something, you morons!* No one was coming in to buy anything. Not that he cared too much about that right now. Unless a miracle happened and some lunatic came in and bought the entire stock. That was the kind of money he needed to sort out his current mess.

Seated in his wheelchair, Dennis Cooper was engrossed in a book of SuDoku puzzles, and that was fine by Daly; he wasn't in any mood for conversation. In any case, he didn't understand most of the shit Cooper talked about, which was philosophy, spouting quotes by people with strange names he'd never heard of.

Augustine Krasniki, whose main use in this shop was humping around heavy items that he'd bought or sold, was upstairs in his flat, no doubt watching some video replay of a football game.

Daly checked horse race after horse race on his phone. In four races today, so far all he'd got was one lousy place. He didn't do *place* bets; they didn't pay out the kind of winnings he was after. High payout trebles were the only thing that would do it for him.

Or that phone call he was expecting.

Then he stiffened as a figure appeared outside, walking with the aid of a stick. 'What the fuck's he doing here?' he said.

Cooper glanced up. 'Gosh, a royal visit!'

Moments later his father entered, and the old man was in an equally foul mood.

'Hi, Dad.'

Gavin Daly's eyes darted around the shop, without acknowledging the greeting. 'You've heard they've arrested someone? Gareth Dupont. Know anything about him?'

Lucas shook his head.

'I had a call from Detective Superintendent Grace. Dupont's been charged with Aileen's murder, as well as robbery. That means he'll be remanded in custody, I'm told, in Lewes Prison.'

'That's good news.'

Gavin Daly's face was thunder. 'What's good about that?

I want the watch back. We need to find someone in the prison who can talk to him. Dupont has to know where it is.'

'I thought you were sure it's in New York.'

'I thought so too, but I haven't heard back – which is not a good sign.'

'Maybe your reward will prompt someone in the prison to talk to him.'

'Maybe.' Gavin Daly's eyes roamed around the displays in the room. Then he suddenly stomped over towards the pair of Chinese vases that Lucas had failed to sell earlier. 'What the hell are these doing here?' he demanded.

'Nice, aren't they?' Lucas said. 'Got a terrific deal on them – bought them for a hundred quid; they're worth a couple of grand, at least.'

'Really?'

'Yeah, Dad! Nineteenth century, Cantonese.'

'I know that. I know exactly what they are.'

Lucas tapped the side of his head, grinning proudly. 'See, some of your knowledge has rubbed off on me.'

'Really?' Gavin Daly picked up one of the vases and examined it closely. 'Knowledge, you say?'

'Yeah.'

'Who did you buy them from?'

'A bloke I'd never seen before. Walked in off the street and asked me to make an offer. He didn't know what he had!'

'Nor did you. You'd sell them for two grand?'

'Be a nice profit!'

'They're Ming dynasty. Got a few chips, which will re-duce their value, but auction them at Sotheby's or Christie's and we'd be looking at north of a hundred grand.'

'No shit.' Suddenly Lucas was really excited, seeing a solution to all his problems. 'Bloody hell!'

There was a crash, followed by several tinkling sounds, as fragments of centuries-old china slithered across the floor.

Lucas Daly's jaw dropped open in numb disbelief. 'You dropped it. Oh shit, Dad, you dropped it!'

'Clumsy me!' his father said, picking up the second one. Moments later that slipped from his fingers, too, and shattered on the floor. 'Whoops!'

For a moment, Lucas Daly wondered if his father was drunk; or worse, in the early stages of dementia, or some disease of the nervous system. There was no shock, or even mild surprise in his father's face. Only anger.

'How fucking stupid are you, Lucas?'

'Stupid? Me? Look what you've gone and bloody done – are you mad?'

'Mad, no. Angry, yes. And disappointed. I'm disappointed in my son's stupidity. Those vases belonged to your aunt. Whoever took them didn't realize their value and chopped them out to some low-grade fence. And then you bought them.' He shook his head.

'I can't believe what you just did!'

'You paid a hundred quid for them, what's your problem?'

'They're worth a hundred thousand pounds – and you just dropped them?'

'Know what they say about family businesses, Lucas? The three-generation rule?'

'What do they say?' he replied gloomily, his hope of getting out of his mess lying in pieces on the floor.

'The first generation builds it up. The second generation screws it up. The third generation puts it down the toilet. You've managed to skip a generation. Congratulations.'

His father stomped out of the shop. As he left, two men in business suits entered. For an instant, Lucas looked at them hopefully; then he started bricking it as he recognized them.

One was six feet, with a shaven head and a face like beaten metal; he looked like he hadn't taken the coat hanger out of his jacket before putting it on. The other, slightly shorter, was dressed even more sharply than his colleague; he had hooded eyes, circled with black rings, and short, fair, gelled hair brushed forward, and was smoking a cigar.

Lucas said urgently to Dennis Cooper, 'Get Krasniki down here, quick!'

'Mr Daly, very nice to see you,' the shorter one said. He took a deliberately slow drag on his cigar.

'I'm sorry, no smoking,' Daly said. 'Business premises – it's against the law.'

The shorter one looked down at Dennis Cooper. Then he took another deliberate puff, blowing out the smoke before he spoke. 'Does the cripple mind?'

Lucas Daly tempered his anger. He wasn't in a position to call the shots here.

'Aggression moves in only one direction. It creates more aggression,' Cooper answered drily.

'Is that right, Quasimodo? Maybe we could apply the same comment to money. That only moves in one direction, too. Into your boss's pocket, but never back to us. Understand what I'm saying?'

'My name's not Quasimodo.'

'Then I wasn't talking to you, sunshine, was I?' He turned his attention to Lucas Daly. 'Nice wife you got. Pretty girl.' He dug his hand into his inside pocket and pulled out an old-fashioned razor. He flicked it and the blade opened.

'I don't think Sarah Courteney would be doing any more broadcasts with her face slashed to ribbons, do you?'

'She's got nothing to do with this,' Daly said.

He turned to his colleague. 'That's too bad, isn't it?'

His shaven-headed colleague nodded. 'Too bad.'

Then he turned back to Daly. 'The thing is, you owe my guv fifty K. I have to persuade you to pay it; that's my job. Innocents sometimes have to suffer, know what I'm saying? But really, they bring it on themselves. Sarah Courteney should never have shacked up with a dickhead like you. Look at your cripple over there – what happened to him? Motorbike crash? Fall out of a loft? Why does he want to work for a jerk like you?'

'Actually, I was in the army and got shot through the spine in Afghanistan,' Dennis Cooper said. 'Since you asked.'

'Oh, great, a bleeding hero.' Then his expression changed from arrogance to fear as he looked past Lucas Daly.

Daly glanced over his shoulder, and saw his henchman, Krasniki, brandishing a baseball bat, and looking like he was about to use it at any moment. 'My boss would like you to leave now,' he said. 'He doesn't like you very much. I'm sorry.'

'Fuck you,' the taller one said.

His colleague shot him a glance, suddenly looking uneasy.

Krasniki took a menacing step towards them, raising the bat. 'Maybe you didn't hear me. Get out.'

The two men backed out of the shop. Krasniki stood waiting until they had exited through the door. They hesitated outside, then walked off.

'Good man!' Lucas Daly said.

Moments later his mobile phone rang. It wasn't a number he recognized. 'Lucas Daly?' he said.

'Pull another stunt like that and you'll be in a wheel-chair like your cripple. You've one week to find the money. Next Thursday, 5 p.m., we'll see you in your shop. Without Boris Karloff. Understand?'

The line went dead.

74

The world had changed in a lot of ways during the time he had been inside, Amis Smallbone was realizing. Technologically more than culturally. He needed to get up to speed if he wasn't to be seen as a dinosaur.

Why was it, he wondered, that the instructions for all electronic equipment were written by someone for whom English was his – or her – fourth language?

The very expensive scanner, partially assembled, lay in front of him on the top floor of his rented town house. He had imagined opening the box, removing the scanner, and bingo!

Instead, the first thing he had to do was install the software, via the CD provided, on his computer. He had done that, although he was not entirely sure he had successfully followed all the instructions, which had been there to trick him at every level.

But finally, he had the thing working, and so far it had picked up little of interest. He had listened in on a banal conversation between Cleo Morey and a girlfriend, comparing notes on feeding babies and sore nipples.

Purrrleasse!

What he was most interested in was Roy Grace's work pattern. He needed a few clear hours when Grace was out of the house and Cleo and Noah were home alone.

He still had not yet decided which one to hurt, or whether to hurt both. His priority remained, as it had all along, to destroy Roy Grace. What would work best? His beloved Cleo disfigured for life? Their baby dead? Both?

He felt a warm buzz deep in his bones.

Both was good.

75

Roy Grace and Guy Batchelor sat in the unmarked Ford Focus estate, in Shirley Drive, a short distance up the hill from Sarah Courteney's house and on the opposite side of the road, giving them a clear view of the property. Her Mercedes SLK was parked in the driveway, alongside the black Range Rover Sport belonging to her husband. It was because of the Range Rover, indicating Lucas Daly was at home, that they had not gone to knock on her door. They knew, from checking with the BBC, that she was on the regional news tonight, at 6.30 p.m. Which meant she would be leaving for the studio very shortly.

After ten minutes, their guess proved accurate. She came out of the front door, hurrying through the drizzle, and climbed into her car. She reversed out and headed away down the hill, towards the Old Shoreham Road.

They waited for some moments, then Grace started the engine and drove after her, pulling up behind her at the lights. She was indicating right. He could see through the rear window that she was making an illegal call on her phone, held to her ear.

The lights changed and she turned right, heading west. He followed, a few lengths behind, as she crossed the junction with Sackville Road and continued heading west. Then he reached out his left hand, switched on the car's blue lights and shot in front of her, braking gently, then pulled over onto the forecourt of Harwood's garage, watching her follow in his rearview mirror.

He climbed out, walked back to the passenger side of her car, and signalled for her to unlock the door. Then, as she lifted her handbag onto her lap, he climbed into the passenger seat and pulled the door shut. There was a pleasant mix of smells: of leather seats and her fragrant perfume. 'Using your mobile phone whilst driving is an offence,' he said, with a grin.

'I'm sorry,' she said, dropping it into the cradle on the dash. 'The Bluetooth isn't working. Is that why you've stopped me?'

'No, but I wouldn't let the Traffic guys see you.'

'Thank you. I wouldn't normally be driving myself, but I need the car to meet a friend later.'

'I thought it might be better to have a discreet word with you away from home – after Tuesday night.' He gave her a quizzical look and she blushed.

'I thought I was going to die from embarrassment,' she replied.

'Let's just make it clear that your personal life is of no interest to me, Ms Courteney. If it was, I'd have knocked on your front door, regardless of whether your husband was in or not.'

'Thank you for not.' She switched the engine off.

Rush-hour traffic swished by on the wet road. Roy Grace turned to face her. 'So, if it's not too personal, may I ask how long you and Gareth Dupont have been an item?'

'It is pretty personal, actually.' She looked at her watch. 'I really can't stop for long – I'm on air at 6.30.'

'I know that. I don't intend to make you late. But Gareth Dupont is a suspect in the murder of your husband's aunt, and you were in bed with him two nights ago.'

'Does that make me a suspect too?'

'Not at this stage, no.'

'But I might be?'

'Excuse me being personal again, but does your husband beat you?'

Shaking, she opened her handbag and rummaged inside it, then pulled out a pack of cigarettes. 'Do you mind if I smoke?'

'I like the smell.'

She offered him a Marlboro Light, but he shook his head. She lit one, lowered her window, and exhaled. 'He's a bastard, if you want the truth, Detective – Superintendent?'

He nodded. 'Is that why you're having an affair with Gareth Dupont?'

'We met at a salsa-dancing class. He was kind to me, fun to be with.' She shrugged. 'It's been a long time since a man was kind to me.'

Grace remembered the trophy in her cabinet. 'He was your dance partner?'

'Yes.'

'Can I ask how long you've been seeing him?'

'About three months.' She looked pensive again. 'Early June, when he turned up at the class.'

'Did he ever talk to you about your husband's aunt, Aileen McWhirter?'

She dragged deeply on the cigarette and flicked some ash out of the window. 'Nothing specific that I can remember. I – ' Then she frowned. 'Actually, yes, now you mention it. I do remember one day, we were talking, and I mentioned that my husband's father was Gavin Daly. Gareth got quite excited about that. Said he was one of the biggest antiques dealers in the country. Gareth had told me he had a passion for antiques. I think, actually, he is quite knowledgeable.'

'Did he ever mention watches to you?'

'Watches?'

'Well, one in particular – a Patek Philippe?'

She shook her head and dragged on the cigarette again. 'No.'

'Are you sure?' Grace watched her face carefully.

'I'm sure. A Patek Philippe watch? They're rather special, aren't they? How does their advertising slogan go? Something like, *You never actually own a Patek Philippe watch. You just look after it for the next generation.*'

Grace smiled. 'He never mentioned a Patek Philippe watch to you?'

She shook her head very definitely. 'No.' Then she held up her left wrist. 'I would have taken note. I love watches.'

'That's a very elegant one. I don't know much about them, I'm afraid.'

'It's a Cartier,' she said. 'A Cartier Tank watch.'

'I've heard of Cartier,' he said. 'Very nice.'

'Thank you.'

He had been thinking, for some time, about getting Cleo a present. Something to make her smile, to lift her spirits with the hard time she was having with Noah. Maybe a nice watch? A Cartier Tank watch? 'If you don't mind me asking, what kind of money would a watch like that cost?'

She hesitated. He watched her eyes. 'Around three thousand pounds, I think.'

She was lying and he wondered why. Probably a gift from her husband, he concluded, and she had guessed the value.

'Okay,' he said. 'I don't want to make you late. Thank you.'

He climbed out of the Mercedes and walked back to his car. Guy Batchelor was looking at him quizzically.

Grace shook his head. 'Sounds like they met at a salsa class.'

'Innocent?'

'Innocent, or else she's a world-class liar.'

'What are your instincts?'

'She was targeted by Dupont. No question.'

76

His mobile phone rang. All that came up on the display was INTERNATIONAL.

He answered. 'Yeah?'

'Listen carefully – don't worry, I'm on a secure phone. You should get one too.'

'I have. I'm on it.'

'It's the same number I've had for weeks.'

'You're the only person who has it.'

'I want you to change it for the next time we speak.'

'Next time we speak I won't need it. We'll be in the same room and I'll have my hands around your fat neck.'

'Temper, temper! Listen to me very carefully, we have a big problem. Gareth Dupont's been charged. He's been out on licence and now he's on remand in Lewes Prison.'

'Tell me something I don't know.'

'Do you understand what it means for him if he's convicted? The rest of his life in prison? I'm worried what the little shit might do to save his skin. He'll shop Small-bone. Smallbone's the weak link.'

'Where the fuck are you?'

'That doesn't matter. What matters is that you silence Smallbone. Permanently. Get my drift?'

'I want my part of the deal.'

'You'll get it when I hear Smallbone's dead.'

'You expect me to trust you? After the way you've behaved?'

'I have low expectations; that's a life lesson you should learn, if you want to be content. Toodle-pip!'

There was a click, then silence.

He stared at his phone in fury. But, he realized, the fat bastard was right about one thing. Amis Smallbone.

77

Gavin Daly awoke with a start, confused about where he was. He heard a drilling sound. For a moment he thought it was men digging a hole. But it was a bell. The phone, he realized. He was in his study, and must have fallen asleep in his armchair. His cigar lay in the glass ashtray, with a ring of ash on the end, next to his glass of whiskey, with the ice long melted. His head ached; he'd drunk too much this evening.

He took a moment more to fully orient himself, then picked up the receiver. 'Gavin Daly,' he said.

'Hey Gavin, it's Julius Rosenblaum here. Apologies for calling so late – hope I didn't wake you?' the treacly voice of the New York watch dealer asked. 'But I thought you'd want to hear this right away.'

Daly looked at his watch. It was 11.30 p.m. 'Yes,' he said. 'Well, no, not really – I'm – I'm still in my office.' He was still feeling a little disoriented, not fully awake, but perking up fast. This was the call he had been waiting for, he realized.

'The guy I told you about, *Mr No Name*, who called me on Tuesday about the Patek Philippe, came in this after-noon.'

'Yes?'

'I've got the pictures of him and the watch, which I've pulled off our CCTV, and just emailed you. Thought I'd give you a heads-up. Do you want to check your mail and see if it is your watch?'

'Yes – yes, Julius. Can you give me a few minutes?'

'Take your time.'

'You're still in your office?'

'I'll be here for another ten minutes, then I have to go to a dinner. I'll give you my cell and you can call on that if you miss me.'

'Thank you. So – what did you think of the watch?'

'He only brought in photographs, but the timepiece looks authentic enough. Quite a bit of damage – the crown and winding arbor are bent, the crystal is cracked and there's a dent in the rear casing.'

'That sounds like it,' Gavin Daly said.

'I asked him about the provenance. Said it has been in his family since the early 1920s.'

'Did he now?'

'Handed down from his grandfather.'

'That's a touching story,' Daly said. 'Remind me of his name?'

'Robert Kenton. Does that mean anything to you?'

Daly thought hard for some moments. 'No.'

'I asked him how much interest he'd had in the watch, and he was cagey about who he had talked to, but said he was expecting offers next week – subject to the watch being what the photographs show – and he would take the best offer by close of business on Wednesday. I told him I was extremely interested, buttered him up a little, and he's going to be bringing it in to me on Monday morning, at 11 a.m. If you could get over here, I could bring you into the room, then you'll be able to see the piece for yourself. If it is yours, I just have to press one button, all the doors will lock, and the police will be on their way.'

'I'm very grateful.'

'Check the photographs and call me back.'

Daly eased himself, stiffly, out of the chair, went over to his desk, sat down and logged on and opened the zipped file. Moments later he was looking at a sequence of low-grade CCTV images. First of a man entering through a door. He was in his mid-sixties, overweight, with short, curly grey hair, and dressed in a blue blazer with silver buttons, open-neck white shirt and paisley cravat. The next image showed a closer and clearer image of the man's face. The third showed the front of the Patek Philippe watch.

He was certain that it was his watch, with the bent crown and winding and the busted crystal. But to be sure he had another hard rummage around for any photographs of it. He opened all the drawers of his desk, rummaged around through all the other old papers in there but still could not find one. He cast his mind back to when he had last seen one.

He was, he knew, getting a little forgetful. A couple of times recently he had lost important documents, or misfiled them inside others. It would turn up; no matter. He looked back at the screen, at the image of the watch, and began to tremble with anger. The bastard. The fat bastard.

Out of curiosity, he entered *Robert Kenton* into Google. There were over twenty hits. He then went to *Images*. None of them remotely matched the face on the photographs he had just looked at. Then he had another thought. Into the Google search he typed *Eamonn Pollock*.

Moments later he was staring at an old *Argus* newspaper headline from 1992.

BRIGHTON CHARITY PATRON SENTENCED

The whole story ran below: how Eamonn Pollock, patron of a leading Brighton charity for disabled children, had been convicted of receiving and handling stolen goods, including a haul of watches. But it wasn't the story that interested him at this moment. It was the man's photograph. Taken twenty years ago, he was marginally less pudgy, and his hair was darker. But there the differences ended.

It was the face of the man who had given his name to Julius Rosenblaum as Robert Kenton.

The man who, the genealogist Martin Diplock had found out for him, was a descendant of one of the men who had come into his bedroom that night, back in 1922, murdered his mother and dragged away his father.

And now he had stolen his father's watch.

78

There were mixed feelings at the Friday morning briefing of Operation Flounder. All the team present were pleased that one suspect, Gareth Dupont, had been charged with Aileen McWhirter's murder. But there was no celebration; they all knew that while one of the monkeys was now potted, the organ-grinder was still at large. Fingers pointed towards Eamonn Pollock, but so far they had no evidence to implicate him in, or even link him to, the crime.

The High Tech Crime Unit had found a series of calls made to Spain from Dupont's mobile number during July and August. The Spanish numbers changed frequently and were all on untraceable pay-as-you-go mobile phones. They were not even able to tell the region in Spain. Neither Dupont's work computer nor private laptop had yielded any useful information. Their hopes at the moment lay with Norman Potting, who had flown out to Marbella to liaise with the Spanish police investigating the deaths of the two Irish expats, Kenneth Barnes and Anthony Macario, and to see what he could find out about Eamonn Pollock. Digging away doggedly was one of Potting's particular talents.

The forensic podiatrist whom Grace had used to great effect on a previous case was due to join this morning's briefing at Grace's request. 'I've asked Dr Haydn Kelly to join us this morning as he has some significant information regarding Barnes and Macario. He will be along soon as he has a Faculty of Surgery board meeting to attend this morning and he's been good enough to come straight over to us afterwards.' At that point there was a knock at the door. He had arrived. Grace nodded at their visitor.

Haydn Kelly, in his mid-forties, had an open, pleasant face, with close-cropped hair, and had a relaxed air about him. He was wearing a navy linen suit, a crisp white shirt with a vivid emerald-green tie, and tan loafers; he could have just stepped out of a villa on the French Riviera. But when he turned to face the group, his demeanour became serious and focused. 'Hi, team,' he said. 'Good to see you all again. The Marbella police have sent me casts taken from the feet of Kenneth Barnes and Anthony Macario. I'll now explain, briefly, the matching I've done to the trainer prints taken from Mrs McWhirter's house.'

Kelly spent the next five minutes explaining the calculations and his computer analysis, concluding that the shoe-prints taken at the crime scene were a match to Barnes and Macario.

Roy Grace thanked him. 'Okay, we now have three people at the crime scene. Two are dead, and the third, Gareth Dupont, is staring into the abyss. I'm having him taken out of prison on a Production Order, and am going to chat to him on an informal basis – see if we can get any names out of him – in exchange for a few privileges.'

'How about a Jacuzzi in his cell?' Dave Green said.

'I wish!' Grace replied. Giving prisoners favours was no longer an option. Any privileges had to be given, unofficially and unsanctioned, while the prisoner was with the police and away from the prison.

Bella Moy reported that one sharp-eyed member of her outside enquiry team had spotted an Art Deco mirror taken from Aileen McWhirter's house on an antiques stall in Lewes. The owner said he'd bought it from a man who walked in off the street. He was sketchy about his description, but it sounded to her like Lester Stork.

'That would fit,' Grace said.

'Presumably before he was dead?' Guy Batchelor said. 'Or did he get it *dead* cheap?'

Several of the team groaned. Then Roy Grace turned to the antiques expert, Peregrine Stuart-Simmonds. 'You have a possible development.'

'Yes, I do. I have a list of all forthcoming auctions around the world for the next three months, which I've pinned up there.' He pointed to one of the whiteboards. 'I've also obtained all their catalogues. The thing is with many of them entry remains open until fairly close to auction time. I've given all of them the details we have of the Patek Philippe, and I'm fairly confident they will notify me if someone tries to place it. At the same time, I've been in touch with all the dealers capable of either buying a timepiece at this price level, or handling the sale of one. So I'm hopeful between the auction houses and the dealers we may soon get some information.'

Glenn Branson raised his hand. 'Mr Stuart-Simmonds, you said at a previous meeting it was likely a number of the items taken would have been presold to private collectors. Might that be the case with this watch – in which case it wouldn't show up on your radar?'

'Well, the thing is,' the antiques expert replied, 'the perpetrators would have had to have prior detailed knowledge of any of the items, if they were stealing them to order. I think it is very significant for Operation Flounder that almost everything that has been taken was detailed on the insurance inventory, while the other pieces missing, some of which appear to have been fenced locally, do not. The watch was not on the insurance, so in my view, it's unlikely it was known about in advance.'

'So do you think it's possible the mastermind behind this still doesn't know about it?' Guy Batchelor asked.

'Yes, very possible. It could be, of course, that whoever took it is not aware of its value.'

Grace said nothing. He was thinking about the concealed safe, and back to yesterday, to his brief interview with Sarah Courteney in her car. She'd acted a little strangely when he'd asked her the price of her own wristwatch – but maybe that was out of embarrassment at the extravagance of it. Yet she had said that she and Aileen McWhirter were very friendly, and that she used to pop in often. Had the old lady shown her the Patek Philippe? If so, did Sarah Courteney mention it inadvertently to Dupont? Pillow talk? What was that old saying? He remembered seeing it on a warning poster from the Second World War: *Loose lips sink ships.*

Sarah Courteney had big lips, very beautiful ones, so full they almost looked unreal. Were they loose?

79

Roy Grace had never harboured any ambition to be a rich man. He'd been to grand houses on a number of occasions, visiting them either for charity functions or as crime scenes; Sandy had been a member of the National Trust, and at weekends they would sometimes visit one of its stately homes. But while he enjoyed the beauty of their landscaped gardens, their architecture and art treasures, what he always found far more intriguing, with his policeman's mind, was where the money had come from to buy everything in the first place. You did not have to go back too many generations with most aristocratic families to find robber barons, he knew.

That thought was going through his mind now, as the wrought-iron gates of Gavin Daly's mansion swung open. He drove along an avenue lined with beech trees for half a mile, and then saw the front of the house looming. It was a truly grand residence by anyone's definition, with a portico of four columns atop the steps, rising almost the entire height of the building, and although Grace did not know much about architecture, the aged stone and fine, classical proportions of the façade gave him the sense that this was the real thing and not some modern pastiche.

Either way, he could not imagine how many millions it would be worth. Tens, probably; yet all his investigations into Gavin Daly's background had yielded nothing criminal. A wily character who sailed close to the wind, but not a crook. Grace felt sorry for him. A lonely man at the end of his life, his sister brutally killed. Did all this wealth give him any comfort or joy?

Parked near the entrance, close to an elaborate fountain adorned with stone figurines, was an elderly navy blue Mercedes limousine with an even more elderly uniformed chauffeur.

Grace rang the front doorbell, aware of the CCTV cameras scrutinizing him, wondering if he would be let in after their previous altercation. A good couple of minutes later the uniformed housekeeper opened it, and greeted him in her pleasant rural Sussex burr. 'Good morning, sir. I'll take you through to Mr Daly.'

He noticed a large suitcase standing by the front door, then followed her as she walked slowly and stiffly across the hallway, and knocked on the door to Gavin Daly's study.

Grace went in, breathing in the dry reek of old cigar smoke, which seemed ingrained in the oak panelling and the furniture. He'd always liked the smell, because it reminded him of his father, who enjoyed the occasional cigar. Daly, dressed in a crisply pressed sports jacket, checked shirt, cavalry twill trousers and suede brogues, stood up. 'How can I help you, Detective Superintendent?' he said, looking distinctly uneasy. He strode across the room with his stick, shook Grace's hand with his own bony grip, then ushered him to a sofa, and perched on the one opposite.

'I hope you don't mind me popping in to see you, sir?'

'No. I apologize if I was a bit short with you previously. This is all very stressful, as I'm sure you can understand.'

'Indeed, sir.'

Grace noticed him glance anxiously at his watch.

'You have a plane to catch, sir?' he asked him.

'Yes – I do – I'm off to France; to Nice. I thought I'd get

away to my villa there for the weekend. I need a break from all of this.' He gave him a smile that was more affable than at their last meeting.

'I can understand. A nice luxury to have. Although if I lived in a house as beautiful as this, I'm not sure I'd ever want to leave it.'

Daly sat stiffly and just smiled. 'Do you have some news for me, Detective Superintendent?'

'We've recovered an Art Deco mirror that we think belonged to your sister – I'd like you to identify it at some point, if that is possible?'

Daly nodded with enthusiasm.

'But that's not my reason for coming. Actually it's a rather delicate situation, sir.' Grace glanced down at the fine inlaid table between them. It was 9.30 a.m. and he craved a coffee, but that did not seem to be about to happen.

Daly looked at him inquisitively.

'We know how well protected your watch was, in the safe with the dummy door. And we've been fairly sure all along that there must have been inside information.'

'From the knocker-boy?'

Grace shook his head. 'I wouldn't have thought your sister would have shown him the safe, would she?'

'Never,' he said fiercely, and glanced at his watch again. 'It was when they tortured her; that's when she must have told them.'

'That is of course one distinct possibility, sir. But I'd like to ask you something. How friendly was your late sister with Sarah Courteney?'

'Extremely. Aileen was very fond of her. She never got on with my son Lucas, but she liked Sarah a lot. Sarah called in on her often, keeping Aileen company.'

'Would you think it possible your sister might have shown Sarah Courteney your watch at some time?'

His face darkened. 'Are you saying what I think you're saying? That Sarah had something to do with this?'

Grace, faced with a difficult decision, looked back down at the coffee table, studying it intently for a moment, as if he might find the answer to what he should do carved there in the wood. 'There's no delicate way of saying this, but it would seem your daughter-in-law was having an affair,' he said, looking Daly in the eye.

Daly shrugged. 'Good luck to her. She deserves better than my son, that's for sure.'

Surprised and relieved by the man's reaction, Grace went on. 'The man she's been having the affair with is Gareth Dupont – who has been charged with your sister's murder.'

There was a long silence. Grace saw Daly clenching both his hands so tightly he could almost see the bones through the thin, white skin. 'This explains a lot,' he said, finally.

'Do you think the two of them might have been in cahoots, sir?'

Daly shook his head. 'Not for one moment, no. Sarah is a decent person. I would imagine this Dupont character would have targeted her, and just gently, gently got the information from her. Have you talked to her?'

'Yes, and I'm inclined to agree with you,' Grace replied. 'I'd say she was used, exploited. Lucas treated her like dirt. She was a ready target for a piece of vermin like Dupont.'

Grace watched his face closely. 'What time is your flight to Nice, sir?'

'One o'clock.'

'Safe travels, and I'll keep you updated on any news.'

'I'd appreciate that.'

*

As he left Daly's house, two things were preying on Roy Grace's mind. The first was Sarah Courteney's uncomfortable reaction when he had asked about the cost of her watch, which he still did not understand. But at the moment, as he pulled into his parking space at the front of Sussex House, there was something more immediate: the suitcase in Gavin Daly's hallway. He had watched a documentary on television some months back, about people with second homes in France and Spain. They talked about the cheapness and convenience of hopping on and off a low-cost flight. The secret, all of them said, was to take no luggage. No wasting time with checked baggage. Just a small carry-on holdall.

That was a substantial suitcase in the hallway of Gavin Daly's house. Very definitely it would be checked baggage – unless of course he was flying in a private jet. But even so, surely a seasoned and wealthy traveller like him did not need to lug baggage around?

Unless of course he had lied about his destination.

His phone rang. It was Peregrine Stuart-Simmonds. 'Roy, I think this will interest you. I've just put down the phone from a friend: a dealer in very rare watches, Richard Robbins, in Chicago's Jewelers Row. This is a man of impeccable integrity. He's heard through the grapevine about a Patek Philippe watch, which sounds from the description very much like our missing one, being hawked around in New York.'

'Does he have any names? Anyone our team could talk to?'

'Yes, several. I'm on it now. Just thought you might want to know.'

'I do indeed, thank you.'

The moment he ended the call, Roy Grace phoned MIR-1 and put in a request for a search of all passenger lists on outbound flights to New York for the rest of the day. The name he gave them to look for was Gavin Daly.

80

The *beep-parp* . . . *beep-parp* . . . *beep-parp* of the siren grew closer, six floors below them, racing along Munich's Widenmayerstrasse. It was a hot, late-summer day and Dr Eberstark's consulting room window was open several inches to let in some air – and with it the traffic noise.

The psychiatrist frowned at Sandy. 'Are you intending to tell him you are actually alive?'

'Roy?'

'Yes, Roy.'

'No.' She felt a refreshing waft of breeze, as the siren peaked right beneath them.

'So you are a dead person?'

'*Sandy Grace* is a dead person. That doesn't make me a dead person.'

Dr Eberstark was a small man, in his mid-fifties, who had the knack, she always thought, of making himself seem even smaller still. It was partly the suits he wore, which all appeared one size too big, as if he was waiting to grow into them, partly the way he sat in his chair opposite the couch, hunched up, and partly the large black-rimmed glasses which dwarfed his hawk-like face. 'Legally you are.'

'Legally I am Frau Lohmann.'

He gave her a quizzical look. 'You told me that you got your German citizenship by paying someone. Was that lawful?'

She shrugged, then said, dismissively, 'No one died in the process.'

The psychiatrist stared at her for some moments. 'No one died, but someone must have been hurt, right?'

She lapsed into one of her long silences. Then she answered, 'Who?'

'Your husband, Roy. Did you never think about what your disappearance might have done to him?'

'Yes, of course, a lot. Constantly, at first. But . . .' She fell silent again.

After some minutes he prompted her. 'But what?'

'It was the best of a bad set of options. In my view.'

'And that still is your view, isn't it?'

'I've made a mess of my life. I guess that's why I'm here. People don't come to a shrink because they're happy, do they? Do you have any patients who are happy?'

'Let's just focus on you.'

She smiled. 'I'm a train wreck, aren't I?'

He had tiny, piercing eyes that usually were steely cold and unemotional. But just occasionally they twinkled with humour. They were twinkling now. 'I would not say that, not just yet. But you are heading towards becoming one, in my opinion, if you go ahead and buy that house.'

She fell silent again for the remaining minutes of the session.

81

'So what's this about?' Gareth Dupont asked, sullenly chewing gum in the back of the unmarked Ford. He had shaved, and was dressed in clean jeans and a freshly laundered blue shirt beneath a suede bomber jacket. Prisoners on remand were permitted to wear their own clothes until convicted.

'I thought you might appreciate a few hours out of prison,' Roy Grace, in the front passenger seat, said. It was midday, and they had to return Dupont by 5 p.m. Guy Batchelor reversed the car out of the custody block bay. The police always had to be discreet when taking prisoners out on a Production Order, to avoid other prisoners finding out. The slightest whiff that one might be a grass, and life inside could be extremely unpleasant and dangerous.

The reason given in this instance was that Gareth Dupont was going to show the police addresses of other domestic burglaries he had done in and around Sussex, in the hope of leniency on that part of his sentence. Even so, rather than collecting him from the prison, he had first been transferred to the custody block behind Sussex House.

'I'd prefer not to be in there in the first place.'

'Your choice,' Grace said. 'Right?'

Batchelor drove down to the electric gate and waited while it slid open.

'I didn't hurt the old lady. I didn't have any part in that.'

'So what part did you have, Gareth?'

He held up his handcuffed arms in front of him. 'Any

chance you could remove these? I'm not going to try to escape.'

'That's very big of you,' Grace said. 'Let's see how co-operative you are, and we might do even better than that – perhaps get you a decent meal?' He raised his eyebrows.

Dupont visibly perked up at that. 'What about prison – can you get me a better cell?'

'One with a sunken bathtub? I think the one with the four-poster bed's already been taken.'

'Haha. I'm sharing with a moron who stinks, and snores like a hog. But like, he really stinks, know what I mean? He's disgusting.'

'I'll see what I can do, but I'm not making any promises – I don't have the authority to. But if you are helpful to us, I'll speak to the Governor. So, what takes your fancy for lunch?'

'Any chance of a Big Mac?'

'With fries and a Coke?'

'Don't get my hopes up.'

'Happy to get you all of those, Gareth, if you're helpful to us.'

They headed along the A27, then up the hill and turned off onto Dyke Road Avenue, a wide road running along the spine of Brighton and Hove, lined on both sides with some of the city's most expensive houses, although some had long been converted into nursing homes. A short distance along they pulled over, outside wrought-iron gates; a large red-brick house sat well back, with a Bentley and a Ferrari in the drive.

'Recognize this place?' Grace asked.

Dupont shook his head.

'It was burgled three years ago. A large haul of paintings

and Georgian silver. No one's ever been apprehended. One of yours?'

'No.'

'You're sure? It'll be better for you to admit other offences before your trial; the judge will be more lenient that way. Otherwise you could find more time being added to your sentence.'

'I don't think anyone can add much time to a life sentence. No, I never burgled this place. And, look, I didn't play any part in hurting the old lady. You have to believe me.'

'Why do I have to believe you?'

'Because – oh shit.' He sighed. 'Those arseholes didn't need to torture her. I already had the safe code, and I knew about the dummy door at the back of it.'

'You knew about the Patek Philippe watch that was in it?'

'Yes.'

'Really? Who from?'

'I can't tell you; he'd kill me.'

'*He?* Are you sure it wasn't *she?*'

'It was *he*,' he said, adamantly. His eyes told Grace he was telling the truth.

Grace nodded at DS Batchelor to drive on, then turned back to Dupont. 'So it's entirely coincidence you were – are – having an affair with Lucas Daly's wife, and then you were involved with burgling her husband's aunt's house?'

Dupont shrugged. 'I might have picked her brains on a few things.'

'Did you specifically target her, or was meeting her just a lucky coincidence?'

'Know one of the things I believe in?' the prisoner responded. 'Serendipity. Sometimes in life you get lucky.'

Batchelor turned right, down tree-lined Tongdean Road, which was even more exclusive than Dyke Road Avenue. Some of the houses were concealed behind walls and shrubbery. They passed one with white columns, the proportions of an ancient Greek temple, then turned left into Tongdean Avenue, considered by many to be the city's most exclusive street. Batchelor steered around three learner drivers in a row practising reversing, then pulled over to the right and halted in front of another gated mansion that, like all the homes on this side of the road, had magnificent views south across Hove to the English Channel.

'How about this place?' Grace quizzed. 'Four years ago the owners were attacked by two masked men, at midnight, as they waited for the gates to open. They were tied up and threatened with a cigarette lighter until they gave the safe code and their bank pin codes.'

Dupont shook his head. 'No, not me, sorry.'

'Think harder,' Grace said. 'Oh, by the way, I do have one more bit of bad news for you.'

'Yeah?'

'My officers have found the Luton van that you rented from a company in Ipswich. I imagine you thought renting from far away would give you a better chance, right?'

Dupont said nothing.

'SOCO found fingerprints of you and your mates Macario and Barnes in there. You're not coming out for fifteen to twenty years. So, just a friendly word of warning, don't piss us about. Shall we make a deal?'

'What deal?'

'We're ten minutes, max, from the nearest McDonald's. Where is the stuff you stole from Aileen McWhirter, and who hired you? Wasn't by any chance someone called Eamonn Pollock?'

'I thought our deal was I didn't talk about the case without my brief. I thought you were taking me around burglary sites.'

'You don't have to talk about it, and we don't have to get you a Big Mac. We can drive you straight back to prison, if you'd prefer?'

'I'm vulnerable in prison,' he said. 'I know that. I'd like a burger, but I'm not grassing anyone up. So if that's your plan, you might as well drive me straight back.'

Grace's phone rang. He raised a finger at him, then answered. It was Norman Potting.

'All good on the Costa del Sol?' he enquired.

'*Costa del Crime*, chief,' he chuckled. 'I have a couple of things to report. Firstly, the post-mortems on Ken Barnes and Anthony Macario. Both men died from drowning, with excessive alcohol consumption a probable cause – their overturned dinghy supports this. However, the Coroner here's unhappy about the men's physical injuries – it looks like they might have been in a fairly brutal fight prior to drowning. But there were no disturbances reported that night to the police and, significantly, none of the people on any of the neighbouring yachts, or in the apartments over-looking the harbour, heard or saw anything. The Guardia Civil have been brought in to investigate more thoroughly and that's where it stands, for the moment.'

'Okay. Thanks, Norman. What is the second thing?'

'The local police had all the outgoing passenger lists for the past week from Malaga Airport checked and Eamonn Pollock's name popped up.'

'Flying where?'

'Last Thursday, August the 30th, domestic from Malaga to Madrid. He must have stayed overnight in Madrid, then on August the 31st he boarded an international flight to New York.'

Grace was conscious of Dupont behind him listening to every word. He stepped out of the car, closed the door and walked a few paces along the street. A blustery wind was blowing. 'Brilliant work, Norman. We need to find out where he's staying in New York. I remember when I went over last year you have to give that information to the airline before you board.'

'I have it, chief,' Potting replied, sounding smugger than ever. 'The Ritz Carlton, five-zero Central Park South.'

'Top man!'

Grace ended the call, his brain spinning. His tip-off from Donny Loncrane in Lewes Prison had been Eamonn Pollock. Just over a week after the robbery, Eamonn Pollock flew to New York. A week after that, Peregrine Stuart-Simmonds reports a Patek Philippe, matching the description of the one stolen, being hawked around New York dealers. Then his phone rang again.

It was DC Exton in MIR-1. 'Boss, I've got a result for you on Gavin Daly. You asked us to find out what flight he was booked on today – it's a British Airways, to New York, JFK, leaving at 1.50 p.m.'

Grace looked at his watch. One hour and twenty minutes. 'Good work, Jon,' he said.

Grace climbed back into the car and turned to Gareth Dupont. 'What was it you said earlier? About serendipity? Sometimes in life you get lucky?'

Dupont nodded.

'Yep, well, you're right. Sometimes in life you get lucky.'

'Does that mean I get my burger?'

'Sorry about that; change of plans. We'll get one on the way back, but I'm going to have to return you to prison right away. I'm afraid it's not your lucky day, Gareth; it's mine.'

82

so – about that chase earlier. We'll go one of the very back, but I'm going . . . to return with vengeance away I'm about it's not your fault . . . but it's is a bitch.

Shortly after 1 p.m. Roy Grace and Guy Batchelor pulled up outside Lucas Daly and Sarah Courteney's house in Shirley Drive. He told Batchelor to wait in the car, then walked up to the front door and rang the bell.

She answered, moments later, casually dressed in jeans and a T-shirt, and blushed when she saw him. 'Detective Superintendent, good afternoon.' She smiled pleasantly.

'I've just been to the shop and I'm told that Lucas is away for the weekend. Playing golf again, is he?'

She looked edgy, but her eyes were steady, telling the truth. 'No. He – ' She hesitated. 'Actually he's had to go away on business.'

'New York, by any chance?'

She again looked hesitant. 'Yes.'

'I need to speak to him rather urgently. Do you know where he's staying?'

Her eyes were still telling the truth. 'I don't, no. He said he would call me when he was there. It was all a bit sudden, actually. Would you like to come in?'

He entered and she closed the front door behind him. 'Can I get you a cup of tea, coffee?'

'I'm fine,' he said. 'Thank you.'

She was a really beautiful woman. What the hell had she been doing sleeping with a total scumbag like Gareth Dupont? Maybe anything was a relief from her bully of a husband. 'Does he go to New York regularly?'

'No. Well – ' Suddenly she looked awkward, and her

eyes were all over the place. 'His father – my father-in-law – has contacts all over the world. Occasionally there are important auctions that he goes to abroad, either to buy or sell pieces. Or pieces he goes to view to possibly buy.'

'Is that what he's doing in New York?'

'As I understand. He doesn't tell me much about his business. We lead pretty separate lives.' She gave him a knowing look. 'As I think you might have noticed.'

This time it was Grace's turn to blush. 'I'm not here in judgement of your private life.'

'Thank you,' she said.

83

Every time Roy Grace entered the grand Queen Anne building, which housed the senior brass at the Sussex Police headquarters complex in Lewes, the county town of East Sussex, he felt himself regressing to childhood. He was once again a small, nervous boy in the headmaster's study.

ACC Peter Rigg, his boss, was a dapper man, with a healthy complexion, fair hair neatly and conservatively cut, and a posh, occasionally caustic, voice. Although several inches shorter than Grace, Rigg had fine posture, with a military bearing which made him seem taller than his actual height. He was dressed in a well-cut dark suit with a striped shirt and what looked to Grace like a club or old-school tie. His office was decorated with framed motor-racing pictures, a passion which Grace shared, and which had given them something in common to talk about in more relaxed circumstances. On his desk sat a photograph of his attractive, blonde wife, Nikki, whom Grace had met recently at a function, and two children, a boy and a girl.

'Thank you for seeing me at such short notice, sir,' Grace said.

'I'm hoping you have more good news,' the ACC said, waspishly. 'Well done on potting Dupont. So, tell me.'

'Well, sir, in the past few hours there have been a number of developments, all of which point to New York. I need to take a team over there urgently, because I don't think I can influence things effectively from here.'

Grace explained the developments of the day so far.

To his surprise, instead of a lecture on police budget cuts, Peter Rigg said, 'Have you thought about how many of your team you need to take with you?'

'I'd like to take a minimum of two, sir: ideally a skipper and a DC. I have a good contact in the NYPD, who is already briefed, but I don't know what to expect there, and I don't want to be dependent on anyone else.'

'Your man Branson seems very adaptable.'

'He has major problems because his wife has just died. But yes, he's a good man. I'd like to take DC Exton – he's an exceptionally intelligent officer, sir.'

'When do you want to go?'

'The first possible flight. There's availability tomorrow.'

'I'll speak to the Chief,' he said. 'But in principle, I'm with you on this, Roy. Just come back with a result, and I think in the current climate of cuts, best not to let the press know.'

'I don't want the press to know in any event, sir. I need the element of surprise over there.'

'Two other things. I know you've had previous experience in the USA, but don't take any independent action without the full knowledge of the New York Police – which I know you won't. And also, I'm up for a Deputy Chief Constable appointment, so don't do anything to embarrass me, okay?'

Grace grinned. 'Good luck with that, sir. And don't worry, my role in New York will be purely liaison.'

'Good luck to you too, Roy.'

Grace had a heavy heart as he walked back to his car. He really did not want to go; he wanted to be at home to help and support Cleo, and he wanted to be with his son. Every time he left the house he missed Noah. The thought of spending several days away from him made him unhappy. But he really could not see any option.

84

His next-door neighbours were arguing! And the baby was crying.

He loved it!

But what Amis Smallbone loved most of all was the news Detective Superintendent Roy Grace had brought home to his beloved Cleo.

'Roy, do you really have to go?'

'I do. I'm the one who has the relationship with the NYPD and we really need their help on this.'

'I really need your help here. Surely with your whole merged Surrey and Sussex Major Crime Branch you have someone else who could take your place?'

Sitting in the big armchair on the top floor of his new house, smoking a cigarette and drinking whisky, Smallbone heard the words through his Bose headset. Detective Superintendent Roy Grace was flying to America tomorrow, at 11.30 a.m. Leaving his beloved Cleo Morey behind. And their son, Noah.

Uh oh.

Not smart. Not smart at all. So many options dancing around in his brain. Disfigure Cleo Morey with acid. Kill the horrid little baby, Noah, who was crying now. Kill Cleo. Kill the baby. Break the little bastard's spine and paralyze it for life.

Then watch Roy Grace wheeling around his little cripple.

So many options. He was spoiled for choice, really he

was. He listened intently over the sound of the little bastard baby screaming.

'*Cleo, darling, you have to understand. It's me who has the relationship with the NYPD, with Detective Pat Lanigan – his help is going to be crucial to this.*'

'*Does he know you have a two-month-old baby?*'

'*I'll only be a few days, I promise.*'

'*I know you. You'll be at least a week. And then probably another week. I understand your work is important, Roy, but you being around to help me with Noah is important too.*'

'*What about getting your mother or your sister to stay with you?*'

'*I can ask my mother, but we'll probably start killing each other after a few days. Charlie's away in Shanghai on her new job.*'

'*Cleo, this is a really important case for me. If I send someone else and they screw up, I'm never going to forgive myself. Come on, you know the score.*'

'*Why can't you send Glenn? He's deputized for you before.*'

'*Because his wife is being buried on Wednesday, okay?*'

Another long silence. The baby was silent, too. Then Cleo spoke again.

'*Who are you taking with you?*'

'*Well, I wanted to take Jon Exton. But the idiot's passport ran out in May. So I'm taking DS Batchelor, and a sharp new recruit on the team, DC Alexander. I'll make it up to you when I'm back, I promise.*'

Oh yes, you will, Amis Smallbone thought. You're going to be making it up to her by buying a beautiful coffin for your son. And I will be there at the funeral, standing a short distance behind you with a smile on my face. So you will know, Detective Superintendent Grace. You will know who made you suffer. You will remember me for the rest of your life.

He crushed out his cigarette, lit another, adjusted the volume level on his headphones with shaking hands, and continued to enjoy the show.

85

As they had cleared immigration at New Jersey's Newark Liberty International airport, Roy Grace had texted Cleo. **Landed! XX**

Then he had phoned the Incident Room and spoken to DC Alec Davies, who gave him an update over the past few hours Grace had been out of contact, but there was nothing significant to report.

Now DS Guy Batchelor and DC Jack Alexander both had their suitcases loaded on their trolleys. Roy Grace, feeling increasingly glum, watched several unclaimed bags make their fourth, or maybe fifth, or perhaps their sixth circuit of the carousel. He held his phone in front of him, waiting equally forlornly for a text back. He was missing Cleo and Noah already, badly.

Then the carousel stopped.

'Shit!' he said.

'Happened to Lena and me last year,' Guy Batchelor said. 'We went on holiday to Turkey. Didn't get my suitcase for three days.'

'Thanks, Guy,' he said. 'That's cheered me up no end.' It was 5 p.m. New York time, 10 p.m. in England. The three of them had sat side by side on the flight, discussing strategy for some time, before relaxing after their meal. Guy Batchelor and Jack Alexander had put on their headsets and watched a movie, but Grace had been too wired to watch a film or sleep. Instead he had been feeling bad about leaving

Cleo, which was distracting him from focusing on the task ahead. Now he felt ragged.

Wearily he trudged over to the British Airways baggage office, joined a short queue, then presented his baggage stub. The man behind the desk tapped the details into his computer then gave him the news he really did not want to hear. 'Sorry, it's not showing up.'

'Terrific.'

His phone pinged with an incoming text. **Great! Now get the next flight home. Noah and I are missing you. X**

No sodding suitcase, he texted back.

Ha! Poetic justice! XX

He grinned and texted, **Call you when I get to hotel. Love you. XXXXXX**

Moments later he got a reply. **Love you too, but I don't know why. XXXXXXXX**

'The best thing would be, sir, if you phoned us around 8 p.m. after the next UK flight has come in.'

'Actually,' Roy Grace said, 'the best thing would be if you phoned me and told me you had my sodding suitcase.'

*

Roy Grace's mood, already lifted by Cleo's text, improved further as the trio entered the arrivals hall and he saw the smiling figure of Detective Pat Lanigan.

Lanigan was a tall, imposing character in his mid-fifties, with broad shoulders and a powerful physique. He had a ruggedly good-looking, pockmarked face, a greying brush-cut, and was wearing a checked sports jacket over a polo shirt, jeans and workman's boots. He was the kind of cop few people would choose to pick a fight with. He greeted Grace with a bear hug, then looking at his attaché case quizzed him on why he was travelling so light.

'Don't ask!' Grace responded, introducing him to his colleagues.

'I'll go sort them out, don't you worry!' he said in his nasally Brooklyn accent. Pulling out his police badge, Lanigan strode in through the exit doors and was gone ten minutes. He emerged with a triumphant smile. 'It'll be at your hotel by ten o'clock.'

'You're a star!' Grace was instantly feeling more confident about his mission.

'Not a problem. I just explained to the baggage guy, the Chief of Police of England doesn't want to have his bag lost. Sorted.' He pinched Roy Grace's face.

'How's Francene?' Grace asked.

'Francene's great! If we get time, she'd love to see you. So, you're a daddy now! Hey, you, congratulations!'

Roy Grace had always sworn he would never be one of those fathers who carried pictures of their babies in their wallets, but he dug his hand into his jacket pocket, and proudly drew out a photograph of Noah and showed it to the New Yorker.

'He's a good-looking fella! Going to be a tough guy, like his dad, I'd say. Can see a lot of you in him!'

Guy Batchelor and Jack Alexander looked at the photograph, too, and Roy Grace felt a sudden, intense moment of pride. His child, his and Cleo's! Their son! He was a part of him, that tiny little pudgy-faced character they were all looking at.

*

Pat Lanigan's private car, a Honda sports utility, was parked right outside, with an ON NYPD BUSINESS card displayed in the windscreen.

Five minutes later they were on the freeway heading

towards Manhattan. 'Figured you guys would like an early night. We'll start in earnest tomorrow, 9 a.m. at my office. Anything you need, you tell me. I've got the antiques experts from the Major Case Squad working the streets. They have sources in New York City from auction houses and confidential informants. I've also got a detective coming along who's not assigned to this squad, but has connections in this field. Keith Johnson, you'll like him.'

Addressing the two detectives in the back, he asked, 'Either of you been to New York?'

'Yes, several times,' Guy Batchelor said. 'My wife was in the travel business.'

'Never,' Jack Alexander said. 'If there's a chance, I'd love to go to Abercrombie and Fitch.'

Grace thought about getting something for Cleo. They'd recently watched the movie *Breakfast at Tiffany's* on television – and he wondered now if there would be anything in that store he could afford.

'We'll make time,' Lanigan said. 'This is a great city, know what I'm saying? Beautiful people. We'll get these bastards, and maybe we'll have time for fun too. First thing on my list to tell you, Roy: we checked out the hotel addresses put down on the immigration forms by Eamonn Pollock, Gavin Daly and Lucas Daly. None of them showed up at those hotels.

'There's a bunch of different ways of searching for a hotel – or *hotels* – the suspects might be staying in. We've checked the US customs forms for all three. They've all given false addresses. But they'll have used credit cards on check-in. I'm having my team check to see if the details are merely held on the hotel records until check-out or if they are put through. If they are put through, then we'll find them that way.'

'And if not?'

'Plan B.'

'Which is?'

'These are wealthy guys, right, Daly and Pollock? They won't be staying in some shithole. We'll start with all the five-star hotels in Manhattan and work our way through them.'

'Makes sense.'

'Okay, so we'll get you checked in. I've booked you into the Hyatt Grand Central, which is a good location for you. Then I was going to take you to Mickey Mantle's – remember it, Roy?'

'You took me there last time I was here, I remember. He was a big baseball star.'

'You guys would have liked it. Great food – simple, nothing fancy; great burgers, great everything – but it's closed. But I know a great Italian. You guys like pasta?'

'Sounds like a plan,' Grace said.

86

Amis Smallbone had a plan, too. It was 10.30 p.m. Earlier in the day he had watched Roy Grace kiss his beloved Cleo goodbye on their doorstep, then walk across the courtyard with his suitcase, and let himself out through the gate. It was a fine, sunny day, and around midday, Cleo had taken their baby out in his pushchair, returning mid-afternoon.

Apart from a brief break at midday to go downstairs into the kitchen and microwave a steak pie and some frozen peas for his dinner, he'd sat up here in his chair, behind the net curtains, watching the courtyard and the front door of the Grace house.

Shortly after 4 p.m. a smartly dressed and quite handsome woman in her mid-fifties had arrived at the house. Cleo's mother. *Mummy*, she had called her. *Mummy* had stayed for two hours. *Mummy* said she would return tomorrow morning at 10 a.m. with *Daddy*, and they would take Cleo and Noah out, looking at houses in the country.

Which meant the house would be empty for several hours. Perfect. He might pop over and take a look around, although, from the plans, he already knew the layout of the place.

He poured himself another whisky and lit another cigarette. *Noah Grace. What was your daddy planning to teach you about life?*

He remembered his own father, Morris. Not with affection, but with respect. His one abiding memory was from when he was a small child; he could not remember his age, exactly, maybe six or seven. His father had stood him on the kitchen table, then blindfolded him and told him to jump into his arms.

Amis had stood there, petrified, swaying, for some moments. His father had urged him, 'Jump, Amis. Just tumble forward into my arms. I'll catch you.'

Finally he had let himself go. His father had not caught him, but had stood, several paces back, with his hands in his pockets. Amis Smallbone's face had smacked so hard onto the kitchen floor he had broken two teeth and his nose.

Then his father had removed the blindfold, dabbing his face with a cloth. 'Let that be a lesson to you, son. Never trust anyone in life, not even your own father.'

Smallbone had never forgotten that moment. His mother standing there, lamely watching. Cowed and bullied by his father into silent acceptance of all that he did to his children in the name of *toughening them up.*

When he was fourteen, his father made him accompany him on his rounds as a debt collector. Knocking on doors of shitty dwellings, opened by tearful women or scared men. Sending them scurrying off into back rooms, scuffling around under mattresses, shaking banknotes and coins out of mugs, tea caddies, pleading. *Scum,* his father told him. *Vermin. Liars, all of them. You have to do what's right. What's right is to collect what's yours. Life isn't going to give it to you; you have to take it. They'll give you every excuse in the world.* 'Me husband's off work, sick'; 'Me husband's lost his job'; 'I've not been able to work because me child's sick'.

Sometimes, Amis Smallbone felt sorry for one of the terrified people. But when he told his father, he would slap him hard on the face and glare at him.

They make me sick, Amis. Understand? They'll prey on

weakness. Show them sympathy and they'll have you twisted round their little fingers. Understand, because if you don't, they're going to shit all over you and ruin your life.

Amis understood. By the time he was eighteen, he was doing rent collection rounds on his own. Accompanied by a barber's razor that he kept in his pocket, and produced at any excuse, on scumbag women as much as scumbag men. Occasionally he would just slash, for the hell of it, to see the crimson ribbons on their cheeks. As he got bolder, he would knock on the door with the razor in his hand, blade open. *Crimson ribbon or your rent?* he would offer.

Maybe a crimson ribbon on Noah Grace's face would be nice, he thought. The little bastard's crying had kept him awake a lot during this past night. How would it be for Cleo to go running up to his cot and find blood everywhere?

How about a slit from the edge of his mouth up to his ears, on each side? It was what other prisoners did to rapists, inside. Depending what prison you were in, it was called *the Glasgow Grin*, or *the Chelsea Smile* or, simply, *the Rapist's Grin*.

He liked that. The Grace baby branded for life as the most vile of all human life forms.

The more he thought about that, the more he liked it. Much better and much simpler than killing Noah.

He toasted himself. It was a great idea.

Genius!

87

Wide awake at 6 a.m. on a New York Sunday morning, Roy Grace rang Cleo. Her mood was subdued; she was with her parents, in their car, heading off to the first of four houses in the countryside, close to Brighton, that looked good on the estate agents' particulars. Noah, she told him, had driven her demented all night.

'I'm sorry, darling,' he said.

'Yes,' she replied flatly.

'Call you later in the day,' he said. 'Love you.'

'You too.'

He pulled on his running kit, took the lift down from his eleventh-floor room, then went out onto 42nd Street and turned right. The early morning air felt fresh and cool. The city felt huge and daunting. Bigger than he remembered. The buildings rising like canyon walls on either side of him. He crossed two sets of lights, then made another right and headed up Fifth Avenue towards Central Park. He ran past smart men's and women's clothes displays in the store windows. Past a street cleaner, brushes swirling, water spraying. On the left he saw the Abercrombie & Fitch store that Jack Alexander had mentioned last night.

He ran on past the Apple Store Cube, breathing in the early morning smell of horses along Central Park South. Ignoring the lights, he crossed the deserted street, and ran on up the uneven paving of the Fifth Avenue sidewalk, looking for an entrance into the park itself.

All the time he was thinking hard. The Patek Philippe

watch was here. Eamonn Pollock was here. Gavin and Lucas Daly were also here.

The Daly family should be working with the police, but they weren't. He felt sympathy for Gavin. He liked the old man. He had always had a soft spot for life's survivors, and there was nothing Daly had done, in all his ninety-five years, that had attracted the attention of the police. He was less certain about his son; a rotten apple for sure. He could still see, in his mind, the bruises on Sarah Courteney's chest.

But it was Eamonn Pollock who worried him the most. Gavin Daly had not lied to him and travelled to New York, aged ninety-five, simply to retrieve an old family heirloom, regardless of its value. If he had just wanted it back, surely he would have given Grace's team all the information he had.

There was another reason.

Another reason why he'd had Ricky Moore tortured. Why two of the burglary team had been found dead in Marbella.

Another reason why Gavin Daly and his son had travelled, in a hurry, to New York.

There had to be.

And he had a feeling he knew what it was.

He ran past the Central Park pond, then headed on, threading his way along the pathways, towards the huge, circular Jacqueline Onassis reservoir, determined, as he had tried to do on a couple of past visits, to run right around the gravel track of its circumference without stopping.

Thinking all the time.

And getting increasingly worried about the task in front of him.

That the watch was merely a sideshow. And the true reason for Gavin Daly's journey here was revenge. The settling of a very old score.

88

At 6.30 a.m. Gavin Daly lay in his fourteenth-storey hotel room, propped up against the pillow, as he had been since 2.15 a.m. when he had woken, and had been unable to sleep again. He could not get the air-conditioning right, so half the night he had been too hot; now he was too cold, and there was a constant tick-tick-tick sound accompanying the air-con every time it cycled.

All the time, his brain had been spinning. He was back in the city of his birth. Back in a place that still, in so many ways, felt like home to him. Back to fulfil a tearful promise he had made all those years ago, on the stern of the *Mauretania*.

A memory as vivid in his mind now as it had been then. And the words just as clear.

One day, Pop, I'm going to come back and find you. I'm going to rescue you from wherever you are.

He ordered English Breakfast tea from room service, with milk, not cream. After he had hung up he remembered how weak they served tea here, phoned down again and asked for an extra teabag. Then he closed his eyes again.

He had woken thinking with deep sadness about his second wife, Ruth, and realized he had been crying in his dream. She was still so vivid in his mind. Some people said that all people only ever really love once in their lives, and he wasn't sure that was true. There had been a time, so many years back, when he had loved Sinead, really loved her. Until the day, ten years into their marriage, when the private detective's photographs showed her startled face, in a bed in some hotel room with her lover, another antiques dealer in the city. It had taken him a long time after that to trust any woman again – many years. Then he had met Ruth, with her red hair and freckles, and the loveliest smile he had seen in all his life.

He could feel her in his arms now. He had loved to stand behind her, holding her slender body tightly, their cheeks pressed together, her hair tickling his face, feeling intoxicated by her scent and by his love for her. She was the most precious gift in all the world. The most precious gift he had ever known since his father. But, it turned out, the poor darling did not have the gift of health.

Firstly she was diagnosed with ovarian cancer; then a few years after her hysterectomy, the cancer came back. Everywhere. He tried specialists around the world. Jetted her in private planes to hospitals and clinics in America, Switzerland, Thailand, to any doctor he could find good words about. But it didn't make one bloody bit of difference.

Money could buy you comfort and luxury, but it couldn't buy you the only thing in the world of real value, which was health. It couldn't buy you a cure. It was ironic, he thought. He was lying in this big bed, in this big suite, with enough money stacked away, in banks, in stocks, in properties, to do almost anything he wanted and to buy almost anything he wanted, and it meant absolutely nothing. Except, right now, just one thing.

His chest pains came shooting back, suddenly, like a firework burning inside his chest. He reached out to the vial beside the bed for a nitroglycerin pill. A few minutes later, as the pain subsided, the doorbell rang.

He climbed out of bed and stood for a moment, in his pyjamas, feeling stiff, shaky, old. Very old. Too old. His eyes were tired. Using his stick because he did not trust his legs or his balance, he let the waiter in, waited for him to set the tea down, signed the bill and tipped him a bunch of dollar bills.

Then he padded over to the huge window and opened the curtains. The view was straight out across Central Park. It promised to be a fine day, just like the little card that had been left on his pillow last night predicted. A light mist hung over the trees. He saw a man, the size of an ant from here, jogging. Keeping healthy.

Gavin had never had truck with exercise. It was all in the genes, he believed. Ruth had been a health fanatic – all salads and fish and just the occasional glass of wine at celebrations; yoga every day; tennis; cycling. But she hadn't made old bones. At least he had outlived the bitch Sinead. And he would go to his grave knowing she wasn't around to dance on it. Although bloody Lucas would be.

And he did not like that thought.

He fiddled with the air-conditioning control, wrestled his way into a bathrobe, turned his attention to the huge parcel with the FedEx label and the customs stamp, addressed in his own handwriting to a New York antique watch and clock dealer. It had been brought to him at the hotel last night by its recipient, Jordan Rochester, another very old friend in this city. Rochester had kindly booked the room in his own name, and used his credit card. Gavin Daly did not want anyone finding him in New York. And particularly not Detective Superintendent Grace, or any of his New York Police Department associates. Not until he had finished his business here.

As a precaution, he hung the DO NOT DISTURB sign outside the door and engaged the security lock. Then he put the teabags into the pot, and while he waited for them to steep, he removed his tools from his suitcase, and began to open the package.

Ten minutes later, he took a sip of his tea, then gently lifted the Ingraham chiming mantel clock from its nest of shredded paper, which lay inside the polystyrene outer casing he had fashioned for it a fortnight ago.

Carefully he removed the round, brass gong from inside the clock's casing. Then even more carefully still, he opened up the two halves of the gong.

And smiled for the first time since his plane had landed.

89

The yellow cab was crossing the Brooklyn Bridge. It was a fine, cloudless morning; Roy Grace, squashed in the cramped rear alongside Jack Alexander and Guy Batchelor, stared out at the sparkling water of the East River. He was all too mindful that it had been less than a mile from here where the horrors of the 9/11 World Trade Center attack had taken place – and that Pat Lanigan had lost a cousin in it.

A short time later the driver, who spoke only mumbling English, pulled over. Grace recognized, from his last visit here, the Brooklyn police HQ office building, housing the Mafia-busting team to which Lanigan was currently assigned. To their left, across the street, was a square slab of a building with a yellow sign on which was written BARCLAY SCHOOL SUPPLIES, and in front of it was an open elevator-system car park that looked like a giant Meccano construction.

They clambered out, paid the driver, then entered the modern skyscraper, and gave their names to the security guard. A couple of minutes later, holding their visitor passes, they waited as the lift stopped on the tenth floor.

Pat Lanigan, wearing a yellow polo shirt, cream chinos and trainers, greeted them cheerily; Grace was relieved, from past experiences with Lanigan, that he'd chosen to dress casually today, as had his two colleagues.

The detective led them through a door with an NYPD shield and combination lock, and along a labyrinth of carpeted corridors, through an open-plan office full of empty cubicles with high-sided partitions. Each little space had a clean waste bin with a neat bin bag and clinically tidy desk. They passed a Stars and Stripes flag with the wording FLAG OF HONOR pinned to a wall, followed by a black and white map of Brooklyn, gridded and numbered, and all the other boroughs of New York beyond it.

Then they passed a wall chart, on which was a family tree, headed COLOMBO CRIME FAMILY – PERSICO FACTION. Beneath were interconnected boxes headed BOSS, ACTING BOSS, CONSIGLIERE, CAPOREGIME, SOLDIERS OF INTEREST, ASSOCIATES OF INTEREST. Grace stared at it intently for some moments, then followed his colleagues into Lanigan's office.

It was laid out in a similar manner to his own, Grace noted. There was a round conference table, a small, cluttered desk laden with piles of documents, a mug full of pens, as well as his computer keyboard, screen, car keys, a photograph of his wife, and a trio of flags. On the wall above it was a photograph of the aircraft carrier on which Lanigan had served in the US Navy, and several group photographs of himself and fellow ratings, and a large, colourful banner proclaiming in bold lettering, **DEFENDING FREEDOM.**

Lanigan sat them down at the table, and offered them coffee. A few minutes later they were joined by the three detectives he had organized for them today, all, to Roy's dismay, dressed sharply in business attire.

Detective Specialist Keith Johnson, a solidly built man in his late-forties, with a trim beard and moustache, and a no-nonsense air about him, wore a beige suit and a dark-brown tie. Detective Linda Blankson, who Grace put in her late-thirties, had Latino looks and a catwalk figure, with sleek brown hair framing a severe but not unattractive face.

She was power-dressed in a black trouser suit and white blouse, and concentrating on typing out a text or email on her phone.

The least amicable of the three was Detective Lieutenant Aaron Cobb, in his mid-thirties, with close-cropped hair brushed forward that reminded Grace of the actor Ryan Gosling. He shook hands cursorily with each of the British detectives, then sat down at the table, chewing gum, with the resigned air of a man who was less than happy about being here on a Sunday morning.

Lanigan began the meeting by asking Roy Grace to detail the history of the circumstances that had brought him and his colleagues over here. When Grace had finished, Detective Lieutenant Cobb asked the first question, in a voice that was even more deeply Brooklyn than Lanigan's.

'We're very happy to help you out but why do you guys need to be here?' He stared pointedly at Grace, chewing his gum hard. 'Like, you've given us the information. Feels to me you don't trust us to do the job.' He dug his finger into his right ear and began an excavation of its interior.

'That's not the case at all, Detective Lieutenant,' Grace said. 'We're here to advise and assist you, and I think we may have information helpful to you.' Although Lanigan was the eldest, he was unsure from the way US detectives did their rankings who was the most senior officer here.

'I don't see it.' Cobb looked down at his notes. 'Eamonn Pollock, Gavin Daly, Lucas Daly. We have their descriptions. We'll find 'em.'

Grace caught Pat Lanigan's eye and saw his apologetic look. 'Pollock is the only one who is an actual suspect at this point, with respect, Detective Lieutenant,' Grace said. 'I believe Gavin Daly and his son Lucas are here with criminal intent. Their motives and their relationship are all very complex. In my view we should be here to help you to understand what is likely to happen. We need to tread carefully if we want to arrest them.'

'Sir, out of interest, why do you think we could not do that by ourselves?' asked Detective Specialist Keith Johnson. He spoke with a strong, clear Midwestern voice.

'I'm not saying you couldn't,' Grace replied. 'But in my opinion there is much more going on than simply the recovery of a stolen watch, and the arresting of the perpetrators. I have a hunch about what is going to happen.'

'I'm intrigued!' said Detective Linda Blankson, abruptly but pleasantly.

'So where do we start?' Keith Johnson asked.

'By finding Eamonn Pollock, Gavin Daly and Lucas Daly,' Grace replied. 'Without them knowing.'

90

Sunday lunch. He could smell it cooking somewhere, in one of the neighbouring houses. That's what most people would be having now, Amis Smallbone thought, bitterly. 1.30 on a Sunday. Families sitting down to a roast. He'd done that every Sunday of his childhood. Roast beef or pork or lamb or chicken. He'd maintained the tradition until he got married to Christine – Chrissie. What a bitch.

He drank some more whisky, feeling a little drunk, but not in a pleasant way. Building up Dutch courage too early in the day.

He and Chrissie, Tom and Megan. That was how it had been, once. She'd been a good cook, Chrissie. He'd give her that, but she was crap in bed. Always blaming him. Taunting him about his manhood. She hadn't minded it when they'd first started shagging – told him she liked it; didn't like men with big dicks because they hurt her. In their divorce she'd got custody of the kids, and buggered off to Australia with them. Melbourne. Maybe he shouldn't have hit her all those times, but she'd deserved it. And screw it, what did it matter now?

What did it matter he hadn't seen or heard from his kids for over twenty years? Good sodding luck to them.

After Chrissie, a long, long time after, he'd met Theresa. The true love of his life. What they had between them was something very special indeed. He'd proposed to her, telling her he wanted to spend the rest of his life with her, start a new family with her, and she'd accepted. They were all set to be married. The church booked, everything sorted, the invitations printed. Finally, he was in a place where he was happy again.

Then Detective Roy Grace had come along. And screwed it all up for him. For *them*. On the morning of the wedding. 5 a.m. A dawn raid.

He'd pleaded with Roy Grace to just let the wedding go ahead and then do what he had to, but did the bastard listen?

No.

Grace had chosen the day of his arrest for maximum humiliation, Amis Smallbone was certain. He could have done it days earlier. Or later. But no, he had chosen his moment very deliberately. And he had not let him make a phone call. So there was Theresa, all excited that morning, having her hair done, getting into her dress, then driving to the Brighton Registry Office. Where Roy Grace let her wait for her groom who wasn't going to turn up because he was in a sodding cell in Brighton nick with no phone. They eventually got married in jail, but that wasn't the point.

Today had been a long time coming. A long time in the planning. The little shit Gareth Dupont had been arrested and charged, and would be grassing him up to get a reduced sentence for himself, for sure. So it was only a matter of time before he'd be back inside. If you committed a crime while you were out on licence, then your licence was automatically revoked; he'd be going back down for another ten years, minimum. But at least this time he would take Roy Grace down with him. The knowledge of Roy Grace's grief would sustain him in the shitholes that faced him now and into old age.

Draining his glass, he stood up unsteadily and left the top-floor room with its view of the courtyard and the front door of the Grace house, and went out onto the landing. He picked up the hooked stick and flailed around with it until he managed to hook the hoop in the loft door. Then he pulled the door down, and hooked the bottom rung of the metal loft ladder, lowering it carefully, until its feet touched the landing carpet.

Then he climbed up it. At the top he reached out and found the light switch. Moments later the two weak bulbs lit up the roof space. Steeply angled wooden beams. Yellow insulating foam, sprinkled with rat and mouse droppings, between the rafters. The water tank. Spiders' webs. An old, empty suitcase covered in dust. He hauled himself up onto his knees, breathing in the dry, dusty smells of wood and the insulating material. Then, supporting himself against the beams with his hands, he trod carefully on the rafters, making his way with some difficulty, because of all he had drunk, towards the roof hatch.

He pushed against it, and moments later, light and fresh air flooded in. He squeezed through the rectangular space and stepped out onto the narrow metal fire escape. It gave him a view across the rooftops down towards the pier and the English Channel. But more importantly to him, it gave him direct access to the Grace house.

What made him less happy was there was just one low, flimsy-looking handrail on one side. This group of seven town houses had been a conversion from a U-shaped warehouse building, and they shared a continuous pitched roof, with a fire escape running the full length of it. The gridded metal of the escape, clearly constructed as an afterthought, zig-zagged across the rooftops between the chimney stacks. To reach the Grace house, he had to navigate a difficult left turn, ducking under a thoughtlessly installed satellite television dish that obstructed his route.

He succeeded and then reached the identical loft hatch to his own. Conscious that he was standing up here, in broad daylight, he looked around carefully, checking who might be able to see him. None of the immediate neighbours, but there were some tall buildings, mostly office blocks, that overlooked them, if anyone happened to be staring out of the window. That was unlikely during a Sunday lunchtime, but not worth taking the risk.

When he did this for real, it would be dark; some ambient glow from the street lighting, but not much. He had to rehearse his steps now, count and memorize the number of steps to each turn, particularly the awkward left by the satellite dish. The important thing would be not to hurry.

Roy Grace would still be in New York. Cleo and the little bastard would be home alone. And he would have all the time in the world!

Amis Smallbone was unaware of one pair of eyes that were watching him, up here on the rooftop. Watching him with the intention of killing him.

91

Keith Barent Johnson, Roy Grace read, as the detective showed his NYPD badge to the front-desk receptionist at the Plaza on Central Park South.

The young Asian woman spent some moments checking her computer records, then shook her head. 'Eamonn Pollock? How do you spell it?'

Johnson spelled it out. 'E a m o n n P o l l o c k.'

She checked again. 'No, we don't have him registered here, sir.'

Grace then showed her a photograph of Pollock. 'This is about twenty years ago, but does he look familiar?'

'No, I'm sorry. No, he does not; not to me, anyways. Can I make a copy and I'll show it to my co-workers?'

'Sure, thank you,' Grace said, handing her the photograph. Then the two detectives repeated the process for Gavin Daly and for Lucas Daly, with equal lack of success.

Roy Grace looked at his watch: 11.15 a.m. He and Johnson had been working through hotels for the past hour and a half, as had Guy Batchelor and Jack Alexander with the other two New York detectives. There was always the possibility that Pollock and the Dalys were staying with friends rather than in a hotel, which would make their current task impossible. But they had to just keep plodding on.

They walked on up Central Park South, past horse-drawn carriages, endless rickshaws and guys standing in their way with bicycle rental placards, and entered the Marriott Essex House Hotel.

Grace and Keith Johnson waited in line at the front desk. They watched a sweaty young couple return bikes to the porter's desk, then a porter wheel a trolley laden with bags into a room behind it.

'Mr Pollock?' the pleasant receptionist said, after studying Keith Johnson's NYPD card. She tapped into her computer terminal. Then, after a few moments, shook her head.

Roy Grace leaned forward and showed her the old photograph he had of the man. She studied it, then shook her head again. Then she turned to her tall, thin colleague and showed him the photograph.

He frowned. 'Yes, I know this man. He is staying here.'

'Eamonn Pollock?' Roy Grace quizzed. 'Is that his name?'

He tapped his keyboard, frowning, then looked back at Grace. 'Dr Alvarez? Dr Alphonse Alvarez?'

'What address did he give you when he registered?'

He looked down at his screen again. 'University College of Los Angeles, Brentwood, California.'

Grace tapped Eamonn Pollock's photograph. 'But you're sure that's him?'

'Oh yes, I'm sure.'

92

How great was this? Perfect or what? Amis Smallbone stared through the net curtains at the darkness beyond the window, and the falling rain. The wind was picking up; he could hear it howling. Which meant it would be hard for anyone to hear him. Not many people would be out on an evening like this, and certainly not hanging around staring up at the rooftops of buildings. But even if they were, they would not see anything.

Not by the time he had finished his preparations.

It was 10 p.m. Mummy and Daddy Cleo had dropped their precious daughter and their super-precious little bastard grandson home five hours ago. Cleo had made them tea, and they'd then discussed the houses they'd seen in the country. There was one they'd all agreed they liked, close to the village of Henfield. But it was more than the Graces had planned on paying.

Mummy and Daddy Cleo had offered to help them. How sweet was that? Would they still help them out if their precious grandson no longer looked so sweet? If the little bastard had scars all over his face?

His bags were packed. By the time anyone came looking for him he would be long gone, down to sunny Spain with the remainder of his meagre stash, and intending to collect from that fat pig Eamonn Pollock what he was owed. Then he'd live it up for however long he had before the law caught up with him. Lawrence Powell owed him a favour; he'd help him out, get him sorted with a new identity. With luck he'd have a few years of freedom, and then he'd be so old he wouldn't care any more. Old age was a prison, so it didn't much matter whether you spent the rest of your time in it or out of it. And at least they took care of you inside.

And he would have one thing to sustain him through those years. The knowledge of what Detective Superintendent Roy Grace would be thinking every time he looked at his son's hideously scarred face.

He delved into one of the cartons of stuff he had bought over the Internet, and pulled out the black jumpsuit; from another, he removed the night-vision goggles and the hunting knife, its blade as sharp as a razor. Then he opened the tin of black boot polish and, using a rag, began to smear it carefully across his face, until all that could be seen was the white of his eyes.

And the hatred burning in them.

*

Out in the street below, Cassandra Jones, a website designer who lived directly opposite Cleo Morey's house in the development, dismounted her Specialized hybrid bike, after returning from a Sunday night stand-up comedy event at Brighton's Komedia Club, followed by a few glasses of wine afterwards with some friends.

She wheeled it up to the entrance, head bowed against the wind and driving rain, feeling a little bit tipsy. Then she tapped in the code, pushed open the gate and, unquestioning, thanked the stranger standing right behind her, who held it open while she wheeled her bike through.

The gate clanged shut on its springs, harshly striking the rear wheel of her bike.

'Sorry,' the tall man behind her said.

93

Eamonn Pollock, his obese body wrapped in a towelling dressing gown, lay back against the plump pillows on his huge, soft bed in his sumptuous hotel suite. He'd enjoyed a painful but invigoratingly glorious deep-tissue massage and was now sipping a glass of Bollinger, toasting himself, toasting his cleverness.

But not feeling quite as contented as he normally did.

He was not at all happy that he had lost his two *lieutenants*, as he liked to call them, Tony Macario and Ken Barnes. Not happy at all. Trustworthy employees were hard to come by, no matter how much he paid them, and he had paid them very handsomely indeed.

Still, he consoled himself, he had much to look forward to. He'd just said goodnight to the lovely Luiza, a twenty-four-year-old Brazilian pole dancer who he could scarcely wait to see again, in just a few days' time. And to bury his face between her breasts! He was in his mid-sixties, but life was still full of delicious treats. How nice it was to be rich. But nicer still to be even richer tomorrow!

But right now he was looking forward to his supper. He had ordered himself a meal from the room service menu. Beluga caviar, followed by grilled lobster and then a naughty key-lime pie, something he always treated himself to in this city. And besides, Luiza had told him she loved his tummy.

And he loved what she could do with her tongue! The thought of it was making him randy.

Later he might phone for a lady from a particularly fine

agency he knew. Or maybe he might just watch a film and go to sleep, ready for a very busy and profitable day ahead. Oh yes, very profitable indeed!

He picked up the Patek Philippe pocket watch from its nest of cotton wool on his bedside table, and cradled it in his soft, pudgy hands. He stared at the metal casing, which, despite a couple of dents, still looked as new as it must have done back when it was made. Too bad about the damage: the bent crown and winding arbor, and cracked crystal that pressed against the tapered black moon hands, stopped at five minutes past four, as they had been for ninety years, and the tiny, motionless double-sunk seconds hand.

For some moments he studied the moon-phase indicator. Then he read the exquisitely written name on the dial. *Patek Philippe, Geneve.*

He was holding a piece of history.

And something, suddenly, made perfect sense to him. His uncle had not taken it from Brendan Daly moments before he, and the other three, had murdered him, and sent it to little Gavin out of guilt. He had sent it because of destiny! It was meant to be! He had sent it on a journey, ninety years into the future, into the hands of his nephew who had not yet been born.

Yes, destiny!

The doorbell pinged. 'Coming!' he called out, like an excited kid. 'Coming! Coming, coming, coming!'

He swung his heavy frame off the bed, slipped his feet – which Luiza liked to kiss; especially his toes, despite the fact that one had been amputated because of his diabetes – into the white hotel slippers. Then he trotted through into the lounge area and across to the door. He checked the spyhole and was happy to see it was the same cheery little waiter who had brought him up the bottle of champagne earlier. He removed the safety chain and opened the door.

'Good evening, Dr Alvarez, how are you?'

'Very contented indeed, thank you!' *Dr Alvarez!* Dr Alphonse Alvarez was one of the several aliases that he used. *Dr Alvarez* was his favourite. He liked it when the hotel staff called him Doctor. Classy. Hey, he was a classy guy!

He held the door, as the waiter stuck a wedge beneath it, then trundled in the food-laden metal trolley. 'You like me to set this up for you, Dr Alvarez, on the table?'

'I would indeed!' Pollock left the waiter and moved through into the bedroom to fetch a tip from his wallet, his mood greatly improved now that his dinner was here, and humming to himself his favourite Dr Hook song. *'Please don't misunderstand me! I've got all this money, and I'm a pretty ugly guy!'*

And he did indeed have it all. And tomorrow, he would have even more. Two million pounds, minimum! How nice! How very, very, very nice!

Hey ho!

In the next-door room he heard the clatter of crockery and cutlery as the waiter laid the table. He was salivating. What a feast! There were flashing red lights on the television. Police cars. Some big incident on the local news. A shooting in the Bronx. Didn't bother him, hey ho.

He trotted back out into the lounge area, holding a twenty-dollar bill between his finger and thumb, like a laboratory specimen he was presenting for inspection. He liked to make sure waiters saw what a very generous man he was, in case they simply shoved the tip into their pockets without noticing it.

Then as he entered the lounge, he froze in his tracks.

The twenty-dollar note fluttered down onto the carpet.

The waiter held the room service bill, in a leather wallet, up for him to sign, with a pen in his other hand.

But Eamonn Pollock did not even notice him. He was staring at the man on the far side of the room, dressed in a thin leather jacket, jeans and black Chelsea boots, who was lounging back on the sofa, removing a cigarette from a pack.

His beady eyes shot to the waiter then back to the man. He scribbled his name, like an automaton, on the bill, noticed the waiter hesitating, but just wanted him out, now.

'Have a good evening, Doctor,' the waiter said, with a forced smile, and lingered.

'Just fuck off, will you,' Pollock said.

The startled waiter removed the wedge from the door and left, closing the door a little too hard behind him.

The man on the sofa lit his cigarette.

'This is a no-smoking room,' Pollock said. 'And what the hell are you doing here?'

'You know why I'm here, you fat jerk. I want to know why your gorillas killed my aunt. And you did a runner with the watch . . . Did you really think I wouldn't find you?'

'Killing your aunt was not part of the plan. That was never meant to happen. And there's a five-hundred-dollar fine for smoking in this room,' Pollock said. 'Put that out or I'm going to call Security.'

'Yeah, why don't you? Ask for those two cops who are standing in the lobby by the elevators.'

Pollock's face blanched. 'What cops?'

94

Roy Grace was nervous. He did not like being out of control, and that was how he felt right now. Although he had a lot of faith in Pat Lanigan, and two of his team, Keith Johnson and Linda Blankson, seemed very helpful and competent, Detective Lieutenant Aaron Cobb had continued to give the impression, at their late-afternoon review meeting, that he considered the presence of the Brits here unnecessary. Cobb was a loose cannon, and in his own manor Grace could deal with someone like him; but here, as a guest in another country, all he could do was to try to win him over – and that was not happening. Further, it was clear that in the pecking order, Aaron Cobb was the senior of the NYPD detectives.

Surveillance had been placed on Eamonn Pollock's hotel, but when Grace questioned Cobb about having only two officers covering the building, he was curtly told that was all the manpower he had available.

By 6 p.m. there had still been no trace of Gavin or Lucas Daly. Door-to-door enquiries on all New York hotels were continuing into the night but, as Aaron Cobb suggested, the old man in particular was probably tired and needed time out to be fresh for the morning.

Guy Batchelor announced to Roy Grace that what he needed, more than time out, was a cigarette and a stiff drink – and that he knew a place in New York where he could get both.

The three Sussex policemen walked the fourteen blocks

from their hotel to the Carnegie Club on 56th Street. On the way Grace called Cleo. It was late in Brighton, and she was sounding sleepy, but pleased to hear from him. Noah was fine, she reported, and he'd been good all day and was now asleep. But, and she was really excited to tell him this, she had seen a house that she loved – and her parents had really liked it too. It was slightly above their price range, but her parents had offered to help them, if they wanted to buy it. The estate agents were going to email the particulars to her in the morning, and she'd send them on to him. It was a cottage, with an acre of land, and surrounded by farmland. 'And,' she added in her excitement, 'there was a hen run!'

Grace, for reasons he could not explain, had always had a desire to own chickens. He had been born and brought up a townie, in Brighton, but there was something that appealed to him about going out in the morning and collecting his own eggs for breakfast. But, more seriously, from the tone of her voice, he knew Cleo had found the house she wanted to live in, and that really excited him.

'Can't wait to see it!' he replied.

'You'll love it, I promise!'

'Is there anyone else interested?'

'The agents said there is a young couple going back for a second viewing on Tuesday. When do you think you might be back?'

'I don't know, darling. Later this week, I hope.'

'Please try!'

'I'm missing you both like crazy! Give Noah a kiss and tell him his daddy is missing him.'

'I will!'

He ended the call, then looked at his watch again. He had been expecting to hear from Peregrine Stuart-Simmonds, to find out which dealers were expecting

Eamonn Pollock in the morning, but it was too late now. It wasn't good news that the man hadn't called.

Five minutes later, as they entered the front door of the club, into the rich aroma of cigar smoke, Roy Grace felt instant nostalgia. This was how bars used to smell, and he loved it. There was a long bar, with two men seated on stools, drinks in front of them, smoking large cigars, watching a ball game on a gigantic television screen. All around the room, which had the air of a gentleman's club, were leather sofas and chairs, some occupied by people smoking cigars or cigarettes, some vacant.

A cheery, attractive waitress, who gave Jack Alexander a particularly flirty smile, showed them to a corner table, then fetched them the drinks menu. Grace glanced at it, and decided on a Manhattan, a drink he had got smashed on one night with Pat Lanigan, last time he was here. He was starting to feel a little frayed from jet lag, so what the hell? It would either slay him or fire him up.

Then Grace's phone rang. It was the antiques expert. 'Detective Superintendent Grace, I hope this is not a bad time?' Peregrine Stuart-Simmonds said. 'Apologies for calling so late, but I've been waiting for information for you. It seems as if Eamonn Pollock is messing everyone around in New York.'

'In what way?' Grace asked.

'He has not confirmed any of his appointments. Which means I can't tell you where he might be going. There's always a possibility he's already disposed of the watch to a private buyer.'

'Great,' Grace said grimly. As soon as he ended the call he rang Pat Lanigan.

'We know he's in his hotel room right now,' Lanigan said. 'We could go in and bust him right there.'

'But if he doesn't have the watch there, we've got nothing on him. We can't be sure he has it with him – I don't think I'd entrust something of that value to a hotel safe – I think I'd put it in a bank safety deposit box.'

'Good point,' the detective said. 'What do you want us to do, Roy?'

'We'll have to follow him in the morning – I'd be grateful if you could give us everything you can to ensure we don't lose him.'

'I'll speak to Aaron Cobb right away.'

That did not fill Roy Grace with confidence. His drink arrived and he bummed a cigarette off Guy Batchelor, feeling badly in need of one suddenly. It was the first he had smoked in several weeks, and it tasted every damned bit as good as ever.

95

Noah was crying. Amis Smallbone, listening on his headphones, looked at his watch: 11.30 p.m. The little bastard had settled into a routine. It would cry, then its mummy would come with her soothing voice, and there would be twenty minutes of breast-feeding sounds. Followed by three hours of quiet, broken only by the occasional gurgle.

Mummy sounded tired; exhausted. Within minutes of finishing and putting him back in his cot, she would go back to bed and fall asleep.

And he would be ready.

Rain was lashing down and the wind was still rising. It was like an autumn-equinox gale out there, not a late summer's night, and that could not have suited his purposes better.

His clothes and equipment were laid out. His night-vision goggles were okay, but didn't give him as much clarity as he had hoped, so he was taking a small torch, in order to see to carry out his handiwork; but that was the only time he intended to switch it on.

He studied the floor plans of the Grace house one more time. Apart from one closet in a different place, the interior was a mirror image of this house he was in now. He had googled several websites to try to see how blind people coped in unfamiliar territory, and he had practised moving around in here, in darkness, every night for the past week. He had done one final practice this evening.

The unknown factors would be pieces of furniture that

he might bump into, something left on the floor he might tread on, and the dog, but the goggles should pick those up.

And the dog should not be a problem.

Mummy'd let the dog out onto the little terrace, where it shat and pissed every night. And tonight it had greedily gobbled up the shin of beef, stuffed with enough powdered barbiturate to knock out a horse, which he had dropped from the fire escape in front of its nose. He had done the same last night, too, as a test, but without the barbiturates. The dog had loved it, wolfed it all down, and then looked up at him wanting more.

It was a simple and effective way of neutralizing guard dogs, and he'd done it plenty of times before in his younger days. Just as he'd broken into numerous buildings in the past, and almost always at night, in the dark.

He removed his clothes, completely, until he stood naked. Then he put on a one-piece body-stocking, leaving only his head exposed, which would reduce the chances of him dropping any skin cells or body hairs for DNA. Over that he pulled on a thin black polo neck, black tracksuit bottoms and a black hooded top. Then he stretched a black Lycra swimming cap over his scalp, pulling it down over his ears and the back of his head, trapping all his hairs, and then pulled black neoprene windsurfer boots onto his feet.

Next he clipped on a webbing belt, threaded through the hoops of a zipped nylon pouch which contained his tools: a glass cutter and suction cup; lock-picks; screwdriver; chisel; small hammer and some small but extremely strong levers; a small roll of masking tape; bottle of chloroform and a small cotton wool pad. His intended route into the Grace house was through the house's roof hatch, but as yet he had no idea how it was secured. If the fixings were the same as his own, it would be a doddle, but he thought it very likely that Grace, with his policeman's mind, might have fitted something more robust. If that proved the case, at least with his kit he had plenty of options.

One final item lay on the floor: a barber's razor he had recently bought for this purpose. No better tool had ever been invented. He put that in the pouch, carefully checked the rest of the tools, then zipped it shut and went into the bathroom to check his appearance.

He could barely recognize himself in the mirror. A black face with panda eyes stared back at him. He grinned. *Oh yes, very good, very good indeed.*

He returned to his post, poured himself a whisky for some Dutch courage and lit a final cigarette. He looked at his watch again: 11.50 p.m. He picked up the headset and listened. It sounded as if the feeding was coming to an end.

He smoked the cigarette right down to the filter. It was now five minutes to midnight. He crushed it out in the ashtray, drained the last drop of the whisky, stood up and said to himself, 'Rock'n'roll!'

As he began climbing up the loft ladder he thought, for an instant, that he heard a sound downstairs, and felt a flash of panic.

The wind, just the wind, that's all, he reassured himself, then reaching out and gripping a wooden support, he hauled himself off the top of the ladder and into the loft.

Downstairs, the front door closed silently.

96

It felt strange that Roy was not here, Cleo thought, as she lay in bed looking at the pictures and details of the cottage in the estate agent's brochure. She loved it; despite its dilapidated state it had such a warm, friendly feeling.

She hoped so much that Roy would feel the same way, and she could not wait to take him to see it. It needed everything doing, but that was why it was almost in their price bracket. It was set a safe distance away from the main road, and backed onto farmland, with glorious views across the valley to the hills of the South Downs. It was the perfect place to raise Noah, and it would be paradise for Humphrey.

She put the brochure down on the bedside table, worrying about that couple who were going back for a second viewing. She wished Roy could hurry home. And not just so he could see the house. This was the first time since they had brought Noah home that they had been apart, and she missed him badly.

Feeling totally exhausted, she closed her eyes, but she was unable to sleep. The television was on, the sound turned low, just for company. An old episode of *Frasier*, which always made her smile, was playing. She picked up the third volume of the *Fifty Shades* trilogy and turned to her bookmarked place, but after only a few lines, she realized she was too tired to read and put it down, then drank some water.

Then she looked at the baby monitor to make sure it was on. She turned the volume up high for some moments so she could hear Noah's breathing. Reassured, she turned it down a little.

She ought to be studying for her Open University degree. Several philosophy textbooks lay piled up on her bedside table, but she had no appetite for any of them at the moment.

The wind was still howling outside and she could feel a draught on her face, through the window pane. Out in the distance she heard a siren wailing mournfully. She didn't really know why, but she felt on edge tonight. Nervous of the sounds of the wind. Nervous for her child. Nervous for their future. Something she had read a few days ago, that Sophocles wrote, suddenly rang true. *To the man who is afraid, everything rustles.*

And yes, tonight, everything was rustling.

She shivered. Cold enough to swap over to the winter duvet. But it was still only early September. Humphrey, who normally slept in his basket down in the kitchen, was asleep on the floor at the end of the bed, and she hadn't the heart to push him out of the room. He suddenly began snoring, loud, deep snores, and for a moment she smiled. He sounded like Roy when he'd had too much to drink.

She closed her eyes. God, she had such huge responsibilities. They told you that your life would change when you had a baby, but they didn't tell you that it was quite such damned hard work, nor that you would be permanently scared of something happening to your child. Her health visitor had reassured her, on her six-week check, that this was quite normal, and so had all her friends who'd had babies whom she had spoken to. But equally, no one had ever been able to tell her the depth of love she would feel every time she looked at Noah, and every time she held him in her arms.

But was he ever making her nipples sore!

Something scudded in the wind across the courtyard below. It sounded like a plastic bag blown loose. She thought about the case Roy was working on. The poor old woman who had been tortured in her home by burglars. What kind of world had Noah been born into? The world was a violent place; it always had been and it seemed it always would be. At least, she thought, both she and Noah were lucky in one respect. Roy always made her feel safe, and he'd always make sure Noah was safe, too.

She turned up the volume on the television slightly. Frasier was trying to get rid of his brother for the night because he had a hot date with his old school prom queen, who was now a middle-aged vamp.

She smiled, feeling a little better.

97

Roy Grace ate the Maraschino cherry, drained the last of his second Manhattan, then stubbed out his second cigarette. The men at the bar, smoking their cigars, continued to be absorbed in the ball game on the large television screen. Guy Batchelor and Jack Alexander were having an animated conversation about Brighton and Hove Albion's prospects for the new football season, while Grace sat, silently immersed in his thoughts, trying to study the estate agent's particulars on their website on his iPhone.

He was missing Cleo and Noah, but it was now half past midnight in England – much too late to call again. And he was concerned about tomorrow. ACC Rigg had made a big leap of faith sanctioning this trip, and they had to deliver. But the fact that Eamonn Pollock had put a false address on his immigration forms was a clear indicator that he was in this city for an illicit purpose. Maybe he should go to the hotel where they knew he was staying, and join the guard. But he had to get some sleep, otherwise he would be useless tomorrow. The best thing he could do, he thought, was get a bite to eat, have an early night and head over there first thing in the morning.

Guy Batchelor waved the waitress over and told her they wanted another round, but Roy Grace intervened. 'Just the – um – check, please,' he said, firmly. Then he turned to his colleagues. 'You might not thank me now, but you will thank me at six o'clock tomorrow morning.'

'Six o'clock?' Batchelor said, looking horrified.

'That's when we're starting. Still want another drink?'

'Maybe not.'

98

Amis Smallbone pushed open the heavy roof hatch. Instantly, he felt the savage wind, hurling rain as hard as grit against his face. Later today he'd be in Spain, in the sunshine, out of all this shit weather. He lowered his goggles over his eyes and the night turned bottle green.

He climbed out, slowly and carefully, onto the narrow metal platform. All around him the wind screamed. He could see the ambient glow of Brighton's street lighting, a vivid green haze. Steadying himself, he once again rehearsed in his mind the short journey ahead to the Grace house. Fourteen paces along the three-foot-wide metal fire escape, with a single handrail to the right for support. Then the dog-leg left, ducking to avoid the satellite dish. Eight more paces and he would be alongside the Grace house roof hatch.

And then, if all went well, he would be in their loft.

In their house.

In their baby's face. Right in it. Making it smile for the rest of its life!

A strong gust buffeted him and he waited for it to pass, gripping the handrail, so much looking forward to what lay ahead. A dream come true. A dream that had been more than twelve long years in gestation. Now he was just paces away from his quarry. From ruining Roy Grace's life. Just as the bastard had ruined his. An eye for an eye, a tooth for a tooth. A baby with a rapist's grin. For the whole of its life!

He took a few steps forward, gripping the handrail and looking around him. Looking down at the deserted courtyard. Looking over the rooftops at night-time Brighton. Well past midnight now, most people asleep in bed.

The metal beneath him was vibrating, as if someone else was walking on it too. He turned his head, but it was hard to see behind him. He continued walking.

Thirteen paces. Twelve. Eleven. Ten. Nine, he counted. His vision through these goggles was less good than he'd thought when he had tried them out. He could see straight ahead, but had virtually no peripheral vision. He glanced round once more, but still his view was restricted. Then he focused dead ahead, continuing to count the paces, to be absolutely sure.

Eight. Seven. Six.

A hand gripped his shoulder, as hard as a steel pincer.

For an instant his brain froze. He turned, saw a hulk of a figure with a balaclava over its face. He squirmed in panic, somehow tore himself free and threw himself forward, feeling the metal gridding vibrating beneath his feet.

Almost instantly, something smashed into the side of his face, like a southpaw's punch.

The fucking satellite dish. He reeled, dazed. His left foot suddenly found only air. He windmilled his arms, the wind pushing him sideways. He tried, desperately, to find the grid again with his left foot, crying out in terror. Then he fell, head first. Struck something hard and wet and slippery. He clawed at the roof slates with his gloved hands. He saw the courtyard looming towards him; he was sliding; slithering. Down a steep slope, face forward. The cobbles were getting bigger.

Bigger.

Racing towards him.

He jammed his hands even harder against the wet roof slates, screaming, trying to get a purchase.

Bigger still.

Then he was falling through air.

99

Cleo frowned. The screen had suddenly gone fuzzy, just as Frasier was about to enter the school reunion with the beautiful former prom queen on his arm. She grabbed the remote and stabbed at a different channel number.

Just then she heard a slithering, scraping noise right above her head. It sounded like a horse tobogganing down her roof. A slate, she thought, blown free by the wind. Then she heard a thud, like a sack of potatoes dropped from a height. For a moment she was tempted to get out of bed and see what it was. But she was cold, and it would be even colder out of bed. And really, it was probably just a roof slate; she would check it out in the morning.

Above the howl of the maelstrom she heard a faint noise, a whisper carried by the wind; maybe it was just her imagination. It sounded like someone had just said, '*Sorry*.'

100

Cassandra Jones hated Monday mornings. And today was a particularly bad one. She had a piercing hangover from the wine she had drunk last night, and she had an important early morning meeting in London with a new client. Why the hell had she had that fourth glass? What, she wondered, was that strange logic alcohol instilled in your brain that insisted you would feel better the next day if you had yet another glass of wine, instead of politely declining, or having a glass of water instead?

She showered, dressed, drank a glass of Emergen-C vitamin booster and forced down a bowl of porridge, then opened her front door and wheeled out her bicycle for the short ride to the station. At least the storm that had raged all night had died, and it was a fine late summer – or early autumnal, depending on your perspective – day.

She closed her front door behind her, then noticed the huddled, contorted figure lying on the cobblestones a short distance in front of her. For an instant she felt a flash of indignant anger. What the hell was one of Brighton's drunk street people doing in here, in this private courtyard?

Then, as she wheeled her bike nearer, she saw the dark stain that lay around the figure's head. The crimson colour of blood.

She stopped in horror at the totally bizarre sight. A small man, dressed in black, with streaks of black mingled with congealed blood on his face. A black bathing cap lay a short distance from him, and a strange-looking pair of goggles were around his chin. Was he some kind of a Peeping Tom?

She dropped her bike, her eyes darting around the houses. Where had he come from? Had anyone else seen him? Then she took several steps closer, trying to remember a First Aid training course she had done a few years ago. But when she got a clearer view of his face, she saw the top of his forehead was split open, like a coconut, and a brown-grey mass had leaked from it, along with the blood. His eyes stared ahead, sightless, like eyes on a fishmonger's slab.

Shaking, she swung her backpack off her shoulders, pulled her mobile phone out of it and stabbed out 999.

101

Roy Grace had set his alarm for 5 a.m., but he need not have bothered. He woke at 3 a.m., feeling totally alert. It was 8 a.m. in the UK, where he would have been up for two hours at this point, and probably completed a run of at least three miles.

Cleo was probably awake, and he was tempted to call her. But in case she was sleeping after a feed, he decided to leave it a while. And, he knew, he needed to try to sleep some more, and get rested before what was likely to be a long and hard day ahead.

He swapped his pillows around and lay back. But after a few minutes, he turned onto his right side. Then his left. Then onto his back again. He was fretting about Eamonn Pollock giving them the slip. He was convinced the man was the key, and that at some point he would have the watch in his possession. And then they would have him.

Detective Aaron Cobb worried him increasingly, and he did not want to leave things to him. He wanted to get to Pollock's hotel himself and find all the possible exit routes – because he was damned sure that Pollock had already established them. With so much at stake, it was highly unlikely the man would be taking any risks.

There was no going back to sleep; he was totally awake, his brain racing. Grace slipped out of bed, showered then shaved. Then he scanned his thirty or so new emails, but there was nothing of any significance. A couple related to the autumn fixtures of the Police Rugby Club, which he ran, and another to a refresher course on Cognitive Suspect Interviewing at Slaugham Manor, the police training and conference centre in Sussex.

He pulled on a T-shirt, tracksuit and trainers, zipped his hotel room card into a pocket, then took the elevator down, emerging into the deserted lobby. A solitary figure stood behind the reception desk, and a tall black security guard, wearing a coiled earpiece, gave him a solemn nod.

He strode along 42nd Street in the darkness for some while, then broke into a jog, turned right and headed up towards Central Park. The traffic was light; just an occasional car or taxi drove past. The sidewalks were deserted. He did not bother stopping at red lights, but just carried on crossing street after street, until he reached the Plaza, where he turned left.

A few minutes later he reached the front entrance of the Marriott Essex House Hotel. He carried on past it, turned left on Seventh Avenue, then left again onto 56th Street and stopped when he reached the rear entrance to the hotel. He tried the door, and to his slight surprise, it opened. He walked down a long corridor, lined with window displays of expensive-looking clothes and jewellery, then reached a bank of elevators.

An alert man-mountain stood guard, eyeing him with curiosity. Next to him, seated on chairs and both fast asleep, were two uniformed cops.

Quietly, not wanting to wake them, Grace showed the guard his UK police warrant card. 'These guys on watch for Eamonn Pollock, suite 1406?'

'Yeah.' He grinned. 'Not much stamina, right?'

Grace raised his iPhone, took a photograph of them, then emailed it to Pat Lanigan with a terse note.

'How many entrances and exits do you have here?' he asked the security guard.

'Two this floor. Two down below. Then we have the fire escapes.' He thought for a moment, then said, 'Six of them.'

Ten exits, Grace thought. Two cops covering them – both of whom were asleep. How great was that?

'Can you show me them?' he asked.

'Sorry, boss, not allowed to leave this station.'

'Mind if I help myself?'

'Be my guest.'

102

Back in his hotel room, shortly after 4 a.m., Roy Grace suddenly felt dog-tired. He undressed and climbed back into bed, and set his alarm for half an hour's time. Almost instantly he fell asleep, only to be woken, what seemed like seconds later, by his phone ringing.

It was Glenn Branson. 'Yo, old timer, you awake?'

'I wasn't but I am now. What's happening?' he said, checking the time. It was 4.20 a.m; 9.20 a.m. in Brighton, he calculated.

'Quite a lot while you've been zizzing away.'

'Tell me.'

'Well, I can't be sure, but it looks like someone might have been trying to break into your house last night.'

'Which house?'

'Cleo's.'

Grace sat bolt upright, fear surging through him. 'What do you mean? What happened?'

'I'm standing outside the house right now. We've got a dead body – looks like he fell from the roof. Got his face blackened; he's all kitted out in black, with night-vision goggles, and a whole set of house-breaking tools on him.' Glenn deliberately omitted the barber's razor, not wanting to worry his friend further.

Grace felt sudden deep dread grip him. 'Is Cleo okay? Have you checked on her and Noah?'

'They're fine.'

'Fell from the roof? Do you have an ID on him?'

'Not yet. He's not carrying a wallet or any other ID.'

'He's definitely dead?'

'Certified by the paramedic. The Coroner's Officer's just arrived.'

'Why do you think he might have been trying to break in, Glenn?'

'He's six feet in front of her house. If he isn't a burglar, then he's come from a fancy-dress party dressed as one.'

'I need to speak to Cleo,' Grace said. 'I'll bell you back.'

His finger shaking, he dialled Cleo's house phone, but it was busy. He tried her mobile but that went straight to voicemail. He redialled the house number and finally she answered, sounding terrible.

'I was trying to call you,' she said. 'It must have been the noise I heard last night – when the television went all fuzzy – someone sliding down the roof. What was he doing up there on our roof, Roy? What the hell was someone doing on our roof?'

His phone was beeping. *Caller waiting* was flashing on his display. 'Darling, hold one sec, okay? I'm just putting you on hold, in case this is urgent.'

It was Glenn Branson. 'Roy, the Coroner's Officer, Philip Keay, says he recognizes the dead man from some years back. I'm not sure you're going to like this much – it's Amis Smallbone.'

Sitting on the edge of his bed, the news was almost surreal. It took a moment for it to sink in. 'Amis Smallbone? Is he sure?'

'Yes, absolutely certain.'

'I'll call you back in a minute.' He switched to Cleo. 'I'm coming straight home – as soon as I can get a flight, darling. I won't be able to get one until this evening – the earliest I'll get back is tomorrow morning. But I'm putting a police officer in the house with you until I'm back. I'll get a Family Liaison Officer.'

'Please come back quickly,' she said, her voice cracking.

'I love you, darling,' he said. 'You're fine, you and Noah. But I don't want you leaving the house until I get back and find out what's going on, okay?'

He could barely decipher her reply through her sobbing. And he was shaking himself. Just what the hell had the little shit been up to?

103

Roy Grace sat on the edge of his bed, shivering from the air-con, his face in his hands, thinking. Amis Smallbone with house-breaking kit. There was no alternative scenario, no other possible hypothesis. Smallbone had been there to break into the house. Period. The unanswered question was, what had he planned to do?

Harm Cleo or Noah, or both? He thought back to the vile, chilling words carved with a chisel on Cleo's car, back in June: *COPPER'S TART. UR BABY IS NEXT.* Smallbone had vigorously denied it was his handiwork. That had been followed by an obituary notice placed anonymously in the *Argus*, shortly after Noah had been born. The person who had done that had still not been identified, but Grace had a pretty shrewd idea it was Amis Smallbone who had been responsible for both.

Did he have an accomplice? Grace thought that unlikely. If Smallbone had wanted something taken from the house, he would have hired someone to do that. No. Whatever he'd planned, he had intended doing it himself. And now he was dead. One less piece of vermin on this planet. He doubted many people would be mourning him. A nasty, futile, squandered gift of life.

His phone pinged with an incoming text. He looked at the display and saw it was from Pat Lanigan.

They're awake now, pal, with pepper up their asses!

He grinned, then phoned Glenn Branson back. 'Has anyone checked Cleo's house for signs of forced entry?'

'We've done that and it's all secure.'

'She's very shaken, Glenn. Can you get someone to stay with her?'

'I'm on it. I'm organizing an FLO to be with her until you get back.'

'Thanks. I thought you weren't going to be at work today – isn't Ari's funeral this week? Wednesday?'

'I wasn't, then I saw the address of the incident on the serial and I came over. I have Ari's sister staying at the house to help with the kids, so it's okay.'

'I really appreciate it. Thanks, matey.'

'I'll phone you with any updates. How's it going there?'

'For half four on a Monday morning, quite lively, so far,' Grace said, wryly. He gave him a quick update, ended the call, then immediately phoned Tony Case, the Senior Support Officer, who was responsible for travel arrangements. He explained the circumstances and asked Case if he could get him an emergency ticket home.

'Hmm, that's going to cost,' Tony Case said. A former police officer himself, he could be a bit of a curmudgeon. 'I got you all a good deal on return tickets, but they're non-refundable.'

'I'll pay it out of my own pocket.'

That seemed to cheer Case a little. 'Well, leave it with me, Roy. May not be necessary. You're on your mobile?'

'Yes.'

'Give me half an hour or so.'

With no interest in – or prospect of – any more sleep, he ordered a pot of coffee, then stepped into the hard, hot jets of the shower, making a mental note to check with Cleo that she had arranged for flowers to be sent to Ari Branson's funeral.

*

Twenty minutes later, invigorated from the shower and from his second cup of coffee, Roy Grace checked his emails. But there were no further updates so far regarding Cleo's house, beyond the information Glenn Branson had already given him.

It was 5.10 a.m. His eyes felt tired, but his brain was wired. In three-quarters of an hour he was due to meet Guy Batchelor and Jack Alexander down in the lobby, and then head up to Central Park South and Eamonn Pollock's hotel.

He called MIR-1 and asked Bella Moy for an update. There were no significant developments, she told him. Then as he ended the call, Glenn Branson rang again.

'You're not going to like this at all,' he said.

'I'm not liking it already!' Grace replied.

104

'I thought in our last session you were going to talk more about the father of your son,' Dr Eberstark said. 'You told me you were having an affair with one of your husband's work colleagues. Do you believe this man is the father?'

'I don't know,' Sandy said.

'And how do you feel about that? About not knowing?'

She was silent for some moments, then she shrugged. 'It's difficult. I'm not sure if I would prefer to know that Roy is Bruno's father, or that he isn't.'

'And if he is, do you not think he has a right to know?'

'I thought I was paying you to help me, not to interrogate me.'

The psychiatrist smiled. 'You keep so much inside you, Sandy. Do you not know that expression, *The truth will set you free*?'

'So how do you suppose I will find the truth? I can hardly ask Roy, or the man I had the affair with, to send me samples for DNA testing.'

'In my experience, most women know,' he said. 'You are a very instinctive person. What do your instincts tell you?'

'Can we change the subject?'

'Why does it make you so uncomfortable to talk about it?'

'Because . . .' She shrugged again, and lapsed into silence.

After several minutes, Dr Eberstark asked, 'Did you

think any more about the house in Brighton that you are planning to buy?'

'It's in *Hove*, actually.'

'Hove?'

'I guess the equivalent here would be Schwabing.'

'A smart area?'

'There used to be a big snobbery between Brighton and Hove residents. Brighton was brash and racy; Hove was more sedate and genteel.'

'Ah.'

There was another long silence.

Dr Eberstark, after checking his watch and seeing they only had a few minutes left, prompted her. 'So, the house in *Hove*, did you make any decision?'

She said nothing, and stared at him with an expression he could not read.

*

As Sandy left the front door of Dr Eberstark's building, and stepped onto the pavement of Widenmayerstrasse, she stopped, staring at the wide, grass bank of the Isar river across the busy street, collecting her thoughts. She had lied to the psychiatrist. She did know who the real father was.

As the traffic roared past in front of her, she wondered whether it was time, finally, to tell Roy about her son. *Their* son. She knew now, for sure, that he was the father. On her visit to the house, two months ago, when she had been taken round by the estate agent, she had sneaked an old toothbrush and a hairbrush from his bathroom into her handbag. From the DNA provided by them, a firm in Berlin had confirmed the paternity of her son, Bruno Roy Lohmann, beyond doubt. It had not been Cassian Pewe's child. She'd had a fling with him, over several months, after meeting him when Roy had attended a crime course he was running, but it had fizzled out.

She was agonizing, too, over the house. She could afford to buy it, but was going back like that the right thing?

Then, suddenly, for the first time in a long time, she smiled, and thought to herself, *I know where I am going now and what I want to do.*

With a spring in her step she took two paces forward and hailed a cab.

105

The same man-mountain was still on night duty in the lobby, beside the bank of elevators in the Marriott Essex House Hotel, when the three British detectives arrived, shortly after 6.15 a.m. To Roy Grace's relief, the two police officers who had been fast asleep when he had been here earlier were now wide awake and nervously eager to give him information. Not that they had anything of significance to report. Last night, at 7.30 p.m., Eamonn Pollock had had a meal delivered to his room. According to the room service waiter, he also had a male visitor. Sometime later, Pollock had pushed his tray out into the corridor. He'd been silent since then, and they presumed he was now still asleep.

Grace asked if he could speak to the waiter about Pollock's visitor. The man-mountain made a call on his radio, and reported back that the waiter had gone off duty and would not be here again until midday.

Leaving the hotel security guard in situ, Grace took his colleagues and the American police officers down to the two basement exits, leaving Batchelor covering one and Jack Alexander the other. He sent one officer up to stand outside Pollock's door and the other to remain down here. Grace went into the front lobby and up to the reception desk, keeping an eye on the main entrance, and asked to speak to the duty manager.

He was finding it really hard to focus on anything since the last phone call he had received earlier from Glenn Branson, telling him that Amis Smallbone had rented the house next door to Cleo's. The little scumbag had been the other side of their party wall. With an electronic eavesdropping device. How had he been able to do that? Surely to God his Probation Officer . . .

But it wasn't the Probation Officer's fault. All he – or she – had to do was to check the address was suitable, and that their charge could afford it. They weren't to know it was next door to where he was living.

But . . . shit.

The night manager, who had already been called and briefed by Pat Lanigan, appeared. 'How can I assist?'

Grace showed him his warrant card and asked if he could view the hotel's CCTV cover of its entrances from 6 p.m. yesterday. He had already noted the cameras at the front and rear of the hotel, giving both interior and exterior views.

A few minutes later he was seated in a cramped, airless room behind the hotel's admin office, in front of a bank of monitors, each numbered and showing different views of parts of the hotel and of the street. Next to him sat a surly, hugely fat security guard, with expressionless eyes, who looked – and smelled – as if he had been up all night. The man was jiggling a joystick, moving and zooming remote cameras; he reminded Grace of the time he had been at a homicide conference in Las Vegas and had walked through the casino on his way to breakfast, past rows of fruit machines, with exhausted people sitting at them who looked like they had been working them all through the night.

Grace sped through the footage, occasionally slowing it down to check out a face; but he did not see anyone he recognized. Finally he gave up and, relieved to get out of this rancid room, returned to the lobby, and took a seat that afforded him a clear view of anyone entering or leaving the hotel from this side.

Moments later, Tony Case rang him. He'd managed to book him on a flight out of Newark at 9 p.m., getting in to Gatwick via a transfer from Heathrow around 9 a.m. the next day; it also gave him the whole day in New York, which he was glad of, despite his concerns to get back home to take care of Cleo and Noah.

The lobby was deserted apart from a woman cleaning, laboriously shifting a yellow slippery floor warning triangle around as she moved. After some minutes, an early-rising businessman strode hurriedly into the lobby, trundling a small overnight bag on wheels behind him, and went up to the reception desk. Grace only watched him to relieve the monotony; he looked nothing like the images he had of Eamonn Pollock from his criminal record. And this man was about twenty years younger.

Ten minutes later a young couple in tracksuits came into the lobby and borrowed the two bicycles by the porter's desk, wheeling them out into the brightening morning.

By 8.30 a.m. he was starting to get concerned. Pollock had flown here from Europe, just a few days ago. With the five hours' – six in Spain – time difference, he would almost certainly have woken early, as he had done himself. He had, much earlier, asked the hotel security to alert him to any action from Eamonn Pollock's room, 1406 – in particular any request for room service or a taxi. The man was going to eat breakfast, or order tea or coffee at the very least, surely?

A few minutes later, Pat Lanigan entered the lobby dressed in a sports jacket and tie, with a warm smile, accompanied by Aaron Cobb, who had the face of a man with a tooth abscess.

'So how're we doing, my friend?' Lanigan asked.

'I'm worried that Pollock's been too quiet.'

'Maybe he popped a sleeping pill?' Cobb ventured. 'People do that to counter jet lag.'

'I don't care how strong a pill I'd taken. If I was about to make two million pounds – sorry, three million dollars – I don't think I'd be sleeping in on a Monday morning,' Grace retorted.

Pat Lanigan sauntered over to the front desk, and spoke to the woman behind it. Grace followed him, and saw him flash his NYPD badge. 'Can you double-check for us that there's been no activity from suite 1406 this morning? I'd appreciate your checking with room service, housekeeping, the concierge, anyone else who might take a call from one of your guests.'

'Of course, sir. Give me a few moments.' She picked up her phone.

A few minutes later she reported that there had been no requests from suite 1406, and a staff member she had sent up there had reported there was a DO NOT DISTURB sign hung on the door.

By 9.10, Roy Grace had a bad feeling. 'I think we should have someone go in,' he said to Lanigan. 'We need to know he's still there.'

The detective agreed and spoke to the front desk again, this time formally commandeering the hotel's manager.

Five minutes later Grace, Lanigan and the manager, an elegant woman in her late-forties, rode the elevator up to the fourteenth floor, then walked along the maze of corridors. The DO NOT DISTURB sign hung on the handle, along with a black bag containing today's *New York Times*.

The manager rapped hard on the door, waited several seconds, then rapped again. Then she rang the number on her phone. Through the door they could hear the warbling of an unanswered phone. Grace's heart was sinking.

Finally, she opened it with her pass key, calling out a cautious, 'Hello, Dr Alvarez? Hello? Good morning!'

Silence greeted them.

A silent room with two sofas, and a dining table on which sat a solitary empty champagne glass.

Grace and Lanigan followed her through into the bedroom. The bed was unmade, the television on, the sound muted, a white towelling dressing gown lay on the floor. Those were the only clues that the suite had ever been inhabited. Its occupant had gone, along with his luggage and toiletries, as the empty bathroom confirmed.

106

The rather tired black Lincoln Town Car the hotel had procured for Gavin Daly pulled up on Madison Avenue, close to a Panerai watch dealership, he noticed. The driver jumped out and opened the door for him, and pointed at the number on the door.

'Excellent,' Daly said, jamming the tip of his walking stick onto the sidewalk, then levering himself out of the limousine, into the hot sunshine. As he stood upright he was conscious of the heavy weight in his trouser pocket. He was tired and jet-lagged, and had slept badly, but was running on adrenaline. 'You'll wait for me here?'

'Yes, sir. If I'm not here when you come out, just wait right here – I may have to go around the block if I get moved on.'

'Of course.'

'An hour, you think?'

'An hour, give or take. Thank you.' He stifled a yawn.

'A pleasure, sir. I'll be right here, sir!'

Gavin Daly had arrived early, as Julius Rosenblaum had advised. It was 9.45 a.m. and Eamonn Pollock's appointment with the rogue dealer was for 10.30. He made his way to the doorway sandwiched between two smart shops, and studied the names on the bell panel. Then he pushed the bell for J. R. Nautical Antiquities, conscious of the camera lens above it.

Moments later he heard Rosenblaum's voice. 'Come on in, Gavin. Take the elevator to the third floor.'

'I remember!' he replied. And he did, very clearly, although it had been ten years, at least, since his last visit here.

It was a tiny, old-fashioned lift, with a sliding metal gate. He pressed the button and ascended to the third floor. A few moments later it jerked to a halt. He opened the door and stepped out into a narrow corridor; the door directly in front of him had a spyhole and bore the name, in gilded lettering, J. ROSENBLAUM NAUTICAL ANTIQUITIES.

Almost immediately it opened and one of his oldest and best customers stood there, beaming, tall and erect, with a military posture Daly had always admired.

Well into his eighties, with finely coiffed white hair and smelling of strong cologne, Julius Rosenblaum looked distinguished, if a little flash and raffish. He had a hooked, Semitic nose, hooded eyes, and a rich, full smile. He was dressed immaculately in a three-piece chalk-striped suit and a flamboyant tie, and wore an extremely ornate and showy Vacherin Constantin watch on his wrist.

'So good to see you, Gavin!' He looked him up and down. 'You look terrific, wow! You haven't changed, you know!'

'Nor you!'

'Come on in. We've time for a coffee, and we have a lot to catch up on.'

Daly entered, stepping onto plush eau de nil carpeting so deep his feet sank into it. Recessed showcases lined the hallway, displaying ship's clocks, a nautical hourglass with a brass top embossed with the wording ROYAL NAVY, and a mounted ship's bell. He followed Rosenblaum into a small room with an antique Georgian table that served as a reception desk. An elegant, elderly woman sat behind it, typing on a keyboard; a pile of antiques magazines lay beside her.

'Marjorie, you remember Gavin Daly from England?'

'Indeed I do!' She smiled at him.

'Would you bring us some coffee, please?'

Then they went into his office. It was furnished with a circular conference table and a large desk, with two leather-covered chairs for visitors on one side, and a large, black leather chair with buttoned cushioning behind it. The walls were lined with fine oil paintings, and the room had the aura of a museum. Daylight entered through a large, frosted glass window. It was quiet in here, well insulated from the traffic down in the street below.

Rosenblaum ushered him to one chair in front of the desk, then sat in the other, shot his cuffs, leaned back and folded his arms. 'So?'

'I really appreciate you informing me about this, Julius.'

On the desk sat a large, silver cigar box, several photographs in silver frames, a huge glass ashtray and a computer terminal. 'What the hell does money matter at our age, Gavin? You know? I need to offload a three-million-bucks stolen watch like I need a hole in my head. I just want a quiet life now – do a few little deals, keep my hand in, and keep me out of the house; otherwise I'd sit at home going nuts with boredom.'

Daly nodded in agreement. 'Still got a yacht?' Rosenblaum, who had served in the US Navy during the Korean War, had always been a keen sailor. Once, many years ago, on a fine summer day, Rosenblaum had taken him on a memorable 360 degrees circumnavigation of Manhattan Island.

'Yeah, but I keep her out in St Barts. Too damned chilly, the waters around here, for me these days.'

Rosenblaum opened the lid of the cigar box and pushed it towards him. 'Help yourself.'

'It's a little early, thanks.'

'Okay, later. We'll have a glass or two and a smoke. Come to my club this evening, if you're free.'

'I'd like that.'

Rosenblaum shrugged, then grinned, almost sheepishly. 'Had my prostate removed. Can't screw any more, so what's left but a fine cigar and fine wine?'

'I'm right with you – same problem.'

'I look on it as a pleasure, Gavin. I used to have these goddamn urges; it felt like I lived much of my life chained to a wild monkey that had some kind of will of its own and just wanted to screw all the time, and wasn't happy when it didn't. Now – hey, you know, I don't miss it. You?'

'I still look, though.' Daly grinned.

Julius Rosenblaum broke into a grin. 'The day I stop looking, I want them to take me out into a field and shoot me. But you didn't come all this way to talk about useless dicks.' He looked at his slim, vintage watch. 'Half an hour until he shows – if he shows.'

'What are your thoughts?'

Rosenblaum pointed up at the wall, and Daly saw the camera, angled down towards the conference table; then he pointed at a door on the far side of the room, with a large gilded mirror on the wall beside it. 'That's my CCTV viewing room through there. That camera is set to give a close-up of whatever is put on the table. I've used it many times to take photographs of items I've been offered, and to check whether they are on any register. And I use that two-way mirror to observe folk in here. You know, you'd be surprised by what you learn from leaving people who are trying to sell you something alone in a room together.' He rolled his lips. 'I figured you might like to observe from in there. If you recognize the watch as yours, you can either hit a button to alert me, or you can step right in. Within ten seconds, either way, Eamonn Pollock's going to find himself locked in. He's not getting out, no which way.' The hoods above his eyes raised, theatrically. 'That okay with you?'

'Just one thing, Julius. What's in this for you?'

The New Yorker raised both hands in the air. 'An old friend like you, Gavin?' He grinned. 'I figure you're not going to leave me empty-handed.'

'Even though you said money does not matter at our age?'

'It doesn't.' He rubbed his finger and thumb together, and gave Daly a sly smile. 'Hey, what's a few million bucks between friends?'

107

Eamonn Pollock was feeling like shit. He sat in the back of the most cramped yellow cab in New York, being thrown around by the city's worst driver – a young Ethiopian who was having a screaming match with someone on his phone the entire way. The maniac drove flat out, accelerating harshly, then leaving his braking to the very last minute, stopping equally violently.

To make matters worse, the creep sitting beside him, sticking to him like a leech, was not cutting him any slack. They'd even bloody slept together. If *sleep* was the right word. Since doing a late bunk from the hotel via the service lift and the kitchen deliveries entrance, Eamonn Pollock had spent the night, trying to sleep, in a narrow armchair in the creep's crappy, cheap hotel room in midtown Manhattan, whilst the leech had snored his sodding head off.

He noticed a Panerai watch dealership as the taxi pulled mercifully to a halt. He might treat himself to one after he had closed the deal on the Patek Philippe, he thought; a nice little prezzie to celebrate. Then he would trot along to Tiffany and buy Luiza a little bauble.

Distracted by his thoughts, he tugged his wallet from his jacket pocket, gave the driver a twenty-dollar bill and told him to keep the change, then opened the door.

Putting his call on hold, the driver said, tersely, tapping the meter, that the bill was twenty-three bucks.

Pollock dug deeper into his wallet. It didn't matter. All being well, in a short while he would be very much richer.

He hadn't yet figured out how he was going to deal with the leech. But he was confident he would find a way. Hey, he'd spent the past thirty years shafting losers. He wasn't about to change his ways now.

They climbed out of the cab. 'It would be best if you waited down here,' Pollock said. 'We'll get a better price if I handle this alone.' He waddled towards the door.

'In your dreams,' the leech replied, lighting a cigarette.

He took two long, deep puffs while Pollock rang the bell. Moments later there was a sharp buzz and a click. Pollock pushed the door open, and the leech followed him in, still holding his cigarette.

'You can't smoke inside here,' Pollock said.

'You can't smoke inside most places,' he retorted, exhaling and tapping ash on the floor.

The lift slowly clanked down towards them and they entered. With Eamonn Pollock's portly shape, there was only just room for the two of them to squeeze in. 'You're not bloody smoking in here!'

'Why are you so fat, Pollock?'

'Because every time I screw your wife she gives me a biscuit.'

'Haha, that's an old one. Tell me, really, why are you so fat?'

Pollock stared him in the face, and shook his head. 'Now, now, don't get personal; we've business to do. Let's not rock any boats, eh?'

The leech took another long drag on the cigarette, then crushed the butt out on the floor as the lift jerked and clattered on upwards.

108

The moment his secretary buzzed to say that Eamonn Pollock was on his way up, Julius Rosenblaum ushered Gavin Daly through the door at the rear of his office into the monitoring room, then dashed back and fetched his cup of coffee for him.

Daly found himself in what was little more than a wide broom closet, furnished with a single, busted swivel chair behind the two-way mirror. The cushioned seat was uncomfortable and felt wobbly, Daly thought, easing himself onto it and propping his stick against the narrow shelf in front of him. He found it hard to believe that he could not be seen on this side of the mirror – his view from the semi-darkness here into Rosenblaum's office was crystal clear.

He sipped his coffee and glanced down to familiarize himself with the volume knob on the complicated-looking control panel in front of him, which Rosenblaum had hurriedly pointed out. Further along was a TV monitor, switched off, mounted on wall brackets, and winking lights on a recording unit. The rest of the space in here was taken up with a row of ancient metal filing cabinets, all of them with boxes and concertina folders of documents stacked on top.

The air was dry and dusty and there was a fusty smell of old paperwork. In contrast to Rosenblaum's office, which had been near freezing from the air-con, this room was hot and airless. He stifled a sneeze, then saw the main office door open, and the secretary appeared for a moment. He watched Julius Rosenblaum rise from his chair, then Eamonn

Pollock entered, dressed in a crumpled beige suit, a gaudy yellow shirt and vulgar brown loafers. The sight of the man made Daly's blood run cold.

For all his adult life, Gavin Daly had studied, with hatred, the faces of those men who had murdered his mother and taken his father away into the night. He'd trawled every major newspaper archive in the world, and his sister's extensive library of books on that period, and, of course, the Internet, looking for new images. Those faces were ingrained in his mind.

And seeing Eamonn Pollock now was like looking at a ghost.

The shapes of the two men were completely different. Mick – *Pegleg* – Pollock was thin and tall; Eamonn, his great-nephew, was pudgy and below average height. But both men had the same wavy hair, and the same arrogant leer. He was imagining Eamonn Pollock thinner, with his cheeks flattened out and the flesh gone below his chin.

Or Pegleg fatter.

Eamonn Pollock was like a Photofit composite.

He could not take his eyes off him. He sat shaking, his nerves on edge, something tugging at the base of his neck, a roaring in his ears, thinking how much he would like to wipe that smug leer from the man's face. Then another figure followed Pollock in.

For a moment Gavin Daly was convinced his eyes were deceiving him. Or that he was hallucinating from tiredness. He stared in total disbelief at the tall, muscular figure in a suede bomber jacket and jeans who sauntered in after Pollock, looking around the room in his familiar, arrogant, bully-boy manner.

'Julius, this is my associate,' Eamonn Pollock said, with clear distaste in his voice. 'Lucas Daly.'

Moments later, Gavin Daly felt the tell-tale fire burning in his chest followed by the tightening sensation. He fumbled in his pocket, pulled out the vial, shook a tiny nitroglycerin tablet into his palm and popped it beneath his tongue. Breathing heavily, shaking with rage and suddenly clammy, he turned the volume up a bit.

'Good to meet you, Mr Daly,' Rosenblaum said with a frown, and indicated for them to sit at the conference table. 'Can I offer you gentlemen coffee – or maybe tea?'

'A coffee would be very pleasant,' Eamonn Pollock said. Lucas nodded. Rosenblaum went over to his desk, raised his phone and spoke to his secretary, then returned to the conference table. 'So, Mr Pollock, I presume you have brought the watch?'

'I have indeed!' Pollock pushed himself upright, onto his feet, with some effort. Then he unbuckled his belt, which had a small black leather pouch hooped through it, unzipped the pouch, removed a large wad of cotton wool from it and laid it on the table. Slowly and laboriously, but beaming with greedy anticipation, he unpicked the cotton wool, lifted free the Patek Philippe watch and placed it in front of them.

Julius Rosenblaum went over to his desk drawer, removed a magnifying eyepiece and wedged it into his right eye socket. Then he sat down, picked up the watch and began to examine it. 'Nice piece, but shame about the condition. Three million you want for this, right?'

'That's the minimum I – we – would accept.' Pollock shot a glance at Lucas Daly, who nodded in agreement.

The New Yorker's secretary brought in their coffees, set them down, then left. Rosenblaum continued to study the watch in silence. He turned it over, then using a thin-bladed tool he opened the back, and carefully examined the interior. 'It's undoubtedly very beautiful, very rare. I've not seen many

431

watches like this in all my life. But I have some issues. What are you able to tell me about its provenance, Mr Pollock?'

'It belonged to my grandfather,' Lucas Daly interjected. 'It was handed to my father in 1922.'

'By my uncle, who came by it illegally and wanted to return it to its rightful owner's family,' Pollock added.

Gavin Daly watched, listening, his fury growing as his angina pains subsided.

'You see, there are a few anomalies,' Rosenblaum said calmly. 'I checked with Patek Philippe, who keep records of every watch they ever made. The production date serial number, 049, 351 – oops – apologies – I'm a little dyslexic; I read numbers backwards oftentimes! The serial, 153,940, would indicate a date of 1911 or later. It should be between 149,100 to 150,000 for a manufacturing date of 1910. Do you have an explanation for this?'

'I do, yes,' Lucas Daly said. 'I understand it was common practice for top apprentices to make themselves a duplicate at the same time as they worked on a particular timepiece, secretly of course. I suspect that's what my father's watch is. That is the reason the serial number is slightly out.'

'I see,' Rosenblaum said. 'But on a watch of this period, every time it was repaired, there would be a little mark of who repaired it, with the date and initials. I don't see any here. Additionally, a watch like this would have been commissioned, and almost certainly the owner would have had his initials engraved on it. Sometimes, of course, when the watch changes hands, the initials would be etched out, but that always leaves a trace. I can't see any trace.'

'This is bullshit!' Lucas Daly said with rising anger. 'Maybe it was stolen way back then, by my grandfather, before any initials were engraved. How would I know?'

Behind the two-way mirror Gavin Daly watched and listened, his brain fogged with fury. Lucas, his son, was sitting there with this fat, sanctimonious, lying shit.

My uncle came by it illegally and wanted to return it to its rightful owner's family.

Oh yes?

His uncle having murdered the rightful owner.

And then Eamonn Pollock had murdered Aileen to get it back, and was now trying to sell it. But where the hell did Lucas fit in?

'This may be a dumb question,' Rosenblaum said, turning to Lucas. 'With such a valuable piece, why did no one in your family get it repaired?'

'I think they believed it might affect its authenticity,' Eamonn Pollock replied.

'No,' Lucas said. 'It's very simple. My father – and my aunt – wanted the watch kept exactly as it was the day they got it back. It was the only link they had with their father, so it had immense sentimental value. It would not have been the same if they'd had it repaired.'

'And how do they feel about you selling this now?' Rosenblaum asked, staring hard at Lucas.

'Well, sadly, they are both dead now.' He raised his hands in a gesture of sad despair. 'The time has come, extremely reluctantly, for the family to sell it.'

A door burst open behind them. All three turned round to see Gavin Daly, holding his walking stick in one hand, and a black revolver in the other. 'I'm dead, am I, Lucas? I will be dead one day, all in good time, you'll be pleased to know.'

He aimed the gun, with a shaky hand, at Eamonn Pollock. 'But this bastard will be dead first.'

109

Detective Lieutenant Aaron Cobb threaded the grimy, brown Crown Victoria through the heavy Fifth Avenue traffic, siren wailing, lights flashing, heading downtown. He cussed at everything in his way, especially the bicycle rickshaws for which he seemed to reserve particular venom.

Pat Lanigan rode up front beside him, while Roy Grace sat in the back, which smelled of feet and rancid kebab, trying to call Cleo, but both her home and mobile numbers went straight to voicemail, indicating she was probably on both phones. He looked at his watch. It was 10.20 a.m.; 3.20 p.m. in Brighton.

'Next on our list coming up, Roy,' Lanigan announced.

Cobb pulled the car up alongside the Flatiron, one of Grace's favourite buildings in the city, and stayed behind the wheel as Lanigan and Grace jumped out and hurried over to the entrance of a small shop. The name was displayed, above the window, in olde worlde script, *The Seconds Hand*. Beneath, in smaller lettering, was inscribed, *Fine watches bought and sold*. The window contained a display of Rolex, Patek Philippe and Omega wristwatches, among the classic brands Grace recognized.

The door was locked, and there was a discreet bell beside it. Lanigan pressed it, and moments later, the two detectives heard a sharp click from the latch. They entered a space that looked considerably bigger than the exterior suggested, and which smelled pleasantly of old leather.

Roy Grace had always liked watches, although most of

the ones he fancied were way out of his price range. There were floor-to-ceiling display cabinets, divided into sections by brand, and more free-standing, glass-topped cabinets around the floor. Without peering too closely, in the one nearest him he could see hand-written price tags that ended in long rows of noughts.

A man in his late sixties rose from behind a desk at the far end of the showroom. 'Good morning, gentlemen. May I help you?' He spoke with a warm, cultured voice, in very slightly broken English, and exuded courtly, old-world charm.

Pat Lanigan held up his NYPD badge. 'I'm looking for Mr Turkkan? Mr Attila Turkkan?'

'You have found him!'

'Detective Lanigan, I called you a little earlier; said we'd be over.'

'This is a good moment, gentlemen – as you can see, we are quiet this morning.' He was dressed for this warm day in a navy and white striped seersucker jacket, a white shirt and an elegant navy and white silk tie, and he carried himself well, with fine posture. His short, silver hair, elegantly cut, was receding at the front, and he had a thin, neatly trimmed moustache, giving him, Grace thought, rather the air of a ladies' man. He reminded him of the actor Omar Sharif.

'My associate here, Detective Superintendent Roy Grace, is from Sussex Police in England,' Pat Lanigan said. 'The NYPD are helping his team on a case involving a rare pocket watch of high value that's been stolen.'

Attila Turkkan frowned, and Grace thought the man looked genuinely hurt. 'Gentlemen, I have been in this business for forty-one years, and to my absolute certainty I have never handled a stolen watch.'

'We're here to ask you for help,' Roy Grace said. 'That's all. Not to accuse you of anything.' He blinked. There was a bright ceiling light with an angled beam striking his face, hurting his tired eyes, and he stepped a couple of feet to the right to get away from it.

The watch dealer looked a little relieved, but was still not comfortable. 'Can I offer you gentlemen some Turkish coffee?'

'I'm afraid we don't have time,' Lanigan said.

'Before I buy any watch, I have to be one hundred per cent sure of its provenance. One hundred per cent, you understand?' A phone started ringing on his desk, but he ignored it.

'That's how you build a reputation,' Lanigan said. 'Absolutely!'

'Precisely. I am known the world over. I pay the best prices; I have the best watches – everyone trusts me. So, tell me about this pocket watch that you are concerned with?'

'It's a 1910 Patek Philippe.'

He nodded. 'There is already an alert out on the wire about this watch, I think. No respectable dealer is going to touch it.'

'That's our problem, Mr Turkkan,' Roy Grace said. 'The man we believe has the watch is called Eamonn Pollock, although he uses a number of aliases.' He pulled out a photograph and showed it to the dealer. 'Do you recognize him?'

Turkkan studied it for some moments, while Grace watched his eyes. Then the dealer shook his head. 'I'm sorry, no, I've never seen him before.'

He was telling the truth.

'I presume there are people in this city who would be less scrupulous than yourself if offered a valuable timepiece?' Grace continued.

Turkkan laughed. 'Some indeed, oh yes, I have no doubt, but I do not know any of these people.'

'Not even by reputation?' Roy Grace asked.

'It is not my world,' he said. 'Not – how do you phrase it in this modern jargon – not the space I inhabit?' He grinned, and Grace saw a flash of gold among his teeth. 'I can't help you gentlemen. I am so sorry, please believe me.' He looked at Pat. 'If you give me your phone number, and this Mr Pollip walks in here, I'll call you instantly and with pleasure.'

Lanigan produced a business card and handed it to him. 'Any time, day or night.'

*

Back in the car, Roy Grace crossed out the circle on the map that had been drawn around *The Seconds Hand*. It was the third watch dealer they had crossed out in the past forty minutes, from a long list of dealers, some totally legit, others less so, that had been compiled by Peregrine Stuart-Simmonds in England, and by two officers from the Major Case Squad here in New York.

Guy Batchelor and Jack Alexander were in separate cars, with detectives Keith Johnson and Linda Blankson working their way through other dealers in the New York boroughs. Grace was about to call and check in with them, when his phone rang. It was Cleo.

'Darling, Humphrey won't wake up,' she said, sounding scared.

'What do you mean?'

'It's half past three in the afternoon here, and he's been fast asleep in his basket all day. I'm really worried about him.'

Humphrey was always awake before either of them,

pulling at the duvet if they'd left the bedroom door open. He would never sleep this long. One possibility was that the dog was sick. But he had always been a believer in applying Occam's razor: that the most likely explanation was usually the correct one. Someone had tried to break into the house last night. Now the dog was fast asleep, hours after he would normally have woken up. It was likely the two were linked.

'Is Humphrey breathing okay?'

'He's snoring.'

'Darling, this might be very important. Is there any way you could take him to the vet?'

'Sure, and leave Noah to mind the house?'

'Yep, teach him to use the vacuum cleaner and washing machine! Look, I'm serious, Humphrey could have been drugged – but we'd need some tests done before the stuff leaves his system. If it's difficult, I'll see if I can get a police dog handler to take him.'

'That would be helpful.'

'Okay, leave it with me. I'll get back to you.'

'You'll be home in the morning.'

'Absolutely. My flight's booked.'

'I'm really scared.'

'You needn't be, darling. I've got the patrols stepped up around the house, and a scene guard on the gates. Has the FLO arrived?'

'Yes, a lovely lady called Linda Buckley.'

'Good, you'll be fine now. How's Noah?' His phone was beeping.

'Noah's fine. He's pooing for England.'

He grinned. His phone continued beeping. 'I've got another call. Love you.'

'Love you, too.'

He switched to the incoming call.

It was Glenn Branson at the mortuary, where he was attending Amis Smallbone's post-mortem. 'I've got some fast-time developments, Roy. Alec Davies, right? He's bright; you're right about him.'

DC Alec Davies was a young officer Grace had recruited to his team a few months back, a young, extremely keen detective who he felt certain had a great future. 'Tell me all.'

'He just happened to notice a serial about a firm of estate agents, Rand and Co., who were broken into on Saturday night. They're the ones that handle Cleo's next-door neighbour's house. He checked with them and found that there was only one thing stolen – ready for this?'

'Ready.'

'The spare keys to the house – Chez Amis Smallbone.'

'Any idea by whom, or for what reason?'

'There's more. SOCO found shoeprints at Rand and Co., and I've just had an analysis done by Haydn Kelly, comparing them to shoeprints found at Smallbone's. They're an exact match.'

Grace thought hard for some moments as he absorbed this. 'So, if Haydn Kelly's right, the implication is that someone helped themselves to a set of keys to Amis Smallbone's house, and then let themselves in. On the same night that Smallbone fell from the roof?'

'You're playing catch-up very well, for an old man.'

'Sod you! So did he fall, or was he pushed?'

'I thought I'd let you work that one out.'

110

Beads of sweat rolled down Eamonn Pollock's face; his Mediterranean tan had vanished and his complexion was now sickly white, as he stared into the gun barrel and at the fury in the old man's eyes behind it.

'Dad!' Lucas Daly said, standing up. 'Put that down.'

'I'll put it down when I've emptied it into that sack of shit,' he said, waving it at Pollock. 'Now you sit back down.'

Lucas hesitated.

'SIT DOWN!'

'Dad!'

Gavin Daly pulled the trigger. In the confines of the room the shot was like a thunderclap. The bullet tore through the tabletop a couple of feet from where Lucas was standing, sending splinters flying, and plugged into the carpet.

In the stunned silence that followed, all four of them were motionless, momentarily deafened, their ears popping, breathing in the reek of cordite.

'I said *sit down*!' Gavin Daly hissed at his son.

Lucas sat down.

'Gavin!' Rosenblaum said. 'What the heck—?'

'I'll pay for any damage, Julius. You have to understand what's going on.'

'Jesus, Gavin! You got some score to settle, do it some-place else – not in here, please!'

Supporting himself on his walking stick, Gavin Daly jabbed the gun at Pollock. 'This piece of vermin's uncle murdered my father.' He swung the gun towards Lucas. 'This other piece of vermin is my son, unfortunately. These two charmers killed my sister to get this watch.'

'I never – I never did – Dad, that was not the plan!'

'Perhaps you'd like to tell me what the plan was, exactly? I'd like to know. I'd like to know why my sister was murdered and why the pair of you are in New York trying to sell my stolen watch? Go on, tell me, I'm all ears, and it had better be damned good.'

The two seated men looked at each other.

The door opened and Rosenblaum's secretary looked in, nervously. 'I heard a – Is – is everything all – ?' Then she froze as she saw the gun.

Rosenblaum nodded, then looked at her, uncertainly. 'Just a little family dispute, Marjorie.'

'Shall I call the police?'

'That won't be necessary.'

She retreated, slamming the door hastily behind her.

'Dad, I can explain,' Lucas said.

'I said I'm listening. But I know what your involvement is, you little shit. Money to pay your debts, right?'

'Because you wouldn't give me any.'

'At your age, isn't it about time you learned to support yourself, instead of sponging off me and your wife? Or are you planning to kill a member of the family every time you need money?'

'Dad, I told you, that was never the plan. It just all went – it went – wrong. No one ever intended to harm Aileen, you have to understand that!'

'I only understand one thing. My sister is dead, and the watch that was in her safe, that belonged to the two of us, is lying on that table. And you two are behind this.'

Daly swung the gun on Pollock. 'I want to hear from

you. I want the whole damned story. I want to know everything you know.'

'Don't kill me!' Pollock pleaded, raising his hands.
'Please don't kill me.' Heavy beads of sweat were guttering
down his face, and he was shaking.

'Why not? Did your thugs show any mercy to my sister?
I don't think so, Mr Pollock.'

'Please, I'll tell you everything I know.'

'Go right back in time. I want to know about Pegleg. I
want to know about the night he shot my mum and took
my dad away. How much do you know about that? What
are your family stories? Did your uncle boast to you about
the night he murdered my mum?'

'I know a little of the story,' he yammered. 'My – my
dad used to talk about my uncle. I grew up in Brooklyn
until my dad was put in prison. My mum was from England
and she took me back there. My dad told me my uncle,
Mick – Pegleg – was murdered a few years after your dad.'

'What a sad loss,' Gavin Daly said acidly. 'Your uncle
was a murderer and your dad a jailbird. And you're a
murderer. What a nice family. You can all have a happy
reunion in Hell.'

'I know a bit about how your dad died.'

Gavin Daly stared at him in silence for some moments.
The words seemed to echo inside his head, and to go on
echoing. He steadied himself on his stick, his hands shaking.
'What do you know?'

'You ever heard the expression, *take a long walk down
a short pier*?'

Daly stared back at him icily.

'My dad told me one day about Brendan Daly – your
father. They took him for that walk one night.'

'Which night? The night they took him from our home? Or did they keep him prisoner for a while and torture him?'

'I don't know.'

'What pier?'

'There was a wharf at the end of the tobacco warehouse beneath the Manhattan Bridge. Almost all of that old Brooklyn waterfront's gone. Redeveloped.'

Gavin stood still, letting it sink in, continuing to point the gun alternately at Pollock, then Lucas. There was no surprise, not now, not after all this time.

'There was snow on the ground,' Pollock said. 'My dad told me it was lucky that the cops weren't very smart back then, otherwise they might have noticed.'

'Noticed what?'

'There were five sets of footprints walking along the pier out into the East River, and only four sets walking back the other way.'

'Three and a half, if your uncle was one of them.'

Pollock looked at him warily, as if unsure whether he should smile.

'Did your dad say anything to you about numbers?' Gavin Daly asked.

'Numbers?'

'Twelve numbers. *9 5 3 7 0 4 0 4 2 4 0 4*. Those mean anything to you?'

Pollock frowned. 'Can you repeat them?'

Daly said them again.

Pollock shook his head.

'I was about to board the *Mauretania*, with Aileen and my aunt Oonagh. Someone, a messenger, came up to me,' Gavin Daly said. 'He gave me the watch, busted and stopped like it is now; he gave me this gun; and he gave me a newspaper cutting with four names written on it – your uncle among them – and those twelve numbers. And he gave me a message. *"Watch the numbers,"* he said, then he vanished.'

Now Julius Rosenblaum was frowning. 'What were those numbers again, Gavin?'

Daly repeated them and Rosenblaum scribbled them down. Then he stared at them for some moments, and frowned. 'I've done it again – I've reversed them! This is really interesting!' He held up the sheet on which he had written, then rewritten, the numbers, excitedly.

'I used to know the waters around New York like the back of my hand,' Rosenblaum said. 'Sailing up the East or West River on a fine day, looking at glorious Manhattan and all the surrounds. Could never tire of it. Go around into the Harlem River, in summer, and all you can see is trees on both banks; you can't see a building at all. You could be in a wilderness anywhere in the world.' He rummaged in a drawer, and pulled out a scrolled sheet of paper that was held by an elastic band.

'4 0 4 2 4 0 4 0 7 3 5 9,' Rosenblaum said. 'I have an idea.' He unrolled the sheet, and Gavin Daly could see out of the corner of his eye that it looked like a nautical chart. 'If I'm right, there are three digits missing. And a few letters and symbols. Okay, first we add an *N* in front of the *40*. Then a *degree* symbol after it. Forty degrees north. We add a minute sign after *42*. That's forty-two minutes. Then the 404. We stick a *W* in front of *073* and a degree sign. And a minute sign after *59*. And that puts us three digits short, as I thought.'

'Short of what?' Gavin Daly asked. 'Three digits short of what?'

'These co-ordinates put you in the area of the Manhattan Bridge, Gavin. But it's a big bridge, covers a huge area. We need those last three digits.'

Gavin Daly glanced down once again at the watch. And then he realized.

It had been staring him in the face for ninety years.

111

In the back of the Crown Victoria, Roy Grace was aware of the minutes ticking away. With each one that passed, the chances were increasing that Eamonn Pollock had offloaded the watch, and was on his way out of town and probably out of America, doubtless under one of his aliases.

'Hey, move it!' Aaron Cobb shouted out of the window at a delivery van blocking the cross-street. 'Just move it, will ya! We're on an emergency!'

Grace could barely contain his anger at Detective Lieutenant Cobb. If he had done his job properly, they would not be in this situation now, and instead would have had a tail on Pollock. The crook could be anywhere in this city, or in any of its boroughs. He wasn't necessarily even taking the watch to a dealer; it could be to a private buyer. Hector Webb, the former head of the Brighton Antiques Squad, had told him there were rich people who got a kick out of buying famous stolen works of art, and hiding them away in private galleries in the basements of their homes – a kind of guilty secret pleasure for the super-rich. The same could apply to this watch.

One thing was for sure, Eamonn Pollock was no fool. He'd showed up on the hotel's CCTV camera when checking in, but he'd managed to evade them when he had done his moonlight flit. The hotel had only one exit not covered by a camera, which was a fire door in the kitchens. How he knew about that was anybody's guess, but no doubt that was the exit he had used. Besides, it was irrelevant how he had left. The fact was, he had gone.

Guy Batchelor phoned in to say they'd had no joy at any of the dealers they'd visited so far. Moments later, Jack Alexander reported the same news.

Grace did a quick calculation. He needed to be at Newark Airport by 7 p.m., which meant leaving Manhattan at 6 p.m. This gave him a shade under seven and a half hours to find Pollock, or return home empty-handed. He intended leaving Batchelor and Alexander out here, but all his instincts were that today was the day that counted.

If they didn't find Eamonn Pollock with the Patek Philippe in his hot, sweaty palm, they weren't going to have a hope in hell, right now, of charging him with anything.

Pat Lanigan turned round to face him. 'Any news from the others?'

'Goose eggs,' Grace said with a grim smile. And that's what this felt like at the moment: a wild goose chase. Eamonn Pollock had done the rounds of the legitimate dealers on Friday, no doubt to fix a value for the watch in the market. But now, very obviously, he was not being stupid and risking walking into a trap.

He peered out of the window at a street vendor, with his stall selling hats and scarves. A cyclist wormed past them, bell pinging. A fire engine honked its way through traffic close by. Then he looked up at a wall, rising sheer into the sky, with maybe a thousand windows. Eamonn Pollock could be behind any one of those at this moment. Behind any one of the millions and millions of windows of this city.

One man and a watch.

A needle in a haystack.

112

Pointing the gun at his son, Gavin Daly said, 'Take the chart, we're going.' Then he turned back to Rosenblaum. 'Julius, I'm sorry for the damage I caused, and send me the bill for whatever it costs to fix. I'm also apologizing in advance for what's about to happen, and any further damage.' He reached forward, picked the watch off the table and dropped it into his jacket pocket.

Eamonn Pollock started to stand up.

'Where do you think you're going?' Daly snapped, pointing the gun at him. 'Sit down! You're not going anywhere. I'm not done with you yet. You know how the Irish punish people? A bullet in the kneecap. I should give you one in each knee – one for what your uncle did to my ma and one for what he did to my pop. Yes? That's what I think I should do.'

Pollock, his eyes bulging in fear, was shaking his head frantically. 'Please. I'll tell you everything I know.'

'Gavin,' Rosenblaum cautioned.

'Julius, this skunk's uncle ruined my childhood. Now this skunk himself has ruined my old age. You think he deserves mercy? This fat, greedy vulture?'

'Gavin, calm down, let's hear him out.'

He turned to Pollock. 'I'm all ears, you piece of blubber.'

'I lent Lucas money – he came to me and I helped him out.'

'How nice of you. Then he didn't pay you back? Did I get that one right?'

'Yes, Dad, he has a moneylending business,' Lucas interjected.

'You're a moneylender, are you?' Gavin Daly's finger was shaking on the trigger. 'A proper little Shylock?'

Julius Rosenblaum took a step towards his desk.

'Don't move another inch, Julius. You hit your panic button and I'll shoot you too, God help me I will.'

'Gavin, you have to calm down!' Rosenblaum said.

'No, I'm ninety-five years old; I don't have to calm down.' He looked back at Pollock. 'You sent two pieces of shit – maybe three pieces of shit – to rob a ninety-eight-year-old lady who'd done no harm to anyone in her life. They tortured the fuck out of my sister, and you want mercy from me? Yes?'

'Those were never my instructions.'

'Oh, really? You had the code to the safe from my piece-of-shit son, so why did they have to torture my sister? They stole ten million pounds' worth of antiques, and they tortured her to death for her credit card pin codes, for a few hundred lousy quid. Did they do it for fun, or is that because you were too greedy to pay them decently for doing your filthy work for you?'

Pollock was shaking. 'I didn't, no, that's not right.'

'Stand up!'

Eamonn Pollock pushed himself upright and stood, cowed and quivering.

Gavin Daly stared at the dark stain around his groin. 'You've just pissed yourself. What kind of a man are you?'

Pollock stared wildly around, as if looking for an escape route.

'Dad, let's be calm!' Lucas said.

'Calm? From a man who beats up his wife regularly, that's rich!' He turned to Julius Rosenblaum. 'She's a very

449

pretty, very smart television presenter. When Lucas hits her, he makes sure it is always below the neckline, so it doesn't show in public, so it doesn't hurt her ability to earn a high salary – for him to squander. He's a brave man, my son is. Know what I've always believed?' He covered all three in turn with the gun. 'You judge a man by the friends he keeps. Eamonn and Lucas, you deserve each other.'

'Hurting Aileen was never intended, please believe me,' Eamonn Pollock whimpered. 'Please believe me.'

'You employed those men, Ken Barnes and Tony Macario. They'd worked for you for a long time. You must have known what they were like, what they would do when you set them loose on an elderly, defenceless lady? What's to believe?'

'Please believe me.'

Gavin Daly pulled the trigger. There was another thunderclap and an explosion of blood in Pollock's right shoulder, sending him hurtling back onto the floor. His mouth was wide open, his eyes looking like they were shorting out.

'Oops, sorry, Eamonn, I didn't mean to do that. Do you believe me?'

'Gavin!' Rosenblaum shouted, in shock.

'Dad!' Lucas shouted.

'That was for my ma; this is for my pop!' Gavin Daly fired again. Pollock jumped in the air, as if a defibrillator had gone off on his chest, and a crimson patch of blood began spreading from his left shoulder.

'No! No! No!' Eamonn Pollock was thrashing on the floor, crying in pain and terror, holding his hands in the air, in front of his face as if they could stop the next bullet.

'Gavin!' Rosenblaum said. 'Stop, man! Have you gone crazy?' He took another step towards his desk.

Daly pointed the gun at Rosenblaum. 'Don't move.'

He swung the gun back at Pollock.

'No, for God's sake, no. Please. Oh God, no!' Pollock squealed, crabbing his way across the carpet on his back.

Daly took careful aim at Pollock's crotch. 'This one's for Aileen.'

'No!' he screeched. 'Please no, please no, please no!'

He fired straight into the dark stain.

Pollock let out an animal howl. He sat up straight, his face contorted, his hands pressing desperately at his groin, his whole body convulsing; a low yammering, which was getting louder and louder every second, came from somewhere deep inside his throat.

'Jesus Christ, Gavin!' Rosenblaum said.

He pointed the gun at Lucas. 'We're out of here, son.'

Lucas was frozen to the spot.

Gavin Daly walked across to the door, swinging the gun towards his son and then Julius Rosenblaum, then his son again. 'I'm sorry, Julius, sorry it had to be here.'

Pollock's screams were almost deafening now.

Daly reached the door, still keeping Rosenblaum motionless with his gun. Then he looked down at Pollock, sheet white, his face a contorted, agonized, clammy mass of perspiration, his eyes rolling; he was breathing in short, fast gasps, still clutching his groin, his hands covered in blood.

'Have fun next time you try to screw someone, Pollock.' Then he pointed the gun at his son, who was holding the chart and looking like a rabbit caught in headlights. 'You, you're coming with me.'

Then he threw the gun on the floor. 'I'm done with it,' he said. 'Maybe my dad sent it to me for a purpose. I don't know. But I'm done with it.'

Followed by Lucas, Gavin Daly stomped past the secretary, who looked frozen in shock, out and into the elevator.

'Dad, this is insane!' Lucas said as the elevator clanked its way down. 'Have you lost your fucking mind?'

'Just shut the fuck up. I've not even started with you yet, boy.'

Lucas Daly said nothing. When they reached the ground floor, Gavin stepped out into the busy street.

The black Town Car limousine was right outside. The driver jumped out as they emerged, and held the back door open.

Lucas climbed in first, then slid across the wide seat.

'How's your day been so far, sir?' the driver asked, taking the cane, helpfully, as Gavin Daly lowered himself onto the seat.

'Pretty average,' he replied.

113

Inside the car, Gavin heard a siren. Anxiously, he looked over his shoulder through the darkened rear window. To his relief it was an ambulance, not a police car. Moments later it went wailing past.

'Driver, go two blocks, make a right, then stop where you can,' he instructed.

'You realize what you've done, Dad,' Lucas said, peering back anxiously at the door to Julius Rosenblaum's offices. 'Shit, you know what kind of a mess you're in?'

'Give me that chart.'

'Why did you do that? Why?'

'You want to know why? Because I might not live much longer and I don't trust the justice system. I'm satisfied now; I've got some justice for Aileen. Some, at least. Give me that chart,' he said again.

Lucas handed it to him, and he scrutinized it carefully. Then he pulled out the Patek Philippe watch, and studied that for some moments, before returning to the chart.

The limousine made a right turn, then pulled over to the kerb. Gavin Daly, keeping a weather eye on his son, leaned forward and said to the driver, 'You have any kind of internet connection in here?'

'Got my iPhone, sir.'

'I want you to look up scuba-diving companies in Manhattan for me.' Gavin Daly pulled out his wallet and handed the man two fifty-dollar bills.

'That's not necessary, sir, but thank you. Scuba-diving companies, you say?'

'Please.'

The driver picked his phone off the seat beside him and began tapping. In the distance, Gavin Daly heard another siren, followed by another. Both of them stopped a short distance away. Then he heard another.

'Got a whole list here!' the driver said, and passed the phone to him.

Daly ran his eyes down them. One in particular stood out for him. *Hudson Scuba. Lessons on our own dive boat, moored in central Manhattan.*

'Call them for me, please,' he asked.

A few moments later, the driver handed him back the phone, just as it was answered by a breezy-sounding male voice.

'Hudson Scuba. How can we help?'

'This may be an unusual request,' Gavin Daly said. 'I need a dive boat, with a trained scuba diver, in thirty minutes – or sooner. I don't know what you charge, but on top of that I'm prepared to give you a ten thousand dollar bonus if you can make it happen.'

114

Roy Grace was in a subdued mood as Detective Lieutenant Cobb drove the Crown Victoria over the Brooklyn Bridge, heading back to Pat Lanigan's office. He'd arranged to rendezvous there with Guy Batchelor and Jack Alexander to discuss their next moves – but he did not know, at this moment, what they should be.

It wasn't helping that he'd slept badly, or that he was in a foreign city – one countless times larger than Brighton, and one that, despite his previous visits here, and his love of it, currently felt totally alien. Although he had the full resources of the NYPD at his disposal, it was hard to work out how and where to deploy them to his best advantage. In England he would have had no such problem.

Glancing out of the window and down towards the Hudson, he noticed a helicopter lifting off from a pad close to the water; then a barge laden with timber making its way upriver, about to pass beneath them on the sparkling, cobalt water. As the tyres bumped almost silently over the joins in the surface beneath him, he was preoccupied with his thoughts. How the hell had Amis Smallbone been allowed to rent the house next door to Cleo? The bloody Probation Service were meant to monitor things like that – why hadn't they? Or was he being unfair to them through his tiredness?

Because the house was in Cleo's name and no one had made the connection, he knew. That was the truth. They'd had a lucky escape. Shit.

He shuddered.

Just how close an escape had Cleo and Noah had?

How the hell could he protect them in the future? What could he do? Quit the police force and spend the rest of his life guarding them? That was how he felt right now.

His thoughts switched to the link that the informer, Donny Loncrane in Lewes Prison, had told him about. Amis Smallbone and Eamonn Pollock, thick together, many years back.

He hadn't given it too much significance at the time, but the latest news about Smallbone was making him rethink, hard. Smallbone had rented the house next door to Cleo, clearly with some very nasty intent, and had installed listening equipment so he could eavesdrop on them. Now he was dead, apparently fallen from the rooftop fire escape the day after someone had broken into the letting agency's offices and stolen the spare keys to his rented house.

How coincidental was that?

Smallbone's house was now a crime scene, and SOCOs would be hunting for any evidence of an intruder. Who had wanted Smallbone dead? It could have been any number of people who the nasty little shit, and his equally vile criminal family, had crossed over the years. But if someone wanted to get Smallbone for revenge purposes, they would almost certainly have had him sorted during his twelve years in prison. That was the place scores were settled.

If Smallbone's death was not an accident, and he had been pushed, it had to be for altogether another reason.

To silence him?

Was the connection between Eamonn Pollock and Amis Smallbone, however historic, a factor?

Pat Lanigan took a call, but Grace barely noticed, he was so deep in thought. Could Pollock have wanted Small-bone silenced? Had Smallbone been involved in this robbery in some way? As a fence? Donny Loncrane had said Pollock was a fence – so were the two of them involved?

One person might know: Gareth Dupont – but would he talk?

He switched to a different track. Eamonn Pollock's two henchmen in Spain had been found dead. Almost certainly, Lucas Daly was involved. Daly had travelled to Marbella with Augustine Krasniki; his golf caddy, he had said. Bollocks.

Intelligence on Krasniki had revealed him to be Lucas Daly's minder. An Albanian immigrant; a thug; Lucas Daly's hired muscle. So had the two of them gone to Marbella to kill Macario and Barnes. For what reason? Why would they have wanted those two men dead? Revenge? To silence them? Or another motive altogether?

And now Lucas Daly, like his father, was in New York. What the hell was going on?

Suddenly, Pat Lanigan was leaning over the front-seat headrest, holding his phone in his hand, terminating a call. 'Roy, I think we've found our man. There's just been a shooting in a Manhattan antique dealer's office. Victim identified as Eamonn Pollock, seriously injured.'

115

The Lincoln Town Car cruised slowly along the vast, ugly, concrete and brick wharf buildings. As they passed the closed steel doors of a loading bay, Gavin Daly, peering out of the rear window, said to the driver, 'Here!'

The car pulled to a halt outside the entrance, marked PIER 92 and with a big yellow stripe around a concrete pillar.

'Wait for us,' Daly said. 'We'll be a while.'

'I'll be right here, sir!' The driver jumped out and helped Gavin Daly to his feet, handing him his cane. Lucas Daly followed his father into the open entrance to the building.

Gavin Daly read the company names on the wall, then went through a door into a huge restaurant. It had a high ceiling with an exposed metal grid superstructure. A window ran the full length, giving a fine view across a small marina, the West River, and New Jersey on the far shore.

Mid-morning, the place was empty. Shiny wooden tables were neatly laid with place settings and bottles of ketchup. To their left was a curved bar, behind which was a row of tall copper beer vats. A balding, middle-aged bartender, polishing a beer glass, gave them a friendly smile. 'Can I help you, gentlemen?'

'We're looking for Hudson Scuba,' Gavin Daly replied. 'They told us to come here.'

'You're in the right place.' The man pointed. 'Go through that far door; you'll see them on the boat, down at the dock.'

They walked through the bar and as Gavin Daly stepped outside, he stopped in his tracks, the memories catching him like a snare.

Something twisted inside his heart.

It was different now, of course it was. Ninety years later. But it was the same, too.

The same place.

His eyes moistened.

He barely noticed the small powerboats and yachts berthed along the marina's pontoons. He was staring beyond them at the ugly, grey, two-storey superstructure of Pier 54 in the distance, stretching out into the calm, muddy-looking water.

The very place he had stood, back in 1922, with his sister, Aileen, and his aunt, Oonagh, waiting to board the *Mauretania*.

The very place where the messenger had pushed through the melee of departing passengers, and handed him the package with the gun, pocket watch and newspaper cutting with the numbers and the names.

And the message.

Watch the numbers.

A sign in front of him in large red letters on a white background read, PRIVATE PROPERTY. OWNERS AND THEIR GUESTS ONLY ON CHELSEA PIERS.

Beyond was a steep, planked gangway down onto the dock. A substantial open fibreglass day boat, with twin outboards and a steering wheel and midship-mounted controls, was moored alongside. One man, in his early twenties, with bleached hair and wearing a wetsuit, stood on the boat, while another, older, stood on the dock passing him scuba tanks, fins, a snorkel, and then a cool box.

'Hudson Scuba?' Gavin Daly called out, as he made his way carefully down.

'That's us!' the older man, good-looking and tanned, said. 'Mr Daly?'

'Yes.'

'I'm Stuart Campbell, and our diver today is Tommy Lovell.'

'Thank you, gentlemen, I really appreciate this. How do I pay you? You take cards?'

'We do indeed, sir.'

Stuart Campbell gripped Gavin's arm and stick, and with Lucas holding his other arm, they helped him aboard. Campbell indicated a wide, cushioned bench seat in the stern. 'You'll be most comfortable there, sir. Driest place, too.' Then Campbell ducked down beneath the helm and produced a credit-card machine, as if by magic. 'We charge seven hundred and fifty bucks the first hour, then five hundred an hour after that, sir; fuel's extra.' He handed Daly the machine.

The old man slipped in his American Express card, then tapped in the information requested, and handed the machine back to Stuart Campbell.

Campbell looked at it, and then said, dubiously, 'I think you've put a zero in the wrong place, Mr Daly.'

Gavin Daly studied it, then shook his head. 'No, that's what I said to the person who answered your phone. That I would give you a bonus of ten thousand dollars for doing this right away.' He put his hand against the raised side of the seat to support himself, as the boat rocked in the wash.

'Well, that's very generous – incredibly so. But with respect, sir, that is a lot of money.' Campbell frowned, as if looking at the two men in a different light now. 'Are you able to give me some kind of assurance there is nothing illegal going on here?'

'Dear boy, I can categorically assure you there's nothing illegal whatsoever – if there was, I'd be giving you ten times this amount. Happy now?'

Campbell nodded doubtfully.

Lucas, standing with a sullen expression, leaned against the windshield support.

'So do you have a specific location, Mr Daly?'

'Manhattan Bridge.'

'Manhattan Bridge? Okay.'

'I'll give you more details when we get there.'

'You're the boss.' Campbell twisted the key in the ignition, firing up the engines. As they burbled, Tommy Lovell untied the mooring ropes.

For some moments they drifted, free, then with a clunk and a sharp change in pitch of the engines, they began moving forward, the water rustling beneath them. Gavin Daly smelled the tang of salt and petrol fumes in the air.

Inside he was jangling.

116

The Crown Victoria raced along Madison Avenue, weaving through the traffic, siren wailing, then slowed as the traffic ahead was heavy and moving at a crawl. Through the windscreen, Roy Grace saw a mass of strobing red lights ahead.

A cruiser was angled across two lanes, and another, a hundred yards further along, was similarly parked. Two further police cruisers were stopped in the middle of the street, and a large, box-shaped ambulance, its doors shut, was parked against the kerb. Not a good sign that the ambulance was still there, Grace thought. From his experience it meant they were working on the casualty in situ; something paramedic crews normally did only when a patient was in a critical condition.

They pulled up alongside the ambulance and he saw yellow and black POLICE LINE – DO NOT CROSS tape blocking off the sidewalk either side of a row of shops. Standing outside the tape were several NYPD cops. To one side, two men in suits, detectives, Grace presumed, were talking to an elderly, flamboyantly dressed and rather distinguished-looking man, who seemed in shock.

Lanigan, Cobb and Grace climbed out of the car, the two New York detectives flashing their badges at a police Captain who came over to them.

The Captain jerked a finger at the ambulance. 'Not looking good,' he said. 'Femoral artery's been shot through. The man's lost a lot of blood; they're trying to give him a transfusion before moving him to hospital.'

'Who's that guy?' Pat Lanigan asked, pointing at the old man.

'Owner of the premises where the shooting happened.'

'We need to talk to him urgently.'

'Go right ahead.'

'Sorry to interrupt, gentlemen,' Lanigan said, nodding at the two detectives, who he clearly knew, before addressing the old man. 'Detective Lanigan and Detective Lieutenant Cobb, and this is Detective Superintendent Roy Grace from Sussex, England. We believe the perpetrator might be an English gentleman, Gavin Daly.'

The man's eyebrows were twitching, and he was shaking. 'That's right. He's normally a – a very – how you say it – calm, nice guy. He went crazy in my office.'

'And you are, sir?'

'Julius Rosenblaum.'

'Can you give us any idea where Mr Daly might be now?'

Despite his shaking, Rosenblaum's voice was calm. 'My guess would be Manhattan Bridge.'

'Manhattan Bridge?' Lanigan repeated.

'Yes, sir.'

'On the bridge?'

Rosenblaum shook his head. 'No, sir, on the water, somewhere underneath it, or close by. His son's gone with him.'

'What's his reason for going to the Manhattan Bridge?'

'He's looking for his father.'

117

As they left the marina, Stuart Campbell opened up the throttle. There was a slight chop on the Hudson, and as the boat came up onto the plane, it hit the waves with a jarring thump-thump-thump. Gavin Daly steadied himself by gripping the seat either side of him with his hands. To his left was a rack of compressed-air tanks, a lifebuoy and a small fire extinguisher secured by two brackets. A sturdy winch handle lay amid a coil of rope close to his feet.

Ahead of them, the pale-green Statue of Liberty rose high into the sky. Beneath, wound all the way around the grey slab of the concrete base, was a long line of tourists waiting their turn to climb to the top.

The further towards the open sea the boat headed, the choppier the water became. The salty wind whipped his face, misting his glasses and making his eyes sting, but Gavin Daly stared resolutely ahead. He was in another world. So many memories now coming back to him. The Wall Street skyline rose to his left, and straight ahead, beyond the white prow of the boat and the green chop of the water, was the suspension bridge across the Narrows.

The bridge hadn't been built in 1922 when, as a small boy, he'd sailed from New York. He could still remember clearly how he had watched that statue receding into the mist and dusk from the stern of the *Mauretania*.

His dad receding.

His life receding.

One day, Pop, I'm going to come back and find you. I'm going to rescue you from wherever you are.

Now he was back.

Finally.

Finally he was going to fulfil that promise he had made, and nothing would stop him.

The boat turned to port, heading around the southern tip of Manhattan. He saw Battery Park; stared at the structures rising on Ground Zero, and the high-rises all around. The Staten Island ferry was passing a short distance away. A few moments later they hit its wash, and the boat thumped hard, twice, pitching and yawing. The winch handle slithered out of its rope nest and clattered past him. He reached down, grabbed it and replaced it. Then, as they entered the East River, he stared across at Brooklyn, where he had lived the first five years of his life. A pleasure boat with teeth painted on its prow thundered past, across their bows, and moments later he had to hold on hard as the wash rocked them. Again the winch handle clattered past him and he grabbed it once more.

A short while later the superstructure of Brooklyn Bridge loomed ahead, its vast, dark-grey pillars rising like monoliths above them. They slipped beneath its inky shadow, heard the roar and rumble above them, and then they were out the other side in sunlight again. Speeding toward the vast, gridded span of Manhattan Bridge.

A sightseeing cruiser was coming through it, heading downriver, passing them wide to their port side. They passed several drab brown high-rises to starboard. The red brick slab of a power station, with one chimney stack, was next. Then the bridge.

His heart flipped. He felt butterflies in his stomach. The

water was calmer here, crunching beneath them, above the whine of the outboards.

Stuart Campbell eased off the throttle as they slid into the wide shadow beneath the bridge, and Gavin felt the boat decelerate.

He looked up at the concrete pillars rising from the water. The steel columns rising from them, holding up the bridge. The vast, dark span of its underbelly.

It felt cold suddenly.

He began to shiver. The boat was rocking in the wash from the passing pleasure boat. This was never how he imagined it might be. And yet, he was here. He could feel his pop's presence. Calling him. His booming voice echoing beneath the bridge. Louder than the incessant traffic roar above them.

Hey, little guy, you still awake?

His gullet tightened. The water was dark, inky dark, ominous. Maybe it was better to leave things be. Better not to disturb its secrets. Was he making a mistake? But he had come too far; he had to go through with this. He had to know. And he had to keep his promise.

Lucas looked at him, a curious, quizzical expression, but he ignored his son. This was about one person. One promise.

Nothing else mattered. It never had and it never would.

The boat was drifting now.

Stuart Campbell was staring at the compass binnacle. 'Mr Daly, we are on the bearings you gave us. Forty, spot forty-two, spot four zero four, north. Seventy-three, spot fifty-nine west. We are three digits short – do you have them? We need them if you want us to pinpoint.'

Gavin Daly pulled the Patek Philippe out of his pocket. Although he knew the numbers by heart, he still felt the need to check.

The hands pointed to 4.05 p.m.

'Four zero five,' he said.

Stuart Campbell tapped the numbers into the binnacle. Then he said, 'Thirty-nine feet of water on this exact location.'

Gavin Daly looked down at the watch, and a shiver rippled through him. Something he had never taken any notice of before. The position of the seconds hand.

It was stopped at 39 seconds.

118

The diver had been down for fifteen minutes. A pink buoy, tethered to the boat and drifting a short distance from them, marked the spot. Stuart Campbell kept an eye on the anchor rope, running down from the prow and holding them steady against the rapid current from the falling tide.

The sonar was on, but the image on the green screen, of the river bed below them, was fuzzy and indistinct. Occasionally when he looked at it, Gavin Daly could see a fish flit past, and from time to time something bigger, moving, which he assumed was the diver coming in and out of view.

There were no *anomalies*, Campbell had told him. That meant the sonar had shown nothing significant down there on this spot.

Had the messenger boy who had brought him the watch and the numbers, and the other items, merely delivered someone's idea of a joke? A cruel, nasty, sick joke? Or had it been someone with a heart?

It was feeling like a sick joke now.

He sat, waiting, clutching the watch in his hands, watching the buoy, occasionally staring across at the mess of slab-shaped buildings on the shore. His eyes drifted over some scrubland, and the remains of the last pier still standing that dated back to his childhood. A black and white tug droned past, a row of tyres as makeshift fenders, hanging down its side. He looked back at the watch.

As he did so, he caught the glint in Lucas's eye. His son

was still standing, looking down at him. Or rather, at the watch.

Gavin Daly held it up. 'It's caused a lot of trouble, hasn't it, this damned little machine?'

'It's beautiful.'

'Beautiful?' Gavin shook his head. 'You're not looking at its physical beauty; you're only looking at its value. That's what's beautiful to you.'

'That's not true, Dad!'

'You killed my sister for it.'

He saw Campbell frown, as if perhaps he had misheard or misunderstood something.

'Dad, you have to understand—'

'NO!' he snapped back at his son. 'I don't have to *understand* anything, boy. Do *you* understand *that*?'

As the noise of the tug receded, Gavin Daly heard another sound, very faint at first.

Lucas heard it too and glanced up, alarmed.

A moment later, Gavin Daly heard the distant, but unmistakable, *thwock-thwock-thwock* of a helicopter. He turned and saw a speck heading low over the water towards them; it was getting bigger by the moment.

'Oh shit,' Lucas said, looking panic-stricken. 'Oh shit!'

Gavin Daly held the watch out over the water. 'This will be for the best,' he said.

'What are you doing? Dad, no! Are you crazy?'

'We're done with it, Lucas. I was done with the gun, and now I'm done with the watch.'

'You can't be serious!'

'What has it done for any of us? What has it brought this family? My dad owned it and he died; my sister had it in her home, and she died. Maybe the damned thing's cursed. I should just throw it into the water, where it should have gone all those years ago with your grandfather. That's where it belongs.'

The *thwock-thwock-thwock* was getting louder.

'Dad, don't, it's sentimental – you can't throw it in the water. You can't!'

Behind Lucas, heading downriver towards them, Gavin could see a launch with a blue hull and grey superstructure. It was travelling at speed, from the size of its bow-wave. He could hear the drone of the engines.

Lucas, hearing them too, spun round. 'Oh shit, Jesus!'

Calmly ignoring the helicopter and the approaching police launch, Gavin Daly said, 'What do you know about sentiment? You couldn't be sentimental for anything. You were born with that gene missing.'

Lucas's eyes were filled with fear and greed. He kept looking at the watch, then at the approaching launch, then the watch again.

The launch, bristling with antennae, reached the bridge and now they could see clearly the NYPD markings on it.

A cold stentorian voice called from a loudhailer. 'This is the New York Police Department. Everyone on board raise your hands in the air. Do not move! Switch off your engines. We are coming alongside to board.'

Stuart Campbell looked at Gavin, then Lucas, in fury. 'What the hell is all this about? You want to explain?' Before either could respond, he grabbed a megaphone from a locker by the wheel, and shouted back, 'We have a diver in the water, I repeat, we have a diver in the water – please keep at a safe distance. I will not move the boat away. I repeat, I will not move the boat away. Please let me get the diver back on board safely.'

He put the megaphone down, raised his hands in the air, and Lucas followed.

Gavin Daly remained seated, ignoring the police, looking at the Patek Philippe in his hand. 'You're right, Lucas. I can't just throw it in the water; that would be stupid.'

'Sir, raise your hands in the air,' the loudhailer boomed, louder as the launch was much closer now, the voice echoing and booming off the superstructure of the bridge above them.

'You know why it would be stupid, Lucas?' Gavin Daly said, ignoring the police.

'Sir, I'm giving you one more warning: put your hands in the air where I can see them.' Aaron Cobb standing on the bridge of the launch, held the microphone in his left hand, and his Glock, at full arm's length, in his right.

Standing close beside him, Roy Grace took the loudhailer and, holding it to his lips, said, 'Mr Daly, this is Detective Superintendent Grace – please do what the officer requests.'

In answer, Gavin Daly picked up the winch handle and raised it in the air.

Cobb's finger tightened on the trigger.

119

On the launch, as it slipped into the shadow beneath the bridge, Roy Grace put a steadying hand on Cobb's arm. 'He's an old man and his emotions are running high,' he said quietly. 'Cut him some slack.'

'Yeah, he's a regular sweet old guy who just happens to like shooting people in the nuts,' Cobb retorted drily, without taking his eyes off Daly.

Grace looked at the water immediately around the marker buoy, looking for air bubbles; meanwhile the police pilot obeyed the request from the dive boat's skipper and kept the launch a safe distance away.

'I'll tell you why it would be stupid, Lucas,' Gavin Daly roared. 'Because you'd have tried to get it back! And you might have done. This way, I won't have to worry about that.'

The diver broke surface a few feet off, but neither Gavin nor Lucas noticed. The old man put the watch on the deck, right in front of his feet.

'Dad, no! No! No!' Lucas yelled as he suddenly realized what was happening. 'No, Dad, no! Don't do that! Don't do that!'

Gavin Daly brought the winch handle down with all the force he could muster onto the watch, shattering the glass and splintering the face. He struck it again, just as hard, then again a third time.

Lucas Daly, Stuart Campbell and the police officers stood watching.

Gavin Daly scooped up the broken, twisted remains, reached across and lifted the flattened crown from under a lifebelt where it had shot. Then with his fingernails, he carefully scraped the hands off the deck, and then a tiny section of the crescent of the moon. Then he tossed everything overboard. 'Done,' he said to Lucas, with a satisfied smile. 'All gone. Feeling sentimental, are you?'

He raised his hands in the air and turned towards the police launch.

'Gavin Daly!' Aaron Cobb called across. 'You need to know that Eamonn Pollock died in the ambulance thirty minutes ago. You are under arrest for murder. You have the right to remain silent and refuse to answer questions. Do you understand? You have the right to consult an attorney before speaking to the police and to have an attorney present during any questioning now or in the future. Do you understand? If you cannot afford an attorney, one will be provided for you without cost. Do you understand?' Aaron Cobb continued to read him his entire Miranda warnings.

Roy Grace stared at the old man, a whole mixture of emotions running through him, but, most of all, sympathy. In the short while he had known Gavin Daly, he'd found him endearing and charming – but tough, too. Doubtless, he had been a ruthless businessman in his day – not many people achieved his level of wealth by being sweet and gentle. Even so, he was unable, fully, to square the horror of what Daly had done, just an hour ago in that Madison Avenue office, with the sad figure he saw in front of him now.

He switched his attention to the diver, who pushed his mask up onto his forehead, spat out his breathing tube, then called up to the skipper of the dive boat, 'Give me a hand, Stu. I got something.' Then, as he paddled towards the ladder hanging down the side of the boat, he was looking around, bewildered, at the scene facing him: the three men on the dive boat with their hands in the air, and the police launch. 'Is this a bad time?' he called up to his colleague as he reached the ladder and gripped it with one hand. 'Want me to come back another day?'

120

Stuart Campbell looked across at Cobb. 'Sir, may I assist my colleague, please?'

The Detective Lieutenant nodded.

Campbell knelt and took the object the diver passed to him in his gloved hand. It was a length of very old, frayed rope, with tendrils of weed on it. Then, with both of them pulling, the diver steadily climbed the ladder, hauling something up by the rope that was clearly extremely heavy.

Lucas leaned over and helped too, while Gavin sat mesmerized.

A bundle of black fishing net slowly broke the surface, covered in weed, with chunks of wet mud sliding from it. There was something inside it that looked like a tarpaulin. A large cement block was tied to the bottom of the net, secured with very old rope wound around it several times in all directions. A crab scuttled off and fell back into the dark water.

Grace watched, equally mesmerized, feeling a lump in his throat for the old man.

Lucas Daly, Stuart Campbell and Tommy Lovell, the diver, finally hauled the whole thing over the side of the boat and lowered it onto the deck. Mud oozed all around it, as water pooled across the deck. Laid out, it was a good six feet in length.

Gavin Daly was trembling. With fenders lowered, the police launch moved alongside, and Grace, flanked by Pat

Lanigan and Aaron Cobb, had to resist the temptation to jump aboard and hold the old man's hand.

The diver produced a sheath knife and began cutting away at the netting. A crew member of the police launch jumped aboard the dive boat with a line, ran it through a mooring eye at the stern, then wound it around a cleat on the launch; then he did the same with another line at the bow.

But none of the three detectives on the launch moved. They all watched. Sensing something that, at this moment at least, they should only be observing.

Lovell, helped by Campbell, pulled away the severed strands of fishing net, exposing the cracked tarpaulin beneath. The diver turned to Gavin Daly, as if seeking his approval. The old man nodded.

Above them the traffic roared. The *thwock-thwock-thwock* of the helicopter continued. Like a surgeon, the diver made a careful incision in the tarpaulin, a few inches at first, then wider, cutting steadily all the way along. Then the two men pulled it open, as if it were the chest cavity of a post-mortem victim.

Gavin Daly fell down onto his knees beside it. Grace could see tears rolling down his face.

He could see inside the tarpaulin now. Bones. A whole tangle of skeletal remains. Every bit of flesh, skin, muscle and sinew gone, picked clean long ago by scavengers that had found ways in through the cracks. And Roy Grace was experienced enough to tell, even from several yards away, that it wasn't animal bones he was looking at.

At one end, he could recognize fibula, tibia, metatarsal, cuboid, cuneiform bones, and wished he had a forensic anthropologist present who could have given them all detailed information on what lay before them.

A few moments later as the two men exposed the full length of the remains, he saw a human skull. Its rictus grin seemed to be saying, *Hey guys, what kept ya?*

Gavin Daly pressed his face into the mud and water beside the tarpaulin, sobbing his heart out.

The three detectives stood watching, as if unsure what to do next.

Gavin Daly raised his head, moved closer to the tarpaulin, and peered in. Lucas went across and laid a hand tenderly on his father's shoulder. Then the old man reached in, and pulled out a short length of thin, discoloured chain. He put it on the deck beside him, then looked inside again, and moments later, lifted out another discoloured chain, with a rusty tiny object on it. He held it up to his neck.

Grace, followed by Lanigan and Cobb, boarded the vessel and walked over to him. 'What is it, Mr Daly?' Grace asked. But he already knew the answer.

'You want to tell us what's going on here?' Aaron Cobb demanded, more than a little insensitively.

The old man, through his tears, turned to him and held up the necklace. Even though it was badly corroded, Grace could make out that it was a tiny rabbit.

'My dad always wore this,' he said, through his tears. 'It was given to him by his dad, who was a member of the Irish Dead Rabbits Gang. I used to admire it when I was a kid and he promised me that one day I could have it.' Then he picked up the corroded length of chain. 'This was the chain my dad had on his pocket watch.' He turned back and stared at the skull. Then he put out a shaking, bony hand, blotched with liver spots, and stroked it. 'They drowned him, the way some people drown a cat. You're detectives. Here's a homicide staring at you all. They drowned him.

They drowned him like a goddamn cat.' He buried his face in his hands and sobbed again.

Then he turned and faced the three detectives. 'Ninety years ago, I made a promise to my dad that one day I would come to New York and find him. That's what's going on here. This is Brendan Daly. He's my pop. And I've found him.'

121

They took away his belt and his shoes and his cane, and gave him prison-issue paper slippers, several sizes too big, so that he walked with a shuffle that made him look like a ninety-five-year-old man might be expected to look.

But Gavin Daly did not care. He was already feeling institutionalized.

Since being taken ashore in handcuffs, he'd been interviewed by an attorney, then arraigned in front of a sour judge who had refused him bail, remanding him in custody as a flight risk, then examined by a prison doctor. Now he was ensconced in a cell at the grandly named Manhattan Detention Complex. His attorney told him cheerfully that it used to be known as *The Tombs*.

He didn't care.

He'd found his pop, and avenged him. On the same day. Nothing mattered any more.

His mood swung from intense sadness to profound happiness. He felt complete, for the first time in his life, as he sat on the hard, blue-foam mattress, writing notes with the ballpoint pen and paper that he had requested, which had been brought by a sympathetic officer.

There was a barred window, high up, through which he could hear traffic noise. Life. Yellow cabs, sirens, horns. A Monday night in Manhattan. People meeting friends in bars, having dinner, hurrying later to catch trains home to the suburbs. Worrying.

So many people worried.

Living lives of quiet desperation.

Had he worried? Had his life been one of *quiet desperation*? What had the ninety-five years, that ended in this tiny prison cell where he could reach out and touch the toilet from his bunk – if he so wished – amounted to? A hill of beans? Anything at all?

Young people who dismissed the elderly overlooked one important thing. The older you were, the less you cared. That was the one, great, liberating thing about old age. Really, you didn't care any more. You were free.

He felt free now, like he had never felt free before in his life. He felt happy. In a way that he had never felt happy before.

Happy in this tiny cell.

Happier than he had ever been in his grand mansion.

There was a clank and his cell door opened. In came the officer who had apologized to him for taking his belt and his shoes. He was tubby, close to retirement age, with the face of a man who had seen it all and had learned that the best way to cope is to smile.

'Lights out soon, Mr Daly, just to give you a five-minute warning to finish your writing. I wanted to check one thing: you don't eat kosher or halal?'

Daly shook his head.

'So, right, just so you know, your next meal will be breakfast. Someone will take you over to the shower room first. You'll be getting cereal, orange – or some other pieces of fresh fruit – milk, bread and breakfast jelly. You have any problem with any of that? You're not diabetic or anything?'

'I won't be needing any breakfast,' he said.

'Well, you'll be getting it anyway.'

Gavin Daly smiled.

The officer hesitated. 'We don't get many folk your age

in here. If you need anything, let me know. But don't miss meals because you don't get nothing in between.'

Daly smiled again. 'Thank you, I have everything I need. Everything I'll ever need.'

That night, for the first time in ninety years, he slept without dreaming.

He slept the sleep of the dead.

122

At 8.45 a.m., Glenn Branson picked Roy Grace up from Gatwick Airport in a pool car. 'Want to go straight to Sussex House, or home first?'

'Home first, please, mate. I want to make sure Cleo's okay, and I need a shower and change of clothes. So how are you? Ari's funeral tomorrow, isn't it? At least I'll be able to come now.'

'I'm glad,' Branson said. 'Thank you. I think she actually quite liked you.'

'She had a strange way of showing it,' Grace replied with a grin.

'Yeah.' Branson sniffed. 'She had a lot of strange ways.'

'But you're okay?'

'Yeah, I am. Her sister's still looking after the kids – she's staying to take care of them until the end of this week, giving me a chance to get myself sorted. To be honest, being at work's the best thing for me. Got a lot to report, old timer, while you've been swanning around the US of A.'

'Haha.'

He felt tired after a cramped, uncomfortable flight, jammed in the centre of three seats, with a bawling baby two rows behind him. And he had been far too wired with his thoughts to sleep, even if the baby had let him. He made a promise never to inflict Noah on any long-haul passengers if he possibly could.

It was a wet day, with a chill in the air, in contrast to the Indian-summer warmth of New York yesterday. The wipers clopped away the water in front of him, although he would almost have preferred it if they didn't, so he couldn't see anything. Glenn's driving seemed to be getting faster and worse the more experience he had. Right now he was accelerating towards a roundabout, when any sane person would be braking. Grace pressed his own feet hard into the footwell, and Branson shot the Ford right in front of a skip lorry that had right of way; he heard the angry blast of the lorry's horn, felt the rear wheels losing grip, and the slide start to happen. Braking hard now, Branson over-corrected and the tail went in the opposite direction. Somehow, miraculously, they came out of the other side of the roundabout still intact, and headed down the M23 slip road.

'Do you have any concept of the laws of physics?' Grace asked.

'Physics?'

'Maybe you should study momentum, get your head around that a little. You could try working out that a car going seventy miles an hour in a straight line has to slow down before turning sharp left, and especially in the wet.'

'That was a controlled power slide. Like Jeremy Clarkson does,' Glenn said.

'Ah.'

'I don't know why you're worried – I've never had a crash.'

'Maybe you're saving it up for the big one.' Switching subjects, Grace asked, 'Anything back from the lab on our dog, Humphrey?' Then he winced as Branson pulled straight across into the fast lane, only inches behind the car in front.

'No, it will take a couple of days. We found a vial of tablets in Smallbone's bathroom that we've also sent for analysis. We've been keeping a careful eye on Cleo; an FLO's been with her around the clock and the Neighbourhood Policing Team's been briefed to be extra vigilant. But from the history, don't you think it likely Smallbone was acting alone?'

'Let's hope so.'

'Okay, we have a significant development regarding the shoeprint found at the letting agent's, Rand and Co. I told you Haydn Kelly had established a match with shoeprints found in Smallbone's house.'

'Yes.'

'We've got a third match – from Eamonn Pollock's yacht in Marbella. The Spanish police sent it yesterday and Haydn Kelly informed Norman Potting an hour ago. There's also other sets of shoeprints – from the patterns it appears three other people, not just Macario and Barnes, were on the boat recently.'

Frowning, Grace said, 'The match is to the ones in the letting agent's and in Smallbone's house?'

'Yes. It's only a shoe match, but if we could find the shoe—'

Suddenly all Roy Grace's tiredness had gone. 'I know who those second shoeprints might have been made by.' He leaned over the seatback and hefted his briefcase onto his lap. From it he removed a small evidence bag containing a USB flash drive, and held it up triumphantly. 'Yesterday, Gavin Daly's son, Lucas, was recorded on videotape in an office in New York admitting involvement in Aileen Mc-Whirter's robbery.'

'Daly's son – her nephew?' he said, incredulously. 'He was involved?'

'Probably the mastermind behind it. Yes, he's a regular charmer.'

'Has he been arrested?'

'No, he's agreed to DS Batchelor and DC Alexander escorting him back to England. But he's asked if they can wait a day or so until he knows what's happening with his father.'

'Result!' Glenn Branson said. 'But – um – how exactly does that help us with the second set of shoeprints on the boat?'

'We'll need to get a search warrant and raid his house. And, I think you are going to like this. If we can put Lucas Daly on that boat, then I think we'll know who the other set belong to.'

'How?'

'Lucas Daly flew to Marbella with his henchman. I suspect they're involved in the deaths of Macario and Barnes. If the shoeprints on the boat match his henchman's, then we have him too. Don't forget there's an historical association between Amis Smallbone and Eamonn Pollock.'

'Yes, I'm aware. But there's one thing still bothering me. All the sets of shoeprints are from trainers: Haydn Kelly's identified the one in the letting agent's and Smallbone's house – and now on the boat – as a Nike shoe, of which there are tens of thousands. The other one on the boat are Asics, again tens of thousands sold.'

'There are a number of ways to put those people at those scenes,' Grace replied. 'In addition to the same make, model and size of the trainers there's also the comparison of wear patterns – Haydn Kelly explained this to me a few days ago and, if we can obtain the trainers, a comparison can be performed of the insoles in the trainers to the insoles in the suspect's footwear as these give an imprint of the person's foot. If there is a match there, then that is pretty much game, set and match! We may also get lucky with DNA deposits inside the trainers.'

'Good stuff! Brilliant! Plenty of options for us.'

'If we stay alive long enough,' Grace said, eyeing the road ahead nervously.

123

In his office at 3 p.m., Grace had just finished a call with Haydn Kelly, discussing in further detail the shoeprints they had. He sipped a strong cup of tea and then yawned. In half an hour a Detective Superintendent from Surrey, whom he had never met, would be arriving to conduct a review of Operation Flounder. It was standard practice, at certain intervals during a major crime investigation, for an experienced outsider to look through the policy book, and all lines of enquiry that the SIO had running, as well as the size and make-up of the team.

It was likely to be a slow and tedious process, Grace knew, and he could seriously have done without this today – particularly with the way things were moving, he was fast getting this whole case wrapped up. With luck the review would be finished by the evening briefing at 6.30 p.m. which he would attend, and then he would head home. He was about to type an email to ACC Rigg to give him a summary, before meeting to brief him fully tomorrow morning, when his phone rang.

It was Pat Lanigan. 'Hey, how you doing, Roy? Home safe?'

'Yes, thanks.'

'Is all okay? Cleo? The baby?'

'Yes, thanks, all is fine. They're safe and well.'

'Hopefully that punk was acting on his own.'

'I hope so, too.'

Then Lanigan's tone changed, becoming more serious.

'I thought you'd want to know this right away. The old guy, Gavin Daly, didn't wake up this morning.'

Grace felt a sudden, deep twinge of sadness. 'He's dead?'

'Seems like he passed away peacefully during the night. He had some heart problems, so maybe the stress of being arrested – it's a pretty big thing for anyone, but especially a guy of that age – maybe that's what did it. I guess we'll know more after the autopsy.'

'I'll never forget the sight of him on that dive boat, looking inside the tarp. Ever,' Grace said.

'Yeah, that was something. You know what? I think he knew he was going to go last night. The prison officer taking care of him said he was very funny about breakfast, saying he wasn't going to need any. Made him wonder if the guy was a bit suicidal, so he kept an extra eye on him.'

'I don't think he was suicidal, Pat. I think he'd done the one thing he had left in his life that he wanted to do. He told me some of his story, about his father and mother, over a cigar in his sister's garden a couple of weeks back. I was moved.'

'Uh huh? Maybe. But you know, he spent the evening, before the lights went down, writing instructions. He wanted his father's remains to be buried in Brooklyn Cemetery as close as possible to his mother's. He wanted restitution paid to the antiques guy, Rosenblaum, for the gunshot damage in his office. And – you'll like this – he asked if someone could contact you and apologize for the trouble you've been put to.'

'Very nice of him,' Grace said, with a grin.

'To me, that sounds like a suicide note, pal.'

'Either way, he's gone, Pat. Does it actually matter? Nothing's going to bring him back – and, you know, I don't think he would have wanted to come back. Life's not compulsory!'

'I like that!' Lanigan said. '*Life's not compulsory*. Think I'm going to use that line next time I have to deal with some total shitbag.'

'Be my guest.'

124

'Good morning,' Roy Grace said to his assembled team in the conference room at the start of the morning briefing. 'Welcome to this briefing on the progress of Operation Flounder today, September the 13th. An unlucky day for some people – particularly our perpetrators.'

There was a ripple of laughter.

'But a lucky day for Operation Flounder,' he went on. 'Lots of positives to report.' He looked down at his notes. 'First up is that our forensic podiatrist, Haydn Kelly, has, through his analysis of Lucas Daly and his henchman Augustine Krasniki's shoes, enabled us to put them on Eamonn Pollock's boat at around the time that Macario and Barnes died.'

He turned to Norman Potting, who was looking better than last time he had seen him; clearly he had caught a little sun while in Spain. 'You have some information for us, Norman?'

'Yes, the Marbella police have found a witness who was close to Pollock's boat on the night of Friday, August the 31st. He was approached for a light by a man who he could not see clearly, but he was accompanied by another man, and their build and height fit Daly and Krasniki. The Spanish police are intending to issue a Magistrate's Warrant for both of them. Just to add to Daly's woes.'

Grace smiled.

Norman Potting continued. 'Spanish police, acting on

490

information supplied by Shoreham Harbour, have raided a warehouse, and found a container filled with antiques matching the majority of the high-value items taken.'

'Brilliant news. Thank you, Norman,' Grace said. Then he looked down at his notes again. 'There's something else which I consider significant. Shortly after the robbery, when we requested photographs of the Patek Philippe watch, Gavin Daly informed us that the photographs he had, and those that his sister had, were missing. Search officers found them late yesterday in a locked filing cabinet in Lucas Daly's back office behind his shop.' He looked up at the Crime Scene Manager. 'Good work, Dave.' He turned to Bella. 'How did the interview go?'

'DC Exton and I interviewed Lucas Daly yesterday, in the presence of his solicitor, as the first of three interviews in our planned strategy. He strenuously denies killing Macario and Barnes. He said that he and Augustine Krasniki did go to Marbella together and went aboard the boat to talk to the men about the whereabouts of Eamonn Pollock and to try to find out where the high-value items were – one in particular being the Patek Philippe watch. He admits they roughed them up a bit, but swears they were alive when they left.'

She paused and checked her notes. 'Now here's the bit that DC Exton and I find hard to believe. Daly claims that they hired a Moroccan to go and talk to the men and see if he could get any more out of them.'

'A Moroccan?' Grace asked.

She nodded. 'Yes, that's what he says. He paid this Moroccan five hundred euros to go and speak to the men.'

'By speak, you mean *torture*?' Potting asked.

'That's the implication, yes. Daly reckons this mysterious Moroccan might have just gone over the top.'

'Does he have a name for this Moroccan, or a description?' Emma-Jane Boutwood asked.

'No,' Bella responded. 'He claims he only saw him in the darkness, on the quay near Pollock's boat.'

'This witness who gave Daly a light, did he see him too?' Grace looked at Potting.

'No, chief. The witness is adamant it was just the two men, presumably Daly and Krasniki.'

'Something is not making very good sense to me,' Roy Grace said. 'Daly and Krasniki are big guys – what would this Moroccan, if he exists, get out of Macario and Barnes that Daly and Krasniki couldn't?'

'Our thinking exactly, sir,' Bella replied.

'So is your view that this Moroccan is an invention?'

'It is, sir, yes.'

Grace nodded. 'Unless someone can physically produce him, it's mine too.'

'What about this Krasniki, boss?' Guy Batchelor asked. 'Has he been arrested yet?'

'No, it looks like he's done a runner. He hails from Albania so he could be hiding in one of their communities here – or gone home – or anywhere.'

'He left a short note in an envelope for his boss, Lucas Daly,' Alec Davies said, and held up a small sheet of paper.

'What does it say?' Grace asked.

'Well, not much at all really, sir. It just says, "*Sorry*".'

125

'Turns out the thirteenth was an unlucky day for Carl Venner!' Roy Grace said. Lounging on a sofa in Cleo's house, he raised his celebratory vodka martini at Marlon. 'What do you think of that, eh?' he said to the goldfish.

Marlon reacted the same way he reacted to everything else in life: by circling his bowl, opening and shutting his mouth.

'That's such fantastic news, darling!' Cleo, seated beside him, set down her laptop and the one small glass of white wine she had allowed herself, kissed him on the cheek and gave him a hug. Noah, lying on his mat on the floor, gurgled happily. Humphrey, asleep in his favourite place – the sofa opposite – did not stir; he appeared to be recovering, slowly, from his ordeal.

'He's got life, with a minimum tariff of eighteen years.'

'You must be so pleased,' she said.

'And bloody relieved!'

'What a week it's been for you!'

'I've had worse.' He smiled and kissed her back, and ran his finger through the delicate Tiffany chain he'd bought her in New York, before heading off to catch his plane.

It was good to be home on a Saturday night again, and this was the first real chance he'd had to celebrate the Venner result with Cleo. Good to be with the two people he loved most in the world. But with one dark shadow hanging over them, the thought of Amis Smallbone and what might have happened had he not fallen – or been pushed. If it was

Krasniki who had pushed him, then a part of him secretly hoped that he might stay free. He deserved that for saving Cleo, or Noah, or both of them.

Cleo picked up her laptop again and showed him a baby outfit with stripes on it. 'Isn't that so cute?' she said. 'It's on this website, Zulily. Don't you think Noah would look so cute in this?'

'It would make him look like a convict!' he replied.

She puckered her face in disappointment. 'No, it wouldn't!'

He continued to look at the estate agent's plans for the house Cleo had fallen in love with, which they were going to see in the morning. But there was a shadow over that, too. He'd had the news in the morning's post that the mystery buyer in Germany of his house had suddenly, and without any explanation, pulled out. They had been relying on his sale, together with Cleo's, to fund the purchase of the new place.

'Darling, do you think there's any point in going tomorrow?' he said.

Cleo smiled and nodded vigorously. 'I was going to tell you this evening my bit of good news. Well, ours, really. Mummy and Daddy have offered to lend us the money for the deposit!'

He looked at her. 'Really?'

'Yes – when you eventually sell your house, then we can pay them back.'

He sipped some more of his martini, closed his eyes for a moment, sinking back into the deep, soft cushions. 'That's incredibly kind of them.'

'They like you,' she said. 'I don't understand why, but they do!' She gave him a cheeky grin. 'A bit the same with me, really!'

'I've been thinking – you know – we were going to get married this year, and then stuff happened and it got put off. Shall we set a date – and just do it?'

'Yes, my darling. Let's make it soon. Like – very soon?'

They kissed again.

Noah was making excited noises on the floor.

'Your turn,' she said.

He put his glass down, knelt, lifted his son in the air, then sat back down, cradling him in his arms.

'Have you seen Lucas Daly's wife, Sarah Courteney?' Cleo asked suddenly. 'This must be a nightmare for her.'

'Can't be much fun for her at the moment, having SOCO crawling all over her home.'

'But I saw her on the news last night, looking as cheery as ever. She's obviously hiding it well.'

'She's a tough cookie,' he replied. 'She's a survivor.' Then he turned his attention to his son. 'Hey, little fellow, have you got something in that nappy for me?'

The rising stench confirmed that Noah had indeed, and he looked very proud of the fact.

126

She sat back, luxuriating in the comfort of her Business Class seat, and enjoying her second glass of champagne.

The cheery young British Airways cabin steward came by with the bottle to top her up. As he did so, he noticed her Cartier.

'Nice watch!' he said, admiringly.

'Thank you!' she replied, and held it up for him to inspect more closely.

'Gorgeous! You can always tell an original – they just have that *je ne sais quoi* about them! A real one speaks for itself!'

'So true. I'm a little confused with the time difference – when are we due to land in Moscow, local time?'

He looked at his own watch, a studded, bronze Hublot. 'Three fifteen. Just over three hours.'

'Thank you.'

He moved on down the aisle. Sarah Courteney unclipped the clasp of her handbag and dipped her hand inside, touching the soft velvet pouch, then lifting it up a few inches, feeling the reassuring weight of the Patek Philippe pocket watch, with the cracked crystal, Arabic numeral dial and the broken crown.

Oh yes, there was nothing to beat an original.

Aileen had shown it to her once, a few years ago, taking it out of the secret compartment at the rear of her safe. And the sweet old lady had never noticed it missing for that week, earlier in the year, when she had taken it to

Dubai, to the little workshop that made such exquisite reproductions.

Clearly, Gareth Dupont had not noticed the difference either when he had stolen the fake in that horrid robbery which had totally shocked her. She had never realized the bastard had been using her.

But all that was history now. Just like Lucas, facing a decade – and probably longer – behind bars, both in Spain and England.

Good riddance, at last.

As the third glass of champagne slipped her into a pleasantly woozy state, she was thinking that, given all that had happened in these past weeks, Aileen would have been proud of her.

She had a buyer in Moscow, willing to pay two and a half million pounds, in cash, and he wasn't concerned about a detail like provenance.

That was good – no hassle. What the hell did proving provenance matter – the watch was real. Just as the cabin steward had said, the real item spoke for itself.

Her father always told her that only two things really mattered in life: health and the time you had left. So, she was in good shape. She had her health.

And she had her time.

ACKNOWLEDGEMENTS

Two important health notes:

1. You will have read in my story of the tragic death of one of the characters from *Malignant Hyperthermia*. This is a real condition that very nearly killed the son of a close friend. It is an hereditary problem causing contracture of muscle and disruption to metabolic functions during general anaesthesia. It is undetectable until a family member reacts under anaesthesia. Diagnosis is by muscle biopsy at the MH Investigation Unit in Leeds. Once diagnosed MH susceptible people can have anaesthesia, provided triggering drugs are avoided and correct monitoring is undertaken. MH is potentially fatal if undetected by the anaesthetist. More information can be found at www.bmha.co.uk

2. One of the characters is diagnosed with Prostate cancer. Information on this disease was kindly given to me by Colin Stokes and John Davies of the Prostate Project, Purbecks House, Grosvenor Road, Godalming, GU7 1NZ, which offers support and awareness. www.prostate-project.org.uk. Tel no: (+44) 01483 419501. The charity supports the local hospitals to improve services and they are now centres of excellence.

*

My biggest research debt is to New York detective Pat Lanigan, grand-nephew of Dinny Meehan, leader of the White Hand Gang, who was murdered at his home in Brooklyn on 31 March 1920. It was through Pat sharing his family history and archive material that this book came into being.

Another huge debt is to the many officers and support staff of Sussex Police, who give me such constant and enthusiastic help and advice. Most of all, thank you to Chief Constable Martin Richards, QPM, for being so very kind and constantly supportive.

Retired Detective Chief Superintendent David Gaylor of Sussex CID, the inspiration behind Roy Grace, not only helps me constantly to hatch my plots, and to ensure Roy Grace and all his team think and act the way real police officers would, he is also my slave driver, making sure I keep up the relentless writing pace through the seven months or so of the first draft . . . and beyond.

Chief Superintendent Graham Bartlett, Divisional Commander of Brighton and Hove Police, has also been immensely helpful on this book. Chief Inspector Jason Tingley has been a total star, helping me both creatively and procedurally on many aspects of this story. As also have DCI Nick Sloan, DCI (retired) Trevor Bowles, Sgt Phil Taylor and Ray Packham of the High Tech Crime Unit, and Inspector Andy Kille of Ops 1.

Huge thanks also to Detective Superintendent John Boshier; Detective Chief Inspector Nick May; Chief Inspector Paul Betts; Senior Support Officer Tony Case; DI William Warner; Inspector Richard Delacour; PC Darren Balkham; DS Simon Bates; Sgt Lorna Dennison-Wilkins and the entire Specialist Search Unit; Scenes of Crime Officers, James Gartrell, Chris Gee, Lucy Steel, Becky Henderson; Sgt Mehdi Fallahi; PC Laura Stanley; PC Jon Anstead; Sgt Gemma Firth; PC Karl Brown.

Retired Detective Sergeant Simon Muggleton, formerly of the Sussex Police Antiques Unit, gave me invaluable information about Brighton's historic antiques underworld.

Thank you to Giles Ellis of the Schofield Watch Company; Richard Robbins; Derek le-Warde; Michael Keehan; Chris Tapsell; David Wiltshire. Hal Mileham; Simon Schneider. Wayne and Vanessa Manley; Steve Reynolds; Danny Reardon; Norman Torrington Genealogy Research; Louise Yeoell; Liberty Taylor.

Forensic Podiatrist, Haydn Kelly; Forensic archaeologist Lucy Sibun; Alan Setterington, Deputy Governor of HMP Lewes.

Thanks also to Michael Beard, Editor, the *Argus*. My terrific researchers: Tara Lester and Nicky Mitchell; Dr Russell Emerson MRCP DM MB ChB; Sarah London; Sherree Fagge, Chief Nurse, The Royal Sussex County Hospital; Rob Kempson; Peter Wingate-Saul; Hans Jürgen Stockerl; Peter Hale MA, MS, FRCS (Gen); Tim Parker; Felix Francis; Graham Sones; Phil Homan; Jeannie Civil; Giles Powell; Bill Shay.

Tony Parker, Director of Engineering of Shoreham Port; David Miller, Deputy Harbour Master; Chris Jones, Dave Smith and Keith Laker.

A very special thanks to Alan Prior MD of the Pinnacle Publishing Group, who so very generously let me into many of the secrets of the arcane world of telesales!

My gratitude as ever to miracle worker Chris Webb of MacService who managed to keep my Mac going after I dropped it, and restore crucial files that had disappeared.

Very big and special thanks to Anna-Lisa Lindeblad, who has again been my tireless and wonderful 'unofficial' editor and commentator throughout the Roy Grace series, and to Sue Ansell who has read and helped me with every single book I have written, and to Martin and Jane Diplock

I'm blessed with a truly wonderful agent and great friend, Carole Blake. And with my dream publicity team of Tony Mulliken, Sophie Ransom, Claire Richman and Becky Short of Midas PR; and there is simply not enough space to say a proper thank you to everyone on Team James at Macmillan, but I must thank my wonderful editor, Wayne Brookes, and my incredibly patient copy-editor, Susan Opie, as well as my great US team: Andy Martin; my editor, Marc Resnick; my publicists Hector DeJean and Tony Fusco, and all the rest at Team James USA!

Massive, massive thanks also to my totally brilliant and long-suffering PA, Linda Buckley.

Helen has, as ever, been unswerving in her support, and putting up with my long nights locked away in my cave. And our three hounds, Phoebe, Oscar and Coco who lie permanently in wait, always ready to remind me that there is a life – and a lot of buried bones – when I care to step away from my desk!

I have to reserve the biggest thank you of all, as ever, to you, my readers. Your emails, Tweets, Facebook and Blog posts give me such constant encouragement. Keep them coming! And I will keep new Roy Grace books coming, I promise you!

Peter James
scary@pavilion.co.uk
www.peterjames.com
www.facebook.com/peterjames.roygrace
www.twitter.com/peterjamesuk

WANT YOU DEAD

**Read on for an extract from the next
Detective Superintendent Roy Grace novel
in the series . . .**

1

Wednesday, 23 October

Karl Murphy was a decent and kind man, a family doctor with two small children whom he was bringing up on his own. He worked long hours, and did his very best for his growing list of patients. The last two years had been tough since his beloved wife, Ingrid, had died, and there were some aspects of his work he found really hard, particularly having to break news to patients who were terminally ill. But it never occurred to him that he might have made enemies – and certainly not that there might be someone who hated him so much he wanted him dead.

And was planning to kill him tonight.

Sure, okay, however hard you tried, you couldn't please everyone, and boy, did he see that at work some days. Most of his patients were pleasant, but a few of them tested him and the staff in his medical practice to the limit. But he still tried to treat them all equally.

As he stood at the clubhouse bar on this late October evening, showered and changed out of his golfing clothes, politely drinking his second pint of lime and lemonade with his partners in the tournament and glancing discreetly at his watch, anxious to make his escape, he realized for the first time in a long, long while he was feeling happy – and excited. There was a new lady in his life. They hadn't been dating for long, but already he had grown extremely fond of her. To the point that he had thought today, out on the golf course, that he was falling in love with her. But being a very private man, he said nothing of this to his companions.

Shortly after 6 p.m. he downed the remains of his drink, anxious about the time, quite unaware that there was a man waiting outside in the blustery darkness.

His sister, Stefanie, had picked the kids up from school today and would be staying with them at his home until he arrived with the babysitter. But she had to leave by 6.45 p.m. latest, to go to a business dinner with her husband, and Karl could not make her late for that. He thanked his host for the charity golf day, and his fellow teammates in turn congratulated him for playing so well, then he slipped eagerly away from the nineteenth-hole drinking session that looked set to go on late into the night. He had something that he wanted to do very much more than get smashed with a bunch of fellow golfers, however pleasant they were. He had a date. A very hot date, and the prospect of seeing her, after three days apart, was giving him the kind of butterflies he'd not had since his teens.

He hurried across the car park, through the wind and rain, to the far end where he had parked his car, popped open the boot, and slung his golf bag inside it. Then he zipped the small silver trophy he had won into a side pocket of the bag, totally preoccupied with thoughts of the evening ahead. God, what a ray of sunshine she had brought into his life! These past two years since Ingrid had died had been hell and now, finally, he was coming through it. In the long, bleak period since her death, he had not thought that would ever be possible.

He didn't notice the motionless figure, all in black, who lay beneath the tartan dog rug on the rear seat, nor did he think it odd that the interior lights failed to come on when he opened the driver's door. It seemed that almost every day another bit of the ageing Audi ceased working, or, like the fuel gauge, only functioned intermittently. He had a new A6 on order, and would be taking delivery in a few weeks' time.

He settled behind the wheel, pulled on his seat belt, started the engine and switched on the headlights. Then he switched the radio from Classic FM to Radio 4, to catch the second half of the news, drove out of the car park, and along the narrow road beside the eighteenth fairway of Haywards Heath Golf Club. Headlights were coming the other way, and he pulled over to the side to let the car pass. As he was about to accelerate forward he heard a sudden movement behind him, then something damp and acrid was clamped over his mouth and nose.

Chloroform, he recognized from his medical training, in the fleeting instant that he tried to resist, before his brain went muzzy and his feet came off the pedals, and his hands lost their grip on the wheel.

2

Wednesday night, 23 October

He held his binoculars to his eyes, in the darkness, focused tight on the woman he loved so much. The night-sight for his crossbow, which he used to keep watch on her when she turned out the lights, lay on the table beside him.

She was drinking a glass of white wine – her fourth tonight – and dialling a number on her phone, again, looking anxious and edgy. With a brief toss of her head, she flicked her red hair away from her pretty face. It was something she always did when she was uptight or nervous about something.

He won't answer, my love, my sweet, really he won't.

3

Wednesday night, 23 October

God, men! What was wrong? Was it her? Them?

There are some things you do in life, Red thought, that are really, really dumb. They don't seem that way at the time; it is only when they go wrong, you realize. It had taken her two years – two years of ignoring the advice of her family, her friends, and ultimately the police. Two years before she had realized just how dangerous Bryce Laurent, the man she had met and fallen in love with from her lonely hearts advert, was.

If she could only wind the clock back two years, with the knowledge she now had.

Please, God.

She would never have joined that online dating agency, and certainly would not have placed that stupid message on it.

Single girl, 29, redhead and smouldering, love life that's crashed and burned. Seeks new flame to rekindle her fire. Fun, friendship and – who knows – maybe more?

Most of the replies had been complete dross. But then she had been warned by her girlfriends that a lot of the men who replied to these things were liars – married guys after a quick shag and not much else.

Well, she had replied to those friends, she wasn't interested in a *quick* shag but she could do with a *long* shag! That wasn't something she'd had for most of the years she had wasted on that introspective dickhead Dominic, who was normally back to checking his emails thirty seconds after a thirty-second bonk.

Besides, Red had reckoned she was smart enough to tell the difference between the shysters and someone decent.

Wrong.

Very badly wrong.

Even more wrong, at this moment, than she knew.

She was unaware that she was being watched, as she took another sip of Sauvignon Blanc and listened to the phone, counting each ring. Three. Four. Five. Six. Then voicemail. It was 8.30 p.m. He was an hour and a half late for their date. Where the hell was he?

She hung up without leaving a message this time, feeling angry and hurt.

4

Wednesday night, 23 October

Van was *the man!* Oh yes. Oh yes, indeed! Van Morrison's 'Queen of the Slipstream' was blasting from his big black Jawbone speaker, flooding his tiny apartment with all those beautiful words he had once felt about Red.

The grumpy old shithead above him banged on the ceiling with his walking stick, as usual when he played his music late at night. But he didn't care.

She had been the Queen of the Slipstream. His queen.

Queen of Hearts.

Red.

The colour of the Queen of Hearts.

And she had rejected him.

And humiliated him.

Did it hurt? Oh yes, it hurt. Every minute of every day and night. Every second.

He had been lucky to get this apartment, with the view it had. Some things were meant to be. Like he and Red had been meant to be. Taking the binoculars from his eyes, he rocked his head from side to side, fury twisting inside him. Okay, so some bad stuff had got in the way of their relationship, but that was all history now – it was too far gone.

He watched her cute lips as she took another sip of her wine. Lips he had kissed so tenderly, so passionately. Lips he had drawn in the cartoon sketches he had made of her, one of which – of her lips pouted in a provocative smile – was framed on the wall. It was captioned, *I'm a five-a-day gal!*

Lips that had kissed every part of his body. The thought of these lips kissing another man was too much to bear. They were his lips. He possessed them. The thought of another man touching the soft skin of her body, holding her naked, entering her, was like an endless bolus of cold water surging through him. The thought of her eyes meeting another man's just as she climaxed made him shake with helpless rage.

But not so helpless any more. Now he had a plan.

If I can't have you, no one will.

He closed the curtains and turned the lights back on. Then he continued to watch her for some moments on one of the screens on the bank of monitors on the wall. She was redialling. Bugging her phone had been simple, with a piece of software, SpyBubble, that he had bought over the internet and secretly installed on her mobile phone. It enabled him to listen to all her conversations, wherever she might be, and whether she was using the phone or not, as well as receive automatically all texts to and from her, the numbers of every call she made or received, all the websites she looked at, all her photographs, and, very importantly, through GPS, know her exact location all the time.

He stared around at the framed photographs of himself covering the walls. There he was in a pink Leander jacket wearing a straw boater at the Henley Regatta, looking pretty much like a young George Clooney, with Red on his arm in a floaty dress and a huge hat. There was another of him in a leather flying helmet in the cockpit of a Tiger Moth. A studious one of him in the Air Traffic Control Centre at Gatwick Airport. Another of him looking rather fetching in a mortar board and gown at his graduation from the Sorbonne in

Paris. Another, also in a mortar board and gown, of him being awarded his doctorate from the School of Aviation in Sydney. There was one he particularly liked of himself in his firefighter uniform. Next to it was one of him shaking hands with Prince Charles. Another shaking hands with Sir Paul McCartney. Impressive? Impressive enough for a queen?

And she had rejected him.

Poisoned against him by the lies of her family. Poisoned by her friends. How could she have listened to them and believed them? She had destroyed everything through her own stupidity.

He turned the music up, drowning out the thoughts raging in his head, and ignored another *blam, blam, blam* on the ceiling from Mr Grumpy.

Then he picked up his binoculars again, switched off the lights, made his way over to the window, and opened the curtains a fraction. It was much nicer to watch her in the flesh, rather than on the screens showing images with sound from every room in her place. He could feel her pain better that way. He looked out and down towards the second-floor window across the alley. Her living-room light was on and he could see her clearly. She was holding her phone to her ear and looking very worried.

So you should be.

5

Wednesday night, 23 October

'Don't do this to me, please,' Red said, as the mobile phone again went to voicemail after six rings.

'Hi, this is Karl. I can't answer just now, so leave a message and I'll call you right back.'

She'd left three messages, and still he had not called *right back*. The first one had been at 7.30 p.m. – half an hour after the time he'd said he would pick her up. They'd planned to have dinner at the China Garden. She'd left a second message at 8 p.m., and a third, trying not to sound angry – which had been hard – shortly before 9 p.m. It was now 10.30 p.m. She'd even checked her Twitter messages and Facebook page, although Karl had never before used them to communicate with her.

Terrific, she thought. *Stood up. How great is that?*

Splitting up with Bryce had been a nightmare that still stayed with her. In those first few weeks after she had thrown him out, with the help of the police, she would often come home to find his Aston Martin parked right outside her old flat. He would be nowhere around, but the sight of the car was enough to give her the creeps. He'd stopped doing it after the time she had got really pissed off at him and let all four of the tyres down. But even after that, sometimes during her solitary training runs for the Brighton Marathon, in aid of the Samaritans, she would spot him watching her, always from a distance, either on foot or in a moving car. For a while it had put her off, particularly the evening runs she used to love across the Downs in the falling darkness.

On the advice of the people she had talked to at the Sanctuary Scheme, she had moved out of her flat into this temporary accommodation, rented under an assumed name they had given to her. The second-floor flat, chosen for its position, had no windows that were visible from the main road, and a reinforced front door. It was in a gloomy, tired converted Victorian mansion block that had once been a grand private residence, close to Hove seafront. Her view from all the main windows was out onto the fire escape of an ugly 1950s apartment block, across a courtyard and an alleyway that led to the car park and lock-up garages behind her building.

Although she was meant to feel safe here, the place depressed her. It had a narrow hallway, dingily lit, that led through into a small open-plan living/dining area, with an old-fashioned kitchen that was little more than a galley separated by a breakfast bar. There was a small bedroom off the hallway that she had made into her den, and a larger bedroom, with a window that looked down onto the lock-up garages and wheelie-bin store at the rear.

She'd given the whole place a lick of white paint which had brightened it a little, and hung some pictures and family photographs, but it did not feel like home – and never would. Hopefully, she would be out of here soon and moving into her dream flat, thanks to the sale of her old place going through, and some financial help from her parents with the deposit. It was airy and spacious, on the top floor of the Royal Regent, a Regency house conversion on Marine Parade in Kemp Town, with a huge suntrap of a balcony facing the English Channel, and fabulous views of the marina to the east and Brighton Pier to the west.

She had been advised by the police not to drive her beloved 1973 convertible Volkswagen Beetle, as it was too conspicuous. So it now sat, forlornly, in a lock-up garage she had rented nearby, and she took it out only very occasionally to keep the battery charged and everything turning over.

She poured the last of the bottle of Sauvignon Blanc she had opened earlier, when it was obvious she wasn't going anywhere tonight with Karl. *Men*, she thought angrily. *Sodding, bloody men.*

But this was so out of character.

After the nightmare of these past years that she had been through, Karl Murphy had seemed a total breath of fresh air. She'd been introduced to him by her best friend, Raquel Evans, a dentist. He was a doctor in the same medical centre as Raquel, and a recent widower. His wife had died from cancer two years back, leaving him with two small boys. According to Raquel, he was now ready to move on and start a new relationship. Raquel had had a feeling the two of them might hit it off, and she'd been right.

Early days, but they'd had dinner a few times, and then last Saturday, with his sons staying overnight with his late wife's parents, they'd slept together for the first time, and spent much of Sunday together. Karl had told her, with a big grin, that he must be quite sweet on her to have sacrificed his regular Sunday-morning golf game.

It was a little bit early in their relationship to be a golf widow, Red had replied, with an equally big – but pointed – grin. They'd spent Sunday morning in bed, then they'd gone to the Brighton Shellfish & Oyster Bar, under the Kings Road Arches, for a seafood brunch of oysters and smoked salmon, followed by a blissful long walk along the esplanade. In the late afternoon, Karl had left to go and collect his boys, and they'd arranged their next date for tonight, Wednesday. He had planned to take the day off to play in a golf tournament and would be over straight after, he had said, to pick her up at 7 p.m.

So where was he? Had he had an accident? Was he in hospital? He hadn't told her which golf course he was playing at, so she had no idea where to begin phoning. She suddenly realized how little she actually knew about him, despite having checked him out. And probably how little about her he had told anyone.

She toyed with phoning the police, asking if there had been any accidents, but dismissed that. They'd heard enough from her over the past few years, with her frequent 999 calls after yet another of Bryce's violent attacks. The hospitals? *Excuse me, I'm calling to see if by chance Dr Karl Murphy has been admitted.*

She realized, though, from her past experience with men, that she was probably being too charitable. He was more than likely pissed, propping up the bar at the nineteenth hole of some clubhouse, and had forgotten all about her.

Sodding men.

She drained her glass.

Her fifth, counted the man watching her.

ABSOLUTE PROOF

By Peter James

'Sensational – the best what-if thriller
since *The Da Vinci Code*'
Lee Child

**From the number one bestselling author, Peter James, comes
an explosive standalone thriller for fans of Dan Brown that will
grip you and won't let go until the very last page.**

Investigative reporter Ross Hunter nearly didn't answer the phone
call that would change his life – and possibly the world – for ever.

*'I'd just like to assure you I'm not a nutcase, Mr Hunter. My name is
Dr Harry F. Cook. I know this is going to sound strange, but I've
recently been given absolute proof of God's existence – and I've been
advised there is a writer, a respected journalist called Ross Hunter,
who could help me to get taken seriously.'*

What would it take to prove the existence of God? And what would
be the consequences?

This question and its answer lie at the heart of *Absolute Proof*.

The false faith of a billionaire evangelist, the life's work of a famous
atheist, and the credibility of each of the world's major religions are
all under threat. If Ross Hunter can survive long enough to present
the evidence . . .